THE EARTH DWELLERS

Book Four of the Dwellers Saga (and Book Four of the Country Saga)

David Estes

ISBN-13: 978-1492226123
ISBN-10: 1492226122

Jacket art and design by Tony Wilson at Winki Pop Design

This book is dedicated to each and every blogger
who has taken a chance on one of my books
and shared what they thought of it with the world.

IMPORTANT AUTHOR'S NOTE BEFORE READING
THE EARTH DWELLERS

The Earth Dwellers will cap off an eighteen month journey that has taken me from unknown Indie author to still-mostly-unknown *fulltime* Indie author. The change is a subtle one for most people, but for me it's a dream come true. To the hundreds (and now maybe even thousands!) of readers who have come along for the ride with me, either by reading *the Dwellers Saga*, *the Country Saga*, or both, I thank you from the bottom of my heart.

Now down to business. There may be some of you who have only read the three books in the Dwellers Saga or the Country Saga, and are now thinking you'll read The Earth Dwellers, which is supposedly the 4th book in BOTH the Dwellers Saga and the Country Saga. Well, that's awesome! However, I must highly recommend that before reading The Earth Dwellers that you read the three books in the Dwellers Saga AND the three books in the Country Saga. Trust me, doing so will greatly enhance your experience, as The Earth Dwellers takes significant characters from both series and crashes them together (yes, like a water country wave) into an action-packed tale of struggle and loss and hope and friendship…and maybe a little love, too ;)

Anyway, that's my advice; it's up to you what to do with it. In any case, thanks for being a part of my own adventure, I'm a better person for having written stories for you!

Recommended Reading prior to The Earth Dwellers

The Moon Dwellers

The Star Dwellers
The Sun Dwellers

Fire Country
Ice Country
Water & Storm Country

A Guide to Slang and Terminology from the Country Saga

Fire Country
Wooloo- crazy or insane

Baggard- an insult, use your imagination...Also, what Perry is!

Tug- a large buffalo-like animal that provides everything from food to clothing to shelter for those who live in the desert

Smoky- attractive (Circ, for example)

Prickler- cactus

Scorch- hell, or the underworld

Searin'- a mild curse word

Blaze- a somewhat-frowned-upon term for human waste

Killer- large wolfish animals that roam the desert searching for food

Burnin'- a stronger curse word

Cotee- Mangy coyote-like animals that hunt in large packs and generally prefer already dead prey

Call- husband or wife previously assigned during a Heater ceremony. "The Call" practice has since been abolished with the creation of the Tri-Tribes.

Bundle- diaper

Grizzed- angry

Pointer- arrow

Fire stick- gun

Fire chariot- truck

'Zard- lizard

Totter- a young child, a toddler

Midder- older kids, but not yet teenagers

Youngling- teenager

Shanker- slacker, lazy person

The Fire- the airborne disease caused by long exposure to the toxic air that has lowered life expectancies substantially

Ice Country

Yag- Large mountain-dwelling creature of ice country legend, not unlike a yeti, bigfoot, or the abominable snowman

Icin'- a mild curse word

Slider- a smooth-sanded plank of wood strapped to one's feet to quickly slide down the mountain. Like a snowboard.

Freezin'- a stronger curse word

The Cold- what Icers call "the Fire." Referred to as the Scurve or the Plague in water and storm country, respectively.

Chill- hell, or the underworld

A Guide to the Peoples of the Tri-Realms and the Countries

The Tri-Realms

Star dwellers- the lowest-ranking people of the Tri-Realms, living the deepest underground and in abject poverty

Moon dwellers- the "middle class" people of the Tri-Realms, although in reality their condition can only be described as impoverished

Sun dwellers- the ruling upper class citizens of the Tri-Realms, they enjoy a lavish lifestyle, artificial sunlight, and beautiful underground cities

Fire Country

Heaters- the original desert dwellers who lived in a small village in the center of fire country

Wilde Ones- a Heater splinter group led by a young woman named Wilde. Comprised of only strong-willed girls, the members of the tribe have been trained to fight.

Marked- another Heater splinter group that broke off in order to avoid the Laws of the Heaters. They are easily identifiable due to their markings, or tattoos, which represent how many lives they've ended, and how many they've saved.

Tri-Tribes- an alliance between the Heaters, the Wildes, and the Marked

Glassies (also referred to as Pasties or earth dwellers)- originally living underground, the Glassies are completely comprised of members of the Tri-Realms who made the trip to the earth's surface, surviving only by building a large glass dome to protect their city from the toxic air.

Ice Country

Icers- the mountain-dwelling people who have long-survived a harshly cold world of snow and ice

Water & Storm Country

Stormers- a tribe that lives on the stormy seaside plains, surviving off the land and riding horses that they refer to as the Escariot

Soakers- a pirate-like people that control a large fleet of ships and prefer living on the water, landing only to replenish their fresh water supply

And now the end begins...

One
Adele

I blink against the blinding sun and the crimson sky and the birds wheeling overhead, and they're still there. My mind is spinning, whirling, remembering: the long journey with Tristan through the rock-surrounded shaft, the exhilarating walk down the tunnel to end all tunnels, the thrill of stepping out onto the surface of the earth, of kissing Tristan, of breathing the real, real air.

I lengthen my strides, the dark skin of my legs flashing from beneath my robe with each step. Muscles tight, heartbeat heavy, mind alive, I race across the storm country plains, determined to surprise my mother with the speed of my arrival back at camp after my morning training run.

And then the three girls appearing, as if from nowhere. But no, they stepped from the shadow of the very rock looming behind us. The middle one asked a question—something about who we are and a sun goddess, right?—one that's still hanging in the air, patiently awaiting an answer.

I open my mouth to speak, but nothing comes out; not a breath, not a word, not a sound.

Thankfully, Tristan answers for the both of us. "I'm Tristan Nailin, a sun dweller, and this is Adele Rose, a moon dweller. We've come from the depths of the earth."

The girls just stare at us for a moment, the two on the sides not smiling, but not frowning either—just staring, like we're covered in filth. The one in the middle, however, is wearing a thick scowl, her eyebrows bent and threatening to pinch her nose. I want to look away, to avert my eyes under their scrutiny, but I don't. I stare right back.

They're wearing very little clothing, just small swatches of material that appear to be some kind of animal skin, around their chests and torsos. They're beautiful and dark and, strangely, remind me of Cole—who I haven't thought of in a long time—not because of their skin, which is several shades lighter than his shadowy complexion, but because of the undercurrent of energy that seems to surround them, both dangerous and exciting and the kind you want on your side. Especially the middle one, the frowner, who is musclier than I am, her toned, tanned arms hanging loosely at her sides.

And then not.

In a split second she's managed to whip out a long blade, glinting in the sun.

"Now, Skye," the tall one beside her says, her voice smooth and almost soothing. She reaches out a hand and touches her fingers gently to the middle girl's arm. Skye, I assume.

"They're *burnin'* Glassy baggards, Wilde," Skye says, her eyes darting between Tristan and me.

"We don't know that," Wilde says, firmness in her tone.

Shaking off Wilde's hand, Skye steps forward, spinning her blade casually. "Yer from the Glass City," she says. Not a question.

"No," Tristan says.

"Yes," she says. "Only the Glassies are vomited from the earth." *Welcome to Earth*, I think wryly.

"No." Tristan again, but there's less conviction in his voice now. This girl's out of her mind, about two pebbles short of a cave-in. She won't listen no matter what we say. She's convinced we're these "Glassies." Whoever they are, they must be her enemies.

For the first time, I'm thankful Tristan and I thought to bring our swords to the surface, for protection. Though I prefer to fight with my fists, or a staff, like my father taught me, when facing the sharp edge of a blade wielded by a crazy woman, I'll take my sword.

Before she can take another step, I reach over my shoulder and slide the deadly steel weapon from the sheath running down my spine. "Back off. We're not who you think we are." My voice is a growl, rumbling from my chest.

The girl called Wilde—who, despite her name, seems the calmest and most in control—steps forward, one hand outstretched toward me and the other once more on Crazy-Girl's arm. "There's no need for that," she says to me.

"Tell that to Short-Fuse over there," I say, pointing the tip of my sword in Skye's direction.

In the time it takes me to blink, I've got an arrow aimed at my heart, nocked on the bow of the third girl, the skinny one, who I'd almost forgotten about. From my training in archery with the star dwellers, I can tell she knows how to use it. I can't count on her to miss.

"Whoa, whoa," Tristan says, extracting his own sword from his belt. "We all need to just calm down."

"Then tell your Glassy friend to stop pointing her searin' sword at my sister," the skinny girl says. So she's the sister of the crazy one. Let's hope insanity doesn't run in their family.

I glance at Tristan and he nods. I lower my sword halfway, but not enough that I can't defend myself if Skye takes a swipe at me.

"Good, that's a start," Wilde says. "Now you, Skye."

Skye flashes an annoyed look in Wilde's direction, but lowers her blade to the same level as mine. Despite her more relaxed stance, the tension remains in her body, her muscles taut, her knuckles splotched with white as they grip the hilt of her weapon.

"And you, Siena," Wilde says. Siena. The sister. Wilde, Skye and Siena. Earth dwellers?

Siena continues to peer at me down the length of her arrow and I can't help but hold my breath. All she has to do is release it and I'm dead. Whose stupid idea was it to come to the earth's surface anyway? Oh right, it was mine.

"Siena!" Wilde says sharply, and the skinny girl lowers her aim, releasing the arrow with a dull *thwock*, embedding it into the dry earth.

"We don't want to fight," Tristan says, lowering his own weapon. *Speak for yourself*, I think. The way Skye continues to glare at me makes me want to crack a forearm shiver across her jaw. Why does she hate us so much? She doesn't even know us.

Skye shifts her death stare to Tristan. "You shoulda thought of that 'fore you murdered our people, 'fore you declared war on the Tri-Tribes."

Murder? War? The Glassies. The people she thinks we belong to. "The Glassies murdered your people," I say.

"Don't play wooloo," Skye says. "You were probably there with the rest of 'em."

"We don't even know who the Glassies are," Tristan says. "I swear it."

"Swear on the sun goddess," Siena says. She pulls another arrow out of the pouch strapped to her back. Doesn't nock it, just holds it. Like a warning. Lie and die.

"I don't know who the sun goddess is," I say, "but I'll swear on her and my life and the lives of my mother and sister, too, if that's what it takes for you people to listen."

Skye suddenly stabs her sword into the ground. Chews on her lip. Sighs, as if exhausted. "If yer not Glassies, who the scorch are you? Yer as white as the snow-capped mountains of ice country, but yer not Icers—not dressed like that. And yer not Soakers 'cause yer not freckly and don't smell like the big waters. With yer pale skin, you can only be Glassies. And what in the big-balled tug are you wearin' over yer eyes and on yer heads? Looks like somethin' them Glassies would wear, ain't no mistaking."

"Dammit!" I say, shoving my own sword into the ground. I'm angry and the sun isn't helping—it's hotter than I ever could've imagined, drawing sweat out of my skin like I've been running laps around the girls in front of us, rather than just standing here across from them. "We're not freaking Glassies!" I rip my sunglasses off, but the light is so bright I have to shut my eyes, so I put them right back on. The brim of my hat casts a shadow down to my chin. Amidst the confrontation, I'd forgotten we were wearing them until Skye pointed it out.

"Adele, stay cool," Tristan says, sliding his sword into his belt. Turning to our adversaries, he says, "Forgive us, we're not used to the heat, the sun. We just came up here to have a look around. We don't know who the Glassies ar—" He stops suddenly, like he's been slapped. "The Glassies…" he murmurs, almost under his breath, trailing off.

"Tristan," I say. "What is it?"

"Adele and Tristan," Skye mutters, "what kinds of names are those?"

I ignore her, my attention fixed on Tristan, whose eyebrow is raised to the red sky. "Oh no," he breathes.

"What?" I ask again.

"I think the Glassies are the earth dwellers," he says.

Two
Siena

I don't know what it is, but I like something about this girl, Adele. She doesn't look like us, certainly doesn't talk like us, but the way she didn't back down from Skye, never so much as looked away, reminds me so much of my older sister I can't help but like her. If there's one thing I learned from all my 'xperiences, it's that you can't judge people until you get to know 'em. The Icers, who I thought were the baggards of the earth, turned out to be mostly okay, 'cept for mad King Goff who was leading 'em. And the Stormers, who at first I had hated hated hated, were really the ones trying to do the right thing. Even the Soakers—despite their roughness and somewhat creepy lust for war 'n blood—weren't so bad once the devil-incarnate Admiral Jones was dead. Scorch, my sister, Jade, even has a thing for one of 'em, and she was a slave for six years, so she'd know the good from the bad.

Now Adele is staring at the guy, Tristan she called him, with such intensity I almost wanna laugh. But I also wanna know what they're talking 'bout. "What's an earth dweller?" I say, thinking of Perry right away. My prickly friend is most definitely stuck in the earth, so I s'pose you could call him an earth dweller.

But Tristan doesn't seem to hear me, or if he does he ignores me, 'cause he and Adele are staring at each other. Adele says, "President Lecter is slaughtering their people?" like it's a question, but the look on her face tells me she's not looking for an answer. She's gone even paler, her cheeks a white sheen even under the shadow of the ridiculous piece of stiff cloth on her head.

"Who the scorch is President Lecter?" Skye asks.

Adele and Tristan both turn sharply toward us, like they're only just remembering we're here. Tristan's hands are tightened into fists, which are turning slightly pink under the hot sun, like he wants to punch someone. If he tries anything, I'll feather him with arrows quicker'n he can say sunburn.

"He's a person, like us," Tristan starts, but then stops suddenly, shaking his head. "Not like us, not really. I mean…" He's having trouble explaining, which isn't helping the tension in the air. I see Skye pull her sword outta the ground slowly. Just in case.

"Let me," Adele says gently, placing a hand on Tristan's arm, which is now trembling slightly. A simple touch, but it speaks so much to me. It's the way I would touch Circ—the way he would touch me. More'n a touch—a feeling. These two

18

mean a great deal to each other, that much is as clear as the cloudless sky above us.

Fingers brushing Tristan's skin, Adele says, "Do you know of the people living underground?"

Wilde looks at Skye. Skye looks at me. I shake my head, say, "All we know is that one day the Glassies popped from the ground. Only they weren't the Glassies, not yet. They were just white-skinned people, like you, trying to build shelters. It was a long time ago. They didn't last very long. They weren't used to the air. It's…not good air."

The guy, Tristan, takes a step back out of the sun, removes his eye coverings. Adele mimics his movements. Her eyes are huge, as big as a full moon, but his are even bigger. "What happened next?" he asks.

I shrug. "They came back. Not the same ones, of course, they were dead, but others. More prepared. Wearing funny suits. Protected somehow. I wasn't even born, but we all know the history. Over many years they built huge structures, constructed a glass dome over everything. Only once the dome was finished did they stop wearing their funny suits. We don't know for sure, but we think the dome protects 'em from the bad air. They live longer'n we do."

"Why did they attack you?" Adele bursts out, like the question's been pushing against her lips for a while now.

Wilde responds 'fore I can even begin to think of what to say. "They're scared of us. Because we're different than them."

"They searin' killed a bunch of us," Skye adds, "but not all. They underestimated us. Now we're gonna kill 'em. Startin' with you."

I watch as Adele's fingers tighten 'round her sword handle. Her face hardens. It's like watching Skye look at her reflection in the watering hole.

"Skye," Wilde says, "we should listen to what they have to say."

Skye doesn't look convinced, but she relaxes her body a little, as if she's not looking for a fight. But I know better. She's still standing on the balls of her feet, still strung as tight as a bowstring, ready to spring into action if she doesn't like what she hears. My fingers dance along the shaft of the pointer I'm holding, too, just in case I hafta use it.

Turning back to our visitors, Wilde says, "Tell us again who you are, how you fit in with the Glassies. You said you're sun dwellers?"

"Yes." Tristan nods vehemently. Says "Yes," one more time. "Well, I'm a sun dweller. We live underground. There are three layers, Sun, Moon, and Star. Adele is a moon dweller, from the middle layer. The deepest are the star dwellers. There's been a massive rebellion; our people have been fighting, because my father was…not a good man…a tyrant."

Don't I know the feeling. Our father was a bad man, too, selling my younger sister, Jade, to the Soakers in exchange for what he thought was a Cure for the airborne disease killing my people. Only he didn't want it for my people. Just for himself and a select group of leaders. Not a good man. I don't cry when I remember his death. Killing him is 'bout the only good thing the Glassies've done.

"And the Glassies?" Wilde asks.

Tristan shifts from one foot to t'other. Is he nervous? "They used to be sun dwellers—at least, most of them. Some of them were moon and star dwellers too."

"I told you!" Skye says. "They're the same. They're the enemy." The tension is back in her arms. She lifts her sword.

"No!" Adele says, practically shouting, speaking quickly. "None of us knew they'd gone aboveground. None of us even knew it was possible. They—the earth dwellers, er, the Glassies—have cut themselves off from us. We had no idea what they were doing to your people. If you don't believe us you can try to kill us, but by God you might die trying."

Things are escalating too fast and I know that look in my sister's eyes. And 'fore I even know what I'm doing, I throw down my bow and jump in front of her, grab her muscly arms, so much stronger'n my own, but she doesn't fight me, doesn't try to break through, almost like she knew I'd stop her and was only moving forward 'cause she felt like Adele's words required an answer of force.

Behind me, Tristan says something I never coulda predicted. "We killed my father because he was evil. If President Lecter is as evil as you say he is, we'll help you kill him too."

Three
Dazz

I don't mind the deepening cold as we trek up the mountain. It's familiar, like an old friend, crisp and alive, even as it creeps through my boots to my toes and reddens my nose.

"Do you think much has happened since we left?" Buff asks.

It hasn't been that long, maybe two weeks. Despite the short length of our excursion away from ice country, there's only one answer to my friend's question. "Yes," I say. The only question we asked Wilde before we parted was whether our families were safe. Knowing that was enough. Now I wish I'd asked more. Like "How is the new government coping?" and "Has King Goff received his sentence yet?"

"Dazz?" Buff says, snapping me away from my muddled thoughts.

"Yah?"

His only response is a hard-packed snowball to my gut. We've reached the snowfields.

I respond in turn, pelting him with a slushball that's filled with gravel and twigs. And then we're both whooping, relishing the powdery snow beneath our boots, our legs churning, suddenly zinging with energy, carrying us up the slope. We reach a rise, laughing, panting, elbows on knees.

This is ice country. This is my home. Wilde's revelation echoes in my ears:

The Glassies spoke of the risk to the Icers too. How now that King Goff has been overthrown they can't trust the people of ice country either. They said they want to cleanse the lands from the desert to the mountains to the sea.

If the Glassies want to kill us, let them try. We'll fight for our lives the same way I fought for my sister, Jolie.

They're forcing us into a war. The Icers too. We'll have to stand together.

Wilde's words grate against my teeth. If it's a war the Glassies want, we'll give it to them. We will stand. We will fight. We will win.

"Hey, relax," Buff says, slapping my shoulder. "Let's get there first, then we'll think about what has to be done." As usual, my friend is able to read me like a book. Hiding emotions has never been my thing.

I flash a false smile and continue on up the mountain.

At some point, the snow starts falling, a handful of lazy flakes meandering on a light breeze, painting everything white. We trudge on, the hours falling under the soles of our thick,

23

bearskin boots. I wonder where Skye is, whether she and Wilde and Siena have met up with their spies yet, whether they're making their way back toward wherever the Tri-Tribes are camped out.

The Unity Alliance. The Tri-Tribes—the Heaters, the Wilde Ones, the Marked—and us, the Icers, joined together as one. Stronger together than apart. Fighting together is our only hope against the Glassies. Now all I have to do is convince the new government. Shouldn't be too hard, especially considering my friend Yo is one of the new leaders, a member of the freshly created consortium. He represents the Brown District. Funny how quickly things change. Just a few weeks ago Yo was just a bartender, a businessman, a tavern owner. Now he's helping to shape the future of my people.

Lost in my thoughts, I barely notice when Buff stops me with an arm. "Wha-what?" I say. Then I see it. The edge of the village, the first houses. The Brown District.

And I can't stop my feet because they have a mind of their own, and Buff is right behind me, and we're able to run fast now because the snow is hard-packed and trampled from people's feet and carts and kids running and playing. Houses blur past on either side, some black and charred, still not repaired from the attack by the Stormer Riders, others being rebuilt by men who are hammering away, clinging to roofs, climbing ladders, bandying together to help one another like people should. A swell of pride fills my chest but I don't stop—can't stop—to enjoy it, because I'm so close…so very close.

A familiar shack of a house appears on the right, and I'm not surprised when Buff manages a burst of speed to pass me, barging through the door like a battering ram, his boulder-like frame thudding solidly against the wood. I follow him through.

A half a dozen kids are attacking Buff, leaping on his back, hugging his legs, toppling him to the floor. His brothers and sisters, welcoming him home. Only the eldest, his sister Darcy, stands back from the fray, her hands on her hips. "Buff, if you insist on charging into the house like a Yag, please at least remove your snowy boots."

But she's smiling as Buff peels his siblings off him, regaining his feet and kicking off his boots in the process. "Always keeping order in the chaos," Buff says, embracing her. "What would we do without you?"

"We'd be forced to eat a lot of raw meat," a voice says to my left. Buff's father lifts up off the bed he was sitting on, using a wooden crutch to get his balance. His leg is wrapped tightly with thick cloth. "Your sister is every bit as good a cook as your mother was."

He hobbles over, nods in my direction. "Dazz," he says.

"Sir," I say. "Good to see you on your feet."

"Good to see you home. Both of you." His voice cracks and I can see the deep lines of worry on his face. And then Buff's arms are wrapped around his neck and they're hugging like only a father and a son can hug.

A pang of desire hits me in the chest, causing my heart to speed up. I can't hug my father, not where he is, but my mother and sister are waiting. Worrying. I can't linger here any longer. "Go," Buff's father says over his son's shoulder. "And thank you for bringing Buff home to me," he adds, as if I was his sole protector.

As I exit into the snow, I call back, "He brought me home, too," and then I'm running up the hill to the next row of houses, where through the light snowfall I can just make out a familiar house—and then I freeze because—

—in front of the house—

—playing in the snow—

—like she didn't spend a week in bed recovering from a knife wound—

—like I never left her—

—is Jolie, building a man out of snow.

And then, as if sensing my presence, she turns, her nose red and her eyes clear and bright. Her face lights up in a smile that's bigger and wider than all the countries of the earth. Her legs pump as she runs toward me and as I crouch down, and then they wrap around my waist as she slams into me.

I pick her up and spin her around and around and around as she peppers my face with kisses and says, "I knew it. I knew you'd come back."

Four
Adele

I can tell Tristan's offer has shocked them, because none of them are saying anything. Even Skye's eyebrows are raised, her mouth slightly open. Gone are the accusations, fired at us with her round words and strange accent.

But does Tristan mean what he said? Can we really offer these people any help? Is it our job, our responsibility? Down below, we've got our own problems. The Tri-Realms are shattered, and without Tristan, leaderless. And Roc and Tawni will be wondering where we are, whether we're dead. And my mother...*my mother*...

"We'll come back with an army," Tristan says, his words cutting into the silence like a knife.

"Come back?" Skye says, and I know from her tone and the pissed off look on her face that coming back is NOT an option…because we won't be leaving in the first place. "Yer our prisoners. Yer comin' with us."

"Like hell," I say, my sword coming up without me even having to think about it.

As casually as pushing back a strand of hair, Siena fits an arrow and aims it at Tristan, half-smiling. "Skye says you're coming, so you're coming."

"But the air," I plead, "you said it yourself: The air is bad, toxic. We'll die if we stay here." I'm surprised how high-pitched and whiny my voice sounds, even to me. But I'm frustrated, tired—of all the fighting, of the nonstop adventure I've been on. We're supposed to be in the Sun Realm changing things, uniting the people. Who knows what the other generals are doing in our absence. If we stay aboveground…will I ever see my mother and sister again?

"Not right away," Skye says. "You can cover yer noses and mouths with cloth until we can find somethin' better."

There's still tension in my muscles, but I drop my sword arm. In this case, a bow and arrow trumps a sword, and I'm not about to die now. Not after racing across the Moon Realm, dodging sun dweller soldiers and killing a deranged psychopath named Rivet to free my sister and father. Not after infiltrating the Sun Realm and assassinating the President of the Tri-Realms. I can't let an arrow from this strange girl be the reason I won't get to see my sister, Elsey, ever again.

Tristan throws his sword on the ground in front of us, also realizing we'll have to make our move later. I follow his lead and do the same. We can't fight arrows with swords. Not now. Maybe later.

"Where are we going?" I ask.

"New Wildetown," Wilde says. "Home of the Tri-Tribes."

~ ~ ~

They cover our faces with thin pieces of cloth, tied tight against the backs of our heads and clamped down by our hats and sunglasses, which they put on over them. I can't see anything except the glow of red light. We can breathe, but I don't believe for one second that filtering our breaths through the cloth will protect us from whatever harmful chemicals are in the air.

What the hell is going on? Who are these girls, so young, so rough, so *here*? With their sun-kissed skin they're clearly not Dwellers, not the ones from the Sun Realm, the Glassies as they call them. But didn't everyone else die when the meteor hit hundreds of years ago? That's what the scientists predicted, that's what the history books say. *But what if they were wrong…?*

My hands are strapped behind my back, but my feet are free so I can walk. Big mistake. All I need are my feet, if I can just get the cover off my eyes…

A firm grip on my elbow. I pull away, struggle against it.

"Everything'll be easier if you don't fight us," says a voice. Not the smooth one, not the rough one, the in-between one. The young, skinny girl with the pack full of arrows. Siena.

When she tries to take my elbow the second time, I don't resist. Not because she told me not to, but because it's not the time to fight. They've got our weapons, we can't see, our hands are tied. Not the right time.

I stumble on my first step, because there are rocks and lumps under my feet, but Siena holds me up. "Careful," she says, like she cares whether I fall or not.

29

"Why are you doing this?" I ask, my voice muffled through the cloth that's over my mouth.

"No talking," the rough one says. Skye, who would sooner kill us first and ask questions later. Siena's sister. I'm still trying to wrap my head around everything that's happening. Is it real? Am I dreaming? Just a few minutes ago Tristan and I were enjoying my first ever glimpse of the earth's surface, and now…now we're prisoners of the people who apparently live up here—who have maybe lived up here for a very long time. What? I repeat: What!?

"Tristan?" I say, just to make sure they haven't separated us, leading us in two different directions.

"Yeah?" he says.

"I swear to the sun goddess if you say one more word I'll—"

"You'll what?" I spout. "Abduct us? Take us prisoner? *Kill* us? Do what you have to do and quit talking about it."

I tense my muscles, wait for the blow. There are scuffs and scrapes and grunts: sounds of a struggle. And then: "Okay, okay, let go of me." Skye's voice.

"We're not going to hurt you," says Wilde, and I almost believe her, because her voice is so calm, so warm, almost like a song. But no, it's not true. Although they stopped Skye from hitting me just now, I can still remember the gleam in Siena's eyes as she looked down the arrow pointed at my chest. If we threaten them, they'll kill us in a heartbeat.

Which is why I'll have to do more than just threaten.

Siena's hand is back on my elbow and we're walking again. The rocks and hard ground disappear, and it feels like we're walking on clothing, on some type of material that sinks down beneath our feet. Everything up here is new and I desperately want to see it, but I can't, because...damn this covering!

"We're on the sand dunes," Siena says, as if reading my mind.

Sand? "Like on the beach?" I ask. Memories of my grandmother's stories flash amidst the red glow leeching through my blindfold. The beach. The ocean. Waves lapping against the shore. Tiny granules of sand, countless, stretching for miles and miles, as far as the eye can see.

"You're thinking of water and storm country," Siena says. "This is fire country. Our sand is much hotter and there ain't no big water next to it."

"I'm not thinking of anything," I say. "I don't have the slightest clue what you're talking about."

I'm hoping saying that will get her to keep talking, to tell me more about what lies above the Tri-Realms, about fire country and water country and storm country, and any *other* countries there happen to be, but she goes all silent on me.

The sand dunes go up and down, up and down, some bigger than others. I can feel the heat on me like a hot iron, pressing down, burning me. My skin's not used to it. I wonder if I'll catch fire. Can the real sun light a person on fire?

Eventually, Siena speaks again. "You swear you ain't never been to fire country 'fore?"

"Will you believe me if I tell you?"

"I might," she says. "Skye, she's…"

"What?" I ask, wondering what her sister has to do with whether I'd lie to her.

"She's tough and brave and'll do everything she can to protect our people. You remind me of her."

Not what I expected her to say. Like, at all. For a moment I'm speechless, dumbfounded, and then I say, "I'm nothing like your sister." I can't stop the words from bubbling up, because I mean them. I wouldn't threaten complete strangers' lives, wouldn't take them prisoner, trudge them through lands filled with air that's toxic to them. No. No way.

Would I?

The doubt creeps in right at the end, when my mouth stops working and my brain kicks in. What if I thought—no, truly *believed*—that those strangers were the enemy, that they'd try to kill my friends, my family, the ones I love? Then what would I do?

The answer comes as hard as a kick to the gut and as trembling as a wizened old man's hand: I might've attacked first and not asked questions at all. Compared to me, is Skye more forgiving, more reasonable? Am I more like her than she is like me?

"Think what you want," Siena says. "But don't judge Skye for trying to protect us the only way she knows how."

Five
Siena

The girl, Adele, goes quiet after that. I keep leading her, on and on, 'cross the desert. And further still, even as the sun turns the red sky purple and orange and sends a bright green flash overhead as it sinks below the horizon.

The sun goddess sleeps, and still we march on in silence.

If Adele won't talk to me, then I'll talk to someone else. "Hey, Skye. You miss Dazz yet?" I ask. It's not a real question, just one of those ones you use to get your fingers under someone's skin, to get a rise out of 'em. It works.

"Dazz? Scorch, Siena, I tol' you a thousand times, he's just a guy," Skye says. That's the rise I was talking 'bout. I snicker.

"But you like kissing him," I say, prodding with my words.

"So?"

"And he makes you laugh like a little Totter."

"He does not!" Finally Skye looks at me, and if looks could kill…well, I'd be deader'n a two ton tug after the last Hunt of the year. But I'm already laughing, and evidently Wilde's amused too, 'cause her giggle escapes her lips, sounding as light and tinkly as rain on rocks.

"I don't know," I say. "I 'spect your head to be sitting just 'bout over your heels right now. And that's all 'cause of Dazz."

"You take it back, baby sister, or I'll take it back with these two fists of mine, I swear it on the moon goddess shining down on us right now."

Her words make me pause, not 'cause I'm afraid of her hitting me—I know she won't—but 'cause I crane my head back to look at the moon goddess, who's hanging high in the sky, almost directly overhead. She's full and bright and…is she smiling?

"Hulloooooo up there!" I shout.

Finally I get a laugh out of Skye. "Sun goddess, Siena. Sometimes I swear you've got tug for brains," she says, which only makes me laugh more, 'cause it sounds like something I would say.

Still tugging Adele with one hand, still staring up at the moon, I say, "'Gardless of my brain constitution, it don't change the fact that you luuuurve Dazz."

And then Skye's chasing me and I'm forgetting myself and releasing Adele's arm and taking off down the dune we've just crested, laughing and laughing and laughing, my feet squishing in the trail of sand lit by the bright, full moon.

And, of course—of course—Skye catches me, 'cause she's stronger and faster and bigger. She tackles me to the ground, pins me there, and shoves my face in the sand. "Take it back," she says, and when I won't, she sprinkles sand in my mouth, which is gaping 'cause I'm still laughing.

I think the realization hits us at the exact same time—maybe 'cause we're sisters and we *both* have tug for brains—and it's only when we hear Wilde's shout that we scamper to our feet and look back up the sandy hill.

Somehow, some way, Adele's got her hands out in front of her and she's taking off her blindfold, her eyes filled with action. I'm already drawing my bow and Skye's got her sword out, but we're both frozen 'cause Adele's charging Wilde, who's holding Tristan with one hand and a sword in t'other, and when she swings at Adele, she ducks under it and kicks low and hard, sweeping Wilde's legs out from under her. Down she goes, dropping her sword in the process. Then, 'fore you can say "spicy 'zard soup," Adele's got Wilde's sword and has freed her hands and Tristan's, and stuck the tip of it into the crook of Wilde's neck.

"Oops," I say, and Skye just glares at me, but I can tell she's not madder at me'n she is at herself.

Maybe not even tug for brains. Maybe nothing for brains. I almost want to rap on my skull with my knuckles and listen to whether it sounds hollow. Stupid, wooloo desert boredom'll get you every time.

That's when I hear a worse sound'n the hollow echo in my own head: A snarl, raw and excited and *close*. A Cotee snarl.

~~~

The moment Wilde and Adele and Tristan come barreling down the hill, I take aim upwards. Not to shoot either of our pale-faced prisoners, but to defend us against the snapping, snarling beasts that are surely 'bout to come over that hill.

I'm not scared; not at all. Five of us against even a large pack of Cotees is doable. I'm ready.

But when Wilde reaches the bottom and I see her face painted yellow by the moonlight, I know we're in trouble. "Killers," she says, her face awash with fear, her breaths coming out in ragged heaves. Wilde doesn't scare easy. None of us do. But that one word—Killers—would strike fear in even the bravest of warriors.

I've lived in fire country my whole life, plenty long enough to know that the bark I heard was a Cotee. So not *just* Cotees—Cotees *and* Killers. Great. We survive the attack from the Glassies, the whims of a mad king, and the brutality of a power-hungry admiral, all to die at the razor-clawed paws of furry wolf-like killing machines?

Burn that. I'll be seared if I'll die now, not when my freshly rescued sister, Jade, is waiting for us back at New Wildetown. Not when Circ is waiting for me.

"How many?" Skye says, her voice firm.

"At least five Cotees, but they're running from maybe three Killers," Wilde says.

"What the hell is a Killer?" Adele asks, but her stricken face tells me she saw 'em.

"A big animal," Skye says. "Get ready."

Steady, steady, I keep my pointer trained on the crest of the hill. 'Side me, I see Skye take out her second blade, hand it to Wilde, feel her tug my short knife out of its loop. She gives it to Tristan. Now's not the time for prisoners, for human enemies. We're in a fight for our lives.

The first Cotee flies over the dune, its four legs moving so fast they're barely touching the sand. Its mouth is hanging open, tongue lolling side to side, eyes wild and wide. It's running for its life. I ignore it, let it come down unscathed. The Cotee won't be stopping to take a snap at us, not when the jaws of death are hot on its tail.

A second Cotee, a third. A pathetic yelp shatters the night. There are no longer five Cotees coming our way.

Just as the first and fastest Cotee is racing 'tween us like we're not even here, like we're no more'n inanimate pricklers standing watch in the desert, the fourth animal soars over the dune in a final, desperate attempt to save itself. A shadow looms behind it, seeming to absorb the moonlight into its dark fur. Massive jaws come crashing down on the Cotee's neck and the sickening crunch of bones rolls down the hill.

"Oh my God," Adele whispers, as the Killer lands on top of the Cotee, twisting its head sharply to snap the animal's neck. Blood oozes from its white fangs, which glisten under the watchful eye of the moon goddess, who I doubt is still smiling.

I can't be frozen, but I am, shocked by the violence I've just witnessed. The last time I faced off against a Killer it was to protect Circ, and in the end, he protected me more'n I did him.

But that was then, and this is now, and I'm a different person. Stronger, more confident. So even as Skye is screaming, "Shoot, Siena! Shoot!" I'm already loosing an arrow, watching it fly straight and true, right into the Killer's eye.

It roars, a mind-rending scream that's filled with anger and pain and maybe surprise, too, like "How could a pathetic, skinny excuse for a human defeat me?" And then it falls, toppling onto its side, skidding down the hill, sending piles of sand rolling down in front of it.

The Killer comes to rest at my feet, as big as five Cotees, black liquid dribbling from its eye. Deader'n…well, just dead, okay? I'm so shocked that I'm plumb out of silly comparisons. I killed a Killer.

One down.

Just as I nock another pointer and raise my bow to the top of the hill, t'other two Killers come charging over the rise. Not distracted by a Cotee—t'other three Cotees are long past us, secure in their knowledge that the Killers'll go for the tasty humans first—they come right at us, teeth snapping, three-inch-long claws out and ready to tear, to rip, to *end*.

I shoot.

One of the Killers—the one on the right—twitches slightly as my arrow slams into its shoulder, but it keeps on coming. I reload, aim, shoot again. The Killer is ready this time, cutting hard to the side, my pointer sailing over its head, which is what I was aiming at.

It's right on top of me, too close to shoot again. No choice but to—

I dive hard to the ground, rolling frantically away, feeling the heavy whoosh of air and sensation of hundreds of pounds of muscle and bone and fur fly past me.

The beast's growl confirms that it missed its mark. I snap to my feet, nock another pointer, release. The shadow snarls, paws at the feathers sticking from it neck. Breaks the pointer in half. Charges.

And then Skye's there, knocking me aside, slashing hard with her sword. The warm splatter of blood sprays my face as I fall to the still-hot sand.

When I push to my feet, all I see is black fur, matted and wet, and blood, pooling at my feet. A groan as Skye shoves the beast off of her. A growl reminds me that it's not over—not by a longshot.

The third Killer is upon us, leaping at Wilde even as she jams her sword upward. The monstrous creature paws aside the sword and knocks her to the ground, landing hard on top of her, snarling and snapping. *Oh sun goddess, no. Not Wilde. No, no!*

But then:

Tristan plows into the Killer, shoulder first, bashing it away from Wilde, simultaneously jamming his blade—my knife—into its side. They roll end over end, t'gether, like they're one animal, a strange mix of fur and flesh and paws and hands. When they stop, the Killer—knife handle protruding from its hide—slashes at Tristan with dagger-like claws, swatting him aside like a pesky desert fly.

I realize I've got my bow raised, a pointer fitted, almost subconsciously, trying to get an angle on the Killer, which is back on its feet, sorta behind the edge of the dune, sorta behind Wilde's unmoving body.

Adele yells, charges, moving quickly and gracefully, swinging the blade she stole from Wilde somewhat wildly, like she's used one 'fore, but's still trying to get the hang of it. She leaps and the Killer does the same, lunging at her 'fore she can get enough strength behind her stab. It's got her 'round the waist, in its jaws, picking her up and crushing her to the ground, her sword skittering away like a skipped stone.

She's as good as dead, but still I can't shoot, 'cause what if she's alive and I hit her? But I don't hafta shoot, don't hafta save the day, 'cause that's what Skye does. That's all she ever does.

And even as I think it, Skye's there, jamming her own blade into the Killer, missing its head 'cause it twists away, but getting it in the upper body, just below its neck. The Killer, even in the throes of death, two weapons sticking from its fur, keeps on kicking, raking its claws first 'cross Skye's cheek and then on her shoulder, throwing her back with the force of the blows.

Impossibly, it's on its feet again, still full of life, standing over Adele's dead body, growling at Skye, who's now weaponless, on her back. I loose a pointer, Skye's last hope, which slams into the beast's hip, but all I draw is an angry snarl.

The Killer leans back on its haunches, preparing to leap, to finish off my sister with its last living breath. It's over. The fight, the part of my life that's worth living, everything.

And then a hand moves beneath the beast. Just a flash of skin and the glint of metal as Adele pulls Tristan's knife—my knife—from the Killer's flesh. The animal's head cocks to the side, such a human expression, as if it's confused at what it's feeling beneath it, and then its eyes widen and roll back as the tip of the weapon emerges from the crown of its head.

It falls, heavy and lifeless and nothing more'n a sack of flesh and bones and blood.

Skye saved Adele.

Adele saved Skye.

Who woulda thought it?

Six

Dazz

"Mother," I say, feeling the word in my blood, in my bones.

Jolie's clinging to my side like she's afraid to let go, but she can't stop me from crossing the room, dragging her with me, embracing my mother, who looks so beautiful, her blue eyes clear, her dark brown hair clean and braided and hanging like a vine over her shoulder.

With the soft glow of the fire surrounding us, her warm arms hold Jolie and me. Although her grip isn't tight, I feel like it's choking me, because our family seems so small now without Wes and my father. We're all we have left in this cold, harsh world.

"Thank the Heart of the Mountain," my mother murmurs into my hair.

"You're still clean, Mother," I say. Not a question, an observation. When I last saw her she had barely gone through withdrawal from the drugs—ice powder—leaving her system.

"Wilde helped me until she had to leave," she says, pulling away from me to look at my face. It's weird to see her eyes so clear, so aware. Strange and amazing.

"And after she left?"

"I helped myself," she says, which makes me gather her up in my arms once more, out of pride.

"I knew you could do it. I always knew."

"We're a family again, right?" Jolie asks from just below my armpit.

"We never stopped being one, Joles," I say. "Not for one second."

~ ~ ~

Wilde didn't tell my mother anything before she left, only that it was an emergency. I don't want to tell her either. How can I when, for the first time in so long, she's happy, truly happy? Still sad about losing Father and Wes, but coping, on her own, without the fog of drugs to blind her to reality. Like the rest of us—coping.

But I know I have to, because she'll find out soon enough anyway, and I'd rather she hears it from me.

"The Glassies are going to attack us," I say through the swirling steam from my cup of tea.

Mother's eyebrows narrow, followed by Jolie's. They look so much alike, their expressions so similar, I almost want to laugh. I would under any other circumstances.

"Why would they do that?" Jolie says. "We haven't done anything to them."

I shake my head, marveling at how my twelve-year-old sister, having gone through so much in her short life—abducted, nearly enslaved by a corrupt admiral, nearly killed by a deranged king—is able to maintain such a childlike innocence. The world would be a better place if the rest of us weren't so jaded by life and experience.

"I don't know," I say. "Maybe they're scared because we're different than them. Maybe they're just bad people."

"Like King Goff?" she says.

"Yah, maybe just like King Goff."

"He's dead, you know," Jolie says, so matter-of-factly it's like she's telling me it snowed today, or she bought bread at the bakery.

"I didn't know that," I say, unsurprised. There was no way the consortium would find the king innocent, considering all the evidence stacked against him. "When?"

"Three days past," my mother says, interjecting. "They did it publicly."

"I wanted to go, but Mother wouldn't let me." Maybe my sister's innocence isn't quite intact after all.

"Mother was right. Death isn't something that should be watched, like a competition."

Jolie shrugs. "Well, I'm still glad he's dead."

I have nothing to say to that because I am too.

~~~

43

I'm nervous. Despite all I've been through—from minor things, like facing pub fights with drunken men wielding shards of broken bottles, to major things, like fighting through hordes of soldiers and black-robed Riders—speaking to a bunch of irate and confused ice country leaders scares me more than anything.

For one, they're men and women, many of them twice my age. And three quarters of them aren't from my part of town, the Brown District. There are four leaders from each District, White, Blue, Brown, and Black. Yo is huddled up with the other three from the Brown District, probably setting the record straight, telling them what I told him earlier, trying to get them all on the same page. The representatives from the White and Blue Districts are sitting together, speaking to each other more with their hands than with their mouths, as if the grandness of each arm gesture determines the weight and strength of the words attached to it.

Lines are already being drawn, even in this supposedly "equal" tribunal.

The Black District reps are sitting alone. Well, only three of the four have shown up and they don't seem interested in anything but whatever card game they're playing—Boulders 'n Avalanches probably. They only turn their attention away from the game to spit wads of tobacco on the dirt floor of the large council room.

I fight back the desire to grab Buff's arm and jump off the raised platform we're sitting on.

Buff seems to recognize my discomfort. "Don't worry, you'll do just fine," he says.

"Whaddya mean, *I'll* do just fine? You're in this as much as I am."

Buff's chuckle is his response. He knows when the time comes, I'll do the talking.

I'm tempted to start the meeting without the last Black District member, but just as I'm mustering the courage to stand, the door swings open and a wiry form fills the entrance. When the man steps into the lantern light, I gasp, my breath sticking in my lungs.

I want to laugh or cry or shout or all three, but I can't do anything as I'm still holding my breath, because…

…because the last Black District rep is Abe, my old friend, as responsible for me being alive as anyone else on this planet. And behind him, filling the entirety of the doorway, is his brother, Hightower, as big and tough as a Yag, but with a heart as bright and shiny as the bags of gold that the two of them stole from the palace when the whole world was being sliced to ribbons by a million swords.

"Hey, Dazzy," Abe says. "I heard you've got somethin' big to tell the consortium."

Seven
Adele

There are fierce red marks where my metal belt dug into my belly and hips. The gashes sting like hell, but I'll take them any day compared to having razor-sharp teeth embedded in my skin. My belt probably saved my life. Well, that and Skye, who threw her own life to the winds of fate and attacked the Killer just before it mauled me to death.

She saved my life. Why? The question zips around my head, but I can't seem to latch onto it to really focus.

Killers. A strangely appropriate name for the enormous beasts that attacked us. Their carcasses lie nearby, dark shadows on the sand. More than once Siena has had to shoot her arrows at the Cotees who've been skulking close by, drawn by the scent of blood and hoping for an easy and satisfying meal. Cotees and Killers: I'm thinking about them like they're normal things that people think about, when really they're as foreign as the sparkling—actually sparkling—stars filling the clear, dark night sky, their beauty dwarfed only by the unbelievably surreal moon looking down like a pale fluorescent eye.

I sit back to back with Tristan, who's got nasty claw marks bleeding down his naked chest, his shredded shirt being torn into strips by Wilde, who's tending to his wounds. Miraculously, she's mostly unscathed, having only had the wind knocked out of her before Tristan saved her from the Killer.

Siena's working on her sister, who took a pair of nasty claw scrapes, one to her cheek and the other to her shoulder.

"We got lucky. Searin' lucky," Siena says.

"I don't believe in luck," I say, not unkindly.

"Neither do I," Skye says, and then, as if realizing she's just agreed with me, clamps her mouth shut and focuses back on her shoulder, which Siena has just wrapped tightly with some kind of animal skin.

"Thank you," I say to Skye. "You saved my life."

She mumbles something I can't make out. "What was that?" I say.

Siena grins. "She said 'Thank you' back. Don't make her say it again, she might not survive it."

I can't help but to grin back. What the hell am I doing? Where the hell are we? It's like Tristan and I are trapped in this strange world of burning suns and fierce sword-swinging, arrow-shooting women, fighting for our lives against creatures that see us only as their dinner.

"Welcome to fire country," Siena says, dabbing at the blood on Skye's cheek.

"What is fire country?" Tristan asks dumbly, stealing the question right off my lips.

Skye laughs. "As if you don't know." She says it like she doesn't believe us, but there's less certainty in her voice than before.

"It's everything around you," Wilde says. "Fire country extends to the great forests in the east, to the cliffs and the waters in the south—where the Killers live in packs—and to the north, to the edge of ice country."

"What's ice country?" I ask.

"Where the Icers live," Siena says, as if that answers everything. "Like my sister's boyfriend, Dazz."

"He's not my boyfriend," Skye says, cringing when her sister dabs her scrape too hard.

"Lover then," Siena says, hiding a smile. I smirk at their banter—the same banter that gave me the opportunity to escape the first time. Now escaping's the last thing on my mind. Not when there could be more Killers—or worse—roaming the desert. Not when there are oceans of sand surrounding us, as far as the eye can see, and I don't have the slightest clue what direction we came from.

"And to the west?" Tristan says.

"What about the west?" Siena says.

"Wilde told us how far fire country goes in every direction but the west."

"Anyone who's gone west has never returned," Wilde says. "As far as we can tell, fire country goes on forever to the west."

~~~

Evidently, we're going to march straight on through the night. They don't bind our hands this time. Or blindfold us. Skye starts to object, but Wilde silences her with a hand. "We're beyond all that," she says.

Skye looks like she wants to say something, but bites her lip instead. Her message is delivered when she points the tip of her blade in my direction. *If I try to run, she'll kill me.*

I guess saving each other's lives didn't change anything. It just goes to show that enemies can be temporary friends in a life or death situation. Then everything goes back to normal.

Siena, however, seems to have softened somewhat. She walks easily next to me, swinging her arms, her bow bouncing against her back. I cast a final glance back at the shadowy forms of the dead Killers, just to make sure they're still dead.

Wilde leads; Skye watches from behind.

Tristan falls in beside me. "You okay?" I say.

He gives me a wry grin. "Yeah, you?"

"Never been better," I say.

"Perhaps a holiday at the Sandy Oasis would've been a better choice," he says casually.

"There's sand here," I point out.

"But no cold drinks."

My mouth seems to go even dryer. "Thanks for reminding me."

"What's the Sandy Oasis?" Siena asks.

Surprised, I look at her. "It's a place where sun dwellers go on vacation."

"What's vacation?" she says, her head tilted to the side like a child.

"Uhh," I say.

"It's taking a break from life to just relax," Tristan explains.

"But then who will do all the work?" This time it's Skye who asks the question. Evidently our conversation has captured even her attention.

"The other people," Tristan says, sighing. "I suspect the world we come from is very different than yours. Some people work harder than others."

Siena's head bobs in understanding. "That ain't different. We got shankers, too. People who just live off the work of others. One of my good friends, Veeva, her guy's the shankiest shanker 'round. I ain't never seen him so much as lift a finger to help out. He's always on—what did you call it?—vaycayshun?"

"Yeah, something like that," I say, suddenly feeling very weary, like my legs can't go another step. We're climbing a large dune, one step at a time, our feet sinking into the soft sand. "How far is New Wildetown?" I ask.

"'Bout a day's hike in the opposite direction," Skye says. "Why? Are you gettin' tired, Glassy?"

"No. And I'm not a Glassy." I'm barely able to make my voice sound strong, when inside of me my heart's settled into the pit of my stomach. A day's hike?

"I thought that's where we were going?" Tristan says.

"We hafta stop somewhere else first," Siena says.

"Don't worry, weak little Glassy, we're almost there," Skye says.

I take a deep breath, hold it, fight off the urge to turn around and punch her. After all, she did save my life. I can be civil.

As we near the top of the mountainous dune, Wilde slows her pace, lowers to a crouch, peeks over. She looks back. "The Glass City sleeps," she says.

We crowd around her, in a cluster, staying low. Sneak a quick look over the sandy peak.

My heart rises from my gut to my throat, trapping my breath in my lungs.

For the sight before me is beyond spectacular, beyond unexpected, beyond real.

A city, domed by glass, filled with metal and stone and glass structures: buildings.

A Glass City. The Glassies. The Earth Dwellers.

The fourth Realm.

Eight
Siena

I've never seen the Glass City 'fore, but now that I have, I wish I hadn't. 'Cause what chance do we got against people who could build such a thing? Their city next to our measly huts and tents is like comparing a Killer to a burrow mouse. There ain't no comparison.

A sudden burst of anger rises to my head and I feel even hotter'n I did 'fore the sun went down. "Why won't you people just leave us alone?" I say. I meant to aim the question at the fathomless glass dome, but for some reason I'm looking right at Adele.

She stares right back at me, her eyebrows heavy in the middle. For the first time I notice how dark her hair is. If her skin weren't so pale, she might fit right in amongst my people. Strange how something as basic as the color of one's skin can make two people seem like they're from different planets. Does it have to be that way? Everywhere I turn it seems like the world is separated by color. Us, the brown Heaters. To the north, the white Icers. To the east, the white, freckled Soakers and the dark-as-night Stormers. No mixing allowed. Maybe that's why Skye won't admit to her feelings for Dazz. Seems kinda silly if you ask me.

And yet…yet I feel my cheeks heating as I glare at Adele. White Adele. Pale Adele. Does the way she looks make her the enemy? Her eyes are wide with wonder as she gazes at the dome. Is she faking her amazement at the size and beauty of the city?

"They're not my people," Adele says. Sun goddess, how I wanna believe her, but I can't. Not yet. Not when I could pluck her 'tween my fingers and stick her inside the glass dome and she'd fit right in. She'd look like she'd been there her whole life. And then she'd come out holding a fire stick and riding a fire chariot, killing my people, killing everyone who's not a Glassy.

I sigh, don't respond. I've got nothing in me but anger.

"My father was a terrible man," Tristan says, gazing out over the Glass City. "The man inside that dome, the one controlling everything, he might be even worse. President Lecter is the one man who managed to control my father."

"You want to prove to us that you're not with them—that you are who you say you are?" Wilde asks.

Adele nods; Tristan says, "Yes."

"Then tell us how to beat them."

Nine
Dazz

"Abe?" I say, because it's the only question hammering through my mind. *Abe? Abe? Abe?*

"Sometimes wealth is power, son," Abe says, smiling that crooked-toothed smile of his. "Especially if you use a little of it to help rebuild the lowliest District in ice country."

"Get that monstrosity out of here," a plump woman from the White District says, looking Hightower up and down. Hightower grunts, but I can't tell if it's a burp or if he tried to say something.

"He's with me," Abe says.

"Consortium members only," a man with a curly mustache from the Blue District agrees.

"You'll have to make him leave, I'm afraid," Abe says. "And I wouldn't advise that at all."

Hightower grunts in agreement.

"He'll sit in the back and won't cause any problems," I find myself saying, as if I'm the one calling the shots.

All heads turn to look at me, which allows Hightower the chance to duck his head slightly and enter, filling a whole corner of the room as he slumps down.

Yo stands as Abe sits with the other reps from the Black District, who go right on slapping their cards down, as if there's not a crucial meeting happening right in front of them. They deal Abe in as he lights a cigarette, drawing glares from the plump woman and the curly-mustache man. The other six White and Blue District members simply ignore the less wealthy side of the room, as if they're not even worthy of complaint.

I clear my throat, trying to open a path so my voice will come out sharp and strong. Yo begins. "Fellow consortium members, we've taken major steps to rebuild ice country and our way of life since the unexpected yet necessary fall of King Goff. However, it has come to my attention that a greater enemy stands at the foothills of our great country, one we cannot ignore. Thus, I have called you here today to listen to the testimony of the witnesses." I realize my jaw has fallen, leaving my mouth gaping open. I've never heard Yo talk like that. It's like outside of his pub, he's a different person.

"What enemy?" a heavyset White District man shouts. I recognize him as the owner of the largest timber yard in the village. He grew up in the Brown District, but found a way out when he founded his business. Of all the White District members, he's the one who's most likely to be sympathetic to our message.

"That's what these boys are here to tell you about," Yo says, waving a hand at us to begin. He sits.

I stand, very aware that Buff remains seated. "The Glassies," I say, but before I can continue, a dozen voices start shouting at once:

"The Glassies are our friends!"

"We trade with the Glassies!"

"I never liked the Glassies, kill them!"

"Who are the Glassies?"

Yo stands again, waving his hands and shouting, trying to quiet the members, while Abe blows a puff of smoke out, half-laughing, half-coughing, as if I've just made the funniest joke in the world.

And I just stand there stupidly, wondering where I went wrong. Perhaps I should've started at the beginning of the story, instead of the end. Leave it to me to mess up in the opening seconds of one of the biggest moments of my life.

Finally, after much arm-waving and a whole lot of red-faced shouting, Yo, with the help of Hightower and his clenched fists, manages to regain order. I take a deep breath, start again.

This time, I start from the beginning. I tell them about my role in taking down King Goff, about how he kidnapped Jolie, how his men killed Wes, about Skye and Siena and the others from fire country. How we went to water and storm country, what happened there. About the information Wilde brought us. "Now that King Goff has fallen," I say, "the Glassies are no longer our friends, if they ever were. A friend to a mad king is no friend to us. Simply put, they want to wipe us off the face of the earth."

When I finish this time, there's silence. I think it's partly due to the heaviness of my words and partly because Hightower has inched his way up the side wall, silently daring anyone to speak over me again.

"Uh, any questions?" I say.

Curly Mustache Man raises a tentative hand, glancing nervously at Hightower. "Yes," I say.

"What do you expect us to do with this information, exactly?"

I raise my eyebrows. Have I been talking to a wall? Did I not make it obvious? We're under attack, for Heart's sake! Or maybe he wants specifics, like what is my recommendation to the consortium. "An alliance," I say. But before I can add "*With the Tri-Tribes*," the man's curly mustache twitches as he speaks:

"I couldn't agree more. An alliance with the Glassies is just the thing we need."

Ten
Adele

Wilde didn't mean for us to literally tell them how to defeat the earth dwellers, at least not right away. Which is good, because Tristan and I need to talk about it, think about it—talk and think about A LOT of things.

"Follow me," Wilde says, and we all do, partly because none of us want to look at the beautiful monstrosity that is the Glass City, and mostly because we're all too tired to argue.

She leads us down the slope and to the right, where a rock formation juts out from the sand. It's large, roundish on one side with sharp protrusions of rock on the other. We head straight for one of the sheer sides of rock, facing away from the city.

As we approach, Wilde whistles, high and clear, and suddenly the rock ripples, folds, opens up to reveal a dark cave. Not rock, an animal-skin cover, stained to look like rock, almost perfect. A secret cave…but why so close to the enemy? There's only one answer: spies.

A young head pokes from the opening, brown skinned, dark eyed. A guy. Shirtless, skin pulled tight across his pectorals and biceps. Basically the male version of Skye. Ripped.

"Hawk, you baggard," Siena says, punching him on the arm.

"How ya doin, Skinny?" the guy answers with a smirk. He straightens up when he sees Wilde. "Uh, Wilde, uh, good to see you."

"We need food and bedding," Wilde says, waving us inside.

"Yeah, sure, right away," Hawk says. He's about to turn, but then notices Tristan and me. "What the—"

"Hawk—meet the pale-faces," Skye says, pushing me past him and inside.

~~~

"Hawk's a durt bag," Siena says with a smile. Her arm's around a bald girl who has tattoos winding around her bare arms, legs, and neck. She was introduced as Lara, an old friend of Siena's. Apparently now a spy.

"A reformed durt bag," Hawk clarifies. "I was sort of a bully growing up. Until I realized I was an idiot—that I was on the wrong side."

We're sitting inside the secret cave, which is quite a bit larger than I expected from the small opening on the outside. Eerie light glows from above us, entering through a largish hole in the roof, which I fully expect is covered with a rock-colored cloth during the day.

My mouth is full of the sort of crunchy, sort of chewy vegetable that Siena called prickler. It's not half bad, although I'm so hungry I could probably eat raw meat from the Killer carcasses right now. Crunch, crunch, crunch. Tristan chews happily beside me, his knee touching mine. Evidently, the food's woken *both* of us up a little.

"So yer Glassies?" Hawk asks, handing a plate of prickler salad to Siena.

"Reformed Glassies," I say around my food. When Skye's chin lifts and her eyes narrow, I hold up a hand. "I'm kidding. We're not Glassies." Skye's lips part, so I say more forcefully, "We're not. For the hundredth time, I swear it. On the sun goddess, moon goddess, rock goddess and every other goddess out there."

"There's no rock goddess," Siena whispers.

"Look, let me explain things once and for all..." So I do. I tell them all about the Tri-Realms. The history. How they were dug out and formed before, during, and after Year Zero. The class system. The rebellion. What we learned about the Glass City and the earth dwellers before we came up. Everything leading up to our arrival except for the fact that Tristan has actually been inside the Glass City once before. Somehow I know that won't help them to trust us.

When I finish, everyone's plate is clean, and Hawk is dishing out bowlfuls of some kind of soup. Tristan takes the first one, raising an eyebrow in question. "'Zard soup," Siena says, which means about as much to me as Cotee steaks would've before I came face to face with a pack of Cotees. "It's better warmed

60

up, but it's too dangerous to light a fire this close to the Glassies."

I nod and take a sip, feeling something slimy roll over my tongue. When I bite down on it, I find it's somewhat chewy. I swallow twice, trying to keep it down. It might not be that tasty, but I need the energy.

While everyone's busily slurp-chewing their soup, Skye looks at me, steel in her eyes. "Why would you help us against the Glassies, if they're the same kind of people as you?"

Her question takes me by surprise. One, because I've never thought of myself as a "kind of people," and if I did, I would most associate myself with moon dwellers, rather than *all* dwellers; and two, because I've been fighting against "my own people," for so long, I've never really had to think about it.

Tristan nods at me. It's a look he's given me many times, that says, "I trust you, I believe in you, I'll follow you to the ends of the earth." If nothing else, it reassures me.

"I fight on the side of life," I say. "For those who are being treated unfairly, against those who would seek to oppress others just because they can. We didn't come to the earth's surface to fight the Glassies. No, we came because we were curious, and because we wanted to give our people the same chance to live above as anyone else. Living in the dark, under mountains of rock, choked by dust, always hungry—that's no kind of life. Not for anyone. We might've won the battle against Tristan's father, but a war still rages below us, and our people are fighting for their lives just like yours. And at the center of it all is President Lecter and the Glassies. So maybe we're not so different. Maybe we're on the same side, after all. Does that make any sense?"

Although I'm looking from face to face as I speak, out of the corner of my eye I can tell Skye's eyes never leave mine, never blink. When I finish, she says, "I understand what you mean more'n you could possibly know."

Then she stands and pushes through the fake-rock flap and into the night.

Eleven
Siena

I can't believe I'm looking at Lara right now. She looks great, tougher'n bones, as always.

Adele and Tristan and Wilde all went to sleep a while ago, curled up on tugskin mats, but although I'm exhausted, I can't waste this chance to catch up with my friend. Even Skye wandered back in and dozed off. Now it's just me, Lara, and Hawk.

"When did you become a spy?" I ask.

"A few weeks back," Hawk says with a smirk.

"Not you, wooloo baggard," I say, but I'm smiling as I say it. Although not that long ago I wished Hawk'd curl up in a hole and die, he's truly turned things 'round for himself. I even sorta like the guy now. Not that that means I'll cut him any slack.

"Almost right after you left for ice country," Lara says. "You know me, I can't sit still for long."

"Don't I know it," I say, taking a sip of water.

"Have some of this," Hawk says, passing me a water skin. I take a sniff.

"Whew! What's this, fire juice? Should you really be drinking on the job, you shanker? Don't you need your wits—however dim—'bout you in case the Glassies do something unexpected?"

"Told you," Lara says, glaring at Hawk.

"You won't tell anyone, will you?" Hawk says, looking scareder'n a mouse under the shadow of a vulture with no hole in sight.

"Nah," I say. "I should just be happy you're not lighting ants on fire and beating up defenseless Midders."

"Defenseless like you and Circ?"

"Circ was never defenseless," I say. "And now, neither am I." I grab my bow and fit it with a pointer faster'n you can say *Reformed bully baggard*. Hawk's hands are up and over his head and he's standing and backing away, but I shoot him anyway, right through the heart.

Only it's a play pointer, made of braided wildgrass for the shaft and bark for the tip. It bounces harmlessly off his left breast.

"Bullseye," I say. "Oh blaze, you shoulda seen your face. Better check your britches, make sure you didn't grizz yourself!" Lara's cracking up, which makes me crack up.

I put up with Hawk's bullying for so long it's nice to see the tents turned on him every now and again.

"Ha ha. Hilarious," Hawk says. "If Lara's staying up and taking my shift, then I'm getting some shuteye. Perhaps you should, too, Skinny."

I ignore the parting shot, his old nickname for me. Somehow, it doesn't hurt the way it used to. We also ignore his advice, talking and laughing and catching up like the old friends that we are, reminiscing 'bout our days spent training with the Wilde Ones, back when it was new and exciting.

We talk until the hole in the cave roof starts getting lighter, the sky above it split with streaks of red and gold. Lara wakes Hawk for his watch shift. Only then do we flop down next to each other and sleep.

~~~

I awake to a scream.

"Holy freakin' son of a—"

I'm on my feet and blinking away the sleep and grabbing my bow 'fore I even have the slightest clue what's going on.

Tristan and Adele are on their feet too, staring at their tugskin mats like they're covered in fire ants. Beyond 'em, Skye's practically going into convulsions, laughing her head off. What the scorch?

Then I see it.

The 'zard. Rough, gray skin with green spots. A pink tongue that's flicking out, almost like a snake. Sitting right on Adele's blanket. I start laughing too.

"You ain't scared of that little thing, are you?" I say. "It ain't even full grown yet."

Adele looks at me, at the 'zard, back at me. "What is it?"

65

"What? You don't recognize it? You gobbled it up last night right quick."

Tristan looks 'round Adele, a look of horror on his face. "Not the soup," he says.

"The soup," I say, holding back another laugh. I rub my belly. "And guess what's for breakfast?"

The 'zard, as if suddenly realizing we're all staring at it, takes off, running right at Adele. She leaps aside and it passes by, scurrying out through the camouflaged skin that apparently didn't fool it for one second.

Although the cave is already heating up from the morning sun, Adele shivers, her face all screwed up like she might be sick. "I can't believe I ate one of those," she says.

"Well, not a whole one. Just pieces of one, all chopped up. The tail, the legs, the eyeballs…" I trail off when Wilde, who's awake now, too, gives me a look.

Adele's hand is over her mouth. "There were eyeballs in that soup?" she says through her fingers.

"Quit messin' with her, Sie," Lara says, rolling over and rubbing her eyes. "There were no eyeballs, just the meat. 'Zards give you long-lasting energy."

Adele doesn't look convinced, but she manages to keep the prickler salad and soup down, so I give her credit for that.

"Do we want to know what pricklers are?" Tristan asks, one cheek scrunched up. Even with the weird expression on his face, he's a good looking guy: wavy, yellow-sand colored hair, sparkling blue eyes—though he's got nothing on Circ, who's smokier'n a bramble fire.

"We passed 'bout a hundred of 'em last night, but in the dark you mighta missed 'em. Some are green, some gray, some brownish. Each one looks a little different, like people, I guess.

But most every one of 'em have these nasty little prickles coming out of their skin. Trust me, you don't want to run into 'em. Once, when my baggard father sent me to Confinement, I managed to break out, but not without running smack into a searin' prickler. It hurt like a thousand fire ant bites, but later I found out the prickler's name was Perry, and we sorta became friends, or at least acquaintances, and I mostly liked him 'cept when he ragged on me, which was most of the time…"

I stop when I realize everyone's staring at me with the strangest expressions, like maybe I've caught the Fire, and it's eating away at my skin. I check my arms, my hands—my skin looks normal. Brown. Just brown. Like always.

"You made *friends* with a prickler?" Hawk says, standing just inside the secret opening, apparently having come inside during my story.

"I'm confused," Adele says. "At first I thought pricklers were some kind of plant, but are they an animal? Or some weird kind of person?"

"We ate your friend?" Tristan says, his handsome face screwed up even more.

Some things you just can't explain, so for the first time since I sprang outta bed, I keep my mouth shut tighter'n a Killer's mouth on a bone.

~~~

When the whole thing 'bout Perry the Prickler blows over, and Adele and Tristan have had a chance to peek outside to see what pricklers look like—they're sticking to eating plants from now on; 'zards are out—we have a real meeting, which is the reason we came in the first place.

As usual, Wilde kicks things off, and she doesn't waste any time with small talk. "You're not going to last long up here breathing this air."

Adele and Tristan nod in unison, their faces even.

"I believe your story. I believe you," she adds. I glance at Skye, whose eyes flick to mine, 'fore returning to Wilde's. Ain't she gonna say something? "Skye and I have talked it over, and we agreed we can't hold you here against your will."

"You have?" I blurt out, once more looking at Skye. She doesn't look at me this time.

"Yes," Wilde says. I raise my eyebrows. I guess Adele saving Skye's life went a lot further with her'n I first thought.

Adele and Tristan exchange a look. "We've talked things over, too," Tristan says. They have? When has all this talking been happening? And where was I? I like talking things over, too. "We don't want to go back yet." I stop breathing. What? "We've got as much to gain as you do from seeing Lecter defeated. We'd hoped there might be a chance to talk to him, to understand his point of view, but it's clear now that he's set on violence. We want to help you."

"But you'll die!" I say, unable to hold it in any longer.

"If we don't help you, you *all* might die. And we won't die right away," Adele says. "We'll last long enough to help you."

I shake my head. "You can go back down and get more of your people to help." You can do anything but stay up here and die! Even as I'm thinking it, I'm wondering why I care so much. I barely know these two. They could be enemy spies for all I know. But something deep inside of me knows they're not, that they're good, that they're really on our side.

"There's no time," Tristan says. "This war is happening now. And if we go back there's no guarantee anyone will follow us. We can't make them. They have enough of their own problems to deal with. We will stay. We will help."

"Sorry to interrupt," Wilde says, an unexpected smile creasing her face, "but we may have a solution to the whole toxic air thing. Show them, Lara."

Then, to my amazement, Lara unfolds a blanket on her lap. And inside are five of the strangest looking objects I've ever seen in my sixteen-year life.

Twelve
Dazz

"No!" I say, not caring that my voice is raised.

Curly Mustache Man looks incredulous. "No? Last time I checked, young man, you're not a member of the consortium. You're here to inform, not to decide."

"This is wrong," I say, pleading. "I've already discussed this with one of the leaders of the Tri-Tribes—Wilde. She's the one who helped save my sister, who helped my mother…but that's not what's important. The point is, we came to an agreement. The Unity Alliance. Us and the Tri-Tribes. It's our only hope against the Glassies. Strength in numbers."

"Not. Your. Decision," the White District rep says. "I put it to a vote. Two options. One: Do the smart thing and ally ourselves with the winning side, to a people who are slightly mysterious, yes, but who have been a valuable and amicable trade resource to us. Namely, the Glassies. Or two: Take this *boy's* advice and ally ourselves with the very people who were involved in the distasteful slave trade that ultimately led to the overthrow and execution of King Goff. Two options, my friends, I need not tell you which option I'll be voting for."

My face is on fire. My knuckles hurt and I realize my fists are clenched at my sides. The old Dazz is back, and if I let him loose I'm pretty sure he'll charge off the platform, break this man's freezin' jaw, and rip every last icin' hair of his curly mustache from his skin, one by one. *Breathe, Dazz. Breathe.* Focus. Words, not actions.

"If I may," I say, trying to keep my voice even, to mimic the air of confidence and slight arrogance my adversary just displayed. "While…"—I almost say *Curly Mustache Man*, but I catch myself—"…our honorable Blue District member has been sitting in his parlor room drinking hot tea and eating bear fritters, I've been in the middle of the action, seeing things that would shock and disgust you all. I might not be as old, might not have as much experience, but I am more informed than anyone in this room. Without the Tri-Tribes, Goff never would've been exposed *or* overthrown. Without the Tri-Tribes, my little sister would be dead. Without the Tri-Tribes, the dictatorial Admiral of the Soakers would still be enslaving Heater children on his ships. So, if you want to make an *informed* decision, I advise you to take option two."

When I finish a shiver runs through me, and I realize my fists are still clenched, my face still on fire, and I'm leaning forward, all the way to the edge of the raised platform. Who was that? Where did those words come from? I almost want to jump up and pump my fist. I never knew words could have such power, not when my fists are so good at what they do.

"Hmm, well met, *boy*," Mustache Man says. "But it will still be decided by a vote. And your plan is still teetering on the edge of crazy and insane. Voting begins now. You can choose one of the two options presented to you today, or you may, as always, choose to abstain." Things are moving much quicker than I expected. Too freezin' quick. "All those in favor of option two, an alliance with the Tri-Tribes…"

I also didn't expect my option to be presented first. I hold my breath.

Abe's hand is the first one up. He even drops his cigarette on the floor, stomps on it with his heel, and folds out of the current hand of cards he's playing. Yo's hand is up a second later, followed by another Brown District member. Although the three other Black District reps seem oblivious to the vote, Abe grab's each of their arms in turn, lifting them above their heads. Six out of sixteen votes.

I stare at the two unvoted Brown District reps. They're looking at their feet. Yo nudges one of them, but she doesn't react, just keeps staring down. The other guy is equally nonresponsive when Yo says something to him. Yo looks up at me, lips pursed, eyebrows narrowed. *I'm sorry*, he mouths.

It's not over. Everyone might just be abstaining, because they're unsure, or scared, or whatever. As long as the other option gets less than six votes we're okay.

"Six votes," Curly Mustache says with half a smile, as if we can't count. "Now for the first option, the *smart* choice. All those in favor of an alliance with our old friends, the Glassies…"

Four White District hands go up. Two Blue District hands. Six votes. All tied. The final four are evidently abstaining. How do they break ties?

But my question is lost on my lips, because just then, very late, a final hand goes up from one of the Blue District reps.

No.

No.

It's not a stretch, or a yawn, or a question—it's a vote. The seventh vote.

No.

This can't be happening. It can't.

It is. It's over.

"An alliance with the Glassies, it is," Mustache Man says. "Fortunately, I had the foresight and intelligence to send a message with our decision to the Glassy leader earlier today. President Lecter should be receiving it any moment, if he hasn't already."

"You can't do that," I say, but the fire's gone from my voice. Was it a whisper? Did I even speak?

"I can and I did. It was a risk, yes, but one that clearly paid off. District reps—please inform the people you represent of the decision. I fully expect the Glassies to send some of their forces to ice country to protect us from any backlash from the Tri-Tribes as a result of our decision. The people will have to get used to having them around."

Thirteen
Adele

"Where'd you get those?" I ask, staring at the gasmasks like they're precious gems.

"Off dead Glassies," Lara says. "The last time they attacked us we killed a bunch of 'em. They were wearing these. There're more in New Wildetown."

"And they're not broken?" Tristan asks, his voice equally full of amazement.

"See for yourself," Wilde says, handing him one. She gives me one too.

I turn it over in my hands, inspecting it for damage. It's a little scuffed, a little dusty, but seems okay. I give it a try, strap it around the back of my head, feel it suction around my nose and lips. Take a breath. *Whoosh!* The air comes in with a rush. It doesn't taste any different, except maybe a little plasticky. "I think it's working," I say, my voice coming out muffled and warped.

Tristan's got his on, too. "Cool," he says, and I can't help but laugh at the way his voice sounds, deeper and garbled. And then he laughs at my laugh, which sounds all husky and throaty.

It'll be annoying wearing the masks all the time, but at least we won't die from the air. "Why don't you wear these?" I ask.

"There aren't enough of them," Wilde says. "And we're not as affected by the air as your people; we're more used to it. Eventually we die from it, but not until we're at least thirty."

Thirty? Gosh, I had no idea. So young. And I thought the moon dwellers dying in their fifties was bad. It's not right that the Glassies, I mean the earth dwellers, should live inside their bubble, unwilling to share their air-filtering technology with the people they share the land with. And worse still, attacking them and trying to annihilate them? A fresh swathe of anger roils down the rivers of hot blood running through my veins. We have to help them. For their sake and for the sake of the dwellers below, who deserve the truth and a chance to live aboveground.

"Thank you," I say, biting back a twinge of emotion. Now's the time to stay levelheaded.

"Don't make us regret it," Skye says, but there's not as much bite in her voice as before. Is that a hint of a smile on her lips?

"You won't," Tristan says.

"Now that you can breathe freely," Wilde says, "we have much to discuss. Hawk, what's the latest?"

Hawk, still shirtless, clears his throat, looking a little awkward. It seems every time he's around Wilde he can't stop fidgeting. Maybe he's got a thing for her. "Well, uh…" he stammers.

"The Glassies have been sending out soldiers," Lara prods.

"Uh, yeah," Hawk agrees. "There are at least ten groups around fire country already, and more ride out on their fire chariots every day."

"Fire chariots?" Tristan says.

"They're very advanced in what they can build," Lara says. "They ride 'em. Metal chariots with wheels. They roll with no one pushin' or pullin' 'em. Dark smoke pours from a tube in the back, so we think they must be powered by fire somehow."

"Trucks," I say. "That's what we call them. It's not fire, not exactly, but you've got the right idea. We have them down below, too, although they're very expensive and not everyone can afford them."

"They're looking for us in these…trucks," Wilde says.

Hawk nods. "That's what we figured, too. And eventually they'll find us."

"And then it's over, like a game of feetball after Circ takes the field," Siena says.

"You have to hit them first," I say. "And harder."

Skye nods, her teeth clenched, says, "That's what I'm talkin' 'bout." At least we agree on something. It's a start, anyway.

"Have the Glassies been riding south, too?" Wilde asks.

"Yeah," Hawk says.

"That explains seein' the burnin' Killers this far north," Skye says. "The baggards are drivin' 'em from their lands."

"They've been killin' off the tug hurds, too," Lara adds. "We've seen 'em carryin' the dead animals back to the Glass City on their fire ch—their…trucks."

76

"They think if they kill off the hurds that we'll run out of food and have to move out of hiding," Wilde says.

"Is that true?" I ask.

Wilde shakes her head. "Not that long ago it might've been. But now, the Wilde Ones have taught the Heaters and Marked to be self-sufficient, to grow their own food, to not rely on meat alone."

"Wilde Ones? Heaters? The Marked?" Tristan says. "Sorry, you lost me there." I'm every bit as far behind and would've asked if Tristan didn't.

"There will be time for all of that later," Wilde says. "You've been very patient with us."

"But first, you want to know what we think you should do?" Tristan says.

Wilde smiles. "You are most perceptive. You know more about the Glassies than we do."

I look at Tristan and he looks at me. This is his call. He's seen them, met them. He gets politics in a way I never will. He might not like the way the world works, but at least he understands it, so he can change it. Me, I'd say let's throw rocks at their damn glass bubble until it shatters. Then they'll see what it means to live in fire country for real.

Jaw tight, he says, "Like Adele said, we have to hit them first and hard. But our only chance is to do it from the *inside* at the same time as the outside."

Skye's eyes light up. "You mean, like a spy?"

"That's exactly what I mean," Tristan says, and I know he's right. And there's only one of us who stands a chance on the inside.

"I'll do it," I say.

Fourteen
Siena

"I'm coming with you," Tristan says.

"No," Adele says. "Two spies will only increase our chances of being caught." Tristan opens his mouth to respond, but Adele rushes on. "And…they might recognize you. After all, you're the President of the Tri-Realms now, not exactly a nobody like me."

"Sounds smart to me," Skye says.

"No," Tristan says. "It's too dangerous. Adele, no." His last two words are less firm, like a desperate plea when you know you've been beaten.

"It was your idea," Adele says, taking his hand. I feel a burn in my gut. It's the way I'd touch Circ if we were in a similar situation. Can we really send her into the belly of the enemy? I know the answer is yes, but I still hafta ask the question.

"Isn't there another way?" I say. "One where she's not all alone?"

"I'd go with her," Skye says quickly, "but I'd stick out like a red bird in a flock of crows."

"No," Adele says. "This is my mission alone."

"Come back to me," Tristan says. "Promise it."

Adele forces a smile. "Have I ever not?"

~ ~ ~

Through the hole, the sky's a mass of yellow clouds, with only the smallest dots of red sky poking through. The wind is heavy, whipping swirls of dust and the occasional brambleweed overhead.

Everything's happening too fast for Tristan, who hasn't said much since the decision was made to send Adele in as the spy. We say spy, but what we really mean is assassin. We want her to kill Lecter, but if she can't, she needs to find a way to help us bring down his forces from the inside.

While Lara and Hawk went looking for an old Glassy suit stripped off of one of the dead soldiers, I've been watching as he holds her in his arms for a long time.

Funny how things can change in a heartbeat. Not funny ha ha, but funny strange, funny wooloo. Just yesterday I had a pointer aimed at this girl's chest, ready to kill her if she tried to do anything to my sister. And now…now she's aiming the pointer at her own heart.

Her green eyes're shining as she looks over Tristan's shoulder, but there're no tears. They're shining with determination, with readiness.

"These will help you blend in," Wilde says, holding some Glassy clothes in her arms. "They should fit."

Adele pulls herself from Tristan's arms, lifts to her tiptoes, and peels back her mask to kiss him on the cheek, 'fore turning to Wilde. "Thank you," she says.

"No. Thank you," Wilde says. "You've given us hope."

"Everyone deserves a little hope. But there's no hope unless I get some information. I need to know more about your countries, about your history. The more I know the better, before I go in."

"Siena," Wilde says. "You know as much about things as anyone. Can you answer her questions?"

"Is Perry a baggard?" I say.

Wilde just looks at me, an eyebrow raised. "Well, yeah, he is," I say. "Sit your butt down and I'll tell you everything you wanna know."

Adele sits and Tristan slides down next to her. I flop down in front of 'em, crossing my legs. "Whaddya wanna know?" I ask.

"How are you even here?" Adele says. "We thought the dwellers were the only humans left."

I laugh. Not that long ago, I thought *my* people were the only ones left. I start from the beginning. "When the Meteor God crash-landed on the earth, my ancestors hid from Him, hoping He'd pass us by. At the time, they lived in these camps, called Rezervayshuns."

"Holy crap, you're descended from Native Americans," Adele says. "We learned about that in school. You were the first people to live here, but then Europeans came and they didn't treat you too well and—"

There's not much time and she's speaking 'bout things I don't think I need to know, not now anyway, so I cut her off. "That all sounds plenty interesting, but I don't know nothing 'bout Or-rope-ians, or whatever you called 'em. All I know is my people hid from Meteor for a long time in caves in the desert rock formations. A long, long time. Like years and years."

"People who didn't get picked in the Lottery…" Tristan murmurs.

"The what?" I ask.

"You mean, you don't know about the Lottery?" Adele says, sharpening her gaze.

I shake my head. "Lot of what?"

Tristan looks at Adele. Adele looks at Tristan. Tristan says, "When…Meteor God…was on his way, the people who used to live here—both our ancestors—picked people to save, those who would go down below. Into the Tri-Realms."

I give 'em my best frown. "That doesn't seem fair."

"There wasn't room for everyone, so they thought it was the most fair," Adele says. "But I don't disagree with you. I can't believe your people don't know about it."

"It's been almost five hundred years since Meteor came," I say. "And most of the years we've been trying to survive, 'specially in the beginning. Some things just get lost."

"Hmm. Well, regardless, some of you survived anyway," Tristan says.

"S'pose so. We called our tribe the Heaters," I say. So I tell 'em as much as I know. 'Bout living in fire country, barely surviving, the Fire killing more'n more of us each year; the Call, where sixteen-year-old girls were paired with guys for the sole purpose of baby-making. I explain how the Wildes broke away from the Heaters, how the Marked were formed, 'bout my adventures in fire and ice and water and storm country. How all kinds of people survived Meteor, forming their own tribes. Anything I forget to tell 'em, they draw out of me with questions.

While I'm talking, some of t'others, Skye and Lara and Hawk and Wilde, pop in and out, sometimes to listen, sometimes to eat, sometimes whispering their own conversations, but I barely notice 'em 'cause I'm reliving the past, almost like I'm creating history all over again.

When I finish, Adele says, "Wow," and Tristan says, "Is that it?" but I know he's kidding 'cause I told 'em a scorch of a lot of stuff. Days and days and days' worth in just a few hours.

"Thank you," Adele says. "It's a lot to take in, but it helps. I hope I get to meet the rest of your people some—"

But she doesn't get to finish that thought, and I don't get to answer her, 'cause Skye comes rushing in, her eyes hard and her fists harder, and she says, "An Icer just showed up at the Glass City…and they let him in."

~~~

We're all peeking over the rocks, blanketed by thick skins that blend right in. It's hot as scorch 'cause the sun goddess is still a long way from sleep. Sweat's running down my forehead and into my eyes, but I endure the stinging so I don't miss anything.

Nothing's happened since the big doors opened and the Icer went inside the city. We've been mumbling the same questions back and forth and up and down and 'round in circles to pass the time.

Why'd an Icer go to see the Glassies?

Is he a Glassy spy, sent to get information for 'em?

Does he know 'bout the Unity Alliance, how Dazz and Buff are getting the Icers to fight with us?

Have they killed him?

Though none of us wanna admit it, it's the last question that's the most important.

When the sun goddess gets tired and starts her long journey home, something finally happens. There's a *whirring* sound, like heavy winds are rushing over us, only there ain't even the tiniest breeze to cool things down. Then, right 'fore our very eyes, the giant metal door in the side of the Glass City begins to open.

"Another group of soldiers looking for us?" I ask to anyone who might be listening.

"Shhh!" Skye hisses sharply, even louder'n I was.

"I betcha my whole skin of water that Icer ain't dead," I say. Is that really what I believe? Or am I just saying it to try to make it true? I think it's what my mother used to call wishful thinking.

"Sister, I swear on the sun goddess that if you don't shut yer tug-lovin' mouth I'll shut it fer ya!" Again, her saying that was louder'n I was.

So, though I've got half-a-dozen other things to say, I stuff 'em down deep, saving 'em for another time. Then I wait.

But I don't hafta wait long, 'cause outta the door comes a fire chariot—what'd Adele call it? A cluck or truck or some wooloo nonsense—spitting up rocks and pushing a cloud of dust in its wake. And on that…truck…there're a bunch of soldiers, all dressed in uniforms splotched with browns and greens. And sitting amongst 'em, like he belongs there, like he's ONE OF 'EM, is that no-good Icer, who I suddenly wish were dead.

~~~

"What the scorch was an *Icer*"—Skye says it like it's a curse— "doin' with a bunch of Glassies?"

We're back inside the hideaway now, setting in a circle. Hawk's drinking fire juice and keeps trying to pass it 'round until Wilde gives him a look that makes him put it away right quick.

"Maybe he's pretending to help 'em," I say, "but really he's spying on 'em."

"That's the searin' woolooist thing I ever heard in my life," Skye says.

I frown, chewing on my lip. Why's she being so tough on me lately? Is it 'cause I gave her a hard time 'bout her thing with Dazz? If so, I'd 'poligize a thousand times—I was just joking 'round to pass the time.

"It's possible," Wilde says, and I give her a grateful smile.

"The bigger question," Tristan says through his mask, leaning forward, his hands on his knees, "is where are they going?"

"Which means starting my mission as soon as possible is even more important now," Adele says.

Now it's Tristan's turn to frown. "That's not what I meant."

"You can go with her as far as a rock outcropping near the Glass City," Wilde says. "Then she's on her own. May the sun goddess be with her."

"Oh, she won't need the sun goddess," Tristan says. "She's got everything she needs with her."

Adele's only response to that is a wry smile.

Fifteen
Dazz

All I want to do is run all the way to fire country and tell Skye and Wilde and the rest of my friends what has happened. That I've failed them. The Unity Alliance never had the chance to become a reality.

But I can't, not when the message has already come back from the Glassies in the form of a dozen soldiers, dressed in thick green-and-brown painted uniforms, toting heavy black weapons—fire sticks Skye calls them—and wearing strange masks over their mouths. Yo told me what the message from President Lecter said. He's accepted our alliance on the condition that we temporarily move to "the New City," which I assume is what they call the glass-domed city in fire country. We'll be protected by the Glassy soldiers as we travel there.

But we can't go there, can we? We can't abandon the Tri-Tribes, my friends, ice country. There has to be a way to cancel the alliance. A revote, a split decision, something.

Yo says it's impossible. We all go or none of us go. The message also said if any Icers try to go rogue that they'll be treated as traitors and killed on sight. For the better part of the morning several of the soldiers have been going house to house, checking to make sure no one's trying to hide. The rest are keeping a careful watch on the perimeter. Yo says maybe it's not a bad thing, maybe this is the only way to survive. But I heard the lie in his voice.

What choice do I have? If I try to run, I'll be abandoning my family, and I might be killed anyway. And if I try to escape with them, they might be killed, too. But if I go along with this plan, at least I can protect Mother and Jolie, Buff and his family, Yo and Abe and Hightower. And the Tri-Tribes might win the war anyway. Then things will just go back to normal, won't they? I could explain things to Skye and Wilde, make them understand the impossible situation we were in.

The only thing worse than lying to your friends is lying to yourself.

I glare at the Glassy soldier walking by and contemplate whether he'd shoot me if I chucked a snowball at his head.

Make that an iceball.

I head inside to give my family the bad news.

~~~

Jolie doesn't understand and I don't blame her. "Why do we have to leave?" she asks.

We're sitting inside the house, trying to keep warm and considering what to pack for the long journey ahead of us.

"The leaders decided it was best," I say, trying to keep from grinding my teeth.

"And they're really smart, right?"

"Wellll," I say. "Some of them are." All the ones who voted *against* the decision.

Mother's gazing absently into the fireplace, saying nothing.

"How long will we be gone?" Jolie asks.

I shrug. "Probably not long. Maybe a week, maybe two. But it could be more than that, too, no one really knows."

"Will Wilde and Skye be there?"

The question hits me so hard it's as if the iceball I wanted to launch at the soldier rebounded and came back twice as hard, smashing me in the gut. "Wellll…" Why do I keep starting my sentences with that word, drawing it out like that? As my father would say, "Sounds like a deep thought." Ha ha. I'm annoying even myself. I start over, ready to face the truth head on with my family by my side. They deserve the truth. "Skye's not coming, Joles. Nor is Wilde. Not any of our friends from fire country."

"Why not? Don't they want to be protected by the Glassies, too?"

Deep breath. Take a sip of hot tea to open my throat. "The thing is, the Glassies are supposedly 'protecting us' from the Tri-Tribes."

Jolie starts cracking up. She doesn't believe me and I don't blame her. "Why would we need protecting from our friends?" Sometimes she's too smart.

I sigh. "We don't, but the leaders think we do."

"We should ignore the leaders and go live with Skye," Jolie says, her face lighting up, like she's just come up with the best idea in the world. Which she has. The best, impossible idea.

"They won't let us," I say. "Trust me, Joles, we have no choice. Now let's get packed up."

"This sucks iceballs," Jolie mutters, and finally Mother snaps her gaze away from the fireplace, her mouth half-open as if to rebuke her daughter's vulgarity. But then her mouth slowly closes and she gives me the saddest look I've ever seen.

~ ~ ~

We're all packed up and ready to go. Mother, Jolie, and I decided to bring just what we can carry on our backs, which isn't much.

As we walk through the snow, leaving final footprints like markers so we don't get lost, I glance back at our house, half expecting it to crumble into ash behind us. But it doesn't, just stands resolute and waiting, the final wisps of smoke from the snuffed out fire snaking from the chimney toward the sky.

A large snowflake lands on my nose, and I watch with crossed eyes as it melts into a tiny droplet that drips to the ground.

I hold Jolie's hand on one side and Mother's on the other, and it's not weird at all like I'd expect it to be. If we must go, we'll go together, as one. We *are* the Unity Alliance, and we'll see it through, somehow, someway, if only in our minds and hearts.

We pass the rigid form of a soldier, red-faced and standing at attention, staring past us as if we're not even there. Are we ghosts? Have we been reduced to wraiths, shadows of ourselves who give in to tyrants? My eyes never leave the soldier's, as if challenging him, but he doesn't so much as change the path of his stare; until, just as we're about past him, his eyes flick to Jolie's and he winks.

The sudden rage that fills me splits me like a logger's axe on a fallen tree. I'm taking deep breaths and clenching and unclenching my fists and thinking happy thoughts—doing all the things I've practiced to control my temper—when Jolie sticks out her tongue. Well—yeah, get ready for another *deep* thought—let me tell you, the soldier's face goes even redder, and it's not from the cold. It's humiliation and embarrassment and for a second I think he might shoot us all dead right here and now. But his hand only twitches on his weapon and then he flashes a smile and goes right on back to staring at nothing and nobody.

I look down at Jolie, and she's grinning up at me. Mother's smiling, too, because sometimes it's the stuck-out-tongue of a twelve-year-old that's the best antidote for arrogance and evil; and my temper, too, I guess.

Down the path we go, making our way to Buff's house. At least we'll be able to travel with him and his family.

I chuckle softly to myself as we approach. It's like all the chaos and insanity that's usually hidden behind the thin wooden walls has spilled out into the snow. They've got a wooden-wheeled cart, full of all sorts of odds and ends, like pots and kindling and water skins and—is that a feathered hat?—and bundles of clothes that appear to be dark with wetness and maybe mud, as if they were dropped a dozen times before making it into the cart-bed. All around the cart are munchkins: two of them are rolling over and over, a boy and a girl, grappling, shoving snow in each other's faces; another one's climbing the cart wheel, screaming "Ayayayayayaya!" with streaks of mud on her face; a fourth kid, who I like to call Baby-Buff, because of his striking resemblance to my friend, has his boots on the wrong feet and is tossing handfuls of what appears to be flour into the air. "It's snowing!" he yells at the top of his lungs. The fifth is being wrestled to the cart by the second-oldest, Darcy, who looks to be about at the end of her rope with impatience and frustration, her dark, curly hair tumbling out of a knit-hat and across her face.

Buff's right behind her, his father's arm looped around his neck. As they hobble over to the cart, Buff sees us and says, "Want to go kid-wrangling? Whoever gets the most in the cart—you might have to tie them up, mind you—gets a rare and wonderful prize."

"Ooh, I want a prize," Jolie says. "What is it?"

"Don't encourage him," Darcy says, shoving one of her brothers into the back of the cart. Within seconds, he's climbed over the food and clothes and leapt off the side, managing to dislodge the wheel-climbing kid at the same time. They tumble through the snow in a fit of giggles and shrieks of delight.

"You get to eat yellow snow!" Buff exclaims, as if *that's* the most original joke he's ever made.

"Eww," Jolie says, but she's giggling.

I swoop down and grab the two kids wrestling, one under each arm. "I'll help with the wrangling, but I'll skip the prize if I win."

"Your loss," Buff says with a tight grin. To anyone who doesn't know him as well as I do, he would almost look happy, like his good old jovial joke-cracking self. But I can see something behind his façade of wisecracks and wide smiles:

fear. For his family; for my family; for this entire freezin' world that's become a huge Heart-icin' mess.

I toss the kids onto a soft pile of unfolded clothes in the back of the cart, and then help Buff lift his injured father. My mother takes his crutch. "What do you make of all this?" she says to him in a low voice.

"Honestly, I don't know. It feels so wrong, but so do so many things nowadays."

My mother nods, takes his hand. "We're in this together. All of us." I give her a boost to sit beside him. "We've got two of the best boys in the whole of this world," she says once she's settled.

I turn away to grab another kid so she can't see the ice water in my eyes.

Sixteen
Adele

Finally, it's just Tristan and I again.

The curving glass dome stands before us, dispersing the last rays of the dying red sun into fragments of light. It's beautiful. Almost doesn't seem real. I still can't get over how big everything is up here. I'd thought some of the Sun Realm subchapters were more enormous than anything in the world, but this land, fire country, makes everything below seem like dwarfs, stunted.

And an entire city contained within a glass dome? Sounds impossible, and yet I'm staring at the buildings rising up like giants made of stone and metal and glass.

The heat of the sand warms my belly, even through the camo shirt, which is tucked into my camo pants.

"Adele…" Tristan says, and I can feel his heat, too, as he looks at me, as his hip brushes up against mine.

I stare straight ahead, as if hoping to cut an opening in the glass with the intensity of my gaze. I can't look at him, can't break down, can't be *attached* to anything but my objectives. Infiltrate, gather intel, sabotage, assassinate.

"Adele, look at me," he says.

"No."

"Adele, I—"

"No." Seriously, no.

Tristan grabs my chin and pulls it toward him and then we're ripping off our masks and kissing, his lips so soft and yet moving fiercely against mine. I wrap a hand around the back of his head, lace my fingers through his hair, breathe him in, kiss him back. My heart blossoms.

It can't. I can't feel this, not now.

I pull away, but can't bring myself to unlock my hand from his head. "Adele, I—I love you," he says.

It's too much—more than I can handle. A raft of emotions fills my chest: a burst of happiness, a swallow of guilt, an icy stab of pain and sorrow.

"You can't say that," I say.

"I just did."

"I mean, you can't say that now."

"Then when?"

"I don't know," I say honestly.

"Too late," he says.

"I love you, too," I blurt out, and when his lips form a huge smile I almost feel giddy, which isn't right because of what I'm about to do, and what might happen and because…

"This won't be the last time you say that to me," Tristan says, serious again. "It won't. Don't think it for one second."

I nod. Swallow. Replace my mask. Go back to gazing at the New City. Where I have to go.

We lay in silence for a while, watching the city from our hiding spot behind the large boulders. The sky grows darker and darker.

When only a sliver of sunlight glows over the horizon, Tristan says, "My father once referred to Borg Lecter as a snake."

I glance at him and our eyes meet. "Takes one to know one." He can't see my smile beneath my mask, but I think it reaches my eyes, because I see his cheeks lift.

"I just mean to be careful. That's high praise coming from my father. He hated and respected Lecter. He must be impressively evil to have wrested power from a Nailin." The way Tristan speaks of his father is so clinical it's like he's discussing the molecular composition of granite. What his father did to him…

"Tristan, I wish things could've been different with your family…" That I didn't have to kill your father, that you didn't have to kill your brother, that your father didn't kill your mother, my father, Cole. So much death—it's almost unbelievable.

"You're my family," Tristan says, still sounding remote, detached. He's got a wall up around his heart now. "Roc's my family. Your father was like a father to me, even if only for a short time. A real father." His voice breaks on the last word, as if the wall around his heart has a crack in it.

I feel my own heart start to crack, too, so I say, "You know, it's funny, people in my town, in subchapter 14, always hated your father, hated the Nailins, but they sort of envied you, too. They wanted to be you. The girls wanted to be with you." I'm trying to lighten things up, but it doesn't work.

"They shouldn't have," Tristan says.

"You were the goodness amongst the evil," I say. "You and your mother. Flowers amongst weeds. That's why she brought us together. Remember? She believed you could change things, and you have. We both have. Only we're not done yet, okay? There's still a fight to be fought."

"But I'll be fighting out here, and you in there." Tristan gestures angrily at the glass dome, glowing now with city lights.

"Perhaps you should be fighting from somewhere else," I say.

"What?" Tristan says, glancing at me sharply.

I point at the ground. "Maybe Wilde was right. Maybe one of us should go back, try to unite the dwellers, gain support for the cause above."

Tristan shakes his head. "I'm not leaving you up here alone," he says.

I take his hand. "Once I'm behind that glass, I'll already be alone. There will be nothing more you can do for me."

"I can fight with the Tri-Tribes. Fight my way inside, back to you." The intensity in his eyes and tone tells me he would. Or at least try. But no.

"They need you down below. You're the one to unite the Tri-Realms."

His head won't stop shaking. "I'm a Nailin who went against the Nailins. The sun dwellers will call me a traitor, and the moon and star dwellers will call me the enemy. I'm an outcast from my own people." It's like an endless chasm has opened in his chest, sucking his soul into a pit of despair. I need to pull him out of it.

I grab his shirt by the collar, pull him toward me, hug him fiercely. Whisper in his ear. "Your mother believed you could make a difference. My father too. And so do I. Just think about it, that's all I ask."

When I release my grip to look at him, one of his eyebrows is raised, and even beneath the mask I can see the cockeyed look of amusement I fell in love with the first time I saw it. He's back. Maybe not all the way, but at least partially. I only hope that's enough.

~~~

Eventually even the city lights begin to wink out, one by one, casting the buildings under a blanket of shadow. The edge of the glass dome shines slightly under the lights of the moon and stars.

It's time to make my move.

Will I ever see my mother again? Elsey? Can't think about that now. Need to focus.

First I need to check out the security situation. I tried to explain it to Wilde, but the idea was foreign to her. "What does 'security' mean?" she asked.

"Like protection," I said.

"Guards?"

"Definitely. Probably electricity and guns and other things, too. Security. I'm just warning you not to be alarmed if you see and hear some crazy things tonight," I told her.

"Okay," she said, but I'm not totally sure she understood.

In any case, it's time to find out what I'm up against. With Tristan watching, I pick up a medium-sized rock and run my thumb and forefinger along its sides, trying to get a feel for it. Tense my muscles in preparation. I pop up, widen my stance, and chuck the rock with everything I've got. Crouching, I watch as it arcs, reaches its peak, and then starts its descent downward, skittering off the hard ground and bouncing short of the dome. I swear under my breath. I've never had that good of an arm. Give me something to shoot—a gun, a slingshot, a bow—and I'll do just fine, but make me throw something and it usually doesn't go that well.

"Sure you don't want me to come along for situations like this?" Tristan says. His comment pisses me off a little, but at least he's joking again, smirking. Himself again.

He picks up another rock, one a little bigger than mine, and crouches beside me. Leans back, his long arm whipping behind his head, and then launches it. We huddle together, watching its flight as it careens farther, farther, farther, and then connects!

Sparks fly as the angry snarl of electricity rips through our ears. The rock is flung back and away from the dome, and a huge spotlight bursts through the glass, illuminating the desert just outside the city.

We duck behind the rocky outcropping, jammed together. My heart's racing, my breath sucked heavily into my lungs. I don't dare to breathe. The light passes over us, cutting a bright arc around the shadow cast by the boulder.

And then it winks off, returning the night to its natural state of moonlit darkness. My breath comes out in a whoosh, but Tristan's is even heavier. Maybe now Wilde understands what I meant by security.

"Guess you'll have to use the door," he jokes.

"Damn. That's so not my style."

We wait in silence for what feels like an hour before risking another peek at the city. Inside the dome, nothing moves, nothing breathes. Silence.

Then we hear it.

A cough.

We look at each other with wide eyes. The cough becomes a hum, then a snarl. A vehicle. Approaching fast. A fire chariot, as Siena would say.

It comes into view when it bursts over a mound, its headlights cutting through the night. It roars down the hill, not fifty feet from us. As it passes, I see them in the truck bed. Earth dwellers, wearing uniforms and masks, not unlike my own, toting black guns. A loud hum fills the air and the black, metal gate swings open, either automatically or because someone is watching for them. The truck enters through the gate and then stops in a glass tube just inside. We can see it through the transparent dome. The metal door closes behind them. There's a rubbery suction-like sound that lasts for a few minutes, and then a door at the opposite end of the glass corridor opens. The truck drives through.

"An airlock," Tristan says.

I nod. "They filter out the potentially harmful air before letting them through." Makes sense. Seems they've got everything figured out to protect their citizens. And yet they refuse to leave the Tri-Tribes alone to live in peace, as harmless neighbors. Why?

It gets later and later as we wait. Or maybe earlier and earlier. Is it the end of the day or the beginning of the next? I'm not tired because of how late we stayed up the night before and how late we slept in today, but my eyes feel stingy, either because of the dust or because I'm not blinking enough, afraid I'll miss something.

Another truck comes and the events from earlier repeat. Door opens, door closes, air is filtered out, other door opens, truck enters.

"What should I do?" I say when the sequence is finished.

"Abort mission," Tristan says, half-grinning, his teeth purple under the night sky.

"Nice try. I'm thinking I just stroll up the next time a truck comes by, slip in behind it."

"This isn't the Sun Realm and these aren't garbage trucks," Tristan says, reminding me of the time when we used a similar tactic to infiltrate the Capitol. "They'd see you right away."

"I don't have many other options."

"Just be one of them," Tristan says. "Pretend you were on a mission, got hurt, disoriented, lost in the desert. Something like that."

I stick my chin out. It's not the worst plan ever. "That could work," I say, "but it'd have to look real. I'd need to have injuries."

"Are you giving me permission to hit you?" Tristan says, and it should be a joke, but he looks horrified.

"I think you'll have to. I'd hit myself, but I'm not sure how effective it would be." Are we really talking about hurting me like it's some tactical problem we have to solve?

Tristan screws up his face.

"We don't have a choice," I insist.

"Not that," he says. "There's something else."

Oh, crap, what? "Tell me," I say.

"Everyone in the city has a microchip inside them, in their wrist." I remember Tristan telling me about how he had to wear a metal armband when he visited the New City with his family.

"To track them," I say. "But I thought they wore bracelets."

Tristan shakes his head. "That was just for visitors. The residents get something more permanent." *Great*, I think. Another chip. I've already got the one in the back of my neck—although it's deactivated now—that my mother implanted to connect me to Tristan. Now I have to get one in my wrist.

"So we have to make it look like someone cut it out," I say.

"Exactly," Tristan says, his lips curled in disgust.

"No biggie. Just make it quick." I hand him the knife I borrowed from another dead Glassy.

He takes it and says, "Right arm. Turn it over. Close your eyes."

"I can watch."

He shrugs as if to say, "If you pass out, at least it'll delay the mission." Slowly, painfully slowly, he digs the tip of the knife into my skin, higher up on my forearm than I expected. At first it's just a sharp prick, almost more like pressure, but as he digs deeper it becomes a searing pain that lances through my arm to my fingertips. Blood wells up and I grit my teeth, grab a jagged corner of the rock with my other hand, fight off the urge to flinch, to pull away, to hit him.

He twists the knife. "Arrr," I growl, keeping my voice as low as possible, so it doesn't rise above the boulder.

And then it's over. He pulls the knife out and presses a corner of his shirt firmly on the wound, which is throbbing wildly. "Sorry," he says. "I'm so sorry. I had to make it as ragged as possible so it would look real, as if someone like Skye cut it out."

I almost laugh at that, despite the fire in my arm. "I think you'll have to dig in one more time to make it look like Skye did it," I say through my teeth.

"If you say so," Tristan says, starting to pull the cloth away, raising the knife once more.

"No, no, no, no, I was kidding," I say quickly.

"I know," he says, slipping the blood-stained knife back in my belt. I don't ask him to clean it; it'll look more realistic with the blood on it, like I'd been fighting the natives before they took me down and cut my chip out.

Tristan tears off a piece of his shirt, exposing his abdomen. He wraps it tightly around my shredded arm, tying it rapidly and somewhat poorly, like how I might've done it myself if I was injured. His sharp mind is working double time, thinking of every detail to give me the best shot possible.

"Do you want me to hit you now or wait a few minutes?" he asks. The wry grin is back, and I know that joking is the only way he can cope with everything.

"I'll barely feel it after the kni—"

His fist comes up so fast and unexpectedly that I don't even have time to think about moving out of the way. The impact twists my head to the side and rocks me back. I slam to the ground, hitting my head on a small stone. My cheek and eye are stinging and throbbing and burning, and I can already feel the pressure of a goose egg rising on the crown of my head.

Tristan's all over me, hugging me, spooning me, kissing the back of my neck. "Adele, I'm sorry. So sorry."

I choke out a laugh, blinking the water out of my eyes. "Don't be. I'm fine. Training with my dad there's never been a question as to whether I can take a hit."

We lay like that for a few minutes, my head swarming with so much fog it's like I'm underwater. Tristan knows how to punch, that's for sure, and he didn't hold back. Again, I know he did it for me and that it probably killed him having to do it. This is the world we live in. Hurting those we love to help them. Hitting me to save my life. A backwards world.

Eventually, I stir, force Tristan off of me, my head spinning slightly. "How do I look?" I ask.

Tristan blinks, his jaw tightening. He manages to compose himself, forces a smile. "Like you just went toe to toe with a brick wall."

"Good," I say, grabbing a handful of dust and smearing it on my face, on my arms. Trying to look as weathered and beaten as possible.

In the distance, there's a cough.

Leaning forward quickly, I give Tristan a kiss on the lips and say, "Showtime."

I push to my feet and step out from the rock. Behind me, Tristan says, "Be careful," but I don't look back. Step by step, I stumble toward the black gates, doing my best to stay in character, which isn't that difficult with my head still floating through the clouds.

The truck is getting closer, the beam of the headlights bouncing just beside me now. I look back, squinting, a hand cupped over my eyes as the glare locks onto me. I stagger…and I fall, first to my knees, and then right on my face. I don't even bother to cushion my landing with my hands, which hurts like hell. But it had to look real—I pray it looked real.

Gravel scraping, tires skidding, voices shouting.

I let the world spin as my eyes flutter closed.

"Soldier! Soldier!" someone shouts. I don't react.

Strong arms lift my arms, my feet, swing-carry me through the air. I play dead.

They lay me gently on something hard. I groan, just like I should.

"Go, go!" a husky voice says, and the truck roars to life, vibrating beneath me, sending jolts through my bones with every bounce over the rough terrain. Humming, humming: I know the New City gate is opening. Can this be happening? Can this be working?

The truck stops and the gate whirs and clicks and hums as it closes.

I'm in.

Seventeen
Siena

So easy. Almost too easy. The Glassies didn't question it, didn't stand 'round scratching their chins and saying, "I wonder if this is some sorta trick." They just grabbed Adele and slung her into their fire chariot and took her inside. So easy.

Are we the fools?

"She's one of THEM!" Skye hisses, stabbing her finger in the dark toward the now-closed door.

"She was acting," Wilde says, but her voice is much less convincing'n usual.

"Ha! See what'd happen if I tried to act. They'd shoot me on the spot," Skye says, stabbing another finger at the Glass City.

Yeah, but... "You don't look like 'em," I say. "She does."

"Exactly!" Skye says, much too loudly, as if I've made her point. "If someone looks like 'em, talks like 'em, rides in fire chariots like 'em, she must be one of 'em."

Her logic makes sense, but that don't mean it's true. "So…what? She was spying on us the whole time?" I say. "She's gonna go tell 'em 'bout the Unity Alliance, 'bout us hiding over 'ere? That's nothing, Skye. If she was gonna spy on us, she woulda waited till we took her back to New Wildetown, then tried to escape." Do I believe what I'm saying, or do I just wanna believe it?

"Then where's Tristan?" Skye says, her eyebrows raised, as if that was the winning argument. Where *is* Tristan? I wonder, looking 'round.

"I'm right here," a voice says from behind us, making us all jump a little.

"You baggard," Skye says, her finger swinging 'round to aim at him now. I'm glad she doesn't have her longblade with her or we'd be constantly ducking to keep our heads on our shoulders.

"I'm the baggard?" Tristan says hotly, staring Skye down. "You're the ones who made her go in there alone. They might've discovered her already, killed her already."

He stomps away, back inside the hideaway. "Don't prove anythin'," Skye mutters.

But it does and she knows it. He came back. And if they were spies he wouldn't've.

~~~

More'n more fire chariots return to the Glass City during the night. Eventually I lose count and my excitement dies down each time Lara or Hawk come running in saying, "Another one!"

When I finally fall asleep, it's so heavy the second coming of the Meteor God couldn't wake me.

It's my nose that pulls me back to life. I awake to the aroma of spiced 'zard. Ugh. Same old, same old.

But my stomach growls anyway, 'cause sometimes it doesn't give two blazes 'bout what I put in it, so long as I put *something* in there.

I sit up, rubbing my eyes. Skye and Hawk are out, lying 'gainst the cave wall at opposite ends. Lara's nowhere to be seen, so she's probably camouflaged up top, watching for more chariots. Wilde and Tristan sit 'cross from each other, heads bowed, having a conversation so low I can only catch snatches of it.

"…has to be a reason they'd…" That's Wilde.

"…found your…" Tristan's response.

"…be ready." Wilde again.

I flinch when Wilde's head suddenly snaps in my direction, like she realizes I've been watching 'em, listening.

"Uh, is it morning?" I say. There's plenty of light coming through the hole in the roof, so it's probably not the smartest question.

"Yes," Wilde says. "Today's the day we go back to New Wildetown."

"What 'bout Adele?" I ask.

"Only the sun goddess can protect her now."

"She'll do her part—now we need to do ours," Tristan adds.

"The fight on the outside," I say.

"Searin' right," Skye says, rolling over. "'Em baggards won't know what hit 'em."

Is she right, or is it just Skye being Skye? Confident, sure of herself, tough as a tugskull. Yeah, we beat the Glassies the last time they came for us, but we surprised 'em. We even surprised ourselves. I mean, the Heaters didn't expect the Wilde Ones to show up, and we sure as scorch didn't expect Feve and the Marked to crash the party. We got the best of our pale-faced neighbors, but the next time they'll come in harder, with more soldiers, with more weapons…

Will we survive? Do we have any chance? With Adele on the inside, maybe, but only half a chance. With the Icers fighting with us under the Unity Alliance, maybe a whole chance. I gotta believe; it's the only way I can stay sane when Circ's not 'round.

I blink away my thoughts when Lara comes rushing in, her eyes bigger'n a Killer's gaping jaw. "Something's happening," she says.

We follow her out of the opening, creep to the top, slither under the rock-colored skin. Even Hawk wakes up and follows us up without asking any stupid questions.

Sure enough, as Lara said, something's happening. But that's a major understatement, 'cause it ain't just something, it's a BIG something. Dozens of fire chariots are setting just outside the Glass City, not moving, just waiting. Half of 'em are full of Glassy soldiers, all wearing masks like the one Tristan's wearing, all wearing uniforms and balancing black fire sticks on their knees. The rest of the soldiers are piling into the remaining empty fire chariots.

I duck my head even lower. If one of 'em spots us…

But no, our cave is pretty far off. Unless they ride right at us, we'll be fine.

Skye curses under her breath. "They musta found us," she says, and I know she don't mean *us* us. She means New

Wildetown. She means all of us. The mothers, the fathers, the children. Circ. Feve. Jade, our younger sister. Veeva. Everyone I care 'bout. My world.

"We gotta get back. We gotta get back now," I say, and I feel my heart racing and a creep of chill running through my veins, almost like I'm back in ice country.

I'm already pulling away, ready to grab our stuff and go, charge 'cross the desert, attempt to outrun the fire chariots, even when I know it's impossible. But Wilde stops me with a hand on my shoulder. "Wait," she says. "Look."

I don't wanna—I wanna run, run, run!—but I hafta look, 'cause when Wilde says something you just do it. I snap my gaze back to the Glass City and see what Wilde's talking 'bout.

The first of the chariots is leaving, spitting black smoke out the back and growling. A cloud of dust plumes in its wake, but the second chariot just drives right through it, following behind. The third, the fourth, and then all the rest do the same. A long line of fire chariots, like a disgustingly long snake roping its way through the desert. We're too late. They're too fast and we're too late.

But wait, look, I think, my thoughts echoing Wilde's simple command from only a moment ago.

The chariots ain't heading west, toward New Wildetown, in the direction most of 'em arrived from during the night. No. They're heading north.

And there's only one thing that's north.

Ice country.

Eighteen
Dazz

There's no easy way down the mountain. Not for the entire village anyway. Why would there be? No one ever goes down the mountain; they have no reason to. Back in the days when Buff and I worked for King Goff—may he rot in Chill—and we went to collect trade items from the Heaters at the border, we used to simply strap our sliders on our feet and zip our way down the snowy slopes. This venture south is quite a different experience.

The wooden cart handle is digging into my shoulder. Next to me Buff is mumbling obscenities as he gets similar treatment from his handle. He's even stopped mocking me and calling me a "sissy-eyed doe-lover" or whatever his usual insults are. Whose idea was the cart anyway?

With each tree root, stone, or bump in the ground, the handles bob up and down, slamming into our bodies, sending shockwaves through our bones and muscles. At least the cold's not a problem, I think. I'm sweating beneath my thick, bearskin coat.

"Freezin', icin', no-good son of a Yag herder," Buff mumbles. "Yow!" he grunts when we hit a particularly large hump in the frozen earth, hidden beneath the ankle-high snow. I grimace, too, switching the handle to the opposite shoulder for about the hundredth time.

"What the chill are we doing out here?" I ask no one in particular, glaring at a Glassy soldier who smirks at me as he passes by.

"The consortium voted and decided to—" Buff starts to say.

"Yah, I get *that*," I say, cutting him off. "But why'd they make such an idiotic decision?"

A voice on my right says, "You should watch what you say, talk like that could be misconstrued as treason."

I don't need to turn my head to know the voice. Abe.

Gritting my teeth—not in anger, but with exertion—I turn to look at him. Of course, he's walking easily, loping along beside me, carrying nothing. His bags are strapped to his ogre-like brother, Hightower, who manages them as easily as the mountain manages us.

"It's not like you voted for this decision," I say through clenched teeth.

"True," he says, tapping a dirty fingernail on his yellow, tobacco-stained teeth. "But it's hard to argue with Glassy soldiers. Hey! Do you want a hand with that cart?"

I know he doesn't mean his own hands. "It's our responsibility," I say.

"C'mon, Dazzy, don't be such a spoiler. It's not like I'm selling my brother into slavery. He likes helping, don't you, Tower?"

Hightower grunts something that sounds enough like a *yes* for Abe's purposes. "See? Take a load off. You, too, Boof."

"It's Buff," Buff says, but he stops at the same time as I do, lowering to a crouch to set the cart on its front stopper. The temptation is too strong.

"Okay," I say, "but we'll take it back when he gets tired."

"What's going on down there?" a voice says from the cart bed. A face appears, hanging over the front. Darcy. "Why have we stopped?" She spots Hightower and shrinks back, ducking behind a barrel.

I move aside, massaging my neck, rolling my shoulders, feeling like I might if I'd gone sliding into a tree. Buff looks equally battered as he stumbles over to me.

"Ain't that better?" Abe says.

I can't say no, so I don't say anything.

Hightower throws Abe's and his bags onto the cart, drawing a squeal from the kids in the back, and then positions himself between the two handles. He takes a moment to scratch his arse and crack his knuckles before stooping to lift the cart, letting out a minor grunt. And then we're moving, Hightower looking as calm and serene as if he's carrying no more than a small child on his back.

"Now we can talk," Abe says.

"About what?" I say, falling in beside him.

He lights up a cigarette.

"When did you start smoking?" Buff asks.

Abe laughs. "From when I could afford to buy them," he says. "When Dazzy here took down the king and made me a very rich man."

"None of us are rich anymore," I mutter.

"This ain't good," Abe says, his mouth hanging open, displaying his yellow-black teeth like trophies.

I'm surprised that he says it. Abe likes hiding things, pretending everything's alright when it's clearly not. For him to say something like that, he must think our situation's pretty bad indeed.

"What the freeze are they going to do to us?" I hiss.

Abe motions for me to keep my voice down, which I thought I was doing already. "I don't know, kid, but I'd expect the worst." The worst? Like King Goff worst, stealing our children—my sister, Buff's siblings—and selling them as slaves? Or like Admiral Jones worst, using the children themselves as slaves, beating them with whips and otherwise making their lives the definition of misery? Or does he mean...

"What are you saying?" I ask.

"Be alert," he says. "Wait for the right time to turn the tables on the bastards." He fingers the knife hanging from his belt. "One way or another, blood will be spilt before the day is done."

~~~

Hightower pulls the cart the entire way to fire country, and I don't think he even breaks a sweat. At the bottom, Abe insists Buff and I take over again. Not because Hightower needs a break, but because he wants his brother to "be ready." Whatever that means. No matter what I ask him, he's being all

113

cryptic with me, talking about "chances" and "lost opportunities" and "winning the day."

Fire country is boiling hot, as if the sun and the sand are in league together, creating the perfect conditions to roast humans alive. Almost immediately, the clothes start coming off. Coats and blankets, boots and socks. Some Icers are even using knives to cut their pants and shirts shorter. Soon we'll be dressed like Heaters.

Most of the Icers have never felt this kind of heat, like they're sitting in a fire. No doubt it'll take a lot of getting used to.

Buff and I trudge along, pulling the cart across the hard, cracked earth, avoiding running smack into pricklers, which have drawn plenty of attention from the other Icers, having never seen such strange plants, all green and spiky and presenting themselves in countless shapes and varieties. I almost wish I was sitting back there with my mother and Jolie, just to see their expressions. There's a whole, wide world out there just waiting to be explored.

But not this way. Not by being forced.

The safety of the trees and the mountain fade away behind us.

After a while, the soldiers stop us, order us to rest and drink, to ready ourselves for the final stage across the desert. They speak with clipped sentences, formal and sharp. Commands, not suggestions. They are our masters, not our allies. I even notice that the curly mustache representative from the Blue District isn't looking so confident in his decision. His face is red, his clothes are streaked with dust, and he has a crying baby in his arms. Should we call a re-vote? I'm pretty sure the Glassy soldiers won't go for that. The alliance has been made.

Abe and Hightower stroll away from us while we're stopped, pointing at a bright, purple flower on a prickler, gesturing and smiling animatedly at a mouse-like creature that pops out of a hole, sniffs around, and then dives back out of the sun. What are they up to?

Be alert, he'd said. I'm trying my best, but Jolie's tugging on my arm, pointing at everything in sight, saying, "Do you see it? Do you?"

And I'm saying, "Yah, yah, Joles," even as I'm watching one of the other reps from the Black District march over to one of the soldiers, waving his arms wildly, screaming at him. I can't make out his words but I can tell they're laced with obscenities and demands. When the soldier just ignores him, gazing off into the desert like the man doesn't exist, he gets all up in his face, sort of bumping him with his chest. Still the soldier ignores him, but I see the Glassy's fingers tightening on his weapon.

A lot of the other Icers are noticing the commotion now too, gawking and pointing. Murmurs ripple through the crowd like a water country wave, picking up speed and quickly alerting the other Glassy soldiers to the plight of their comrade. They've got us surrounded, but now they're looking at each other, unsure of themselves.

One of them starts moving around the circle in the direction of the soldier being harassed, but another soldier yells at him to "Hold position!"

Be alert. I scan my surroundings, looking in all the places the soldiers aren't. Abe's up to something—that's the only thing I'm sure of. Then I see him.

Outside of the ring of soldiers. Not Hightower, just Abe. Surprisingly, Hightower is nowhere to be found. Although he stands a foot above everyone else from ice country, Abe's brother is missing, which means he must be crouching or sitting or hiding somewhere.

Abe's on the move, staying low to the ground, moving silently behind one of the soldiers, who's completely oblivious.

A distraction. That's all the Black District rep is. He's pushing the soldier now, and the soldier is finally paying him some attention, pushing back and shouting a warning at him. Now raising his weapon, pointing it at the guy, who finally backs off, his hands in the air…

Abe grabs the other soldier from behind, around the neck, twisting his head viciously to the side. The Glassy drops and Abe bends down to pick up his weapon.

No one notices except me, as the Icers and Glassy soldiers are equally distracted by the continuing scene with the man and the soldier. Now the man's moving forward again, his arms out, as if trying to reason with the soldier. He points to the sky, at the sun, as if trying to say that the heat's making everyone a little crazy, a little quick-tempered.

My eyes flick back to Abe, who's striding around the arc of the human circle that is the entire population of ice country, all three thousand of us. He doesn't run, just walks calmly, confidently, deadly.

A large form draws my attention on the other side of the circle. Hightower, having risen up from wherever he was crouching, is walking in the opposite direction, closing in on another soldier, who's looking the other direction, toward his comrade who's dealing with the irate villager.

And then, and then…

—Tower's arm is raised, his clenched fist like a club, high above his head, and he

—drops it like a falling tree, right onto the crown of the soldier's head.

The soldier crumples without so much as grunting.

I whip my head back to the other side, where Abe is swinging the fire stick like an axe at a tree, cracking it off the next soldier's skull.

Finally, someone besides me notices. A scream, loud and shrill, pierces the murmurs of the crowd. Heads turn and feet scramble as everyone tries to figure out what's happening. Who screamed and why? The remaining soldiers are doing the same, turning, realization flashing across their faces, because three of the other soldiers are missing, out of sight below the height of the people.

And they're shouting, too, trying to make their voices carry over the rumbles of the village, growing louder and louder and—

—there's a CRACK! sharp and like thunder, and right away, even though I've never heard it before, I know what it is. The sound of a fire stick being used. One of the soldiers has hurt an Icer, maybe even killed them.

Everyone's screaming and running now, leaving everything—their carts and packs and everything—behind as they try to get away. CRACK! CRACK! CRACKCRACKCRACK!

The noises come fast and furious and provide the perfect, gruesome accompaniment for the fearful screams of the crowd.

"Dazz!" Jolie yells, clutching my leg. I grab her and throw her up onto the cart, where Buff is already corralling any of his brothers and sisters who clambered off when we stopped. They'll be safe from the stampede up there.

People are charging around us, trying to get away, running back toward ice country, and I'm craning my neck to see what's happening, who's dying, where Abe and Hightower are.

The mob parts and there he is: Abe. He's got the stolen fire stick raised and there's a soldier lying flat on her back before him, her own weapon discarded to the side, her hands held out in front of her. Abe goes right on up to her, shoves the tip of the fire stick to her head, and

CRACK!

I see a spray of crimson liquid from her head and she slumps, unmoving. Dead. Abe killed her with the Glassy weapon. He knows how to use it. Somehow, he knows.

As the villagers continue to rush past, between them I see the bodies behind Abe. Two more soldiers. As lifeless as sacks of rocks. The cracks I heard weren't from the Glassy soldiers— or at least not *all* from the soldiers. They were from Abe's stolen fire stick, as he killed them.

Abe marches forward, his weapon raised once more. I follow his aim. There's one soldier left, the original one, the distraction. The Black District rep is lying motionless in the dust in front of him. The Glassy's pointing his weapon, but not at Abe, at Hightower, who's stomping toward him, looking every bit like the giant that he is. Behind him are a few more fallen soldiers.

CRACK!

The soldier shoots and Tower's shoulder twitches back slightly, like he's been punched, but he keeps on coming, grabbing the Glassy's fire stick, yanking it out of his hands, and bashing him over the head with it.

It's over.

No, not yet. Abe approaches his brother, gently nudges him aside, points his stick at the head of the final soldier.

CRACK!

Now it's over.

Nineteen
Adele

The truck lurches forward once more, but I don't open my eyes. Can't open my eyes because it's too soon and I'm afraid they'll betray me, show the lie.

The metal truck bed rumbles beneath me, and it's a welcome distraction from my pounding head and throbbing arm. Tristan didn't hold back, not one bit, for which I'm glad. The tenacity of his attacks might be the very thing that saves me.

I feel the truck turn and a wave of nausea fills my throat, either because of Tristan's blow to the head or the vehicle's movement—or perhaps a combination of the two. Even as I swallow it down, I wonder whether I should succumb to the urge, whether lifting my mask and vomiting on the soldiers' feet will add further credibility to my story.

I hold it in. Is it my first mistake?

I don't have time to wonder as the truck shudders to a stop and I feel the scramble of the soldiers as they jump out. "What the hell happened?" a gruff male voice barks.

"She's not one of ours," a female voice answers, stopping my heart. It's over already. How did they know? "Must be part of another platoon." My heart continues beating, albeit twice as fast as normal. I force myself to breathe evenly. She just meant I'm not part of her squad.

"Scan her," the gruff voice orders. My jaw clenches. I've got no chip.

"Shouldn't we get her to medical first? She's hurt pretty badly, looks like a blow to the head. They'll scan her there."

There's silence for a couple of seconds. "Okay, move her." My jaw unclenches and I focus on keeping my eyes closed, my body relaxed and rubbery.

Someone pries off my mask. Hands pull me from either side, sliding me along the truck bed and onto something hard. I'm tempted to tighten my arms to my sides, but instead I let them flop down, hanging lifeless over the edge of the backboard. Someone lifts them up and crosses them over my chest. "Soldier, accompany me with her to medical," the female voice orders.

"Yes, ma'am!"

And then I'm floating, drifting through space, being spirited away. What's my next move? They don't know I don't have a chip—that it's been cut out of me by the "enemy". They don't suspect a damn thing yet. But when I get to medical things will cascade pretty fast. When there's nothing to scan, they'll have plenty of questions for me, and I can't fake unconsciousness forever. Nor is there time to. The Tri-Tribes and Tristan are counting on me to make a difference as soon as possible, maybe immediately.

I need a new identity. A chip.

I risk opening my eyes, just slits, seeing only darkness through my eyelashes. Close them again.

There's a slight jolt and a quiver as I feel my legs angling higher than my head. We're going up a ramp or steps. My legs drop back to level, and the heavy black behind my eyelids gives way to a dull yellow glow. Lights. I sneak another peek and see fluorescent lights above me, stark white walls on both sides, and the green-brown back of a dark-haired soldier in front of me. The woman who temporarily saved me, her hair falling halfway down her spine.

Is she the one who has to die so I can live?

I grit my teeth and silently promise myself I'll do whatever I have to do to stop Lecter. After all, could any of his followers really be innocent? Surely many of the citizens are, but the soldiers?

But the first thing I have to do is ditch my escort. We turn a corner, head down another bright hallway, lined with doors on either side. They have signs on them. X-Rays, Exam Room C, Administration, Maintenance, Electrical Room, Exam Room D, etc. It's the middle of the night and this place is empty, save for us, the hollow footsteps of the soldiers at my front and back echoing away. Do I make my move?

I wait, like a spider, watching my web for the perfect moment to pounce on my prey.

We pass through a doorway, into a large room, sparkling clean and smelling sterile with antiseptic. "Where is everyone?" the male soldier behind me says.

"At night they're on call, and since there hasn't been much action lately…" the senior officer says. "We'll get her to a bed and then call someone."

No one's here. Not a single person except us. This might be my only shot. The doctor will have questions. Hard questions. I have to act now. Now. NOW!

I snap my eyes open and kick my legs back, clamping them to the head of the soldier behind me. Then I whip my ankles forward, pulling him over my head and onto the gurney with me. He cries out as our combined body weight brings the board down on top of the woman soldier, who stumbles.

His head's in my lap, and I don't waste any time. Two hard punches to the head and his tongue lolls out, his eyes rolling back in his skull.

The woman scrambles, tries to roll, to kick and fight her way out from underneath us, where her legs are pinned. I easily twist away first, push to my feet, and shake my whirling head to try to center myself. Then I kick her solidly in the face and she stops struggling.

My mind is cycling through my options. If I don't kill them, it could really come back to bite me. But what if they're like the sun dwellers, mindless drones operating under a system where the only thing they know is their little world, following orders without question. Do they deserve to die the same way that President Nailin did? The way Lecter does?

Time's running away through my fingers as I comb a hand through my hair. Think, think, think. I need a chip. Should I take hers? Will she be missed right away? If I don't kill them, will someone find them?

First, I take the backboard and lay it in a stack against the wall, trying to buy time, my mind racing.

I withdraw my knife, approach the woman. Hold it close to her neck. Take a deep breath. Lower it to her right arm, where Tristan sliced me open. Withdraw the blade.

No. She's the leader of her platoon. People will know who she is. Her soldiers. Her superiors. I'll be discovered too soon.

I should probably kill them, and I may be making my second mistake, like when I chose not to throw up in the truck, but I can't. Not with them lying here, defenseless, when all they were trying to do was get me medical attention. I scan the room, locate a locker with a large cross on it. Supplies. Medical supplies. I rush over and thrust it open, quickly reading the labels. I recognize some of them. For pain. For fevers. Ah! Anesthesia. Needles with plungers, full of the stuff. Perfect.

I don't know where to inject the fluid, so I roll up their sleeves and pick out the largest vein I can find in each of their arms, jam the needles into them, and press down hard on the plungers. Then, for good measure, I give them each a second dose. I hope it won't kill them, but I need them out as long as possible—it's a risk I have to take.

Next I rip the sheets off one of the beds and use my knife to methodically cut it into strips. Bind their hands and feet, tie them together. Gag their mouths. Remove their weapons: guns and knives and grenades.

Now where to stash them? There are plenty of closets around, but surely those are used on an almost daily basis. Not a good spot. The other rooms in the hall we came from? Probably used regularly, too, except for maybe…Electrical

Room. Unless there's a problem with the electricity, no one would go in there.

Feet first, I drag the guy to the doorway, peek to my right and then to my left, up and down the hall. Quiet. Empty. I slide him out, across the bare, white tile. There! Electrical Room. I jiggle the handle but it doesn't open, feels locked. In frustration, I twist it again and shove with my shoulder.

It gives way and I barge through into darkness. Except for…a green, blinking light with shining letters above it: Effective.

We're in business.

I drag the soldier inside, stop, feel around with my hands. The equipment with the green light has plenty of space behind it. I stuff him back there and return for his superior officer, doing the same with her. When I close the door behind me, I take a deep breath, steady myself against the wall, close my eyes for just a second.

I can do this.

Next step: get a chip. It has to be one from someone who won't be missed, who won't be able to rat me out.

I stride off down the hall, as if I belong, stopping only briefly to collect the weapons left behind by the unconscious soldiers.

The medical building is eerie at night, even more so because it's so brightly lit and yet so empty. Surely there's illness and accidents in the New City. Surely the residents need medical attention sometimes, even at night. Perhaps this is only for the army, whose actions, according to Wilde, have been confined to searching for the Tri-Tribes. Nothing particularly dangerous. No casualties, no injuries. Thus, an empty army medical ward at night.

I pass through a wide room labeled Eatery. There are long rows of white tables, benches on either side of them, attached with metal piping. I'm partway across when I hear it. Music. Well, sort of. Someone singing, just loud enough for the sound to carry through the unoccupied hallways.

Do I run in the other direction?

It's a woman's voice and I need a chip.

I make for the singing, crossing the rest of the cafeteria on tiptoes. Down another passage, the singing getting louder, clearer:

Rest, my darling,
Sleep, my darling,
Dream your cares away,
Do not fuss,
Do not cry,
The night is here to stay.

It's coming from one of the rooms branching off from the hall I'm now in, but I can't tell which one, the echoes distorting the direction of the sound.

First room, door closed. Move on.

Next room, open. Peek inside. Empty, except for shelves of supplies. A bucket. A mop. Cleaning liquids.

Third room, also closed. Singing getting louder still:

Travel down roads of gold,
My darling, Charity,
Don't be scared, for you are bold,
Find your way back to me.

A lullaby. I recognize it. My mother sang it to me when I was little. A moon dweller lullaby. Could this woman be…a moon dweller? Tristan said many moon and star dwellers were tricked into coming above, to be used as the servants of the earth dwellers. To do all the work that the migrant sun dwellers didn't want to do—that they weren't used to doing. Cleaning, trash collection and disposal, food preparation…

I peek in the fourth room and she's there, holding a mop, dabbing it in a water-filled bucket, squeezing it out. Sweeping it back and forth in circles on the floor, until the surface shines under the fluorescent lights. Wearing white linen pants and a white shirt, blond hair spilling down her back. Clearly not a soldier. Her back is to me. A cleaner. A servant. A chip.

Would anyone miss this woman? Maybe, but not the same way they'd miss an officer. Has fate brought me to her to use for my purposes? Do I have it in me to cut her open, to spill her blood, to stain her brilliantly white clothes? My earlier silent promise to myself rattles through my head. *Whatever I have to do…*

I take a soundless step inside the room and she goes on mopping the floor, whistling now.

My fingers tighten on the knife in my belt, brush against the gun strapped beside it. Hot blood rushes through my veins, my heart pounding.

I take another step, my shadow trailing behind me.

A noise, high-pitched but not overly loud, rings out. Sort of throaty.

I freeze, take two quick steps back into the hallway. Duck behind the doorframe.

The woman stops whistling, props her mop against the wall. "Hush, my darling," she coos, stepping to the side and reaching down over the railing of a small bassinet on wheels that I hadn't noticed while focusing on the woman.

She picks up a child, a baby, no more than a few months old. Gently, ever so gently, she rocks it in her arms, once more singing the moon dweller lullaby, whisper soft.

I hold my breath the whole way through, barely blinking, entranced. When she places the baby back in the portable bed, I empty my lungs, the sound louder than I expected it to be.

The woman turns sharply, startled. "Oh," she says. "I'm sorry, I didn't realize anyone was here." She looks embarrassed, guilty, like *she's* the one who's not supposed to be here, rather than me.

"I'm," I say, trying to keep my voice steady, like a soldier, "just making my rounds."

She smiles, but it doesn't reach her eyes. A grim smile. What is she so worried about? Surely being here is her job.

"I—I know I'm not supposed to bring Charity to work, but I—" Her voice trails away as she looks at the baby sleeping beside her.

"Rules are rules," I say in the sternest voice I can muster. I realize my hand's still on my knife. Was I really considering slicing this woman open, potentially killing her? Baby or no baby, have things gotten so far out of control that I'd do that? Hurt an innocent woman?

"My husband—he's not well. He can't look after her while I'm at work. He can barely look after himself. I don't have any other choice," the woman pleads.

Does it matter if this woman dies? I wonder. Like the rest of us, her life is falling apart. Is one life more important than another? If I'm destined for greatness, to save lives, to kill a corrupt president, to overthrow a dictator, does that make my life more valuable than a woman who does nothing more than raise a child, care for a sick husband?

As long as blood's running through my veins and my heart is beating, *yes*, it matters. Maybe more than anything. This woman is exactly who we're fighting for. The Tri-Tribes, yeah, them too. The dwellers below. But not only them. This woman. Her child. Her sick husband. Those who can't fight for themselves.

"It's okay," I say, softening my voice. Her eyes widen like it's the last thing she expected me to say. "I won't tell anyone."

And then I move on without another word, no doubt leaving the woman speechless, alone with her baby again.

Down the hall I run, feeling more and more tired with every step. At some point I have to sleep, or my exhaustion will no doubt cause me to make a mistake. But where?

I pass a door and the placard on the wall catches my eye. Morgue.

Stopping, I return to the door, which is windowless. Soft, white light pours through a tiny crack at the bottom. Slowly, slowly, slowly I turn the handle, push the door open. Cold air rushes out, instantly sending a chill through my bones. I freeze when I catch sight of a foot.

Not moving. On a table. I push further in, slip inside, turn the handle and close the door, as quiet as a sleeping baby.

Thankfully, the dead soldier's eyes are closed, not watching me.

She's naked, dark lines drawn on the entirety of her body, as if in preparation for an autopsy. White light from panels above gives her skin an unnatural sheen, almost as if she's glowing from within. I shiver, the cold biting through my stolen uniform.

Is this my chance for a chip? The woman's right arm appears unmarred, so apparently they haven't taken her chip out, if they will at all. I could easily extract it, but would that lead to too much suspicion? The last thing I want is a massive manhunt within the dome. It would distract the earth dwellers until they caught me, but my mission would still fail. And they'd likely kill me.

But wait. If she's here, in the army medical building, she must be a soldier. Again, not the type of person's identity I want to steal. I need someone who can blend into the background better…

I sit down on an empty slab, hug myself, trying to create heat by running my hands up and down my opposing arms. A wave of exhaustion hits me. I need sleep.

Well, if nothing else, they'd never expect me to be hiding out here. I stand, walk to the wall, where there are rows and rows of large drawers, rising all the way to the ceiling. Grabbing a handle, I say a silent prayer that this particular "bed" is unoccupied. Slide it out, cringing until I see the blank and empty darkness inside.

Goodnight, Tristan, I think as climb into the drawer that's meant for a dead person, use the top to slide myself in, closing it completely, save for a sliver of soft, white light shimmering through a crack at the end.

Twenty
Siena

All we can do is follow the fire chariots as best we can, wondering why in the name of the sun goddess they're rushing off in the direction of our friends to the north. Whyohwhyohwhy.

Nothing makes sense. Nothing good anyway.

Thankfully, the dunes slow them down, as they have to take the long way 'round the big ones, while we—Skye and Wilde and Tristan and me; we left Lara and Hawk back at the cave—can just go over 'em, careful to wait 'til they can't see us anymore. But soon the dunes give way to flat, hard ground, and they race away from us, the only evidence of their passing the lingering clouds of dust and the cracked-earth tracks from their wheels.

We run along the track, and I'm impressed that Tristan is able to keep up. His forehead is red from the sun—unprotected by the half-mask he's wearing—but he ain't slowing, ain't complaining. "You run well," I say between breaths.

"I've had to do a lot of running recently," he says.

We pass the cave that he and Adele first emerged from and I see him staring at it. "No one's stoppin' you," Skye says, noticing it too.

Tristan just grits his teeth and keeps on running, only looking back once.

The sun reaches its midpoint and still we run, clinging to the tracks like a baby to its mother, as the ground pops up in mounds. And then we climb a mound and the fire chariots stand 'fore us on another hill, strangely still, like a hurd of grazing tug. As if they're trying to decide what to do.

A loud CRACK! rings out and we see the Glassy soldiers diving behind their fire chariots, clustering near the wheels. I know that noise. It was a fire stick going off. Invisible killers. Not the fire sticks themselves, but whatever comes out of 'em, the little metal pods we found stuck in the sides of our shelters after the last attack.

But who would be shooting fire stick pods at the Glassies? Only the Glassies know how to use 'em.

Shouts in the distance. From the Glassies. Screams further still. From someone else.

CRACK, CRACK, CRACK!

More shots, the soldiers still ducking. Now some of 'em are sticking their fire sticks underneath their chariots, 'round the sides, aiming at whoever's doing the screaming and shooting.

CRACKCRACKCRACKCRACKCRACK!

A flurry of shots, fire exploding from the soldiers sticks, which is why we named 'em the way we did. And then the soldiers are jumping back into their…trucks, and they're racing out of sight, over the hill, attacking someone…

Skye yells for us to go and we do, racing down one mound and up the next, peering through a dust cloud as we crest the hill, seeing the chariots flying across a flat, barren field, right toward—my heart stops 'cause I can't believe my searin' eyes— a massive group of people, as many as we have left in all the Tri-Tribes.

And I can see right away that they're…they're Icers. All the Icers.

Most of 'em are screaming and running, but some of 'em are standing, holding fire sticks like they know what to do with 'em—and they must, 'cause I heard the CRACKS.

And the only thing standing 'tween the Icers and the Glassy soldiers are…

Bodies.

Scattered on the ground like stones.

Twenny-One
Dazz

It took a chill of a lot of running around and talking to people to get them to calm down. Buff agreed to stay back with our families as I worked with Abe and his conspirators to collect all the weapons from the fallen soldiers. Curly Mustache Man looked like he was about to complain, but after a quick glance at Abe's fire stick, he backed off.

The minority reps are suddenly controlling the show. "We're going back," I say to Buff and the others as I approach them.

"I don't understand," Buff's father says. "Why did they kill the soldiers? Weren't they protecting us?"

"Yah, protecting us right off a cliff," I say. "We can't trust them. They want us all dead, or controlled, or both. They think we're savages."

"The people need to rest," Mother says. "They're tired, they're scared."

"No time. We have to go now," I say. "We can rest when we get home." Then I have to find Skye, tell her what's happening, and figure out what to do next. Rekindle the Unity Alliance.

Abe and his people are giving the message to the rest of the village. Questions are met with rebukes. No time for questions. Finally, everyone gives in, start to shoulder their packs, get their carts moving back the way we came. "Let's do it," Buff says, positioning himself under a cart handle.

Growls in the distance.

No.

Coming fast.

No.

Getting louder.

No.

And then they're there, a dozen vehicles, standing on a hill, looking down at us like desert gods. Someone screams, "Oh, Heart, no!" and then a lot of people are screaming and shouting and running.

No. Please, no. Not my family. Not our people. Not this.

"Run!" I shout to those in the cart. My mother scrambles down, helps Jolie, then Buff's injured father. The kids spill out, tripping all over themselves, fleeing in front of everyone, joining the stampede. Jolie looks back at me. *C'mon!* her face says.

"Go!" I yell. "Go with Mother!"

"Not without you," she cries.

"Now!" I say, turning back the other way, blinking her scared face out of my head.

Abe and his people are aiming fire sticks at the top of the hill.

CRACK! The first report of a weapon, probably Abe's, the one who seems the most confident with them. Our enemies dive for cover and three more shots hammer away.

Buff and I run to Abe and he tosses us each a weapon from a pile. I catch it awkwardly, gaping at the hot metal. I fight with my fists, not with knives or swords or clubs…certainly not with fire sticks. But what choice do I have? I can't fight fire with punches and kicks. I have to try.

I don't even know how to hold it, but I watch what he does. "Point and press this thing," he says, showing me a little lever. I mimic his motions, try to hold it like him, wondering how he figured this out all on his own.

Half a dozen shots slam into my eardrums, raining down from the hill. A guy directly to my left slumps over, blood pouring from a hole in his forehead. Down the line from Abe, another man falls.

Then the fire chariots growl and come roaring down the hill.

"Ruuuun!" Abe bellows, taking off in the other direction. We do, pumping our legs as fast as we can, and at some point I realize we're all trying not to be the slowest one, because the slowest one will get caught first, killed first. And I glance back, and the slowest one is…it's Buff.

The vehicles are gaining on us. A shot rings out and I hear the whine as something screams past my head. A miss. No. Fifty feet beyond us a little girl falls, her hand slipping away from where it was clutching her father's as they fled. He looks back, his face a sheet of white terror and then he stops, falls to his knees, slumps over her. Curly Mustache Man.

None of his slanted words can save her now.

I look back again. Buff passes someone, one of the reps from the Black District. CRACK! The guy stumbles, falls, dies.

Why are they doing this? Is it because we broke the alliance, killed their soldiers, shot at them? Doesn't make sense. Why would they send so many soldiers to meet us when we already had an armed escort? Was this always the plan? To slaughter us as we crossed the desert wasteland? I suspect the answer is yes. Abe knew it and he tried to do something to change our fates, but it was too little, too late.

We can't escape. We have no choice but to stand and fight. Try to give the rest of them a chance. Our families. My family.

"Abe!" I yell. He's ahead of me and looks back. "We have to fight!"

He nods and stops. "Turn and fire!" he yells.

We do. We turn and fire.

The CRACKS! explode in my ears and my fire stick rocks against my shoulder, sending spears of pain dancing through my already sore muscles. Sparks fly against the metal vehicles as they rush toward us. One of us gets lucky and a soldier tumbles from the back, rolling away in a cloud of dust.

They respond with shots of their own and another one of us dies, I'm not sure who. We keep firing even as they roar closer, and the weapon dances in my hand, like it's alive. I force it steady against my shoulder, although I know it's going to hurt, and aim at one of the vehicles. CRACK! Shards of rock shiver through my bones, but it works! Cracks form in the glass at the front and I can see someone slumped inside, his arm hanging awkwardly out the window.

The vehicle lurches sharply to its right, slamming hard into the flank of another one. There are more sparks as the domino effect continues, ratcheting across three or four other chariots. The one on the end loses its center of gravity and rolls, throwing men and women and guns around and off it like a folded hand of cards. The other vehicles follow, crashing into each other, bouncing around and eventually slamming into the overturned one. The soldiers in the back aren't moving.

"Shoot at the front windows!" I scream, even as another one of us gets hit, falling almost right in front of me.

I fire and another window shatters, but the soldiers inside are still alive, staring at us. One of them aims a weapon and blasts away…

Abe goes down, blood spilling from his neck. This can't be…this isn't…

Buff and I fire in short succession, and both men in the front die. But the vehicle lurches the wrong direction, away from the other enemies, angling off harmlessly into the desert.

A half a dozen enemy carriers, still coming, shooting…

Another Icer slumps over and I swivel my head from side to side. Everyone dead. Everyone except Buff and me. I shoot. Nothing happens. Buff shoots and a soldier rolls into the dirt.

Enemy shots crackle.

Buff groans and falls.

No.

His chest is covered in blood.

Not my brother.

He's trying to speak, but his lips are red and slick.

Like Wes. Just like Wes. Not a brother by blood, but a brother just the same. I wasn't man enough to save him.

Shots ring out, but this time they're different. Not hammers in my ears but punches in my chest. Sharp pressure. My legs fail me. The last sounds I hear are muffled and unreal, like maybe this was all a dream. A very bad dream. A nightmare.

Screams and growls and cracks like thunder.

Just a nightmare. A bad dream.

Go back to sleep, Dazz.

But they're screaming—the children and the people and my sister. They're all screaming.

Just a dream. I close my eyes and sleep.

Everything goes black.

Twenty-Two
Adele

I know I've overslept when I hear a noise outside my drawer. The door opening with a click. My intention was to sneak in a few hours sleep and creep out before anyone was the wiser.

I don't move, just blink in the dark, listening.

"We'll have to finish with this one and get the place ready for a large intake," a woman's voice says. "Just in case there are casualties." *Casualties?*

"But I thought the mission was scheduled for later today?" another woman says. I close my eyes, concentrating on not missing a word. *What mission?*

"It is, but we have to be ready early. You know how Lecter likes things."

A laugh. "Don't we all. Clean and organized. A clean city is a happy city. I've heard the ads. Hey, you want to grab a coffee before we get started? I feel like it's going to be a long one."

"Sounds perfect."

I hear the door close, and once more I'm alone in silence. No time. I've got to move now or I might not have another chance.

I guide my hands along the top of the drawer, pushing myself out. My skin is cold, but I feel refreshed. Ready.

My friend the corpse-woman hasn't moved since last night, which is a good thing. Eyes closed or not, I try not to look at her.

I'm about to exit, when I see them. A pile of white linen clothes that weren't there the night before. Brought by the women I heard talking. Preparing for a potentially large intake. These must be the clothes they dress the bodies in after they've finished each autopsy. They don't look all that different than what the cleaning woman was wearing as she mopped the floor, singing to her baby…

I've never undressed so quickly. The first set of clothes is way too big, covering my hands and feet. The second: perfect, or close enough, the sleeves plenty long enough to cover my cut arm. Do I take my dirty, bloody, and torn soldier's uniform with me? If someone asks me about it I can probably lie my way through an interrogation, but I'd rather have my hands free. And what about the weapons? Do I take those?

The clock is ticking…

Making a split-second decision, I use a knife to cut off a piece of fabric from one of the other white clothes, wrap it four times around the blade of the knife, and shove it inside my boot. Unfortunately, there are no shoes to wear, so I'm stuck wearing a dead soldier's boots until I can find something else. But for now it makes a good spot for the knife. Everything else—the uniform, a couple knives, and the guns I took from the drugged, bound and gagged soldiers in the electrical room—I shove in the highest corpse drawer, hoping they won't be found anytime soon.

When I turn to leave, the door handle rattles, turns and…the door opens.

I freeze.

"I heard the president bathes three times a day," a woman says, looking back as she enters. Her hair is bright orange and tied up in a bun. She's somewhat wide, but it's more pudge than muscle. Right away I know I can incapacitate her if I have to.

"I heard four times," another woman says, her voice carrying through the door. The two from before, back with their coffees.

"Oh!" I exclaim, trying to sound as surprised as possible, which isn't that hard considering my heart is in my throat.

The woman turns sharply, her coffee spilling over the side and onto her hand. "Dammit!" she says, cradling it with two hands and pushing it onto one of the tables. "What the hell are you doing in here?"

The other woman—as skinny as a rod, her dark hair also tied up and away from her face—rushes in behind her, immediately grabbing a towel to wipe up the mess.

"I—I—" I stammer. I should've been born a sun dweller. I could've been an actress.

"Well, spit it out, girl," Meaty-Bun says, kindness absent from her voice.

"I'm sorry, I was under the impression there might be a large intake today, that this room needed to be cleaned and prepped," I say, staring at my feet. Eye contact shows strength, and strong people draw attention. I want to be like a piece of furniture, just part of the room.

"You heard right, but that's part of our job," Skinny-Bun says, her tone less serious. "It's not a normal cleaning job. It takes a special kind of training."

"Oh," I say again, like I'm an idiot who barely understands the simple concepts she's explaining. "I'm sorry. Really sorry. I'll check with my supervisor to see what I'm supposed to be doing." Like I can't think for myself, requiring direction for every little menial task. Do I even have a supervisor? I hope so.

"What's your name, girl?" Meaty-Bun says. "I'll have to report this." Uh oh. Don't make me introduce you to right-fist.

"Aw, c'mon, Sandy," Skinny-Bun says, "there's no need for that. It's probably her first day on the job."

"It—it is," I stutter.

Meaty-Bun frowns, but waves her hand. "Fine, fine. I don't have time to file a report today anyway. Those forms are so damn long. Just don't come back, you hear me?"

I nod sheepishly. "Th-thank you," I say as I'm opening the door and slipping through. Before the door closes I hear the fat one say, "Must be a star dweller," and then they both laugh like it's the funniest thing they've heard all day.

Unable to control myself any longer, I slam the door and bolt down the hall. How can there be so much ignorance in the world? A star dweller? Just because I acted a little simple, a little scared, a little shy? I've met star dwellers who could outthink sun dweller engineers if given the chance. Hell, my mother is an honorary star dweller, considering how much time she spent in the Star Realm. And Trevor…a burning bubble wells up in my chest and I have to take a deep breath to push it away…Trevor was a star dweller and one of the smartest, most capable people I've ever met. Quick-witted and sharp-tongued. Another casualty of ignorance, a life—if it was ever really a life to begin with—cut far shorter than it should've been.

I turn a corner, feeling queasy, following a sign for EXIT. Pass a woman in a white coat who doesn't bother to look up at me from the papers she's reading. Dressed like a cleaner, I'm invisible.

My thoughts continue to roll and tumble and spill over each other. Why have we rebuilt the world this way? Was it ever different? Did people ever just accept each other, regardless of race, religion, gender or social status? If the President Nailins of the world were born in the Star Realm, would they turn out differently? More tolerant? Better? Does something as simple as the place you're born change everything about you, determine what kind of person you'll be? As my face grows hotter and hotter, I know I'm losing control, which is something I cannot afford to do. Maybe my questions have no answers, or answers I'll never be willing to accept.

One more turn and I see the exit, a set of glass-paneled double doors, bright outside light pouring through them. Closed, locked, impossible to push through. There's what appears to be a chip scanner on the wall, next to a sign that says, "Do NOT exit building without scan." Feeling light-headed, I slump against the wall, right next to the scanner.

There's a beep and the door opens. A man enters, striding past me as if I don't exist. I wait a second until he's further down the hall, and then grab the nearly closed door, holding it open. I slam through with a shoulder, gulping at the air, my hands on my knees. Trying to get control.

Someone pushes past me, into the building. "Watch where you're going," he says gruffly, and I almost laugh.

The ridiculousness of everything I've seen—from the squalor the star dwellers are forced to live in, to the bright-costumed and well-perfumed lives of the sun dwellers, to this new world, stark and sterile and cold-hearted, the home of the earth dwellers—snaps me out of my temporary funk, because despite all that, there are people out there like my mother, like Roc and Tawni, like Tristan—who had it all and gave it all away—who *are* on the right side. And regardless of the mistakes I've made, the people I've failed along the way—Cole and my father and Trevor and my little sister, Elsey—I'm on the right side. If nothing else, that's a truth I can cling to when I'm feeling weak at the knees.

So I stand up straight, take a deep breath, and march on, more determined than ever to bring down Lecter.

~~~

This is a strange place. Beautiful, in a way, with the sun shining through the glass dome, raining down in spots on the pavement as it penetrates the massive sun shade that runs along the curving atrium. But it's ugly, too. Almost too clean, everything brand new and untarnished. From the paved, unlittered streets to the clear, shiny glass windows on the buildings—constructed of light-colored stone and white-painted metal—the New City is pristine. It almost looks…unlived in, like everyone's just a visitor, like me.

Evil wears many disguises, some that can be mistaken for beauty.

I shrink against the wall of a building to let someone, dressed similarly to me, pass by, using some kind of machine that appears to be cleaning the already spotless street. He winks at me as he passes, as if he knows just what I'm thinking.

"Excuse me," I say, and he stops. As he shuts off the machine and turns, I wonder where he's from. The Star Realm? The Moon Realm? Could he be from the subchapter I grew up in, number fourteen? The possibility excites and scares me.

"Yes?" he says. "Are you okay?" His eyes flick to my battered face.

"Oh yes—yes. I just fell yesterday, I'm fine. I'm sorry to bother you, but I'm sort of lost. You see, my chip is malfunctioning and I need to get it replaced. Do you know where I can do that?"

The man chuckles. He has a friendly face. "Are you new around here? I thought the Lower Realms were done sending workers." Definitely not a sun dweller. His subtle use of "Lower" rather than the derogatory "Lesser" Realms tells me that much. Someone I can trust perhaps?

"You could say that," I say. "Seems I'm always the last one to arrive."

He takes it as a joke, his thin, brown beard chasing his cheeks into a smile. "And to think, I thought I'd won some lottery!" he says. "I guess it was, in a way. This place isn't exactly what I was expecting, but it sure beats the darkness of the Star Realm." So he's a star dweller. Or was, I guess. "I'm Avery," he says.

I shake his offered hand. "Uh, Tawni," I say, grabbing onto the first name that pops into my head, the name of my good

146

friend. "Tawni Sanders." I lock it into my memory. Can't change it now.

"Nice to meet you, Ms. Sanders. I have a daughter about your age. If our paths cross again, I'll have to introduce you."

"I'd like that," I say. "About those directions…" I've got to get going; I can't linger here, chip-less and exposed. Several other people have passed in the few short moments we've been talking.

"As I'm sure they told you during initiation, the city's set up in blocks, numbered and lettered. Not the most interesting way of doing it, but it makes getting around easy enough. You're at the corner of twenty-sixth and J, and you want to get to thirty-third and P."

"Sooo…" I say, looking up and down the road.

"That-a-way," he says, motioning down the road I was heading. "Seven blocks, turn right, and then…"—he looks at the dome above us, his lips moving as he counts—"…uh, another six blocks. There's a big sign on the door, 'Get Chipped!'" He pumps a fist in the air, which makes me smile. "You can't miss it."

"I remember now," I lie. "Thank you, Mr…Avery."

"You're welcome. And it's just Avery. See you around, Tawni Sanders."

He turns his machine on and begins pushing it down the road, toward the army medical building.

I go the other way.

~~~

I don't talk to anyone else until I reach the "Get Chipped!" building. I take in as much of the New City as I can along the way. The sights—uniformed kids walking with their arms folded reverently in front of them, eyes forward, lips closed; soldiers patrolling the streets with automatic weapons held with both hands, like they're expecting to have to use them any second; cleaners, going about their business, keeping the city scrubbed and buffed to gleaming perfection—to the sounds— the whir of huge turbines set in the dome above, pumping in fresh air that's apparently gone through some sort of filtration system, probably something similar to what we've used for centuries in the Tri-Realms; the hum of various cleaning machines being used by window cleaners, and street cleaners, and everything-else cleaners; the clear clop of the parade of people moving down the streets, rarely stopping to talk, or even look at each other.

The whole thing is giving me the creeps, so I'm glad when I reach my destination.

I enter through a spotless glass door.

A woman with a pointy nose and thick horn-rimmed glasses looks up from a screen. "May I help you?" she drones in a dull, nasally voice, as if she hopes the answer is no.

"Yes…please. My chip was malfunctioning, you see, and I—"

"Name?"

"Uh…Tawni. Tawni Sanders. I went to the medical center and they—"

She silences me with a finger in the air, typing with her other hand. "There's no Tawni Sanders listed. Spelling?"

"My chip was malfunctioning, deleting inform—"

"Spelling?" she repeats, as if I hadn't been talking.

I spell it for her and she taps at her keys, with both hands now. "No. Not here. Proceed to the right, to malfunctioning chips." She goes back to her screen. I take the whole experience as a win.

The door to the right doesn't have a window. The room beyond is—surprise, surprise—white and sterile, without even a splash of color anywhere. And empty, save for a little window with a circular hole cut in it.

Behind the glass, a balding man with two chins and a bulge in his neck looks up at me. "Name," he says.

"I already told the other lady my—" I start to say.

"Name," he repeats. I've really got to stop fighting this, just go with the flow.

I sigh. "Tawni Sanders." I spell it for him before he can ask.

"You're not in the system."

"I was," I say. "My chip was—"

"Your chip must be malfunctioning," he says. "Doesn't happen very often, but it does happen. The specialist will call you in shortly."

He goes back to his screen, but I can't imagine what he could be looking at considering I'm the only one here. For all I know he might be sending a message to security, who could crash through the door at any moment, fully prepared to shoot me on the spot, a team of cleaners behind them, ready to mop up the blood and gore before it even hits the mirror-like tiled floor.

I sit down thinking about my blood and guts on the floor and wondering whether someone will come by to clean the plasticky chair the moment I remove my butt from it.

Probably.

As I wait, I remember what Avery said, about how this might not be the best place to live, but that it's better than living in darkness in the Star Realm. Is it really better here? I've been to both places, and, although it took some getting used to, I still might choose the Star Realm. At least the people there are real. Dirty and messy and real. Everyone here, except for the cleaners I've spoken to, are more like clones…or machines. Inhuman. Fake.

But if Avery likes it here enough to prefer it to his old life, would I really be helping him by removing Lecter from power? By helping the Tri-Tribes win the war? *Yes*, I think, nodding to myself. Why can't the people have *everything*? A good place to live and a life they enjoy, one that makes them truly happy. That's what this is all about, isn't it? Giving all people what they deserve?

A door opens next to the window and a tall man with a long neck sticks his head through. "Tawni Sanders?"

"Yes," I say, standing.

"You're not in the system."

"So I've been told," I say sarcastically, drawing a strange look from the guy. Blast my loose tongue. "I mean, I know. My chip's malfunctioning."

He nods. "Come with me."

I follow him through the door and down a wide hallway. He leads me into one of a half-dozen rooms off to the side. Gestures for me to sit on a paper-covered cot.

"What seems to be the problem?" he says.

I consider pulling up my sleeve and ripping off Tristan's makeshift bandage, but I think better of it, and explain things first. "My chip wasn't working, it was—"

"Malfunctioning," he says, nodding, as if he's already two steps ahead of me.

"Yes. Malfunctioning. Wouldn't scan. Kept deleting my information, my identity. So I went to medical."

"That's not protocol," he says.

"I didn't realize," I say, "but that's what I did. They cut the faulty chip out of me, and then sent me here."

"That's not protocol either," he says.

"I know, but the guy was new and I'm new and we messed up."

"Messed up?" he says, cocking his head like I've just said something so impossible that he can't comprehend it, like I'm a hundred and twenty years old, or my father's President Lecter.

I shrug. "It happens, right?" I say, trying to smile, trying to get him to smile.

"Not really." No smile. No expression. "You're a star dweller?" he asks, like it's a foregone conclusion given the mistakes I've made.

"A moon dweller," I say, holding my right fist with my left hand. If I let go, I'm afraid I'll punch the blank look off his face.

"Hmm," he murmurs. "Show me."

So I roll up my shirt, peel off the bloodstained bandage...

"Oh my God!" he cries, covering his mouth with a hand.

"I know," I say, silently relishing the effect my ragged wound is having on him. "I had to report him to his superior. I hope they never let him near another human being."

He nods, his eyes wide, and I feel like we're bonding over my made up story. "I'm sorry for my reaction," he says, as if it was a terrible offense. "I just wasn't expecting..."

"It's okay," I say, reassuringly. Suddenly we're best friends. "Can you fix it?"

"We'll have to recreate your identity on a new chip, implant it in the same spot. Wrap your arm and let it heal."

"Good, good, whatever you have to do."

And then he does it. Like there's no way I could be anyone but who I say I am, because how could I be? Who would sneak into the New City? Who *could* sneak in? He numbs my wound, cleans it, activates a new chip, and inserts it, capping the procedure off with a fresh, white bandage. The whole thing takes twenty minutes.

Then he says I'm too new to understand the system, so I'll have to fill out a bunch of forms by hand. He promises to enter everything in the system as soon as I complete them. Drowning me in a mountain of paperwork, he leaves me alone to complete the forms. Who I am, who my parents are, siblings, friends, date of birth, my whole history. And since we're best friends now, he explains how it'll be programmed onto my chip, how if I have any problems I should come right back to him.

Everything I write is a lie, but because I'm starting from scratch, theoretically their system won't know that. I'm an orphan; the rest of my family is dead. I was recently selected to come above to the New City. I haven't made any friends yet. I haven't had time—been working too hard at my job. Little white lies.

I leave as a new person, literally. Legal and accounted for. Oh, and in the occupation section, I checked the box for "Presidential Cleaner." I don't know exactly what that means but I suspect it'll help me at some point along the way.

Twenty-Three
Siena

Skye tries to take off down the hill, chasing after the trucks like she has any chance of catching 'em, like she'd be able to make any difference even if she could, but Wilde grabs her from behind, pulls her back, screams at me and Tristan to help her.

We do our best, clutching at my sister, who's fighting like a Killer, thrashing and screaming and scratching at us with her nails. "Let go of me! Burn you all! It's my choice…mine!" And the whole time I'm pinning my sister to the ground, I'm staring at the desert in front of me, unable to look away, as the Glassies and their fire chariots and their fire sticks tear through the Icers like a dust storm through a village.

And I'm crying, tears streaming down my face, 'cause I see him, Dazz. Buff, too. They're at the front and they're fighting, using the Glassies' weapons against 'em, but it's not enough—not nearly enough—and they fall. And the chariots keep going, into the fleeing villagers, women and children and men, fathers and mothers and sisters, like Jolie, who we fought to save, nearly died to save. I know their screams will fill my nightmares for the rest of my days. They're all cut down, until none are left standing. Not a single one.

And Skye, even though she can't see it—thank the sun goddess she can't see it—knows it, too. That it's over. That they're all…

I can't even think it.

We're wrapped up t'gether, Skye and Wilde and me, broken and sobbing, falling apart, 'cause they were our friends and to Skye, maybe more'n that.

I feel a firm hand on my back. Tristan, his mask ripped off. "We have to…go," he says, his voice a shattered-whisper. I look up. His cheeks are wet, too. He didn't know any of the Icers, but still he hurts for 'em, for us. He ain't no spy. "We have to go," he repeats. "If they realize we're here…"

He's right, and as much as I want to lie 'ere all day, want to dig a hole and crawl into it, we have a whole village of people that are depending on us. We hafta be strong for 'em, even if we're broken inside.

Wilde stands first, her cheeks shining. She helps me up. The three of us try to pull Skye to her feet, but she resists, the opposite of 'fore. Then we had to force her down, now we can't get her up. "No, leave me," she says. "Just leave me." Her voice is weaker'n a sick Totter's, barely coming out, like it's

154

stuck in her throat. Seeing her like this stabs through me like a knife. But I can't listen, can't let her have her way, or she'll die.

"Get up, Skye. Get up." I pull harder, and t'others do too. We force her to her feet, although her legs are as wobbly as a newborn tug's. "Yer not dyin' on us," I grunt, pushing her arm 'round my neck. "Carry her," I say.

Wilde takes her other arm and Tristan grabs her feet, and we start down the opposite side of the mound, but 'fore we're even halfway to the bottom, Skye's twisting outta our arms. "I still got two feet," she mumbles.

So we let her down, let her walk on her own, but I keep close to her, 'cause she's stumbling, not lifting her feet high enough, and muttering under her breath, tears continuing to trace meandering streams down her cheeks. And she's making soft, whimpering noises, but no, that's not her. It's me. I'm sobbing as I walk.

Broken. So broken. And yet only half as broken as Skye must be.

~~~

When we're far, far away from where it happened, we sit down in a cluster, Skye and Wilde and me. Trying to pick up the pieces. Trying to remember why we hafta keep going. Tristan has replaced his mask, hiding his expression. He gives us our space, sitting a little ways off, just staring at the red sky above us. Every now and again he wipes a tear from the corners of his eyes.

Eventually, the tears stop, for all of us, like we've run out. Is that even possible? To run out of tears? Another time I thought so, too, when I'd believed I'd lost Circ. That was the worst of

155

the worse, every bit as bad as things are now, and yet I picked myself up and came out stronger. And then my mother died. With almost her last breaths, she saved me. Did it break me, destroy me, end me? No. Again, I came out stronger.

But Skye, she ain't crying anymore, but the hurt's still there, in the dark brown of her eyes, in the quivering curve of her lips, in the clenched lines of her face. Will she come out stronger? She's already the strongest person I know, so what does that mean?

I tuck a hand 'round her head, pull her into my chest. For once, I'm the stronger one. I hafta be, for her. She lets me do it for a little while, until I feel her body tense up. She squeezes her fingers into fists, releases 'em, squeezes again.

And when she looks up, well…I've seen Skye hardened and raw and rougher'n prickler skin plenty of times 'fore, but I ain't never seen her like this. Her eyes are dark and her chin like stone. Even with the dried tears on her cheeks, she looks unbreakable. And yet beneath the impenetrable fortress she's desperately trying to build 'round herself, I sense she's more broken'n shattered glass. I don't know what to do for her.

"I'll kill every burnin' Glassy baggard there is," she growls. "They started this war, but we'll finish it."

~ ~ ~

The trek back to New Wildetown feels longer'n it is. It's like what we saw is sucking us back with each step. Three steps forward and two back. But still we soldier on. Skye's starting to scare me with those eyes of hers, darker'n ever 'fore with her angry eyebrows so low over 'em it's like they're a part of 'em.

156

I feel awful for having given her a hard time 'bout Dazz when we were trudging through the desert 'fore. Even if it was just a bit of fun, I still shouldn'ta done it.

When the familiar three-peaked tower of rocks comes into view, I heave out a ragged breath and will my legs forward one at a time. Everything is suddenly catching up with me as I see the place I called home for a short time 'fore we left for ice country. It wasn't that long ago, but it seems like miles and miles and miles and years and years and years. Lifetimes. Tears blur my vision as we pick up the pace.

All I want is to see him, to have a soft place to land, to have a shoulder to fall into, to cry into. Skye can have my shoulder, but I want his. I need his.

And then he's there, emerging from a hidden break in the rocks, running, sprinting. Circ. Graceful and perfect and mine.

Feve's right behind him, and as they approach I can see in their expressions that they can tell something's wrong. Probably 'cause the tears on my cheeks are shining from a mile away.

I'm running. Skye and Wilde are, too, I think. Tristan's the only one who's still walking, or maybe just standing there, gawking. I don't know, 'cause I'm too busy crashing into Circ and he's holding me fiercely, tighter'n a clenched fist, like he was worried I wasn't coming home at all, regardless of how many pieces I'm in. "Oh, sun goddess," I breathe, 'cause even Circ's love can't bring 'em back. Nothing can.

Feve's got Skye and Wilde, one in each arm, and it's the scariest thing in the world to see Wilde so shattered, tears running down her cheeks, clinging to Feve like a wet shirt.

"They killed 'em," Skye says, and I finally realize she ain't crying. She's the only one of us three not crying. "They killed 'em all." And her words, they're like the hard, cold ice in the mountains to the north, a home for a people who no longer need it. "It's time for war."

~~~

We're setting in a circle. Lots of other folk are 'ere too, mostly just to listen, to hear the tragedy that Wilde's recounting. The news from ice country.

I'm leaning into Circ and his arm's 'round me, and it feels so searin' good that it feels awful.

'Cause Skye's got no one to hold her.

'Cept she does, 'cause our younger sister, Jade, is huddled up against her, and you know what? For once, Skye lets her, doesn't push her away, doesn't tell her to scram, like she always does if I try to show her affection. And I'm glad for it. So glad.

Feve's asking questions of Wilde every so often in that low, warm voice of his. He's got a baby in each arm and his wife, Hela, at his side. Feve the family man. Even after I witnessed it the first time, after we settled in New Wildetown, I could barely believe it. But it's true, and I was shocked that the dark warrior was a pretty searin' good father.

The odd one out is Tristan, whose eyes are shooting all 'round like darts, just taking everything in, looking like an alien wearing his mask. Answering any questions that are asked of him, mostly stuff he's already told us. Where'd you come from? Who are you? Why are you here? Your girlfriend really went inside the Glass City alone? To help us? And you swear you're not a Glassy? His voice sounds strange through the mask as he answers each one.

He looks so out of place it's almost funny, and I might laugh if I felt like I could.

But laughter's just not something any of us got in us right now. Maybe tomorrow.

~ ~ ~

When all the questions and the conversating pretty much ends, me and Circ go for a walk. I need to be with him right now. Just him. Even if only for a short time.

He's got his fingers laced in mine and I'm grizzed at myself for enjoying it so much. My footsteps are heavy and loud, while his are as graceful and lithe as one of the fire dancers who sometimes perform at the evening meal.

"Siena," he says, his dark brown eyes even darker in the shadows, his skin like night. Under the cloudy sky, he could almost be a Stormer. "Tell me."

And that's Circ. Knowing me every searin' bit as well as I know myself. Knowing when I got something to say and when I don't.

"I'm afraid I'll be a hot mess if I try to talk 'bout it," I say, squeezing his hand harder just to make sure it's still there.

In less time'n it takes Perry to hurl an insult, Circ's got me in his arms, carrying me, like I'm some helpless little doll of his.

"Put me the scorch down!" I hiss. "I got two feet like everbody else."

But he just laughs, goes right on carrying me, and I don't fight him too hard, 'cause it's kinda fun and kinda what I need.

We go to the left, into darker darks, through some sorta cave cut into the side of the canyon. I feel us rising…up, up, up…twisting one way, then t'other, Circ's strong arms holding me like I'm as heavy as a Totter, which ain't that far from the truth.

I breathe him in and he's the desert and the heat and a bit of that crushed prickler-flower powder I gave him one time as a gift. He said it was a gift for a woman, but now he uses it more'n *any* women I know.

When we emerge from the dark I lose my breath, even though he's been the one doing all the work, 'cause the sight is beyond imagination. We're high up, unimaginably high, looking out over the vastness of fire country, spreading wide and dark and mysterious under a cloud-filled sky.

Still carrying me, Circ sets himself down and holds me on his lap. "I wanted stars," he grumbles.

"Never mind the stars," I say.

Circ looks into my eyes and the warmth and familiarity of 'em are too much, too much. I duck my head into his shoulder and my body shakes, tears trailing silent tracks down my cheeks. "Why are they doing this?" I sob. "What'd any of us ever do to deserve this?"

There are no answers, so Circ stays silent, just holds me, his cheek against my hair.

When the tears stop falling and I'm able to pull away to look at him, his eyes are glistening. He considered Dazz and Buff friends, too. Fought beside 'em, travelled to foreign lands with 'em. Never again.

"Everything's so burnin' screwed up," I say. "We're the only thing that's right."

"No," Circ says.

"No?" I echo, feeling fresh tears well up. We're not right?

"Not *only* us," Circ explains and I blink the tears away. "Your sisters. Wilde. Feve. My family. Everyone down there, sitting around that fire. They're right, too. We've got something—a world, a life, a happiness—worth protecting."

160

And his words are so perfect and so beautiful that I want to grab 'em and bring 'em to my chest and never let 'em go…but instead they slice through me 'cause…

"You weren't there," I say, my words numb. "You didn't hafta watch 'em die. You don't know."

There's fire running through my belly and suddenly it's like I wanna be somewhere else, anywhere else, but I know there's no place I can hide from the past. From the truth.

Circ kisses me so suddenly I don't have time to take a breath, but then I'm kissing back and breathing when I can, and realizing this is a place I can go, 'cause when we're doing this I'm far, far away and maybe I don't ever hafta come back.

His hand's on my back, in my hair, tugging at my hips: they're everywhere at the same time, like he's got more'n two. He's all I need.

How can one person, whether male or female, or young or old, or friend or family or lover, make you feel so good, send sparks dancing through your very being? It's a question only a heart can answer.

His lips, painting a picture on mine. And I'm gone, gone, gone, drifting away…

…finding a better place.

Twenty-Four
Tristan

Where the hell am I? What the hell am I doing?

I watched those people die today, and I knew I was watching the hand of evil. It cracked my bones, splintered my soul, shattered my heart. I didn't know any of them, but I didn't have to, because they were mothers, fathers, children, brothers, sisters, friends. Like Adele and Roc and Tawni and Elsey and no different than the ones I love down below. They were people—slaughtered like animals.

If the Glassy soldiers doing the killing are the hand of evil, then Borg Lecter is the face, the mouth, the one giving the orders. And I've pushed Adele right into his gaping maw to be crushed with a single bite.

She could be dead already. But I'd feel it, wouldn't I? Instead I feel nothing, empty. Is that because of what I saw today, or because she's gone? No. No, I felt something completely different when my mom disappeared, when my father admitted—bragged even—that he'd killed her. Sadness and rage and loss. I don't feel any of that. So that means Adele's still alive, right?

"Yes," I whisper under my breath. Even if I'm lying to myself, I feel better having said it out loud.

"What's that?" the tattooed guy, Feve, asks. His wife took one of the babies he was holding, but he's still got the other one tucked under his arm like a package. When I first met him, all dark and tatted up and ripped like he spends every day, all day lifting stones, working out, I'd never have guessed he was a family man. And yet somehow…it suits him.

"Uh, nothing," I grunt, my voice coming out raspy, phlegm in my throat.

New Wildetown stands before us, the towering, sheer cliffs of the canyon rising up on either side, framing a long line of tents and shelters, constructed of a combination of wood and thick animal skins. Activity buzzes through the village. Talking, laughing, shouts of mothers and fathers disciplining their children. It's all so…normal. Like there aren't people killing each other less than a day's journey from here. Like there's no war, no evil. They might not have a towering glass dome, or the technology to raise it, but the people of the Tri-Tribes have created a bubble of their own. Even being a foreigner, a stranger, I already feel safe here.

My gut clenches. Adele should be here.

"There was another Wildetown," Feve says, leading me between the rows of tents, past a young boy (clothed in just a tiny skin around his torso) chasing an even younger boy (buck naked). Their mother is chasing both of them, a tub of water standing nearby. I guess kids run from bath time here, too.

"What happened to it?" I ask through my mask.

"Nothing," Feve says, using his non-baby arm to help a struggling old man to his feet. The man nods at Feve and we keep walking. "The Wildes abandoned it when we formed the Tri-Tribes."

"The all-girl tribe," I say.

Feve looks at me curiously. "They've told you about our history?"

"As much as they could," I say. "But it's easier to understand now that I'm seeing it in real life."

He nods, swings the child into both arms in front of him, rocks it gently. "The first Wildetown wasn't as well-hidden or well-protected. This place is almost impossible to find, even if you know where to look."

I remember how my jaw dropped when we squeezed through what looked like an impossibly small opening in the rocks that surely led to nowhere, only to find a canyon so large it could, apparently, fit the peoples of three tribes in it.

"This canyon is much larger than the one the Wildes used to live in. There are almost three thousand of us."

"Is that enough to win the war?" I ask, ignoring the stares of a group of children who are laughing and pointing at me. Then, just as we pass them, I crouch down with my hands held out like claws and go, "Rawr!" and they run away shrieking.

Feve raises an eyebrow. "Get the children on your side and you'll do quite well here," he says, before going back to my question. "Not nearly enough," he says. "Not with the firepower the Glassies have. Do you know anything about those weapons they have? The fire sticks?"

I almost laugh, but I don't want to insult him, nor do I mean to. It's just crazy that these people are living so primitively they don't even have a basic understanding of guns or electricity or any of the things I always took for granted. Heck, even the moon and star dwellers understood technology, even if it wasn't always readily available to them. But these people, they're happy if they have food and water and each other. Is that so wrong? Is that a reason to kill them?

My almost-laugh turns into a clenched jaw. If anyone can get to Lecter, it's Adele.

I slip a hand under my mask and massage the tension out of my face, answer the question. "We call them guns," I say. "They shoot small pods of metal—we call them bullets"—I raise my thumb and forefinger to show him the approximate size—"at speeds so fast they're invisible to the human eye."

"Are they magic?" Feve asks, and I think he's joking, but his eyes are dark and serious.

"Uh, no. Just technology. Like the glass dome. Like the trucks—I mean, fire chariots."

Feve stops. "This girl, Adele…will she be able to help us?"

I want to believe. I have to believe. "Yes," I say. "She will help you."

~~~

I'll be staying with Feve's family until they can find me something more suitable. I feel awkward at first, as his wife, Hela, prepares a bed for me, but soon I'm holding his kids and

165

they're grabbing at my mask, playing with it, and I feel right at home.

It's the safest I've felt since arriving on the surface.

After a day that was longer and more traumatic than most, the soft skins and blankets suck me in, and, hoping Adele's found a place to sleep, too, I drift away to the muted coughs and babies' cries and whispers of a camp at rest.

~~~

Shouts shatter the night. I claw at the blankets, drowning in them, trying to get to the air. A sliver of light flashes into the tent and I remember where I am. New Wildetown. Guest of the Tri-Tribes and Feve's family.

Did I dream the shouts?

One of Feve's babies starts crying, and I catch a glimpse of Hela picking him up, bringing him to her breast to feed. "Shhh," she whispers.

"What happened?" I say.

"Feve went to find out," she says, her eyes barely visible in the dark.

I scramble to my feet and out the door, into a brighter night, the stars twinkling through the top of the canyon, a long rectangle of glittering night sky. The clouds have moved on.

Sucking a filtered breath through the mask, I hear the shouts again, arising from the direction of the secret entrance. Too far to make out the words or the voices. I run in their direction, past the tents from which there are more babies crying and mothers shushing them.

And then I see them: A group of people, men and women, shouting, arguing.

"We should kill the Glassy baggards 'ere and now," a woman's voice says. I identify the speaker immediately. Skye. Her back is to me, but to her left I see Circ, holding a torch, and Siena, too. And on her right, Wilde and Feve. "I'll do it myself if I have to."

"Skye, please, we need to talk about this." Wilde says that, reaching out to calm her friend, but Skye slaps her arm away.

"We've talked enough. Did the Glassies just *talk* to the Icers? Ha! They squashed 'em like ants."

"Where'd you find them?" Feve asks. It's clear he's not asking Skye.

I move closer, craning my neck to see past Skye, to see who they found, and who did the finding.

Hawk's face comes into view. What's he doing away from his post? I wonder. "They were wandering in the desert," he says. "Dead on their feet. If we hadn'ta found 'em when we did, they'da probably died."

"Good riddance," Skye says.

I'm getting closer now, almost able to see past Skye, where there's a shadow on the ground, maybe two shadows. A voice freezes me in place, widens my eyes. Cracked and tired, but a voice I'd recognize anywhere. "Please. We're just trying to find our friend."

In a burst I rush forward, shove my way between Skye and Siena, and look down.

Impossibly, he's there.

My half-brother and best friend.

Roc, staring up at me with the most surprised eyes ever.

And beyond him: Tawni, breaking into the biggest smile in the world, a flash of blond hair framing her face under the torchlight.

Twenty-Five
Adele

I'm tired. Which isn't a surprise. Sleeping in a cold, metal drawer meant for dead people doesn't lend itself to the most restful kind of sleep.

At the same time, however, I'm energized. Even as my eyes are trying to close and my feet are screaming at me to "Sit down!" my blood is running hot and fast through my veins. Because things are going so right at the moment. I've got my chip, my new name, a friend named Avery cleaning a street somewhere, and, most of all, a chance. A mission that originally meant to be bordering on suicidal is suddenly full of possibilities.

And I can't fail. I can't. I don't know how.

The first step is to get my bearings. And who better to help with that than my new friend. My stomach growls as I make my way back the way I came, down twenty-sixth street, left on J. I'm hungry, but not desperately so. I clench my abs and try to swallow the dry, thick spit in my mouth. Another seven blocks and I'm back where I started, where I first met Avery and got the directions. I head in the direction he went with his cleaning machine, stopping at each intersection to look both ways, see if I can spot him.

I reach the army medical building, past which the city ends at the main gate, the one with the double doors and airlock system. The edge of the dome rises up from the desert floor. Thick glass separating me from Tristan.

I turn around, retrace my steps, and pick a random road to turn onto. People move down the streets: some wear white like me, which I'm starting to realize means they're from the Lower Realms, moon dwellers and star dwellers; some wear camo uniforms, the army obviously; and others wear gray and black. What is their role, I wonder? Most of the people enter glass-walled buildings, and I watch as they scan their wrists on a transparent plate before pushing through metal turnstiles, almost like scanning your ticket at the underground train stations in the Tri-Realms.

I come to a long line of people, waiting patiently to enter a door. The hearty aroma of cooked food wafts out. My stomach grumbles again. I stop to watch.

Every so often someone exits, and another person is allowed to enter, scanning their wrist on the glass plate at the door. A red light flashes and then turns green. The man at the door gestures them inside. Red light flashes. Turns green. One out, one in.

I'm about to move on—my main goal is still to find Avery—when I see something different happen. Red light flashes. Stays red. "You've already received your ration for today," the burly man at the door says.

"C'mon, I'm still hungry," says the kid trying to get in. He's younger than me, maybe fourteen.

The big guy looks at a screen in the side of the scanning machine. "You've tried this before. Twice."

"No," the kid says.

The man points to the machine, taps the screen. "Two warnings in the system. And you're supposed to be in school."

"No," the kids says again.

"There are no third warnings," the man says.

"Stay away from me," the kid says, backing away. "I'm just hungry. I just want more food."

"Everyone shares equally," the man says.

And then I hear them. Heavy footsteps from behind, running. I glance back. Two soldiers, dressed differently than the others I've seen so far, still in camo uniforms but in shades of blue. Carrying guns, but even their weapons look different. And yet so familiar…

My father slumping to the floor, the Taser having sent a shock of electricity through him.

The Enforcers turning on me, on my mother. Taking her. Taking them. Taking us.

The beginning of everything.

"No!" the boy screams behind me, and when I turn to look, he's already halfway down the block, charging away. He's got a good lead on the…I don't have any other word for the soldiers than the one I know from before…*Enforcers*, about to turn the corner. Maybe he'll be able to find a place to hide, to escape…

He looks back as he cuts sharply to the right…

Slam!

Another Enforcer comes out of nowhere, cracking something long and thin over his head—some kind of a stick. The boy flops to the ground, still. So still.

The other two Enforcers catch up, lift his rubbery body, and carry him away.

No one in the food line even turns to watch. None of them say a damn thing.

Where are they taking him? To a place like the Pen in subchapter 14, a kid prison for troubled youths? All for what? Asking for more food when he's hungry, skipping school? If those offenses warranted imprisonment, every kid I grew up with would've been hauled away.

What kind of city is this? Rations, food lines, bland colors representing your standing…

"Hey," a voice says from the side, jerking me around.

Avery. Thank God. "Hi," I say.

"Did you get your chip malfunction sorted out?" He leans on his cleaning machine.

"Yeah, yes, thank you," I say, still too shocked at what I just witnessed to think of anything more.

"That happens sometimes," he says, motioning to where the boy had just been beaten. "Your first time seeing it?"

I nod. "How often?" I ask.

"Once, twice a week," he says. He lowers his voice. "Usually to moon and star dwellers, since our rations are less than the others. Every so often the hunger makes someone snap, but most of us just learn to tighten our belts and ignore it."

"Less?" I say.

He doesn't answer, just looks at the food line. "Haven't you eaten since you've arrived?"

I'm getting into dangerous territory. "Uh, yeah, but I guess I, uh, just never noticed."

He looks back at me and I do my best to meet his gaze. Try to look honest. "My daughter's over there, in line," he says. "She's on her break. Do you want to meet her?" He motions to a girl wearing white like me and Avery. I only now realize she's watching us closely.

"Sure," I say.

We walk over together and Avery makes the introductions. Her name's Malindra. Lin, for short. I shake her hand, meet her eyes, which are a mesmerizing mixture of blue and green. With each movement, her reddish-brown hair bounces in curls on her shoulders. She's got a nice, warm smile, like her father, although she doesn't really carry any of his other features.

"I've got to get back," Avery says, as two blue-clad Enforcers eye his unattended machine as they pass by. He rushes off, leaving us alone…with all the other people standing in line.

"No line jumping," someone yells from the back.

"Oh, I'm not—" I go to say.

"Shut your mouth, we're just talking!" Lin yells back sharply. I gawk at her, her smile temporarily falling, but coming back just as quickly. "Have you had your afternoon ration yet?" she asks.

Uh, what? "No," I say.

"C'mon," she says, pulling me away from the line. "The food here sucks anyway."

I let her drag me down the street. A guide is exactly what I was looking for.

When we cross the road that leads back to the main gates, I hear a commotion to our left, somewhere behind the army medical building. "What's going on?" I say aloud, my thoughts spilling from my lips.

"Who knows, who cares?" Lin says, still pulling at my arm. "The army's always up to something. Supposedly protecting us from the big, bad savages, or some such nonsense."

I stop, pull back, listening. It sounds like something big is happening, or has already happened. *The mission*, I remember, the one Meaty-Bun and Skinny-Bun were talking about when they entered the morgue. Just beginning or just ending?

"Can we check it out?" I ask Lin.

She looks at her watch. "I've only got twenty minutes before I have to get back to work…" she says. "Ah, screw it, let's go." She releases my hand and we stride quickly toward the building and then past it. "Why the interest?" she asks. "You got a boyfriend in the army or something?"

"Not exactly," I say, smashing my face to a fence that's blocking our progress. She does the same, grabbing the metal links with her fingers. We crane our heads far to the right, trying to see what's happening at the gate.

Vehicles are pulling in, one at a time, soldiers spilling out. Blood on their uniforms, on their faces, on their hands. Backboards being carried to the trucks, loaded up with bodies, hauled away. "What the hell?" I say.

"Looks like the natives might've got the best of them this time," Lin says beside me. "There aren't usually this many casualties, but it's happened before. Once. Maybe twice."

"What?" I say, even though I completely understand what she's saying. She thinks they've been fighting the natives, but does she mean the Tri-Tribes? "Who?"

173

She shrugs. "I dunno, they don't tell us much. Only that we're safe and that the army is doing everything they can to protect us from the savages. But it's not like the natives are just going to roll over and let us take their land. Nor should they. It's all a load of rubbish if you ask me. We should just leave them alone and maybe they'll leave us alone."

My mind is whirling. If there are this many Glassies…I mean, earth dwellers…dead, then how many "savages" died? Skye and Siena and Wilde and…oh, God, Tristan. Could he have been in the battle? Here I thought I was the one taking the risks, going inside the dragon's lair, when really the dragon was outside hunting. A pit widens in my stomach.

"Can we climb this fence?" I say, looking up, already sticking a foot between the links. I have to see if they've got any prisoners, if any of the dead bodies are the enemy. (Or Tristan.)

"Only if you want to get shot," she says, grabbing my arm. "It's a restricted area; they won't hesitate." Her eyes are serious enough that I step down.

But I can't just do nothing, can I? I try to swallow, but my throat's too dry.

"What's this really about?" Lin asks, ducking slightly to catch my gaze.

Tristan. It's about Tristan.

"Nothing," I say.

~ ~ ~

She has to go back to work, so we agree to meet later on. I promise to answer all her questions. But I can't, can I? She doesn't seem to have any love for the army, or the way the city is run, and she *is* a star dweller, or at least used to be…but what if she turns me in? I barely know the girl, and as feisty as she seems to be, if she gets her mind to do something, there's no doubt in my mind that she'll do it. It's a risk but…

I could really use an ally.

Before Lin left, she took me back to the food line. I'm halfway to the front but my appetite is long gone, replaced with the dark hole in my gut. Who did the soldiers fight? Did they discover the spy cave used by Hawk and Lara? I cling to the hope that whoever killed so many soldiers didn't suffer any deaths. Or maybe it was those wild beasts, the Killers. Yeah, maybe the soldiers ran into a huge pack of them. I'll take anything other than Tristan fighting.

I'm at the front of the line, having forgotten to watch the person in front of me to see what they did. Scan your wrist, do it quick, like you know what the hell you're doing. I lower my arm to the glass. Will this work?

A red flash. Please turn green, please, please, please…

Green!

The burly man, who somehow contacted the Enforcers to arrest the hungry boy, motions me inside. I resist the urge to spit in his face.

Inside, it's way too quiet to be a place where people eat. Food involves conversation, and conversation involves stories and laughs and some level of fun. Even in the Pen it was like that, although the fun sometimes included fistfights and insults about mothers.

I see them. Burly men wearing black, standing in the corners. Watching everything, scanning the room, eyes roving back and forth. Back and forth. Fun-killers. People are sitting, eating, most of them in silence, some talking in voices so low I don't know how anyone can hear them. It's eerie, like I'm in a cave full of sleeping bats.

The line moves forward and I look for a plate, a tray, something. Everyone moves forward empty handed. I watch as a woman wearing dark pants and a black shirt at the front of the line scans her wrist on another plate, and is handed a dish with a glass of water and four rectangles on it: one green, one red, one yellow, one brown. What are those? Surely not food. She takes her plate and sits down at the first seat she comes to.

The next person, an old white-clothed man with a cane, scans his wrist and is given a similar plate, only with just three rectangles. The same as the lady's, but without the brown one. "No meat ration for the Lowers today, I guess," he mutters as he sits near where I'm standing, looping the curved part of his walking stick on the corner of the table. Despite his complaint, he dives right in, using the side of his fork to smash the rectangles into something that looks—at least slightly—more like food. He shovels the resulting paste in his mouth with a large spoon, pausing only to take long gulps of water.

It's almost my turn, but my mind is on anything but food. *No meat ration for the Lowers today.* The man's muttered complaint. By "Lowers" did he mean…those from the Lower Realms? The star and moon dwellers? The ones wearing white, doing all the jobs the former sun dwellers don't want to do? I pay attention to the three people in front of me. Two of the three are wearing dark clothes and get the brown rectangle. The last one, wearing white, doesn't. A Lower. So what does that make the others? Uppers?

Feeling disgusted, I scan my wrist. A chubby woman wearing a white cap over her hair hands me a plate. No brown rectangle for me, the Lower.

176

I take the first seat I come to, fighting back the rising urge to scream.

~~~

I meet Lin later on where she told me to. The corner of W and 2nd. The streets are full of white-clad people, presumably returning home from whatever crap jobs they've been assigned. I'm surprised—the sun is still streaming through the glass, an hour or two from the horizon. Are their jobs really that bad if they get to go home this early? Maybe they start really early too.

Despite having made sure I'd be at the designated meeting spot well before six, the time we'd agreed on, Lin's already waiting, smiling broadly.

Without any kind of greeting, she grabs my hand and pulls me through the press of the crowd. It's the loudest I've heard the earth dwellers. They're talking and gossiping like normal human beings. Like they're alive and not the zombies I've seen walking around all day.

"Lin?" I say, still being dragged.

"Yeah?" she says, not looking back.

"What's going on?"

"They let all the workers out early, for an—"

A three-toned sound rings out somewhere above, cutting her off. Instead of continuing whatever she was going to say, Lin sticks a finger in the air and keeps on leading me.

A loud voice blares, immediately silencing the people. "Please return to your sleeping quarters and power up your vids for an important announcement from President Borg Lecter. I repeat…" The command loops three times, until I can't help but to mimic it, mouthing each word. What sort of announcement? Is this about the injured soldiers we saw today?

After eating lunch, I'd gone back to the army medical building, looked through the fence. The soldiers were gone, all of them, the injured likely receiving medical attention, the dead taken to Meaty-Bun and Skinny-Bun in the morgue, one of them probably stuffed in the very drawer I slept in last night. Hopefully they didn't need to use the drawer I stashed the weapons in. The uninjured would be back wherever they live, resting and preparing for the next mission. If there'll be a next mission. But if they won the war already...

Lin practically yanks my arm off as she cuts to the side, out of the human flow, leading me through a door that clicks and opens automatically when she scans her wrist on a plate at the front.

We stop in front of a row of shiny, metal doors. Lin presses a button in the middle of them, which lights up bright yellow.

Only then does she turn to me. "Everyone's speculating what the message will be about," she says, "but I can tell you from experience that Lecter"—I like the way she says his name, irreverently, just his last name with no "President" attached—"only makes city-wide announcements if he's trying to gloat or influence us."

"So propaganda basically," I say.

"About right," she says as one of the doors opens. I follow her into a small closet, barely wide enough to fit both of us. Buttons with numbers from two to thirty-two are poking from one of the walls. Lin scans her wrist again and presses eighteen. The button lights up.

The doors close and the closet hums under our feet. There's a lurch and we start to rise. Even as I put a hand on the wall to steady myself I can't help but think of the long ride up to the surface with Tristan. Up to check things out and back down to the real world. That was the plan. I shake my head, wondering how the hell I ended up as a spy in the New City.

"What?" Lin says, eyeing me curiously.

"Life is funny," I say, meaning something else.

"No. Life is crappy," she says, meaning exactly that. Her word choice is closer to what I was thinking anyway.

When we stop and the doors open, we step out into a long hallway with many doors on each side. Like *a lot* of doors. There have to be at least a hundred. Weird.

Lin turns left and goes to one with the number 1808 on it. Scans her wrist, waits for a click, and then pushes through. "Avery?" she says. Funny she doesn't called him "Dad" or "Father." A lot of things about Lin are kind of funny.

"Here," the familiar voice answers. She holds the door for me and I step into a long narrow room that ends in glass. Through it I can see the sun reflecting off the side of another building. Avery's inside, fiddling with some kind of plastic wrapper.

"I brought Tawni," Lin announces, and I almost look around for my old friend. But no, that's my name now.

"Hi there," he says, to the both of us.

"Hi Mr…Avery," I say.

"Just Avery," he says, ripping the plastic off a green rectangle. "Want to have dinner with us?"

My stomach clenches at the thought of more rectangle-food, but I know I need the energy. I can't just not eat because the food is tasteless and shaped like bricks. "Sure," I say.

I close the door behind me and take in my surroundings…or rather, lack of surroundings. There's nothing to the place. A small counter runs down one side, with small metal squares, like cabinets, set into the wall—no handles, no knobs, no way of opening them. Just in front of the glass window at the end is a small table with two chairs. Running back down the other side is a bare wall, gray, with strange lines cut into it. This is where they...live?

Avery peels off another couple packages and adds a brown and a yellow rectangle to his plate, holds his wrist up to one of the metal rectangles and it opens. He shoves the plate inside and shuts the door. Yellow light glows from the edges as it hums. Maybe ten seconds later, the machine goes dark and the door pops open. Steam rises from the rectangle-food.

"You can have this one," Avery says, handing me the plate. *Rations*, I think. I can't possibly take their rations, can I?

"That's okay, you have it," I say.

"Here, I'll trade you," Avery says, setting the plate on the counter and grabbing my wrist. Why do he and Lin love to do that? He lifts my wrist to a different metal plate and then pulls it back. The door slides open and inside are three clear, plastic pouches, each with a colored rectangle inside—green, brown and yellow.

Down the counter, Lin has scanned her own wrist and is already unwrapping her food. So it's like...unlimited food at night but rations during the day? Why would that kid have been complaining about being hungry?

I lift my wrist to try scanning it on another metal square, but nothing happens. Did I do it correctly? Is there some special technique to scanning I haven't quite mastered, that I would have learned had I been through the proper welcome-to-Earth orientation?

Avery laughs. "I try that sometimes, too, just for kicks, hoping there will be an error with the system and I'll get a double ration. But it never works."

I laugh like that's exactly what I was trying to do. Trick the system. Like I'm not the clueless idiot who doesn't know how anything works.

But Lin's not buying it. "You're different," she says, grabbing her steaming plate out of the weird-super-fast-cooker-thingy. Avery sticks the next plate in.

"I could say the same about you," I say. "Both of you."

"How so?" Lin asks, sitting at the table.

"Have a seat," Avery says with a wave. I take the only other seat and Lin passes me a fork, the question still in her eyes.

"Well…" I start, choosing my words carefully so as not to offend the only two friends I have at the moment. "Lin, you're…not a zombie, and Avery, you actually talked to me on the street."

"Score! Not a zombie," Lin says. "That's what I was hoping for. Compliment of the year."

"So I *am* a zombie?" Avery says, standing and eating.

Smiling, I shake my head. "No, I just meant that I walked around all day and no one seemed the least bit interested that I existed. Except for you two."

Oh, and the two Enforcers that had stopped me on the street and scanned my wrist. "Why didn't you just tell us it was your Anything Day?" one of them had said before they moved on, leaving my heart to return to normal speed, my knuckles to unclench.

"See, there you go again," Lin says. "People don't talk like that up here."

I look out the window, but it's not a window anymore, it's a black screen, spotted with static.

"The announcement's starting," Avery says. "Let's see what our esteemed and fearless leader has to say." I like the way he says it. He sounds startlingly like Lin did when she spoke of the president.

The window-that's-now-a-screen suddenly blazes to life, filled with a man set against a blue background. He's wearing a dark coat with a dark shirt underneath. The only splash of color is a red flower in his breast pocket. His face is lined and weathered, like he's been through a lot in his life but come out on top. He's not that old, but has silvery hair, parted just to the side of center, accented by blue-gray eyes. He wears an easy smile, but it doesn't look natural, like it's been pasted on.

This is President Lecter? He could be someone's grandfather. He probably *is* somebody's grandfather.

"Citizens of the New City, earth dwellers, pioneers," he says slowly, like each word is of the greatest value and deserves perfect pronunciation and attention.

"Why does he always start that way?" Avery asks, almost to himself.

"Because he's a tool," Lin mutters.

Staring right at me, Lecter continues. "We've won a great victory today in the fight for our children, for our liberty. The savages that call themselves the Icers have been destroyed!" My heart blinks, once, twice, thrice, stuttering before returning to normal speed. Not the Heaters. Not Tristan. I hate myself for the excitement that flutters through me because *other* people have died.

"We couldn't let any of them live, because even with their last dying breaths, the bloodthirsty natives were trying to kill our soldiers. They even brought their children to fight, arming them with guns stolen off the bodies of our loyal protectors."

They killed them all. Wilde had talked about the Icers like they were their only ally. So where does that leave them? A bubble of pressure forms in my throat. My mission has just become even more important. I cannot fail or they'll all die. What's left of them anyway.

"But we suffered losses too," Lecter says, his face softening. "Twenty-two of our brave men and women were killed in the battle, and many more were injured. Let us have a moment of silence for them and their families." The president bows his head, clasps his hands. We just stare at him.

I speak over the silence. "Do people here really believe the natives are savages?" I blurt out.

Lin stares at me and I know I've been too obvious. "Who are you?" she says.

~~~

I wait until Lecter concludes the announcement—raising a fist and promising to eradicate the rest of the savages that threaten the good people of the New City, or some such nonsense— before answering.

"I—I'm a moon dweller," I say, desperately trying to decide where to go from here. Can I really tell them? Can I really trust them? I said it myself: Avery and Lin are different. But are they allies? If I just leave, walk out the door, will they forget about me, that I ever existed? They know my name—my fake name, yeah, but the one that the damn chip in my arm is linked to. They could tell someone about me.

"Yeahhh…" Lin says, urging me on. "But you're not *just* a moon dweller, are you?"

At some point, I'm going to have to trust someone, or I'll never learn the ropes. And if I don't know the ropes, I'll stick out more than a star dweller in the Sun Realm.

I stare at Lin, mulling over my decision.

She rushes on. "Look, we have NO love for Lecter, for the way things are run around here. Whatever your game is, I want in. I can't take another second of this creepy, God-forsaken city. I know Avery thinks things are worse down below, in the Star Realm, but they're not. Not really. At least down there we can live life the way we choose. Whatever you're hiding, tell us. You won't regret it."

The conviction behind her words is as hard as steel. Either Lin's a really good actress, or she's being honest.

I take a deep breath. This is it. My best or worst decision. My gut says I can trust these people, and I've learned to trust my instincts. The truth.

"I snuck into the New City because I'm helping the natives," I say, holding my breath.

Twenty-Six
Siena

Tristan's staring at the prisoners and they're staring back up at him.

And then Tristan jumps on the guy, right on top of him, like he might strangle him to death. Only he's not strangling, he's…well, I think he's hugging him. "Roc," he says. "You crazy son of a—"

The prisoner—I s'pose I hafta call him Roc now—groans and says, "My gut, you're gonna rip it open…"

Tristan rolls off of him, shifts to the girl with the sunny hair, says, "Tawni." She hugs him and we're all just standing there staring at Tristan hugging the Glassies. Or, wait, if he knows 'em, then either they're not Glassies or Tristan is, and I think we decided Tristan's not, right? Things're getting more wooloo than a prickler casserole made from Perry's left arm. Sorry, Perry, but you know it's true.

"What's with the mask?" Roc asks Tristan.

"Like we always knew, the air's not good up here," Tristan says. "Especially for people like us who aren't used to it. We'll need to get both of you masks too."

"What the burn is goin' on?" Skye says. At least she and I are thinking the same way.

"These two," Tristan says, getting up and pulling the girl, Tawni, up after him, "are my friends." He helps Roc to his feet, too.

"I say kill 'em anyway," Skye mutters, but no one pays her any attention, and for once I think she's joking.

"And why are they here?" Wilde asks.

An arm 'round each of 'em, Tristan says, "Now that's a good question."

Roc, the one with the brown skin who almost looks like he could belong with us if not for the strange britches and shirt he's wearing, says, "To find you. It was easy. We just spoke to the scientist you introduced us to before you left, arranged transport to the surface. You put me in charge, so he couldn't refuse me."

"We were worried," Tawni adds.

Tristan shakes his head. "You shouldn't have come."

"What? We were just going to do nothing when you and Adele didn't come back?" Roc says. "It took all of two days for everything to start falling apart again."

Tristan smirks, pushes Roc's shoulder. "So you came to get me because I'm needed below?"

Roc's eyebrows lift and he pushes Tristan back. "Oh, wait, you didn't think we came because we were worried about you? No, no, no, the Tri-Realms, Tristy. Personally, I was hoping you were taking an extended vacation, that maybe I could kick back, sit on the throne for a while…"

"Bastard," Tristan says, but there's no anger in his voice and I finally realize they're joking, like friends do.

"*Roc*," Tawni warns, using her eyes like weapons. Turning to Tristan, she says, "We were worried about you and Adele both, regardless of what my idiot boyfriend says. He could barely sleep when you didn't come back."

"That's the last time I share my secrets with you," Roc mutters, but he moves over and puts an arm around Tawni. Not a "friend" embrace, like the one Tristan gave her, but something more intimate. "Speaking of Adele, where is she? Not as light a sleeper as you, I guess?"

Tristan's chin falls to his chest. His eyes close. "She's…not here," he says.

"What do you mean, 'not here'?" Tawni asks, her voice about as hard as it's been since she started speaking.

Tristan doesn't seem as talkative all of a sudden, so I figure I can be helpful and I blurt out, "She's in the Glass City."

"What?" Roc says. "You don't mean the…" He trails off.

"The earth dwellers," Tristan says, eyes still closed, head still down. "She infiltrated the New City to try to stop them."

"Stop them from what?" Tawni asks.

Tristan looks up. "From killing everyone who's standing around you right now."

~~~

We give the prisoners, who I guess ain't really prisoners any more—except to Skye, who keeps muttering that we should at least tie their hands t'gether—water and food and a place to sleep. Wilde also manages to scrounge up a couple more masks, stolen off of dead Glassies. Tristan tells 'em 'bout all the stuff they missed, and even though he skips over the part 'bout the Icers quickly with only a few words, Skye leaves the tent and I hafta blink a few times when my vision goes all blurry. Roc and Tawni, whose eyes've been wide for most of the story, are suddenly interested in their hands.

"God," Roc breathes when Tristan finishes.

Tears are making tracks down the tops of Tawni's cheeks, disappearing beneath her mask. These two ain't Glassies. Glassies'd be cheering right 'bout now, wetting their britches with delight.

"The sun goddess only watches us, gives us hope," I say. "But we hafta make our own choices. The Glassies made theirs today."

"The Glassies?" Roc says. "You all kept calling us that. You thought we were from the New City?"

"Yes," Wilde says. "Before Tristan and Adele, anyone that looked like you were Glassies. The enemy."

"That's why that crazy girl who was here earlier wanted to kill us," Roc says.

"I'm pretty sure she *still* wants to kill you," I say. "And watch what you say 'bout her. She's my sister and she's grieving something awful right now. Looking for revenge."

"Because of the…Ice—Icers?" Tawni says.

I nod. "They were our friends," I say. "But one of 'em was more'n a friend to Skye, and she doesn't let people in very often."

"That's horrible," Tawni says. "The earth dwellers are horrible. Like ten times worse than the sun dwellers." She looks at Tristan. "No offense."

"None taken," Tristan says. "I want things to change as much as anyone. That's why I didn't come back. I have to do what I can to help these people, the Tri-Tribes. We can't let Lecter get away with mass murder."

Skye steps back in. She's been listening the whole time and her eyes are on me, softer'n 'fore, but still twice as hard as the canyon walls. "Now yer talkin'," she says. "If I don't get to kill you all, then I wanna kill Lecter."

Twenty-Seven
Tristan

I still can't believe Roc and Tawni are sitting in front of me, lifting their masks to sip water out of a skin and eat prickler, and learning all about what's happening up here. They've been asking questions, just like Adele and I did, for near on an hour now, and Skye and the rest of them have been answering every single one, taking them through the situation. There's a bloodthirsty gleam in Skye's eyes every time Lecter's name comes up. I don't blame her.

"Without the…"—Skye's voice cracks slightly, and she takes a deep breath—"…our friends to the north, even if Adele can take care of things on the inside, we still don't have the numbers to beat 'em."

She's right. Adele could assassinate Lecter and it probably wouldn't make one bit of difference. The soldiers would get orders from some other follower of Lecter and do the killing just the same. We simply need more bodies.

"Roc," I say. "Tell me about below."

Under the torchlight, what I can see of my half-brother's face looks orange. "The generals have been asking to meet with you since the moment you left. Their troops are angry, frustrated. They were winning the battles in the Moon Realm when you ordered them to withdraw. They want the green light to start the bombing again. The generals say the delay is giving the rebels time to regroup, to refortify."

"What did you tell them?"

"That you decided to become a hermit and live the rest of your days in a cave, letting your hair and beard grow to your knees," Roc says with a straight face. I give him a look. "What do you think I told them? I lied, held them off as best as I could, said you were dealing with a lot right now, in talks with the leader of the Resistance, General Rose."

"And that worked?"

"Hell no. They left me alone for an hour, maybe two, and then they were back on me like a bad hair day." Roc's still cracking jokes, but his eyes are grim. He's stressed. "They finally said they'd take matters into their own hands if they had to. We caught the first scary-box-rocket thing to the surface, fell outside the cave like a couple of newborn babes, and wandered the desert for almost a day before we ran into your new 'friends,' who immediately began discussing whether to kill us now or later."

"They tend to do that," I say, trying a smile but not quite getting there. Crap. The Glass City is the rock and the Tri-Realms is the hard place. I'm stuck.

But there's really no choice. "We've got to go back," I say.

"Yer leavin' us?" Skye says, her eyes eating me alive.

"No…yes…it's not like that."

"I knew you were a baggard. Yer woman's probably burnin' us 'round too."

"No. Skye, no." She seems surprised that I said her name, like I know her; her face lights up for a second before returning to a dark frown. "Skye. Seriously, I'm with you." Her hands are clenched at her sides and I can see the hurt on her face. There's a person beneath the hard shell she's built around herself. Human feelings. Pain and loss. I can almost see the goodness seeping out through her pores. "Skye," I say again, pulling my thoughts together. "I have a plan. No one's abandoning you."

She purses her lips, breathes deeply through her nose, slowly unclenches her fists. "Spill it, dweller," she says.

Looking right into her eyes, I say, "In three days' time, we attack the Glass City."

~~~

Even Skye seems satisfied now. Everyone's happy, or at least as happy as possible given there's a good chance we'll all be dead in less than a week.

After some rest, Hawk and Lara will escort Roc, Tawni, and I back to the cave, where we'll return to the Sun Realm. Our mission: to convince as many soldiers as possible from the Tri-Realms to accompany us back to the surface to fight with the Tri-Tribes. We'll be counting on Adele to help find us a way into the New City by then, or at least create a disruption in the earth dweller chain of command.

Skye and Wilde will lead their own forces northward, toward ice country, looping around the edge of fire country and then moving south. While the Glassies are searching to the west, they'll be northeast.

If all goes according to plan, we'll converge on the New City in three days, from the two places they'll least expect to be attacked from. There are a million variables in the plan that could go against us, but Skye's right about one thing: we have to act first, not wait for Lecter's army to hunt us down and massacre us like they did to the Icers.

With Roc already snoring softly beside me, his arm draped around Tawni, I finally stop staring at the tent roof, which is turning from black to brown with the rising sun.

~~~

"Git up you lazy, wooloo baggard!" a voice says, shoving me out of a dreamless sleep. The voice sounds familiar, but the words don't make sense coming from his mouth.

Someone shoves me for real, and I grab at the arm, blinking my eyes open. I pull Roc hard, throwing him off balance. He tumbles over me, cracking his head on one of the tent poles.

"Ow!" he hollers, lying in a heap, rubbing furiously at his skull.

"Serves you right," I say. "What were you saying to me? Something about being lazy and wooloo and—what was that other one?"

"A baggard," Roc says, popping his mask off, grin-grimacing, one eye closed. "Siena's been teaching me all kinds

193

of new words while we waited for your no-good tug-lovin' butt to wake up."

"Well, this butt is awake," I say. "The rest of me too."

Roc replaces his mask. "Yeah, I found that out the hard way. I risk my life to come find you, and you throw me into a tent pole. Some friend you are."

"We ain't searin' friends," I say, doing the Siena-impersonation now. "We're brothers, and I'll be burned if I won't chuck you into tent poles and pricklers if I have a mind to."

Roc laughs. "Not bad," he says, "but you've had time to practice. Now let's go, the day's a-wastin'." He crawls out of the tent.

Sighing, I roll away from my blanket and follow after him, squinting when the blinding light hits me. It could be years before I get used to how bright everything is up here. On Earth. Where I am. Not in it, but on it. It still doesn't feel quite real.

Brown-skinned people are milling about, carrying stones, logs of wood, bags of what appear to be cut up pricklers, babies, and all sorts of other things. Men are building tents, stacking stones. Women are tending fires and stirring pots. Kids are playing, stopping to stare at me as I pass them.

Roc's already sitting beside Tawni on a stone bench, next to a crackling fire. Circ and Siena are side by side, smashed together so close they almost look like a two-headed person. Hawk and Lara are there, too, but they're on opposite sides of different benches, like they see plenty of each other on a daily basis to want to get too close.

I sit next to Roc, jabbing him lightly in the ribs.

"Morning," says Tawni brightly.

"Good morning," I say. "Sleep well?"

"Like a rock," she says. "No pun intended." Roc grins.

"Yeah, he does seem to fit in up here," I say, motioning to the stone seat our butts are on. "Maybe we should leave him."

"Do your worst," Roc says. "But I'm growing to like the food up here already." Balancing a bowl in one hand, he shovels a spoonful of soup under his mask and into his mouth. "This 'zard stew isn't half bad."

"Ain't half bad," Siena corrects. "Remember what I taught you?"

"You might not be saying that if you knew what a 'zard was," I say.

Roc gives me a look, but I don't elaborate. I'll show him a live one on our trip back to the cave.

"So you don't want the soup?" Circ says, offering me a bowl.

I shake my head. "If you've got any prickler salad, I'll take that." He hands me a wooden plate with green chunks and some sort of dressing on it. "Mmm," I say, taking a bite, "at least this wasn't creeping in the dirt before it ended up in my mouth."

Roc, having just taken another bite of his soup, looks down at his bowl curiously, as if it might be looking back at him.

I finish off the salad and stand up just as Skye, Feve and Wilde approach. "We met with the rest of the Tri-Tribe council," Wilde says. "They've agreed to the plan. We'll march north shortly after you leave for the East."

"Good," I say, my eyes meeting Skye's. I can't read her expression, except I know I'm gladder than ever that I'm not a Glassy. "I hope we meet again soon."

Twenty-Eight
Adele

They don't call the Enforcers, don't turn me in to Lecter. At least not yet. Although I'm not denying the possibility that the moment I fall asleep they could very well turn me in. I wouldn't necessarily fault them if they did, considering I'm trying to, in a fashion, bring down their perfect little city.

Instead, they ask me questions and I give them answers and they shake their heads in bewilderment.

"I know this is an impossible request," I say, when there's a break in the questions, "but I need your help. Not directly."

"Anything," Lin says.

"Lin," Avery says.

"No, Uncle. We can't do nothing. You know as well as I do that Lecter's gone too far." *Uncle?* But I thought…Avery called Lin his daughter, so I assumed he meant from a biological standpoint.

Avery sighs. "He went too far a long time ago," he says. Something clicks inside me. Why these two are different than the others, maybe.

"Lin, where are your parents?" I ask.

She scowls at the table, drums her fingers on it lightly. Her half-eaten plate of mushed brown, green and yellow insta-food has long been pushed away from her.

"My sister, Lin's mother, died in the Star Realm a long time ago," Avery says.

"I'm—I'm sorry," I say, following Lin's gaze to her hands.

"She was supposed to come with us," Lin says, her voice tight. "We'd been 'hand-selected to start a new life as sun dwellers.'" I can tell she's quoting something. A message, a person. She looks up at me. "We were so excited, my mother more than anyone. She'd been sick for a long time, but she was always worrying over me, concerned I wasn't eating enough, wasn't hanging out with the right sorts of kids, wasn't smiling enough. But when we were picked, she couldn't stop smiling. Not because she was going to what she thought was a better place, but because *I* was going to a better place, going to have a better life…" Lin's voice trails off and she looks away, out the window that's just a window again.

"She died a few days before we were scheduled to leave," Avery says, looking at Lin with concern.

"Because of me," Lin says, and her words are cracking so much I get the feeling she wants to cry, but she doesn't. "She only held on as long as she did because she was worried about me. Now that I was taken care of—or so she thought—she gave up. It was my fault."

"Lin, no," Avery says, putting a hand on her back. "It was just life."

Lin turns to look back at her uncle, her lips quivering but her eyes like steel. "Well this 'just life' has been awfully rotten to us. You can't deny that." She looks back at me. "We went to the Sun Realm, all right, but then they said we'd been further selected to go above. 'Above?' we said. There were nothing above the Sun Realm, or so we'd all been told. Only toxic air and a dead world. Not that different than the Star Realm really. But they were so excited when they told us. We even got another letter, this one from President Nailin himself, wishing us luck on our great adventure."

She slams her fist on the table so suddenly I flinch back.

"They lied every step of the way. The moment we got up here they shoved a chip in our flesh and put us to work, told us where we could go, what we could eat and how much, where we could sleep and how long.

"My father...was a stubborn man—guess there's no surprise where I get it from." Finally a tear falls and she wipes it away quickly, as if frustrated by it. Blows a few stray hairs out of her eyes. "He asked a lot of questions and they don't like questions up here. He questioned the rules and the honor of the president, and then one day he didn't come back from his craphole job cleaning toilets around the city."

Reflexively, my hand goes to my face, covers my mouth. Does my heart have room for one more tragedy?

She continues numbly. "We got a letter three days later saying there'd been an accident, that he was dead, that his body was...*unviewable*—whatever the hell that means. But there was

198

no accident—they killed him. The bastards killed him." She laughs, shakes her head.

"You know, the funny thing is that it was just a day earlier that my dad and I were joking about how he'd better watch his mouth or Lecter might come down off his throne and shoot him. This 'just life' that we have isn't life at all. It's as good as death. So yeah, Uncle, when I say I'll help Tawni in any way I can, I mean it."

"My real name's Adele," I say, finally trusting Lin and Avery with every bit of my being. "Under the orders of President Nailin, my father was shot and killed and my sister, Elsey, maimed. I'd be honored to have any help you can give me."

Lin looks at me, manages a smile, and then sticks out her hand. I shake it firmly. "Avery, you with us?" I say.

He scrunches up his face like he wishes he'd never spoken to me in the first place, but then says, "Yes, but please don't let anything happen to Lin. She's all I've got left." *And he thinks of her like a daughter*, he doesn't have to say.

"Don't worry," I say. "I'll do all the dangerous stuff. Now tell me what 'Presidential Cleaner' means."

~ ~ ~

Turns out you can find out a lot about a person if you're able to scan their wrist onto your vid screen.

The first thing that pops up is a way big photo of my face, complete with the Tristan-inflicted black eye. It's the photo the chip guy took earlier today and it's completely blocking our view of the building next to ours. TAWNI SANDERS it reads in black block letters.

Avery's shaking his head. "I don't know how you did it, Adele."

"Luck, mostly," I say, grinning. "And a little help with directions from you."

He shakes his head again and the screen changes. Lin is using a small pad which is showing her whatever's on the screen. There are some stats about me. Height- 5'7". Weight- 130 lbs. Eye color- green. Hair color- dark brown. Boring stuff.

Lin uses her pad-thingy to flip to the next screen: Occupation and Schedule. A photo of a large building appears, fully glass and rising higher than any of the buildings around it, coming to a sharp point, like a spike. Near the base, there's a large iron door with a couple of armed guards standing in front of it. A sign above the door reads: Presidential Offices.

Below the picture it says "Presidential Cleaner."

"Seriously," Lin says. "How did you land this gig?"

Now even I'm shaking my head. "I just saw it on the forms and checked it off as my job. Evidently because all my information was supposedly 'lost' on my malfunctioning chip, they just believed me."

"Well it's perfect for our mission," Lin says, sounding almost eager.

"I think you mean *my* mission," I say.

"That's exactly what she means," Avery says.

"I just want to help," Lin says. "That freak president killed my father."

"You already *are* helping," I say, motioning her back to the screen. "What does all this mean?"

"Well, you're to report for duty tomorrow at seven in the morning. Whoever implanted your chip made your Anything

Day today, so you'll have to work nine days straight before you get another break."

"I heard an Enforcer say that—*Anything Day*—what does that mean exactly?" I ask.

"It's just a normal day off. One in ten days we get one, and we can do practically anything we want, within the laws and restrictions of the city, of course."

I'm not planning on sticking around long enough to experience my next Anything Day, but at least I know it's there if I need it. "Okay, what else?"

"You have a consistent schedule. You'll start at the same time every day and finish at six in the evening. Today we all got out at five because of the presidential message, but most people work seven to six."

They're long hours, but not to the point where people will rebel, I think to myself. It seems everything in this city pushes people to the edges of frustration, but not quite over the brink. Definitely part of Lecter's strategy. It's like he's obsessed with efficiency, organization, cleanliness. And he pretends to believe in equality, with the rationing of food, of resources, etc, but it's an act, because those originally from the Sun Realm get slightly greater rations than the "Lowers."

"Hey," I say, "what do they call the people who used to be sun dwellers?"

"The Uppers," Lin says. "Why?"

I grit my teeth. "No reason, just curious." It's the Tri-Realms all over again, just packaged, shined up real nice, and hidden amongst a bunch of other shiny things on a shelf. Where Tristan's father liked to flaunt the huge gaps between the haves and the havenots, Lecter is more subtle. Tristan was right.

President Lecter is the one man who managed to control my father.

He's dangerous, that's for sure. I can't just charge in there, guns blazing. I'll have to be every bit as subtle.

"Where is this place?" I ask.

Lin swipes her finger and a map appears on the window, a red dot pulsating in the direct middle.

Avery says, "The city center, 20th and M. It's the tallest building, rising to just below the apex of the Dome. It comes to a point at the top."

The screen flashes back to a close-up of the main doors. "It says you won't be entering via the main entrance. There's a side entrance down an alleyway in the back somewhere."

"Will you take me tomorrow?"

"Hell yeah, I will," Lin says.

~~~

After Lin turns off the screen, I drink a liter and a half of water, my entire ration for the evening. I even force down the cold slop still on my plate. Avery says he can heat it up, but I don't think it'll help the taste much, so I just stuff it in my mouth and swallow without chewing. I have to stay hydrated and keep my strength up.

When I finish, Lin asks, "Where will you sleep?"

I look around at the thin room, the flat wall with the grooves on one side. "I'm guessing these fold down into beds?" I say.

Avery scans his wrist on a glass plate set in the wall. Instantly, the wall begins to move, folding in on itself to reveal a thin bed and a solitary pillow. The covers are pulled tight and tucked underneath the mattress.

"We've only got two beds here," he says, "and as you can see they'll only fit one person each. When Lin's father…was gone, we were forced to move into a smaller place. And anyway, if you don't check into a bed you'll be flagged in the system. Only night workers are expected to be out and about."

"They'll know I'm not in bed?" I ask incredulously. This is even worse than I expected.

"Something like that," Avery says. "They might activate your tracker, come looking for you, break down our door, that sort of thing."

"Where do I go?"

"I don't think Gripes' old place has been filled yet. It's a single flat," Lin says.

"Who's Gripes?" I ask.

"A—a friend," Avery says.

"He died?"

"Might as well have," Lin says venomously.

"He was taken to the detention center," Avery says, looking like he'd prefer not to talk about the details. But then he goes on anyway. "He was old, good to Lin, almost like a grandfather to her." Beside him, Lin nods earnestly, looks at her feet. "He was assigned to be a janitor at the army barracks. Showed up late for work once…"

"It was at the complete other side of the city," Lin says, scuffing her foot on the floor. "Gripes only had one leg."

"They sent an old one-legged man to prison for being late one time?"

"Three times," Avery says. "First they gave him a warning, then something more like a threat, and finally…"

"They dragged him away in the middle of the night," Lin says, looking more and more like she wants to hit something.

"I'm sorry," I say. "Maybe he's still alive. If I'm successful, we might be able to find him."

Lin nods. "You know something funny? We never found out how he really lost that leg. He'd always make up stories about fighting for the Resistance in the Tri-Realms." She blows her hair away from her face, but it settles back down in the same spot. "Anyway, you can sleep in the place he used to. Now that he's gone, it's up for grabs. You should get some shuteye; you've got an early start tomorrow."

I yawn, feeling exhaustion hit me like the Enforcer's club hit that boy today—hard and out of nowhere. Tomorrow I get one step closer to taking down Lecter.

"You'll take her over?" Avery asks Lin.

"Sure. Get to sleep, I'll be back soon."

"Thanks," I say to Avery as we exit. "For everything."

"You remind me a little of my brother-in-law," he says, shrugging. "And I could never say no to him either."

Lin leads me down the hall, and I scan the number plates until she reaches 1819, one of the doors on the other side of the hall, which are closer together. Even smaller places. Meant for one person rather than two.

"Scan your wrist," she says.

I do and the door clicks open. I raise my eyebrows appreciatively. "So is this, like, officially my place now?"

She smiles wickedly. "More like your base of operations. But yeah, until you claim another empty place, or are cracked over the head and hauled away by the Enforcers, or are captured and tortured by President Lec—"

"Lin, I get the picture."

"Right. So, do you need anything else?"

"I don't think so."

"We're just down the hall if you do. I'll meet you out here at six-thirty tomorrow morning. The bed will make sure you get up on time." And before I have the chance to ask what the hell she means by the bed getting me up, she's heading back down the hall at a half-jog.

Feeling suddenly alone and almost naked in the dimly lit, empty hallway, I enter the flat, closing the door behind me. I lean my back against the shut door, take a deep breath. Sure, things are bad in the New City, but things below were bad too, and we did what we had to do—*I* did what I had to do. And I will again.

The room is small, basic, similar to Avery and Lin's place. I try scanning my wrist on the food dispensers, but nothing happens. I've had my rations already, no midnight snack for me. It's not that different from living in the Moon Realm, where all the food left in the house was eaten for dinner and then you prayed you'd be able to scrounge up enough Nailins to buy more the next day.

My room has no window, just a wall at the end that I assume doubles as a vid screen. There's a glass plate on the empty wall to my right, and I scan my wrist. A bed appears, barely long enough, barely wide enough. Good thing I'm not as tall as the real Tawni, I think.

Not even bothering to undress, I slip under the covers and close my eyes, the lights turning off automatically behind my eyelids, perhaps triggered by my weight on the bed. What a strange, strange world.

Where is Tristan sleeping tonight? On an animal-skin blanket in a cave or a tent or just under the million-star sky? Wherever he is, I wish I was with him, feeling the warm touch of a real breeze, in a world so bright and so real that it can't possibly be a dream. Is this the last fight? Or will another, more powerful, cleverer enemy rise up after Lecter is gone? Is there always another evil to do battle with? Will I be fighting my whole life?

I once spoke of the inherency of good and evil, but now I realize it's so much more complex than that. And yet so much simpler at the same time. Although there are hundreds of shades of gray between right and wrong and good and evil, in the end it comes down to a single choice: to care or not. To care about humanity, about the pains and fears and sorrows of others, or to ignore them, to look the other way, to say "it doesn't concern me." I know I haven't always made the right choices, but I hope I haven't chosen completely wrong either, and in the end, we all die. But we don't die equal.

Not even close.

Twenty-Nine
Siena

Tristan and his friends—the funny one, Roc, and the nice one, Tawni—head east with Hawk and Lara, back to where they came from, deep underground or whatever. I hope we will, but I don't 'spect we'll see 'em again anytime soon. After all, who would purposely join a war?

The day is hot as scorch, go figure. The ground's so dry that the trod of their feet is already kicking up a trail of dust in their wake.

"See you soon, ya wooloo baggard," Roc shouts back with a wave.

"You know, if I wasn't so coolheaded, I might shoot a pointer through your heart for a comment like that," I say, smiling.

"But then you'd lose your star student," Roc says.

"Don't ferget yer side of the agreement," Skye hollers.

"We won't," Tristan says. "Before the end of the third day, I'll finally prove myself to you."

"Maybe you will, maybe you won't," Skye mutters, "but I'll kill me some Glassies either way."

"C'mon, Sis," I say, "we've gotta say goodbye to Jade." I grab her elbow and steer her back into New Wildetown. She's cursing under her breath, something 'bout how only someone with rocks for brains would trust people who live in holes in the ground.

"Jade's waiting," I say, urging her forward faster. We've barely spent a lick of time with our sister since we arrived home. Scorch, we've barely seen her since we rescued her from a life of slavery on the Soaker ships. In a normal world we'd be spending every moment of every day with her. But this ain't a normal world. Least not now, if it ever was 'fore.

As we approach the line of tents, I see her, sleek black hair braided in a single spine down her back, sitting cross-legged in the durt, playing with a baby, who's crawling 'round in front of her.

Skye stops me with an arm in front of my chest. "Promise me," she says, looking at me.

"Promise you what?"

Skye's eyes are like glittering brown stones. "That you won't die. That you'll be more careful than me. That you'll stay alive to take care of Jade."

I chew on my sunburnt bottom lip, feeling it sting a little. What's she saying? "Skye, you ain't gonna die neither," I say. "Yer the roughest, toughest person I know. Yer—"

"Sie—"

"I ain't finished." I put my hand on her shoulder, squeeze a little. Skye doesn't even flinch back from my touch, like she usually does. "Yer my idol, Skye. Always have been. When I lost you…"—I pause, fight back the emotion that's rolling through me—"…I thought I'd lost me too. But then I realized that I was who I was 'cause of watching you. And I was stronger'n I ever knew 'fore. You're a part of me, always will be. So I'll promise you I'll do my best to stay alive for Jade's sake, but I won't promise you I won't do anything wooloo out there, 'cause if you're in trouble, I'm gonna do everything I can to save you."

And then she's pulling me into her chest, harder and fiercer'n she's ever done 'fore, and I can hardly breathe but I don't need to, don't want to, 'cause I got exactly what I need.

We only release each other when a voice says, "Skye? Siena?"

Jade's looking at us with those big, brown eyes of hers and she looks so grownup, well, 'cause she is. I mean, scorch, she's got a foreign boyfriend back in water country. I didn't even start thinking 'bout Circ in that way 'til I was near on sixteen. She's had to grow up faster'n any of us.

She's got that baby in her arms and I recognize it, 'cause it's got a nose so flat it's like someone smashed it, which I think is kinda cute, but which his mother thinks is uglier'n the back end of a tug. Polk. Veeva's kid.

"You babysittin'?" I ask.

"Yep," she says.

"You wanna hug?" I ask.

"Yep," she says, smiling broadly, setting Polk in the durt and opening her arms wide enough to reach 'round the both of us. And we hold each other for as long as Skye'll suffer us, 'cause we're family, and we're all we got.

~~~

"How'd you end up with that Soaker boy?" Skye asks, picking Polk up and turning him 'round so he'll crawl in t'other direction. She's had to do it a dozen times already, but Polk always seems to head back toward her, like he knows she don't like babies much.

"Yeah, you never told us the whole story," I say.

Jade's face goes slightly red. It's nice to see her like this, acting her age a little. Usually she's just like a mini-Skye, all rough'n tumble.

I owe Circ one for this. We should be getting ready to leave, both Skye and me, but he agreed to pack for us, so we could spend this time with Jade.

"I told you, I chucked a scrub brush at his head," she says.

Skye laughs loudly. "That's always my favorite part." It's nice to see Skye like this, cracking jokes, laughing, like she don't have the weight of the world on her shoulders.

"But what happened after that?" I ask. "You know, up until that baggard Admiral Jones tied you to the pole and whipped you."

She picks up Polk, cradles him in her arms, and tells us the whole story. 'Bout how she tormented Huck every chance she got, but then eventually realized he was trying to do the right things, how he did unspeakable things to save her life, how he saved her from drowning. Huck Jones sounds like a real hero. It's no wonder she's got feelings for him.

"So that's why Admiral Jones beat you? 'Cause his son was fallin' for you?" Skye asks.

We've both seen the wounds, which have a long way to go 'fore they're fully healed. She'll always have the scars. Red slashes down her back, puffy welts, her perfect, beautiful skin made to look like a battlefield.

"I haven't been completely honest with you," Jade says slowly.

Me and Skye look at each other, then back at her. Polk's got a handful of her hair and is pulling on it.

"Whaddya mean?" Skye says.

"It's true that the Admiral Jones you're thinking of ordered me to be beaten, and he even got a lash in…" She closes her eyes, a long blink. When she opens them a single tear drips out of each eye.

"Then who did the rest of it?" Skye asks, her fists balling in her lap. Sun goddess help him if it's someone who's still alive.

"He had no choice," Jade says, "Admiral Jones would've killed us both if he didn't…"

"Who?" Skye says through locked teeth.

"The new Admiral Jones," Jade says, clutching Polk to her chest. "Huck."

Skye stands, her chest heaving. "Then how are you…how could you…why do you…" She can't get the words out, and I understand completely. Anyone who'd hurt our sister this way deserves the worst.

But we don't know the circumstances, do we? Could there ever be a reason to hurt the ones you love? Would I ever be able to whip Circ, if I knew his life depended on it? I know the only answer is yes.

"Skye, she's alive and that's all that mat—"

"I'll destroy him," Skye growls. "If I ever see that runt again, I'll beat him ten times worse'n he beat you."

She stalks out of the tent, leaving Jade crying and Polk playing with her hair.

~~~

Eventually I'm able to calm Jade down. We both know how Skye is. She'll come 'round. I mean, she might get a few licks in on Huck Jones if she ever sees him again, but surely she won't kill him. Least that's what we tell ourselves.

We say our goodbyes and I leave Jade with Circ's family, who she's been staying with.

I take Polk back to his mother, my old friend Veeva, who I haven't had a chance to catch up with yet. She's outside her tent, hanging wet bundles on a line, 'bout a dozen of 'em.

"Sun goddess, Siena," she says, and it's like I never left. It's always been that way with her. "Take that spawn of the devil right back wherever you found 'im; I ain't ready to clean another bundle. He's down to his last one."

"I think he's hungry," I say. "He's been fussing something fierce."

"He's *always* hungry," she says, but she whips out one of her large breasts like there ain't dozens of people walking 'tween the tents. I try not to look, but it's hard not to. I notice a few other heads turning, too, mostly men. When I hand Polk to Veeva, he goes right for the food. Guess I was right 'bout him being hungry. "I heard all the warriors'll be leavin' soon," she says. "Guess that means you."

"Yeah," I say, wondering when I became a warrior. I still almost feel like I'm playing a child's game when I start shooting my pointers. Only in this game people really die.

"Grunt's going too," she says.

"What?" I say, genuinely shocked. Her guy, Grunt, ain't no warrior. He's the shankiest man I ever met. I can't imagine him marching through the desert, much less fighting against the Glassies.

"Everyone who don't have a good reason not to is going," she says. "I'm still feeding Polk 'ere, so I don't have to."

"You mean, you woulda gone if not for Polk?"

"What, you think I can't take care of myself?" Veeva says. "I've slapped Grunt many a night when he's come home drunk on the fire juice, gropin' at me with those magical hands of his. I might not be the ladylike type, but I won't lay with a man in that kinda condition, even one as talented as my Call."

Hearing the words "magical" and "talented" associated with Grunt makes me wanna throw up my breakfast, but I swallow hard and say, "Well, I'm glad you're not going. I'll be fighting for you, Veevs."

"Yeah, that's what Grunt says, too, only he looks much scareder'n you when he says it. You'll watch out for 'im, won't you?" There's something in her eyes I'm not used to seeing.

"Of course I will. He'll be just fine. I'd better get running. Circ's been doing all the hard work to get ready."

"Be safe," Veeva says. "Yer probably the only person that really gets me, so I can't lose you."

That's when I realize what I saw in her eyes: fear.

213

"They deserved better," Wilde says. I look at her eyes, which are full of hurt. "We have to defeat the Glassies for them."

I was surprised when she pulled me aside, just 'fore it was time to leave.

I stare at her, unblinking. "I don't know what to say."

"I just need to talk to someone," she says, and I realize what a searin' fool I've been. While I've been trying to help Skye get through what happened, and Skye's been trying to get herself through it, no one's been helping Wilde.

I guess everyone just 'spects her to do things on her own, the way she always does. But this hurt must run too deep, even for her.

"I'm sorry," I say. "I'd forgotten."

Her eyes soften. "It's okay," she says. "I didn't love Buff, not in that way. We never would have worked out together, but he made me laugh. I still cared about him, about all of them…Dazz, his mother, Jolie. I loved them like family."

I know. I know. I did, too, but maybe not as strongly as Wilde did, 'cause she spent so much time with 'em.

I still don't know what to say 'cause I'm helpless. I can't bring 'em back, can't fix anything. But that's not what she wants, is it? Suddenly the answer is obvious. Even the strongest of us are like little children sometimes, and just need someone to hold 'em.

I put my arms out and Wilde practically falls into me. "I'm here," I murmur as her tears stain my neck.

I'd hold Circ's hand as we leave, but I'm s'posed to be a warrior, and I don't think warriors hold hands. So I settle for walking next to him, occasionally brushing up against his side. The wind's heavy, picking up clusters of sand every now and then, tossing it into our faces. Thankfully, not strong enough for a sandstorm, but plenty strong enough to be searin' annoying.

Skye strides up ahead with Wilde, who looks nothing like she did when I last spoke to her; once again, she's her calm, composed self, every doubt and hurt and fear having dried on the skin of my neck, leaving faint, white tracks. T'gether, they lead us northwards.

Early on, I tried to talk to Skye 'bout Huck Jones and how Jade wouldn't want her to hurt him, but she just told me to "Shut my tughole" and kept walking. As much as I admire her, sometimes I wish I was stronger'n her so I could give her a piece of my mind.

There are maybe a thousand of us, maybe a few more, in a long column. Feve's next to Circ, his long blade swinging from his belt. Circ and I try to make our eyes and face look like his— serious and dark and fierce—but we crack up every time we try. Feve just shakes his head.

"This look isn't something you can learn. It's something you're born with," he says, which makes us crack up even more. It's the weirdest thing to be laughing with Feve, who I hated not that long ago. He saved my life once, but then it turned out he was working with my father. But he's made up for his mistakes tenfold ever since, and I can't hold a grudge for something he did that he didn't really understand the repercussions of. These days I trust Feve as much as I trust Circ.

215

Some of t'other warriors are joking and laughing, too, but most of 'em I recognize as Heater Hunters, those who used to bring home tug meat for the village, and those who have fought against the Glassies twice 'fore. They're used to the thrill of battle. It's just another day in their dangerous lives.

But most of t'others—excluding the Marked and the Wilde Ones, who look as serious as Feve and Skye—are just normal people, used to taking care of kids and preparing food and living full and ordinary lives. I can see the fear in their eyes, just like I saw in Veeva's, 'cept it's a different fear. Not the fear of people they know dying, but of themselves dying.

Grunt's one of 'em and, remembering the promise I made to Veeva, I keep one eye on him even as I'm joking with Circ and Feve. His face is already red and sweaty and it looks like he's struggling to put one foot in front of t'other in the sand.

I feel bad for him. He shouldn't be here. None of us should be. Why are there so many wooloo, power-hungry people in this world? Why can't they just live like the rest of us, have a few laughs, help those that need it?

Not caring whether it's something a warrior would do, I grab Circ's hand and swing it along beside me. He raises an eyebrow, but doesn't say anything. Just squeezes my hand back.

Thirty
Tristan

It's dark when we reach the cave Adele and I stepped out of what seems like years ago.

Most of the way, Roc was practicing using the words Siena taught him. He only shut up when I pointed out what a live 'zard looked like, sunning itself on a rock. Tawni was pretty grossed out, too. Hawk laughed, said, "You survive offa what the land gives you."

As we shake hands with Hawk and Lara, say our goodbyes, and step into the cave, it hits me that I'm leaving Adele in another world, while I return to the one so familiar to me. What if something happens and we can never get back to the surface? Will she find a way back down? Does she even want to come back? After all we've seen, all we've experienced, can any of us just return to a life of phony light and absolute darkness?

But I can't stop my two feet from taking turns, stepping—one, two, one, two, one, two—moving me forward. Because they know: It was my plan and if I don't follow through with it the earth dwellers will win, and Adele will die, along with every last person in the Tri-Tribes. And it will be on my head and mine alone.

We reach the pod that will take us home, step inside, remove our masks. Press a button to turn it on. Artificial yellow lighting hits me full in the face.

"What floor?" Roc says, smirking, knowing full well the pod only goes to one place.

"H," I say. Roc looks at me quizzically. "For Hell," I explain.

"Oh, c'mon, Tristy. It ain't all that burnin' bad," Roc says, still practicing his—what do we even call it? Desert language? He pushes a button.

"I know," I say. "I just can't believe we're leaving her."

"We're doing it to save her," Tawni says. "It's the right thing."

They're simple, but her words help to comfort me. For a long time, Tawni's been our moral compass in a world where the shades of gray are as abundant as the shadows. Once she stopped us from killing unarmed and defenseless soldiers. Ever since, I've been thankful she did. So if she thinks this is the right choice, then it probably is.

I close my eyes and the pod drops, sending an airy thrill through my stomach. Adele…Adele, where are you? When I reopen them, Roc's holding Tawni's hand, his foot directly next to hers. And, of course, he's grinning, his teeth yellow in the fake light.

"What?" I say.

"Do you think anyone will be waiting with tea and biscuits?" he asks.

I'm as far from a laughing mood as I could possibly be, and yet I laugh. That's why Roc's my best friend. That's why we've survived this long. By laughing and joking and not taking ourselves too seriously when the rest of the world seems to be only serious.

"I hope so," I say.

"Do you think they'll have the little flower-shaped ones filled with the red cream?" Tawni asks.

"If they don't, heads will roll," I say. "After all, I'm the President of the Tri-Realms now."

"You're sounding more like your father each and every day," Roc says in a dramatic voice. "It's a beautiful thing to see."

That was a low blow, but it doesn't hurt as much as it probably should. My father destroyed my whole life, but he didn't destroy me. My mother, even with her last act, gave me a chance at a real life, and a chance to make things right, to cleanse the Nailin name. And then my father killed her for it.

"Sooo," I say after the longest stretch of silence, where the only sound was Roc's incessant tapping of his toe.

"Sooo what?" Roc says.

"What exactly will we be facing when we step out of this pod?"

Roc cocks his head and taps his teeth with a finger, like he's taking my question seriously. He's not. "Let's see, there will probably be an old, crusty scientist—bald, of course—and four walls of rock."

"You mean walls with pictures of you all over them? My worst nightmare is coming true."

"Hmm," Roc says.

"That *would* be a nightmare," Tawni says drily.

"Ganging up—not fair," Roc says. "And my own girlfriend…"

"Seriously," I say.

"Seriously," Roc says, mimicking me.

"Did Trevor give you, like, a whole bunch of tips on how to annoy me?" I ask.

I don't mean to dampen the mood, but speaking our dead friend's name does the trick. The laughter ceases and Roc momentarily stops with the jokes. He takes a deep breath. "We have to do this, Tristan. We have to do it for Trevor and Ram and your mom and my mom. For Cole and Ben and Elsey. For everyone that's been hurt by your father and by Lecter."

"We will," I say, trying to sound like my old, confident self. "Especially with your fighting skills on our side." I can't help it, the laughter a moment ago felt so good, like maybe we weren't all doomed because we were doing something normal and light.

"You shouldn't mock," Roc says. "I'm still injured because I couldn't figure out which way to aim the sword."

I laugh ten times harder, because that's Roc. Cracking a joke about the bravest thing he ever did, when he stabbed himself to save my life.

"I'd take your sword by my side every time," I say, wiping away a bit of moisture from my eyes that's mostly happiness.

Roc smiles. "Just as long as it's not *in* your side, eh?"

"You stab me, I'll stab you back."

Tawni shakes her head. "I'm not sure I'll ever fully understand you two," she says.

"That's because we're mysterious," Roc says, wagging his eyebrows.

"So back to the situation below," I say, because I feel like the half-hour ride is at least halfway over already. "How bad is it? Am I walking into guns pointed at my head, swords thrust into my neck, or fists swinging at my gut?"

Still smiling, Roc says, "All three."

I groan.

~~~

There was no car waiting for us when we exited the secret cave onto the streets. Roc apologized for forgetting to arrange it, calling me "Your Highness." I told him he should keep doing that.

So we're walking, which is fine by me. I need time to prepare myself for the uphill battle I'm about to face. The streets are dark, lit only by the artificial moon and stars, which look so pathetically inadequate after seeing the real thing. The buildings, on the other hand, seem so grand compared to the tents and basic shelters used by the Tri-Tribes. And yet I can't hear the crying of any babies or the shushing sounds made by their mothers. Lifeless. Empty.

When we arrive at the palace gates we get guns in our faces. So Roc was wrong—not all three—swords and guns and fists—just the guns. But when they see who I am, the guards apologize quickly and profusely and let us in, asking if we'd like them to send a car down.

"We'll walk," I say.

The road snakes through the palace gardens, and after seeing so much sand and rock and brown, the trees and plants and flowers almost look impossible. I have to take deep swallows a few times to catch my breath.

As if reading my mind—like he does—Roc says, "At least we have some happy memories of this place," and he's right, because when I think of the gardens I'm always happy.

We reach the main entrance, framed by a half-dozen black-marble pillars. White, spike-like spires rise up toward the lofty cavern roof, pointing at the fake moon.

As I stride inside, I remember: I'm the President. Here I have power, and it's my responsibility to use it the right way. "Gather all the generals together," I say.

"But it's the middle of the night," Roc says, feigning concern.

"Then wake them up."

"I was hoping you'd say that."

"Tawni, can you try to get Adele's mother on the main video screen?" I ask.

"I'll do what I can," she says.

While Roc scurries off to pound on a few generals' doors and Tawni goes to the communications office, I make my way to the place my father always liked to refer to as "the throne room." Lavishly adorned walls flash by on either side, but I barely notice them. After all, I grew up in this kind of luxury. It doesn't mean anything, not to me.

When I enter the throne room, it's empty, save for the dozens of black-marble pillars holding up the balcony above and surrounding the lone, grand seat in the middle. The throne, constructed with a thick, sturdy oak-wood frame and cushioned with generous red-velvet pads on the seat, back, and armrests, stands as a reminder of the difference between my father and me. The old President Nailin would spend as much on a place to rest his rear as a moon dweller miner made in ten years. The new President Nailin has the urge to take an axe and chop the chair into splinters to be used for firewood.

Distorted shards of memory slice through my head and I see this room as it was on the night my father died. The floor slick with blood. Steel weapons flashing, clanging, killing. Bodies falling. Trevor falling, dying. My father's great victory, cut short when Adele shot him in the head not long after in his grand council room.

The fall of a tyrant. One down, one to go.

Although I'm tired from the trek across the desert and the midnight stroll from the hidden cave to the palace, I resist the urge to sit in my father's plush throne. The generals would probably respond well to that kind of normalcy, but I just don't have the stomach for it, not when so many of the decisions that exacerbated the inequality in the Lower Realms were made from this very chair.

I remain standing as a video screen lowers from a crack in the ceiling. Evidently Tawni found a palace technician to help her get things set up. Hopefully General Rose isn't too angry with me for waking her, although I take comfort in the fact that you can't kick someone through a screen. Even my father wasn't able to develop that kind of technology.

I hear the first grumbling voice, echoing from a hall outside of the throne room. "If this is some kind of a joke, I'll have you whipped a thousand times!"

I almost laugh, but the thought of facing the generals makes me feel slightly ill. I may be the president, but these are men who have done things a certain way for a long time. They're used to winning, to crushing the enemy, not to signing peace agreements. The ceasefire pact I signed with the Lower Realms before we went above will only hold them off for so long.

A large man with a thick, gray beard stomps in wearing a heavy frown. His eyes widen when he sees me. "Good God, it's President Nailin," he says. I don't miss the mockery in his tone. Not a good start. "You do exist."

"General," I say, not taking the bait. When all the generals are here I'll make things very clear.

Three other men enter behind him, blinking sleep out of their eyes and registering surprise when they see me. They whisper to each other behind their hands.

"We ask for meetings with you a dozen times, and then you roust us from our beds in the middle of the night?" says the large, sarcastic man, General Aboud. "All hail, President Nailin!" He almost sounds drunk. Maybe he is. Maybe he passed out, rather than going to sleep.

I ignore him, watch as six more generals shuffle in, standing beside their comrades. Roc steps in behind them, winks at me. I rest an arm on the top of the throne. Even if I don't have the audacity to sit in it, perhaps just having it near me will set the right tone.

I start to speak, but General Aboud beats me to it. "Where the *hell* have you been? We've got a war to fight and your own generals can't even get an audience with you."

This is one question I'll most definitely answer. "Above," I say. The men stare at me with blank faces.

"Above?" Aboud says. "There is no above. *We* are the above!"

"No," I say calmly, although the red-faced man before me makes my blood boil. "We are not." I go on to explain everything to them; everything my father would not. The secret project my great-grandfather started, recruiting the best and smartest engineers, keeping them separate from the rest of society, monitoring them to ensure no one talked; the early failed expeditions to the earth's surface, everyone dead; the continued attempts, the construction of the Dome, reengineering the air filtration system to allow for life on earth; the slow but effective wresting of power from my father by Lecter. As I speak, there's utter silence. Even Aboud knows when to just shut up and listen.

At some point Tawni comes in and gives me a nod, holds up a controller. She's ready with General Rose.

"Any questions?" I say as I finish.

A bald man with blue-tinted glasses says, "Why didn't your father tell us? We were his most trusted advisors."

"Well, General Marx, you'll have to ask him," I say.

"What kind of answer is that?" Aboud bellows. "Your father is dead."

"He took a lot with him to the grave," I say. "I can't answer for him. I'm not my father, or my grandfather. They kept things from you, secrets. I refuse to do that."

"Why?" Aboud again, his frown deepening.

"Because I think you're more than what my father made you into. You're more than mindless killing machines who see missions of murder simply as missions, lines on a page with checkmarks next to them. You were chosen because of your brains, not your hearts, but that doesn't mean your chests are empty."

"What are you asking of us?" General Marx asks.

"Just to listen. Make up your own minds. If you disagree with what I propose, we'll take a vote. This is not a dictatorship. That was my father's way, not mine."

There are raised eyebrows and more whispers, but no one, not even Aboud, objects.

I turn, nod to Tawni. She raises the control and presses a button. I gesture for the generals to look at the screen, which goes from black to fuzzy gray to an orange-lit room, a textured brown-rock wall in the background. Adele's mother sits at a desk, wearing a blue uniform. A flashing red light above the screen indicates our cameras are working. She can see us.

"Tristan," she says, her face not showing even the slightest degree of surprise. I wonder if this unflappable woman has ever been astonished by something. Adele's got so much of her mother in her, but has a softer side, too, a side that clearly was a gift from her father. She got the best of both her parents. "Where is my daughter?" She asks the question as if I'm the only one in the room, as if there aren't ten generals staring at her. It's a question I've been dreading.

"In the New City," I say. Unlike the generals, we told her everything before we went above. "She's on a mission."

"But she's alive?" she asks. She makes the most important question in the world sound like any other question. She might as well have asked *Is my uniform blue?* for all the emotion she put into her words.

I want to, but I can't lie to her. "I don't know," I say. "But I'm operating under that assumption."

Aboud raises a fist in the air. "I want answers and I want them now. What the *hell* are you talking about?"

I nod slowly, but my eyes never leave General Rose's. Is that a glimmer of fear I see? She blinks quickly and it's gone, once more replaced by steel and fire. "I need your help," I say. For the next hour I recap everything that happened from the moment Adele and I stepped onto Earth. When I finish, I ask, "Will you help me defeat Lecter?"

Aboud looks me in the eye and says, "Not with her." He spits at the screen. "If you want us to do this, we're doing it our way, the right way, the way we've always done it. Your father's way."

I glance at Roc and Tawni. And then I draw my sword.

Thirty-One
Adele

I awake to a shaking bed. Not hard, more like a buzz beneath me. "Your bed will wake you up." Now I get what Lin meant.

When I roll over and put my feet down, the bed stops and the lights flash on. The moment I take my weight off the mattress, the wall shifts and the bed disappears. I blow a sharp breath through tight lips. This world is really starting to freak me out.

My white corpse-clothes are wrinkled and smelling far less fresh than they were when I stole them yesterday. I'll have to check with Lin to see if she has some clean ones I might be able to borrow. She's shorter than me, but it'll have to do.

Or not. When I scan my wrist on the metal ration dispenser, two things happen: One, the metal door opens and out pops a white-yellow rectangle, steaming hot; and two, another part of the wall moves behind me, revealing several sets of white clothes and a narrow cubicle with a metal fixture at the top and a drain at the bottom. There's a handle on the wall in the middle. Some kind of cleaning device.

And I don't need to inspect the clothes to know: they're all in my size.

Suddenly I realize the power of the chips in our wrists. Not power for us, but power for him. For Lecter. Control. We have to use them for everything, and therefore, he can track and control everything we do. He doesn't need cameras set up to monitor us, because we tell him what we're doing each and every time we scan our wrists.

I clench my fists and resist the desire to rip off my bandage and dig out the chip. I have to be like everyone else if I want to win this fight.

Sitting down at the table—which only has one chair, I guess guests are frowned upon—I eat the egg-like block in front of me. It tastes too salty but I force myself to swallow, washing it down with the single glass of water the liquid dispenser will allow me. Finished, I stare at the wall, which has gone from white to black in an instant, like someone turned off the lights. Only the lights are still on and the rest of the room is bright.

There's a flash and numbers appear. 6:30. A voice drones from a speaker built somewhere into the ceiling. "You have fifteen minutes to read this morning's announcement." Another flash and the numbers disappear, replaced by an image.

My chest heaves and the eggs rise up in my throat. I cough, choke, look away. Try to breathe. Slowly, slowly, slowly, I return my eyes to the screen, breathing through my nose. Tears blurring my vision. Seeing only bodies. Not a few. Not hundreds. Thousands, scattered in the sand, spotted with blood. Men and women and kids. A lot of freaking kids, their bodies so much smaller.

A group of soldiers stand in front of the carnage, mugging and smiling and giving thumbs up signs for the camera.

It was murder. No, even that is too soft a word for what the Glassies have done. What Lecter ordered them to do. Genocide. It's a word I learned in school. A word that captures the very essence of the hate and the fear and the mass killing the Glassy army is set on carrying out, has already carried out.

I raise a fist, intent on smashing it through the image, but then it falls limply to my side, defeated. It's just a picture; I can't hurt the soldiers by breaking my hand on the wall. But I can hurt them other ways, and I will.

The image vanishes, text appearing in its place:

Yesterday's victory was decisive in the fight for the liberty of the good citizens of the New City. The savage Icers will never threaten us again. The army's efforts now turn to the desert mongrels who have consistently avoided peace talks, using brute force as an alternative. President Lecter has stated publicly that he's confident good will prevail. "Because of the sacrifices of our brave men and women, the Earth will once more become a civilized world, where our children can grow and prosper, where Godless savages exist no more," Lecter said in a recent interview. A memorial service will be held to honor the courageous souls who perished in what has been coined as The Battle for the North.

I turn away. If there's more, I don't need to read it. They're just words, lies, propaganda. In reality, all the savages in the world are gathered inside the very glass dome that has become my prison.

There's a knock on the door. "One minute," I say, hurriedly changing out of my disheveled clothes and into fresh ones, ignoring the cleaning I so desperately need.

When I throw open the door, Lin's there. "Did you read the announcement?" she says. No greeting, just a question.

I don't have to respond; the look on my face says enough. "You did," she says. "Want to go throw rocks at the presidential building?"

I offer up a grim smile. "I want to do a whole lot more than that," I say.

"Then let's go. We've got a sicko to kill."

We make our way out of the building, just two birds in a flock of many, each bird with white wings and silent beaks. Are they too defeated to even talk to each other? Doesn't anyone have a comment about the announcement?

When we get on the street, I want to run, to sprint, to feel my muscles working, my blood flowing, as if maybe that would cleanse my mind of the image I saw on the screen, help to focus me. But we can't. There are too many people. And it would look strange, anyway, draw attention when that's the last thing I need. Just be like everyone else. Walk at a normal speed, silent, going about my business. Another fish in the school. Another zombie in the...what do you call a group of zombies? A pack? A herd? A gaggle? My slight chuckle draws a stern look from Lin. Is laughter not allowed? Will I be Tasered and hauled off to prison for laughing at my own, admittedly bad, internal joke?

We pass a building on our right that looks familiar. Large iron doors, guards standing next to them. The Presidential Offices. "We're here," Lin says, smiling back at me. Note to self: smiling allowed, laughing not. Check.

I crane my head back and let my gaze travel up the side of the magnificent building. It's like a glass stalagmite, broad at the base and pointy at the top. Like a shard of glass.

She leads me past the doors and to the right, along another main street. Halfway down the block, we follow a man into a small, dark alley. I use the term "alley" loosely, because it's nothing like the alleys in the Moon and Star Realms. It's dark, yeah, but only because the buildings rise up so high above it, blocking the rising sun. But it's not strewn with litter, doesn't have any dirty, ale-drenched beggars shoving their hands in your face, doesn't make me feel unclean just being in it. Instead, it's spotless, a thinner version of the main road, just another thoroughfare for people going to work.

Lin slows and lets the man in front of us get ahead. "I can't go with you all the way to the entrance—it will look…weird," she says. The man stops at a door with another guard. "Just follow him, and act like you know what the hell you're doing."

I nod. "Thanks, Lin. Promise not to turn me in?" It's a bad joke, but she laughs anyway.

"I'd go in there and strangle Lecter myself if I had any chance of getting past the dozen or so layers of security. Even for you it'll be a longshot."

"I have a history with longshots," I say.

"Good luck, see you tonight." And then she's gone, off to her own job, and I'm alone again.

I take a deep breath and stride up to the door, which is already closing behind the other guy. The guard ignores me.

What am I supposed to do? Of course, there's a glass plate. Self-service. Why would I expect the guard to act like a gentleman and hold the door for me? I scan my wrist. A red light flashes and then…stays red. I swallow hard. I can tell the guard's paying attention now.

"Damn cheap machines," I say, like it happens all the time. I scan my wrist again. Red light tries to penetrate my shirt, the bandage, my skin…

Green. It turns green and the door clicks. The guard goes back to ignoring me as I open it, not letting out my held breath until I get inside.

Right away, I see the guy that entered first. His arms are extended outwards, his feet apart. Two men with black wands are waving them over every inch of his body, presumably checking for potential weapons. I'm glad I ditched my stolen semi-automatic rifles back at the morgue, I think wryly.

They finish with him and he walks into some kind of machine with another red light. It flashes green and a door on the other side opens, lets him through, and then closes.

The guards turn to me. One of them smiles, his white teeth shiny and totally unexpected. I frown and step forward, spread my legs, put my arms out at my sides, trying to mimic what I saw the guy do.

"Mm mm mm," the smiley guy says, "I've never seen you before."

I don't respond, just watch them from the bottom of my eyes as they start with my feet, their black wands slipping over my shoes and around my ankles with deft, practiced movements.

"You new around here?" he asks, moving up my leg.

"First day," I say, my voice monotone, my heart hammering.

"Hopefully not your last." The other guard chuckles. Their wands slide up the inside parts of my thighs. "This might tickle a little," the smiley guard warns. I freeze as his stick jabs into my crotch. I stare straight ahead. "Does that feel good?" he asks. "Because we might have to check again. Women like you are known to hide dangerous things in unlikely spots."

My leg starts to quiver and I clench my muscles to stop from giving in to the instinct to knee him in the crotch and slam my forearm into his nose. That would be a quick way to put an end to my mission.

Their wands move on, over my hips, around my abdomen, and to my chest, where once again they linger. I open my eyes and stare right at the guy as he rubs his damn stick against my breasts, which, thankfully, are completely hidden beneath my high-collared white linen shirt.

And then it's over. "See you tomorrow," the guard says, unable to resist smacking my butt with his wand as I step forward into the machine. I'm quivering with rage, but I bite my lip and clench my jaw until the door opens in front of me.

I step through, wondering if all the guards are like those ones, whether the women of the city have to put up with that kind of treatment on a daily basis. If so, I give them credit for their restraint. I'd lose it within two days. Whichever guard was wanding me on the second day would undoubtedly have at least one less testicle when I was done with him.

On the other side of the door there's a hallway, curving away to the left. The other employee is already gone, which doesn't surprise me considering how long my "security check" took.

Breathing deeply to push down my anger, I stride along the hall, which doesn't go far, just around a bend and into a large room with half a dozen people moving around, carrying towels and bottles of blue fluid, pushing mop buckets, all turning their heads to watch a plump woman with a clipboard, who's giving them orders. I stand in the doorway to listen.

"Benson—outer atrium," she barks.

"On it," a woman with a blond ponytail says.

"Holly—lower meeting rooms."

"Yep," says the guy with the mop bucket, the one who entered just in front of me.

"Bridges—bathrooms."

A guy with a shaved head cringes, but says, "Yes, Boss."

"Sanders—you're coming with me to do the upper suites."

Silence. The woman looks up from her papers. Frowns. "Are you Sanders?" she says to me. Everyone turns to look my way.

Sanders? Who the hell is Sanders? "I—" Sanders, you moron! As in the last name you invented not a day earlier. "Yes, that's me. Tawni Sanders reporting for duty." My voice sounds high and ridiculous and way too freaking eager. It doesn't impress the woman.

She rolls her eyes, mutters, "I don't know why they even sent you; I didn't order any new workers..."

I look at the floor, trying to look pitiful, hoping she won't send me back to…wherever they send unneeded workers.

After a few seconds of silence that seem to stretch into eternity, she sighs and says, "Well, you're here, so we might as well put you to work. We use last names only. When I say your name next time, do yourself a favor and respond immediately. I don't like waiting."

"Yes, ma—"

"And don't speak until I'm done." She looks down at a watch. "You're right on time. Tomorrow, be five minutes early. The normal rules don't apply in this building. President Lecter expects more."

I wait a few seconds to be sure she's finished. "Yes, ma'am," I say.

"Grab those things and follow me," she says, exiting through a door at the back of the room. I look down to find a pile of stuff, way more than I can possibly carry on my own. I sigh. I have a feeling it's going to be a very long day.

~~~

Thankfully, the guy I followed in has a heart and helps me load up a cart with all the cleaning supplies. He also shows me the way to the elevators. Of course, my boss is already gone. I shouldn't have expected her to wait for me.

"Go to Level 50," he says. "You'll find her there."

"Thanks," I say, pushing my cart onto the elevator. I'm pretty sure it's some kind of a special elevator to be used by building workers only, as it's exceptionally large and could easily fit four carts. Scanning the numbered buttons, I mutter, "Level 50, 50, 50…"

I find the right one and almost press it as the doors are closing. But then I stop myself. The numbers go all the way up to 55. If Lecter is in this building, surely he'll be all the way at the top.

I jam my thumb into the button marked 55. It lights up blue.

What am I doing? I'm being reckless. But this could be my only opportunity to get a close look at Lecter, maybe even kill him right here and now, and it's not like the war is going to wait for me to slowly gain the trust of my employer. And I've got a card to play, one I can only play once.

The elevator whirs to life and climbs, climbs, climbs, shuddering every now and then. The doors open and I half expect Lecter to be sitting in front of me, his silvery hair set atop his fake smile. No, it's just a lobby, with stark white walls like everywhere else in this city.

The door begins to close automatically and I block it with a hand, peek out to the right. There is a set of glass doors with a desk behind them. A woman is rummaging through a cabinet, momentarily distracted. Two guards are on either side of her, but they're looking away too, talking to her. One says something lewd about how she should wear shorter skirts to work. The other just laughs. Do I have time to slip through the doors and past her? There's no way I'll make it with my cart.

I glance to the left to find a single door. Will my cart fit through? This is my one shot, I remind myself. Grabbing the handle, I pull the cart over the bumpy transitional bits from the elevator to the lobby floor, cringing when a few cleaning bottles rattle against each other. The lady is oblivious as she tries to find whatever she's looking for, and the soldiers only have eyes for her backside.

Heading to the left, I pray the door's unlocked. I turn the handle, feeling the satisfying give as the door opens. Pull my cart through...

Crap!

The sides of the cart slide along the sides of the frame and then stop. It's wedged. Past it, the woman pulls something from the cabinet, scans it, and then starts to turn...

I wrench the cart sharply, trying to force it through the doorway. It makes a nasty scraping sound, but then it's through, rattling ten times worse than before as it follows me into a hallway. The door closes behind me. Did the woman or soldiers see it? Did they hear it? I'm not sticking around to find out.

Heart thudding like a bass drum, sweat trickling down my back, I push the cart hard down the hall, just under jogging speed. Turn a corner and—

—bright light blinds me, seeming to go straight into my eyes, into my brain, and

—even as I slam my eyelids closed I can see the fiery red of the sun through them.

Funny little spots dance amongst the red. It's like I'm emerging from a life spent underground all over again. *What was that?* I wonder, even as I'm thinking, *Gotta find a place to hide, in case that woman…*

Ever so slowly, bit by bit, I open my eyes, shielding them with a cupped hand. A wall of glass stands before me, angling sharply, creating the building's pointed top. The panes face the rising sun, letting in an extraordinary amount of light. And above me and around me and everywhere, is the Dome, impossibly enormous and almost glowing as the morning sunlight pours through it.

Beneath that, spreading out in every direction, is the city, the buildings' dwarfed by the larger presidential offices. It's a spectacular sight, and yet…there's not a splash of color anywhere, and I might as well be back in the gray oblivion of the Moon Realm.

I tear my gaze away and turn back to my cart and I'm about to move on, when I hear a voice. "Failure is not an option!" it roars, muffled as it cuts through glass and wood to reach my ears. And although the voice is different, angry, not in the least bit constrained like how I heard it before, I know without a doubt who the voice belongs to:

Lecter.

Thirty-Two
Siena

Grunt's stumbling every few steps by the time night falls on the desert. I almost want to go over and let him lean on me, but I don't wanna disrespect his manhood. And if I'm being honest, I don't really want his sweaty, hairy arms touching me. A good night's sleep will do him some real good.

Unfortunately, that ain't happening, 'cause if we wanna make the wide loop 'round fire country and back to the Glass City, we'll hafta march well into the night.

As the day has trudged on, there's been less and less talking. Even I shut up eventually, stamping out the urge to drink half my water skin with each step. I'm still holding Circ's hand, but Feve's moved up ahead to walk with Wilde and Skye.

Long after the sky turns completely black and littered with starlight, we stop to rest. Half the group, including Grunt, just drop where they stand, falling asleep without eating or drinking anything. Grunt must be awfully tired, 'cause it ain't like him to miss a meal, even one as unappetizing as dried 'zard and raw prickler.

Me and Circ lean up against each other, the sand warm and rough beneath our bare legs. Chew slowly, drink slowly, listen to each other's heartbeats. Forget 'bout why we're here and where we're going and who we're fighting. Just exist, as one, like so many times 'fore.

A familiar voice shatters the silence, one I haven't heard in a long time. A voice from the past, tossed through two sets of bars, comforting in the dark. "We're almost there," he says.

I turn to see Raja, still as skinny as a tentpole, like me, but with slightly more meat on his bones'n the last time I saw him. Raja, who shared his secret with me. Raja, my wrongly imprisoned neighbor the two times my father sent me to Confinement. He's holding a torch and grinning widely.

"You—you look better," I say.

"Thanks," he says. "Hey, Circ."

"Raj," Circ says, passing him the water skin. Raja takes it and presses it to his lips.

He hands the skin back. "Fightin' the good fight, eh?" he says.

"Searin' right," I say.

"You know, we ain't that far from…you know," he says.

"Where?" I say. Somewhere north…ice country? No, not that far yet, but close. Confinement. We ain't that far from Confinement.

241

Raja must see it click in my eyes, 'cause he says, "Wanna go see our old stomping grounds?"

No, I think. But I wouldn't mind going to see good ol' Perry. I should be sleeping already. "Yeah," I say. "Be back soon." Circ gives me a look but doesn't try to stop me.

Me and Raja weave through the sleeping bodies, out into the dark of the desert, his torch freezing 'zards and burrow mice in their tracks 'fore they scamper outta our way.

"Wooloo, isn't it?" Raja says.

"What?"

"How things change so quick, like they's strapped on a bolt of lightning, or the wind, or the back of a Killer."

"Yeah," I say, blinking back the reminder of what happened to the Icers. "But everything stays the same too."

"How so?" Raja asks, holding his torch up to see my face.

"We're still friends, ain't we?"

"Guess yer right," he says, and we stop to let a brambleweed tumble past.

"Can I ask you something, Raj?" I say when we get moving again.

"Me sayin' no's never stopped you 'fore."

I laugh. Ain't that the truth. "We've both been in a hopeless place 'fore. Like *hopeless* hopeless, where we thought the world could end and we mightn't even care or notice. But we pulled through, didn't we?"

"Is that the question?"

"No," I say, thinking of Skye. "I'm just asking whether we got lucky. I was never the strongest person 'fore, but then I found something inside me I didn't even know I had. And I got through it. You did too. Do you think everyone's the same like that? The strong ones, the weak ones, the in-betweens. Or will some of 'em stay stuck down in that hole, seeking out revenge and death?" What I don't ask is: Will Skye stay stuck down in that hole? If Lecter dies, will she be satisfied? Or will she be angry all the time, boiling from the inside out, like a 'zard egg in bubbling water?

Raja chews his orange-and-red flickering lip. "I s'pose it comes down to whether the person *wants* to climb outta that hole."

His words hit me so hard I almost stop walking. 'Cause holy 'zard skins! He's exactly right. I never realized it, but that's the truth, ain't it? After I'd thought Circ'd died, I loathed being so miserable all the time. I coulda stayed that way, coulda plunked down in that hole of despair and chewed on durt and earthworms and all kinds of nasty stuff, but I stood up, my legs skinny and shaky and barely holding up my body...

But still...

I was standing, and that makes all the difference.

"Raja, you're searin' smarter'n you look," I say.

"Uh, thanks. Was that s'posed to be a compliment?" he says. "'Cause it was the worst one I ever heard."

We both laugh at that, only stopping when we see it, dark and spindly and almost like the skinless bones of giant long-dead monsters, picked clean by carrion and sharp-toothed animals.

The empty cages of Confinement rise up against the dark sky.

Home, sweet home.

~~~

While Raja picks his way over to his old cage—he says he wants to see what it's like to look in from the outside, rather'n t'other way 'round—I head along the backs of the wooden shells, remembering the first time my father sent me to this place. How Bart looked me up and down, made a rude comment. Everything came full circle when he tried to force himself on me and my mother killed the baggard.

Am I past Bart's old cell already? Am I past mine? I'm squinting in the dark trying to see my own hand in front of my face. Raja's torch is somewhere on an angle to the right. I've gotta be close.

"Oww!" I run smack into something thick and rough and spiny as all scorch.

No. It can't be. Not again.

But it is. And it's happened again.

I've run smack into Perry the Prickler.

Nice of you to pay me a visit, Siena, he says, looking more black'n his usual gray-green in the dark. *But I wouldn't recommend going straight for the hug next time.*

"Siena!" Raja shouts. "You alright?"

"Fine. Just fine," I mutter, feeling wet tears of blood in the dozen or so holes Perry opened up in my arms and stomach.

"Did you move since the last time I saw you?" I ask Perry. I coulda sworn he was more to the left, not so close to the cages.

Do you see any legs? he says.

"Shut up, Perry," I say, for old times' sake.

Do you see a mouth? he replies, 'cause his wit's always been just a hair quicker'n mine.

"It's night," I say. "I can't see a searin' thing, but you're talking enough for the both of us, ain't you?"

I'm glad you're here, Perry says unexpectedly. *It gets awfully lonely out here in the desert.*

"Don't I know it," I say. "But I'm glad to be here too.

Does that mean I get another hug?

I groan, my skin still stinging from the last one. "Hey, Perry?" I say.

Yeah.

"I saw this tall, skinny prickler with bright red flowers back a-ways. She asked 'bout you."

You're lying.

"No, really, she'd heard all 'bout you. How you're so good at standing really still, not moving the slightest bit, even when the wind's blowing something fierce."

Now you're just being silly.

"She was really impressed. Said she might stop by sometime."

Hey, Siena. You gonna try any daring escapes while you're here?

"Changing the subject won't work, Perry. We're talking 'bout you and the smokiest prickler I ever laid eyes on."

"Siena, did you say somethin'?" Raja asks, peering through the bars of his old cage."

"Naw," I say. "What're you doing in there?"

"Seeing what it's like now that I don't hafta stay in here."

"And?"

"And what?"

"What's it like?" I ask.

"Amazing," he says.

"C'mon," I say. "Let's go get some sleep. We got a long day ahead of us."

245

I turn to go, but over my shoulder I say, "Take care of yourself, Perry. If I survive this war I'll pop by every now and again."

I'd like that, Perry says. *And Siena?*

I turn back. "Yeah?"

Take care of yourself, too. Don't do anything I wouldn't do.

"Sure," I say, even though that pretty much eliminates doing anything 'cept standing and poking holes in clumsy people. I walk away from Perry for what might be the last time.

~~~

The sun goddess is shooting a hole through my head.

We've been walking for hours and it's like the sun and the clouds are in league with the Glassies, dead set on stopping our march. The sun goddess seems bigger and more fiery'n ever 'fore, and the clouds, well, they're scarcer'n a burrow mouse under the shadow of a vulture. It's a 'spiracy, I tell you.

As per my promise to Veeva, I'm watching Grunt like a hawk, just waiting for him to keel over, to eat the sand with his dried lips. But he doesn't, just keeps trudging on, back bent. Maybe he's got more mettle'n I ever gave him credit for.

I tried to talk to Skye earlier, but she's like a rock-person now, all sharp edges and stone-faced, determined to crush anything and everything in her path. I hafta believe she wants to get outta the hole of anger and sadness she's digging. Like Raja said, she hasta want it. The only person she seems willing to talk to is Wilde, and though it hurts a little, I understand it, too. Wilde's a hard one to ignore. Her calm presence comforts us all.

Wilde said a few words 'fore we departed this morning. She talked 'bout how we're doing this for a lot of weaker people depending on us back in New Wildetown. How we hafta be strong for 'em. Right away I thought of Jade. Not that she's weak, 'cause she ain't, but 'cause she's only barely old enough to be a Youngling, and 'cause her childhood's been snatched away from her once and I won't let it happen again. She deserves something good in her life. We all do.

Feve is doing what he does best: giving us courage. He roams 'round the edges of the group, watching for anyone lagging or tiring. When he spots someone, he says a few words to 'em and they buck up right quick. Having a steel-boned warrior like him by your side gives you confidence.

And Circ is Circ. My rock, my best friend. Other'n when my father threatened my life and forced him to fake his own death, Circ's been there for me, as consistent and never-changing as a mountain.

I hold his hand as we walk, sometimes in silence, sometimes with me going on and on like a chatterbox. And he always laughs at my jokes, even the bad ones, not 'cause he's just being nice, but 'cause he thinks they're funny. We're cut from the same mold, he and I, only his came out strong and graceful and beautiful, and mine came out, well, like me. Perfect in an imperfect kinda way.

The wind picks up as we reach the edge of ice country, blowing a slight chill down from the mountains. I enjoy watching the many of us who haven't seen trees 'fore, as they ogle the stalwart defenders of the border. I remember the first time I saw 'em, the first time I felt the crunch of their dry, fallen leaves beneath my feet, touched their rough skin. It's like yesterday and like forever ago.

A thousand thousand footsteps and the day is gone, the sun goddess mercifully dipping below a thick wall of yellow clouds building along the western horizon, behind us as we head dead east. And just as she starts throwing purples and oranges and pinks into the sky overhead, we turn south, toward the Glass City.

Will they see us coming? Will they expect us to sneak in the back? Was Tristan right?

I hafta believe this is our only choice. We all hafta, or we're as good as dead already.

Purples and pinks turn to navy blue as the second day since Tristan and Roc and Tawni left comes to an end.

In three days' time, we attack the Glass City.

Time's moving too fast, leaving me feeling breathless all of a sudden.

We march on, Circ and my footsteps in sync without even trying.

We're at the head of the column, just behind Skye and Wilde, who're still leading the march. And as I'm looking out in front of us, watching the rise and the fall of the dunes as the desert breathes, I see something that ain't right, ain't natural.

The sky is full of what at first look like black clouds…but no, they're moving too fast, much too fast, and diving at the earth and fighting with each other, and croaking and cawing and carrying on. And beneath the clouds-that-ain't-clouds…

"Circ…" I say, my voice fading away like the last light from the dying sun.

He sees it, too, 'cause he grips my hand harder.

And then I know what I'm seeing, what ain't right, what'll never be right, and I know Skye knows what we're seeing too, 'cause she stops, dead in her tracks. Wilde steps in front of her, trying her best to block my sister's vision.

We're not nearly as far east as I thought we were, 'cause I see 'em like the images burnt forever in my mind. Only they're not images, they're real, setting in front of us like a nightmare.

Carts and packs of supplies and hundreds and hundreds of bodies.

An army of vultures and crows fighting over the spoils, feeding, feeding, cawing and screaming at each other…

We've come to where the Icers were slaughtered by the Glassies.

Skye pushes past Wilde and starts running toward 'em.

Thirty-Three
Tristan

"Kill me if you must," Aboud says. "But I won't fight with the likes of her."

My sword is catching the light and reflecting it in a slash of white on the general's chest. He's weaponless—there's no way he could stop me from sending him to whatever hell my father is surely in. I'm sure the ex-president would love the company.

If I do it though, am I just like my father? Killing anyone who disagrees with me, who challenges me? Would that make me a dictator too? If this man had something to defend himself, would it make any difference if *I* was the aggressor?

Even if I want so badly to ignore them, I know the answers to those questions like they're a part of me. Maybe that's why my mother believed in me, why she trusted me with a responsibility that seems well beyond what I'm capable of. She could see the truth in my heart. I'm not like my father—will never be.

Would she be proud yet? Or do I have dozens more moral decisions to make before I can proudly declare "I lived up to my mother's expectations!"?

I shove my sword back in its sheath. The heat of a dozen stares burns my cheeks, but the one I feel most is from the screen. Is that…a hint of a smile on her lips? Surely not. If General Rose were me she'd slash through the generals in an instant, wouldn't she? Maybe she's not all kill-strokes and snap decisions like I thought. Maybe she's got a bit of Ben in her too.

"That's what I thought," Aboud snarls. "We'll take Lecter down, that's for damn sure, but we'll do it without the help of the traitors."

"No," I say calmly. "You won't." Aboud's face turns red and he's about to speak, but I step forward and cut him off. "You will follow my orders or be dismissed from your position."

"I was appointed by your father for life," he says. "We all were."

"For *his* life," I say. "Which is over. You remain generals only on my command now."

He laughs, but there's no joy in it. "*Your* command. You're a child, regardless of whose son you are. We'll run the army as we see fit."

"Your choice," I say. "Commit to fight against Lecter with a united Tri-Realms, or you can leave right now."

The general's smile is as ugly as a bat's. "I'll leave. But I'll take the rest of the generals and our army with me." He spits at my feet and stalks off. "Follow me," he says to his comrades.

Three of the men follow immediately, then a fourth. A fifth turns halfway, and then turns back, looking at the remaining four generals, as if torn.

I meet his eyes. "Do what you have to do," I say, "but I'll show you no mercy on the battlefield."

"And neither shall I," he says, and then exits behind the others. Nearly two-thirds of my leaders are gone in the blink of an eye.

The four left look like they want to throw up. One of them is the man with the blue-plated glasses. General Marx. "What do you want us to do?" he asks.

"Prepare for war with the other generals," I say. "We must defeat them tomorrow or there might be no one left to save by the time we get above."

Through the speakers, Adele's mother clears her throat. I look at her. Is that pride in her eyes? "I'll get together with the leaders of the moon and star dweller armies. We're coming to the Sun Realm."

"Get here fast," I say, motioning to Tawni.

She raises the controller and cuts the connection, and I'm left with two of my best friends and my four remaining generals.

~ ~ ~

The communications technician looks at me and nods. A red light blinks above the camera.

I look down at the script Roc and Tawni helped me compose over the course of an hour, after only managing to grab about two hours of sleep. I fight off the urge to yawn as I skim the fancy words and the calls to action and the "together we are strong" line that I liked so much at the time, but which now just sounds like a bunch of fake nonsense. Halfway through preparing the speech, the reports started coming in that large portions of the sun dweller army had abandoned their posts under the leadership of the six deserting generals. *Good riddance*, I think, lying to myself.

I know I should be saying something, because I'm live and the entirety of the Tri-Realms is watching me right now. But I don't, I just stare at the paper for a few seconds, and then crumple it in my fist. When I look to the side, Roc's there, barely out of the range of the camera, grinning that I-told-you-so look that's so annoying but is so justified in this instance, because he's the one who told me to just speak from my heart when I asked him to help me write something.

I chuck the balled-up speech at him and he ducks, letting it hit the wall behind him. That Roc: He's a wily one, all right.

Turning back to the red blinking light and the glass circle that means millions of people are watching me, I place my hands on the table, trying to steady my nerves. "My—my father lied to you his whole life…" I can imagine the gasps from the sun dwellers, the nodding heads of the moon dwellers, the shouts of "No surprise there!" from the star dwellers. "He told you the earth's surface continues to be uninhabitable, and in some ways it is, but"—I pause, knowing even the moon and star dwellers will be waiting in anticipation for my next words—"there are people living there."

I wait for it to sink in, if that's even possible. I remember the outraged cries of denial from my friends when I told them. Hell, I don't think Trevor ever believed me. How could a secret so big be kept from everyone?

I go on to tell them about the New City, about the Tri-Tribes, about the good people I met who just want to live their lives in peace, like we all do. When I tell them about what I saw, about how the earth dwellers massacred the Icers, I hope their eyes are wet, that they feel something. If not, then the fight is already lost.

"And now I ask you…no, I *implore* you, to unite as one, to cast aside your differences for another day, to help me and the other leaders of the Tri-Realms build a new world. A better one." I pause again, praying my words are more than just the dry rock dust I feel in my mouth. "There will be those who even now are plotting against us, who will tell you a disparate, separate world is a good world, but don't listen to them. That was my father's way and it only ever led us to rebellion and war. I can show you a new way. Be ready because it's coming."

The light blinks off and I slump back in my chair, sighing deeply. Roc comes over.

"Not bad," he says. "Maybe you won't be as crappy a president as I expected."

I don't even have the energy to punch him for that comment. Public speaking takes a lot out of you. Just another thing I'll have to get used to. "Any word from the generals?"

"I got a note that said two more have left and taken their troops with them."

"What?" I say, my fists clenching.

"Just kidding," Roc says, chuckling to himself. Now I do find it in me to punch him in the gut, soft enough that he'll keep his breath but hard enough to tell him what I thought of his joke. "Ow! Okay, okay, the note said they've briefed their soldiers and that they're ready. It also said the other generals are marching their armies to the border tunnels. Looks like they're going to try to stop the moon and star dweller armies before they can get here."

In other words, everything's a huge mess, and I'm the one who caused it.

~ ~ ~

The day is half gone and the anticipation is killing me. The non-military citizens are hiding inside their beautiful flats and apartments and homes, peeking out their windows as we pass through the streets.

I'm at the head of one of the platoons from the portion of the army that I still command, marching toward one of the border tunnels that leads to the Moon Realm. General Marx is by my side in the back of a truck. We received a comm from the moon dwellers that they're transporting several of their own platoons through this tunnel.

Evidently the enemy generals intercepted that comm, because even before we reach the cavern wall, I can hear the whisper-roar of a large crowd. When we round a bend with our force of at least five thousand soldiers strong, we see an ocean of darkness, standing stock still and going silent when they spot us.

The deserters have cast off the red uniforms that the army behind me wears, and replaced them with black clothes, as dark as oil.

Presumably on a command from one of their generals, they raise their guns, pointing them right at us. All around me, not needing a command from Marx or me, our soldiers mirror the enemy's movements, clicking and shouldering their weapons. Maybe I should've ridden in the back like Marx suggested. No, that's what my father would've done; or worse, he would've stayed in his palace fortress, safe while his men and women died for him.

If anyone must die, I'll die with them.

A voice bellows from the black swarm, amplified by a bullhorn. "President Nailin. Before we kill each other, may I have a word?"

Even distorted by the electronic ting of the amplification device, the voice is recognizable. General Aboud.

Marx hands me a bullhorn. I raise it to my lips. "The time for talking is past. You have abandoned your posts, committed treason against your own people, your own government. Stand down or face the consequences."

Before Aboud can respond, there's a shout from further back, somewhere near the cavern wall, where a massive inter-Realm shipping tunnel sinks into the rock like a huge, black eye. "They're coming!" More shouts, loud and wicked and almost excited, but even they're not loud enough to drown out the echoes from the tunnel. Drumbeats. No, not drumbeats—feet marching in unison, spilling out of the tunnel mouth.

The Lower Realms have arrived.

~~~

256

There's a flash of red fire and more screams. An explosion rocks the city, sending shards of black and red through the air amidst a thick fog of gray smoke.

A grenade. The moon and star dwellers are coming in firing.

Shots ring out and at first they're distant, like Aboud's soldiers are firing into the tunnel, but then they're closer. A dozen soldiers cry out around us, the air spotted with tiny pink clouds. And then the cracks of weapons exploding are so loud it's like they're in my ears, as our force returns fire. Black-clothed soldiers fall, but are quickly replaced by the next line, illuminated by flashes of orange explosions from the muzzles of their weapons.

Marx pulls me off the truck, behind a shield of metal and rubber. My head is buzzing; I can't hear properly. My heart is racing and I realize I'm clutching my own gun to my chest with two hands. I've fought plenty of times, but not like this. Not when I'm just one speck of dust in a mountain of dirt. Not when the enemy might kill me even if they're not aiming at me.

I take a deep breath as Marx sticks his gun out the side of the vehicle and shoots. He doesn't even look, just pulls the trigger, again and again and again, until his gun starts clicking. He withdraws his hand, pops out the spent cartridge, reloads.

"This is what you wanted, isn't it?" he says. His voice sounds muffled, like he's speaking underwater. He doesn't wait for my response, just rolls to the side and starts shooting again, like it's as simple as going out back to take a leak.

What am I doing? I'm no soldier. I know how to shoot, yeah, because my father made me spend hours on the range, but not when the enemy is a black wall, individual people as indiscernible from each other as a single ant atop an anthill.

This might not be what I wanted or what I expected—what did I expect, exactly?—but it's what I *made*. So now I have to live with it, whether I like it or not.

Gritting my teeth, I roll to the side opposite from Marx and start shooting.

Thirty-Four
Adele

Every last instinct is urging me to run-run-run as far away from that voice as possible.

I run right at it, leaving my cart behind, and staying on my toes to ensure my approach is soundless. Down the hall past empty offices to the other side of the room, my feet carry me toward him.

Even as the voice gets louder, I wonder what I'm going to do when I reach him. Will I barge in, attack him, try to kill him on the spot? Presumably he has some form of security that will stop me. But I could try. Killing Lecter would end the war pretty quickly, and *quickly* is exactly what we need.

I slow my pace as the voice becomes softer and clearer, the sound slipping through a crack in a door to a corner conference room. There's frosted glass on both inner sides so I can't see a damn thing, but I can hear every word.

"We can't find them, sir," says a new voice. "It's like they disappeared into the sand."

"That's the best excuse you have to offer me?" Lecter says, his voice rising once more. "That the desert dwellers have sunk into the sand?"

I creep close, right up to the door, stay to the left of the hinges, in case it opens. I might get lucky and have the chance to hide behind it.

"No, I'm just saying—"

"You're just saying that you've failed to destroy the savages. Do you know what that means?" Lecter again, his tone once more full of the calmness he displayed during last evening's announcement.

"Yes," the man says.

"Do you?"

"It means they're still out there?" the man says, like it's a question.

"Wrong!" Lecter scoffs.

"They're *not* still out there?"

"You idiot, of course they're still out there, but that's not the important thing. The important thing is that the people— my people—know that we've won, that we've done what we set out to do. *Cleansed* the earth so we can start over. What citizen of this good city is going to agree to ride out into the desert to be a part of the next city we construct if there are savages still running around somewhere?"

I'm pretty sure Lecter isn't expecting an answer, but the man says, "No one."

"You're damn right no one. Look, we suffered the partnership with the Icers only because their king was…unstable…and because he provided us with a fair supply of wood and meat. But even had he survived their little rebellion, we still would have had to kill them all eventually anyway. For the good of the earth. His death was merely the perfect excuse."

"I've heard Goff's death wasn't caused by a rebellion," the man says, his voice filled with a little pride.

"Oh have you?" Lecter says, a sliver of sarcasm in his tone.

"I heard dark warriors came from the sea."

"Dark warriors?" Lecter's words are full of mockery now. "Sounds like you've been reading too many sun dweller novels, Gomez."

"I'm just saying what I heard."

"You think I don't have all the same information as you? I've heard the same thing, only my sources called the eastern people *savages*, not dark warriors. Just more savages. Don't give them more prestige than they deserve. One day our coastal cities will be built on the graves of these so-called dark warriors."

A firm hand grabs the back of my shirt and I almost cry out.

"What do you want me to do?" I hear the man ask Lecter, even as I'm looking back at my attacker, preparing for a fight.

It's my boss, her face like a red balloon. *Uh oh.* She doesn't say anything, just points down the hall, to where I left my cart.

I walk away from the room, feeling her behind me the whole way.

Lecter's final words hit me in the back. "Kill them. Kill them all."

~~~

"What the *hell* were you doing?" boss lady says. I swear a wisp of steam escapes her ear. We're down on the 50ᵗʰ floor, where I was meant to go in the first place.

"I got the floor wrong," I say innocently. "I'm sorry."

"Why'd you leave your cart?" Big hands on big hips.

"I was looking for you."

"So when you didn't find me you decided to crouch outside of a conference room?" she asks. She doesn't say "President Lecter's conference room," but I can tell that's what she means. It was a major offense.

"No, I…see, the thing is…I saw a smudge on the glass, so I went to inspect. And when I got closer, there were more smudges, LOTS of smudges, so I was contemplating what to do about those smudges when you snuck up behind me."

"I didn't sneak," the boss says. "I don't sneak."

I don't doubt that. I must've been pretty engrossed in what Lecter was saying to not notice her approach. Building new cities. Cleansing the earth. Killing the savages. The themes of the conversation were anything but comforting.

But my conversation with my boss is going nowhere. Time to play the card under my sleeve.

"Look, it's my first day, I was just trying to figure things out. I promise, it won't happen again."

She smiles at me, which scares me a little. I wither under the scrutiny of her gaze and the strangeness of her unexpected smile. "Oh, you're right about that," she says, and I can tell she's not in any way, shape or form agreeing with me. "It won't happen again because your employment here is terminated, effective at the end of the day. Your rations will be cut off starting tomorrow, until you are assigned a new position."

~~~

That could've gone better. Not only will I be unable to get close to Lecter again after today, but boss lady is watching me like a parent watches their troublemaker kid on the playground.

First we clean the long hallways on floors 50 to 54, using strange machines that evidently suck the dust off the fuzzy, soft floors that almost look like blankets have been sewn into them. I think they had them in Tristan's palace in the Sun Realm, too—he called them carpets. We stop there, leaving 55 to clean itself, I guess. So much for the smudges on the conference room glass.

Next we clean every last window on those same five floors. It's truly backbreaking work, and I have to constantly switch the hand that I use to scrub with so my arms don't get too tired. What am I doing? I'm on a clandestine mission to help stop a ruthless dictator and I'm scrubbing windows until they're so clear you can barely tell they're windows. It's quite a different experience to when we took out Tristan's father.

The day can't go fast enough, because under boss lady's scrutiny there's no hope of learning anything else. And even the stuff I already learned is of no real value; it just supports what I already knew about President Borg Lecter: that he's a good candidate for a bullet to the head.

Finally, my back aching and my arms sore and my fingers ready to fall off, we're dismissed for lunch.

On the way out, boss lady stops me. "You know what? Cancel the rest of the day. You're fired now. You'll be able to eat lunch but not dinner. Report to the employment office immediately if you want to eat tomorrow."

I don't respond, just walk away, my muscles tight from the cleaning and anger. And frustration. I was right there, a pane of glass and a cracked-open door the only things separating me from him! So freaking close! I screwed up. I should have barged in, taken my chances with any guards that might've been inside, gone for Lecter's jugular with my teeth. I should have sacrificed my own life for the greater good. Tristan might disagree, but only because he cares about me. Now I'm back to square one, the weight of regret on my shoulders.

When I exit into the alley, Lin's already waiting. "What took you so long?" she says. "I've already lost ten minutes of my break."

"I got fired," I whisper.

"What?"

"Shh, I don't want to make a big deal about it."

As we walk to lunch, I tell her what happened.

"You got that close to Lecter on your first attempt? You *are* on a mission!" Lin says.

"Shh," I say, "keep your voice down. I've lost my best chance—the chance that I was lucky enough to stumble upon—to get close to him. I messed up, Lin, went for too much, too soon."

We stop talking for a few minutes as we scan our wrists at a different eatery than yesterday. Inside, it looks the same. The same food, the same guards in the corners, the same bored, expressionless citizens sitting and eating, barely talking. It's really starting to creep me out. These people have lost the will to live.

"So what's your next move?" Lin whispers when we sit down. A purple rectangle stares up at me from my plate. I mash it with my fork, mix it in with the yellow and green ones on either side. Maybe together they'll taste better than apart. I take a bite.

Blech. Maybe not.

I ponder Lin's question. It's just a setback, not failure. I've still got options and my identity is still secure, which is the most important thing. But clearly I'm running out of time. The soldiers I left in the electrical room will be found soon, and then I'll be presidentially screwed. I'm still convinced the fastest way to end all of this is to get to Lecter.

"Where does Lecter live?" I ask.

~~~

Lin insists on sharing her dinner with me, because, no matter how many times I try scanning my wrist, the food dispenser just looks back at me with a single red eye. She also wants to come with me to Lecter's place.

"No," Avery and I say at the exact same time.

"Why not?" Lin says. "I've been helpful so far, haven't I?"

"You have," I say. "But there's a curfew?"

She nods.

"And they check that everyone's where they're supposed to be using their chips?"

Another nod. Avery's nodding along with his niece, apparently in complete agreement with where I'm going with this.

"So you'll be caught before you get half a block. The Enforcers will Taser you and haul you away."

"What about you?" Lin asks. "You have the same problem."

I take a deep breath, roll up my sleeve, and peel away the bandage.

"Yuck, what died in there?" Lin says, covering her mouth with the top of her shirt.

"What in God's name?" Avery says.

I almost want to throw up, too. My arm's a mess, the wound Tristan inflicted jagged and torn, filmed with black-red-brown dried blood, oozing with cream-colored scabbing, still moist. Beneath it is the small welt from the fresh chip injection I received on my first day.

"You want to help me, Lin? Dig out my chip."

"You can't be serious," Avery says, still staring at my mangled skin.

"I'll do it," Lin says.

"Wait just a minute," Avery says, "there has to be another way."

"I'm listening," I say. "If you know another way to trick the system, I'm all ears."

He bites his lip, cringes, says, "I know someone who might be able to help. I could talk to him tomorrow."

"I don't have time for tomorrow," I say. "I've got to do this tonight, keep things moving. The sooner I figure out whether killing Lecter is a possibility, the sooner I'll be able to either end this or move on to the next option."

"And what's the next option, Adele?" Avery's hands are in the air. "You going to smash through the Dome, destroy the city, throw grenades into the army barracks?"

"I'll do what I have to do," I say.

"Even if it means dying?" I'm surprised because the question comes from Lin, not Avery. She's looking at me intently, watching for my reaction.

Meeting her gaze, I say, "Yes. Even if it means dying."

Avery groans. "Don't go filling her head with that suicidal nonsense."

"It's not suicide, Avery. My mother, my sister, my boyfriend, my best friend…they're out there, counting on me to do this. They believe I can do this."

"You're one crazy girl, you know that?" Avery says, breaking the tension with a grim smile.

"So I've been told," I say, quirking up the side of my lip. "Now will you let your niece dig out my chip?"

"No," he says, and I'm about to protest, but then he adds, "I'll do it."

~~~

My arm hurts like hell, but at least the bleeding finally stopped. A thick bandage and a long-sleeved shirt hide any evidence of the ad hoc procedure. Avery had to use the tines of my fork to get the chip out, and the only thing that stopped me from screaming like a banshee was Lin stuffing a towel in my mouth.

Not my brightest moment.

But it's done now, and we scanned the removed chip into my bed, laying down chairs on the mattress to try to trick it into thinking I'm sleeping.

Time to go.

"Be careful," Avery says. "No unnecessary risks."

"They're all necessary at this point," I say wryly.

"You know what I mean."

267

I give him a quick hug, because it just feels right after everything they're doing for me. Lin goes down with me, because the exit door won't open without someone scanning their chip, and my chip needs to stay in my bed with the chairs.

When we reach the bottom, I give her a hug too. "Knock when you get back," she says, but I get the feeling she's just saying it to make us both feel better. It's not likely that I'll be coming back. "And kick some presidential ass."

"I will," I say. She scans her wrist on the door, which will raise some alarms, but then they'll assume she just poked her head out for some fresh air the moment she scans it upstairs and gets into bed.

I slip out, a blind spot on Lecter's radar; like a ghost, I'm invisible.

"There will be night patrols," Avery told me before I left. "The city's broken up into eight quadrants, each with a separate patrol pattern. You'll have to make your way across three of these to reach your destination. Watch each patrol to get a feel for it, and then make your move."

I didn't ask him how he knows of all of this. I'll just have to take his word for it.

The first patrol is in our quadrant, and I won't have a chance to observe it because I'm already in the thick of it. My only chance is silent speed. My white clothes flash around me as I race down the street, and, not for the first time, I wish for a darker wardrobe.

Reaching the first cross street, I turn right. I'm halfway down the block when I hear voices and footsteps, just ahead, perhaps around the corner. I slam on the brakes, bolt across the street, duck into an alley. It's full of shadows that grab me and pull me under, cloaking my presence.

Across the street, two Enforcers stroll by, carrying semi-automatic weapons and talking and laughing. They look completely relaxed. I'm guessing they usually get a pre-warning if someone's out on the streets who shouldn't be. Because they won't get that warning, they'll think it's just another boring night on the job.

They pass and I slip behind them, sticking to the route that Avery and Lin mapped out for me. Two more blocks and then left, leaving the first quadrant. I look for a place to hide, to observe.

There are no nearby alleys, but there is a military truck, parked near the corner. It's not safe enough to prowl behind it, so I dive to the ground, roll underneath, peer out.

Silence.

If the city is strange and sterile and somewhat frightening during the day, at night it's downright spooky. Not a soul in sight. Utter silence. Dim lighting from lamp posts, sheening everything with a luminescent white glow.

Voices. Footsteps. The next patrol. Different than the last one. Four Enforcers, two on each side of the road, shining lights in alleyways and at the shadows as they pass. I'm lucky I didn't try hiding from these ones. My only choice here is to avoid them completely. They're coming right for me, but Avery promised they wouldn't cross over into our quadrant, so I'm holding my breath and biting on my thumb and hoping he's right…

They turn right at the intersection, away from me. I let out a silent breath.

There's no time to waste. I roll out from hiding, scramble to my feet, and bolt across the road, running hard, secure in my knowledge that the patrol is behind me. Three blocks, make a right—

WHAM!

Something hits me; or rather, I hit it. Not a wall, because it gives way, groaning and collapsing in front of me as I stumble over it. A person. No, an Enforcer. Another patrol in the same quadrant? Avery must've forgotten to mention that.

But I've hit him from behind and landed on top of him, and though I'm shocked, I'm already recovering, raising my hands like a club, ready to bash his skull in…

When I see the blood.

It's already pooling around us, escaping from somewhere in the front of his head, which he must've hit on the stone-block street when he fell. My head's on a swivel, looking for his partner, who's probably right behind me about to—

Nothing. We're alone. Which really means that I'm alone, because I'm pretty sure this guy is dead.

Crap, crap, crap!

This was not part of the plan. I could try dragging him away to an alley somewhere, but I won't have time to clean up the blood. Do I go back, find a way to break into Avery and Lin's building, knock on their door, start over fresh in the morning? Or do I continue on, really turn this into a suicide mission, doing everything in my power to kill Lecter tonight?

I go on, grabbing only the dead guy's gun, which thankfully clattered away in front of him, several feet out of range of the blood.

I leave the body, dashing into the night, being more careful, peeking around corners before turning them. The second quadrant disappears behind me and I don't stop to observe the patrols in the third quadrant, because at any second someone might raise the alarm that there's a dead Enforcer in the streets and a crazed, disgruntled, chipless citizen on the loose.

It might be luck, it might be fate, or it might just be that the entire patrol had to take a bathroom break, but whatever it is, I don't see a single Enforcer in the third quadrant.

And just like Avery said, there was no chance I'd miss Lecter's house. House is a loose term—it's more like a mansion or palace. Not quite as grand as the Nailin Palace—after all, it's still as sterile and white as everything else in the city—the presidential quarters are surrounded by a head-high brick wall—easily climbable—with a tall, glass sheet above it—impossible to climb.

I creep along the wall, looking for a break, a gate, something.

There's nothing on the side I'm on, so I turn the corner and head down the next section of wall. Ahead there's a blank spot in the wall. An entrance?

Tucking my stolen pistol under the waistband in the small of my back, I stride toward the gap, like it's the most normal thing to be doing in the middle of the night. When I risk a quick glance through the entrance, I see a guard station. There are three guards this time, each toting black weapons.

Things are about to get even messier.

I turn the corner, advancing without caution, like I belong. One of the guard's shouts and then there are three guns pointed at my head. "Hiya, boys," I say.

"How the hell did you get onto the streets?" one of them asks, a tall brute with a chest like an iron statue. There's no way I'll be able to take him one on one.

"A little gift from Borgie," I say, rolling the made up pet name for Lecter off my tongue like syrup. "He made it possible so I could pay him a little visit." Although I know I'm just playing a role, my own words make me want to spew up the half-dinner I ate.

"No one told us," the second guard says, a guy with a face so wide it almost looks stretched.

"He doesn't always tell us," the third guard says, his dark skin like chocolate, his white teeth flashing with each word. It's music to my ears, not that I'm surprised. I'd expect a man like Lecter to take advantage of every last bit of his power. Maybe he likes the young ones the best. The only question left: Will they buy it?

"Lecter's not even here," Iron-Chest says. "Something happened. He rushed off with his guards."

My heart sinks. Now I've got myself a real problem. How to talk my way out of here, away from these guys, who are still pointing their guns at me, although they've dropped them a little, more toward my legs. But *should* I talk my way out?

"We'll send someone to escort you home, ma'am," Wide-Jaw says, the polite one in the group.

I make a decision. Screw getting away from here. I'm only going to have so many chances. "Maybe I could wait inside," I say. "Borgie won't like it if he doesn't get a chance to *see* me tonight."

White-Teeth's mouth flashes open to speak, but I hurry on. "I could even keep you boys company. We could take turns." Vomit, vomit, spew, vomit. I let my thoughts hurl—no pun intended—through my head, but my face is relaxed, my lips pouted out slightly, as I look at them through lowered lashes.

"Ma'am, I think we'd better get you home," Wide-Jaw says.

I close my eyes. Either I have zero sex appeal, or Lecter's chosen, trained, and paid his guards well, because these guys aren't falling for it. Which leaves only one option. Brute force.

The moment Wide-Jaw steps within my circle of reach, I snap a kick hard and high, rocking his monstrous jaw back, his teeth clacking together as his open mouth bites shut. One of the other guards shouts something, but I'm not listening because I'm already drawing my pistol, aiming it at Iron-Chest's bulging left pec, pulling the trigger…

BOOM!

The gunshot rocks the silence like an explosion, and even as he's raising his gun he's falling back, a red hole in his chest, which apparently isn't made of iron after all.

I dive to the side, because I know—*I know*—that when you fight three guys, the one to be the most worried about is the third.

Bullets whine through the air around me, ricocheting off of the brick wall and the cement walkway. I scrape against the ground, the impact stinging my arms and legs, feeling a particularly sharp burst of pain where Avery stabbed me with a freaking fork earlier, but I ignore it because it's nothing.

Turning, I fire three shots, each of them into White-Teeth's gut. Even as his eyes widen and his mouth opens to reveal his pearly whites, he raises his arm to take a final shot. I'm a sitting duck and it's all I can do to turn my body, hoping to get hit somewhere that won't kill me, like an arm or a leg, just not the head…

There's a thud. No gunshot. Just a thud.

Slowly, I roll over. White-Teeth is down, his fingers still closed around the trigger, even though they didn't have enough strength left to pull it.

Nearby, Wide-Jaw is groaning and rolling around. Blood's pouring from his mouth, from his teeth—which are probably broken and shattered—and his tongue—which he might've bitten off.

Images of bodies…children and men and women…

Lying dead in the desert…

Grinning soldiers, mugging for the camera…

I shoot Wide-Jaw in the head.

And then, even as voices and lights rain down from the building above me, I run past the guard station and dart along the side of the structure, into a narrow space between the outer wall and Lecter's house.

In the shadows, I stop, because I'm shaking and breathless and freaking crying uncontrollably, my hand over my mouth to muffle the sound. What did I just do? When did I become a cold-blooded killing machine? Is this what my mother and Tristan's mother were hoping for when they chose me? Is this what my father intended when he trained me?

Back against the wall, I slide to the ground, trying to get control, trying to justify my actions. There are bad people and good people. Those were bad people, right? Do I know that for sure? Do I know anything for sure? But they were polite and they didn't even try to take me up on my lewd offer…

Tristan. His name pops into my head and at first I cry harder, but then I grab onto him. He's something I know for sure, and if he was here, I know he'd trust that what I did to those men was necessary. Anyone carrying guns for Lecter is undeserving of mercy. I use the back of my hand to wipe away the tears, grit my teeth and clench my fists and pull every last muscle in my body tight.

I. Get. Control.

There are voices in the front now. Scared shouts and calls for help. They've discovered the bodies. They'll be searching the premises. I have to find somewhere to hide.

And Lecter's not even here. Where could he possibly be? What could be so urgent that he'd rush off into the night? Did they find the Tri-Tribes? Will we get an announcement about another massacre in the morning?

I have to believe we won't.

Above me, the building rises three stories. Those searching for me will check the lower floors first; the higher I can get the better. I start to climb, starting with a windowsill and then grabbing onto a pipe, tightening my feet around it and pulling myself up. My muscles are still burning from all the cleaning I did this morning and my arm hurts like Avery is *still* jabbing it with the fork, but all of that is just pain. I bite it away.

Reaching the second floor, I find a foothold on another sill, and then reach up to grab a third-floor window. I shove upwards with all my might, but the window doesn't budge, doesn't move one inch. Locked.

There are more windows on either side; I'll have to try those ones, hope for a miracle.

But before I can step across to the next sill, the window above me opens and a head pops out.

I have to jump—I have to—no other choice—just drop and hope I don't break a leg and then run as hard and as fast out of this place as possible, because I'm caught.

I'm caught.

My muscles tense as I prepare for the fifteen foot fall.

"Adele?" a voice says from above, stopping me just before I step off the ledge.

I look up and gasp.

It's impossible. No, not impossible, unless I'm dreaming, because though—

—her cheeks are slightly thinner and—

—her eyes dark with tired bags under them—

—I'd recognize this woman anywhere.

I've never seen her in person, only on the telebox.

But my mother has, years ago, when she plotted and schemed to implant the very microchip in my back that would lead me to Tristan, and Tristan to me.

Tristan's mother, Jocelyn Nailin, stares down at me. "Come inside," she says. "They're looking for you."

Thirty-Five
Siena

With crows a-cawing and vultures wheeling lazy circles above us, I chase after Skye.

She's almost to the bodies and I don't want her to see 'em close up, but I'm afraid it's too late, 'cause though I'm faster'n her, she got a good head start on me and she's searin' motivated. Black-winged birds scatter in front of her, taking flight in a swarm, Skye screaming at 'em, using words so colorful I wonder where she even learned 'em.

And I know she's looking, looking, looking for one body in particular, and that's the one body I don't want her to see. I mean—I don't want her to see any of 'em, but please, sun goddess, not that one—not him.

The birds keep lifting off 'round her, melting into a swarm of black, almost disappearing against the darkening sky. I'm amidst the carnage now, too, and I lift my hands to shoo the birds off the bodies, which are stained with blood, both old and fresh, from the Glassies and the crows. If anyone had survived the attack, the birds finished 'em off.

"Skye, wait!" I shout, and she stops. I think I've done it, that I've gotten through to her, but she don't turn 'round, just stares ahead at something. She's found who she's a-looking for.

I take off running again, 'cause maybe I can catch her now that she's walking slowly, toward a body laying off from most of t'others in the durt. There's a line of 'em, like they were defending the rest of the village, which I know they were, 'cause that's what Dazz'd do.

Skye stops when she's nearly there, and I stop, too, 'cause there's a—a—a huge searin' bird just setting on Dazz's chest. A vulture, with a hooked beak and old, gnarly face, and the blackest eyes you've ever seen. It looks at Skye and she looks back at it, and then it ducks it's head and goes right back to pecking at—I can't hardly say his name again, much less think it—at him.

Well, Skye lets out the loudest yell—more like a ROAR!— I've ever heard from her, and charges at that nasty ol' vulture. The beast-bird hangs on till the very last moment, as if it'd rather face my sister's wrath'n pull itself away from its meal, but then it goes, lifting off, pumping its wings with a *whoomp whoomp whoomp!* and it's gone, soaring 'cross the desert, in search of something else dead to snack on.

Skye kneels, drops her body on top of Dazz, whose body is pocked with holes from fire sticks, riddled with fierce red peck marks from that burnin' vulture. Skye starts shaking, her muscled body convulsing in waves.

No. Everything is so wrong, so searin' wrong—can it ever be right again? Can any of us ever be the same after seeing this, the way the Glassies killed 'em all and then left 'em to be picked clean by the birds?

I whirl in a circle, the world spinning 'round me, full of death and pain and more'n more birds taking flight as Wilde and Circ and Feve and a few others chase 'em off. I'm overwhelmed with feelings, but the one that's the strongest is...

—I turn to see Skye standing, still shaking—

—turning toward me, and there ain't no tears on her face—

—and her face ain't torn and broken, no, it's strong, like mine—

—'cause in that moment I realize she's feeling *exactly* what I'm feeling:

. . .

. . .

RAGE.

~~~

I can't believe they just left the bodies in the desert. I've said it 'bout three times and thought it a million. Even when we defeated the Glassies when they attacked our village, we disposed of their bodies. They were still people, after all, and no one deserves to become the next meal for a scavenger.

But the Glassies couldn't be bothered to do more'n loot the carts and the bodies, taking everything of value—there ain't a weapon to be seen—and leaving 'em to the crows.

Evil.

Searin' evil.

As I've been helping to carry, pull, and drag the bodies into one place, I've let my rage subside, dropping the anger into a hole somewhere deep within me, somewhere hidden. I'll save it, let it simmer…until I need it.

Skye carries Dazz's large, strong body herself, over her shoulder, refusing help, like it's her duty. I think we're all a little afraid she'll bite our hands off if we ignore her and try to help anyway.

Instead, I help Wilde carry Buff, and then Dazz's mother. Her cheeks are streaked with tears but she doesn't say anything, just gets on with it.

Afterwards, as we continue to search through the dead, I find her. Jolie. Dazz's sister. She's almost Jade's age, but her skin's white like snow where my sister's is as brown as a bog hole. I try not to look down as I pick her up in my arms, but I can't help it. Wow. She takes my breath away and shatters my heart with just that one peek, 'cause she looks so peaceful, angelic, her face unmarked, unbloodied, her eyes closed and her mouth turned up in an almost—is that a smile? What'd give her cause to smile even as her family and friends were being slaughtered, I may never know, but maybe, just maybe, as she was dying, as the life was draining out of her—too soon, far too soon—she was seeing something that the rest of us living folk can't. Something beyond this world: a better place, a better life, where folks don't go 'round killing each other. A place where there ain't sandstorms and the Fire and Killers. Maybe she could see her brother, Wes, who died trying to save her life, and her father, dead years earlier from the Cold. Maybe she could even see Dazz, who'd died moments earlier protecting her. And if they were all beckoning to her, showing her this magical place where no one's dead, then why wouldn't she be smiling even as she took her last breath?

Even as I'm setting her down with the rest of the bodies, I'm wondering: Do any of us have cause to fear death? It's not like we should be seeking it out, but if it comes to us, should we spend our last moments screaming and crying and worrying over it, or should we do like Jolie did, and smile, one last time, letting happiness form on our faces for ever and ever?

I almost share what I think with Skye, but unlike me, her rage is still rippling over the surface of her skin, forming a hard shell on her face, filling her already strong body with extra power.

She carries two bodies, one over each shoulder, past me and adds 'em to the growing pile. I know she sees Jolie, 'cause she hesitates for just a moment, but then she goes back to collecting the dead. She don't want nothing to distract her from her anger.

When the bodies're all t'gether, all piled up, we do what we hafta do. It's a risk, setting a big ol' fire in the dark, but these people are our friends, our neighbors, our allies, and whatever bad decision someone made for 'em to march out 'ere in the desert don't change that.

If the Glassies see the flames licking high over the dunes, notice the puffs of dark smoke creating a cloud above us, well, they can come, and sun goddess help 'em if they do. I wouldn't be surprised if Skye, the way she is now, killed every last one of 'em.

Wilde says a few words, but they're lost to me as I watch the bodies burn, Circ's arm 'round my waist. I'm hoping with every beat of my shattered heart that whatever Jolie saw when she died is where she is now.

'Cause maybe that means I'll see my mother again someday, too.

And when I get up, Circ doesn't say anything, doesn't try to stop me. I plonk down next to Skye and I know she wants to be alone, but I ain't letting her, rage or no rage. I put my arm 'round her and her body is so hard, all clenched muscles and protruding bones and I can feel her stiffen even more beneath my touch. But she doesn't try to stop me, just lets me hold her, even if she doesn't have it in her to hold back.

We stay there like that, just being sisters, for long after everyone's gone to bed and the fire has dwindled down to a hot pile of ash.

Just being sisters.

~~~

The morning is full of heaviness, as if we're weighed down by the thick yellow clouds hanging low in the sky. Clouds're s'posed to be light, ain't they? After all, they float, don't they? Well, these ones look like they're full of boulders, doing everything they can not to fall from the sky, crushing everything beneath 'em.

It don't take any of us long to eat a few bites of breakfast and pack up to go. The pile of ash is still there, but there's less of it, the night winds scattering the Icers, carrying what's left of 'em off into the desert to become a part of the dunes.

And Skye's still frowning, shredding holes in everyone with her eyes. I know she ain't angry at us, but I still duck and shimmy to try to stay outta the way of that stare of hers. You can never be too careful these days.

"Day three," I say to Circ as he shoulders his pack.

"About time," he says, like he's been wishing it here from the beginning.

"You can't protect me the whole time during the battle," I say.

"I can try," he says, warming the pieces of my broken heart.

"Side by side?" I say.

"Where we belong."

We leave, heading further east, Circ and me walking hand in hand, knowing that today we'll either die in defeat or live in victory, and for some reason, the details don't matter nearly as much as they used to.

We don't get far 'fore we hear it.

"What is that?" I say, and I hear similar questions being asked along the column.

"Oh, blaze," Circ says.

My first thought is: the Glassies are coming; they saw the fire and smoke and they've been riding through the night to ambush us in the morning.

But it's not the growl of a fire chariot or the boom from a fire stick that we're hearing. It's high-pitched and coming from a dozen mouths, one after another.

Everyone's stopped now, looking to the south, past the mountains of dunes that block our vision more'n a half mile or so.

Yips. That's the only way to describe the noises we're hearing. And that means only one thing: Cotees.

As I pull my bow off my back and fit it with a pointer, I'm almost excited. No one's gonna die. A Cotee pack, even a large one, won't stand a chance in scorch against the size of our force. Consider it a warm up for the fight with the Glassies.

Those 'round me are drawing their weapons, too, swords and knives and bows. Circ's blade screeches out of its scabbard.

I aim at the top of a large dune, waiting impatiently.

The yips grow louder, a chorus of voices, loud and sharp and desperate. They *are* desperate, I remember. The tug hurds are gone, finished off by the Glassies, so they've got nothing to eat, least nothing sustaining. They've been driven from their homes, in search of food.

Wait. The noise gets louder still and something 'bout it doesn't sound quite right…

They're making more noise'n I've ever heard a single pack of Cotees make. And maybe it ain't the cry of a dozen mouths, or even two dozen, maybe it's a hundred, some kind of a super-pack.

I hold my breath—wait.

The animals appear over the dunes, not stopping even when they see how many of us there are. Instead, they pour down the hill, yipping even more, almost like the sight of potential food gives 'em energy. And there ain't hundreds of 'em…

…there's thousands.

I loose a pointer and I can't see where it lands in the army of Cotees, so close t'gether it's near impossible to tell where one animal ends and the next begins.

A bunch of people are screaming now and I can see some of 'em turning to run, but most stay, I think. I don't look though, as I'm trying to block everything out 'cept nocking another pointer and aiming and—

My bow sings and a Cotee at the front drops, cutting a line through the animals as they stumble and crash over it.

They're getting closer, the air filled with pointers. Surely some of 'em must be dying, but it's impossible to tell 'cause there's so searin' many of 'em. Even as I shoot again, I see Circ's hand tighten on the handle of his sword beside me.

Will we really die now? Having come this far, having endured so much?

I load, aim, shoot, right into the snapping jaws of a big one, with gaunt cheeks, saliva crusted on its maw. Desperate and starving and now dead.

Drawn by.......what?

It hits me. Perhaps the funeral fire last night wasn't bright enough or high enough to draw the attention of the Glassies, but with the wind blowing hard south like it was, surely the scent woulda carried a long way, reaching the noses of this army of Cotees, whipping 'em into a frenzy of hunger.

Making 'em run all night till they reached us. And now they want to eat us.

My next pointer rips into a Cotee's eye, jerking him back and leaving him twitching on the durt.

They're too close now and I frantically swing my bow 'round my neck, withdraw a pair of short knives, even as Circ is pulling his sword back, preparing to...

He swings and so do I, snapping my knives forward in quick succession, jamming 'em into the neck of a leaping beast, feeling warm blood spatter on my face as it lands on me, its fur swallowing me up like a blanket.

"Siena!" Circ shouts, but I can't answer him 'cause I'm eating matted, smelly fur and tasting coppery blood from the dual wounds I inflicted.

People are screaming to the left, to the right, behind and in front; some are cries of war, of violence, of attack, and others, well, they're the screams that nightmares are made of.

I gotta get up, but I'm drowning under the carcass of my victim. "Argh!" I cry out when I feel something grab my ankle, its teeth sinking in deep, cutting into me. I kick at it, shake my leg, try to dislodge it, and the pressure releases. The dead Cotee falls off of me.

Circ grabs my wrist, my hands still clutching the knives. He doesn't have time to say anything 'cause there's a shadow jumping at him—

—and he turns

—and slashes

—and the dismembered head of the attacking Cotees goes flying past me, spraying crimson life in a surreal arc.

My ankle's on fire, but it ain't gonna kill me, and there's more Cotees running toward us. I throw down my knives and draw my bow in a flash, sending two pointers off in short succession, ending the miserable lives of a pair of mangy Cotees.

A third one leaps over its dead comrades and is coming right at me and I'm struggling to nock another pointer and Circ is too far away, slicing at three or four Cotees that are surrounding him…

Acting on instinct without really knowing what I'm doing, I drop my bow—the Cotee's leaping at me now—and fall backward. As the Cotee is flying over me, I shove the pointer in my hand up as hard as I can, feeling my wrist bend backwards when the momentum of the beast carries it past me.

I leap to my feet, stumbling slightly as my two left feet both decide to turn the same way, but maintaining my balance enough to see the Cotee slump over and die, the feathers of my pointer sticking out of its flesh, right above where its heart should be.

My bow's at my feet, and I grab it, fit another pointer, whirl 'round to locate another Cotee, and see—

Circ's down, animal bodies piled on all sides, a beast chewing on his foot and another on his arm, even as he's slashing at 'em with his sword. I'm not thinking, just acting, like that time I almost got us both killed during that Killer attack so long ago. But this time I have something to offer more'n my two left feet and tentpole skinniness.

I shoot and shoot and shoot, the first pointer cutting into a Cotee's ear, the second into one of their eyes, and the third, well, that one goes right down the throat of another Cotee that was looking to bite Circ in the head.

Circ's still slashing at them, yelling himself hoarse, not realizing they're already dead. I rush to him, crying, "Circ, Circ!" and he stops, looks over.

His eyes widen and I spin 'round, thinking maybe he sees something scary behind me, like a dozen Cotees snarling and leaping, but there's nothing. The last few Cotees are dying at the hands of Skye, who seems to be the only one still fighting, like she's somehow attracting the final, desperate attackers. I watch her slash one across the neck and impale another one through the gut 'fore I turn back to Circ.

He's clutching at his arm and at his leg at the same time, which is 'bout as awkward as I've ever seen Circ look, but he's smiling while he's doing it. If my heart weren't still pounding so much and if I weren't still hearing the cries of the injured, I'd almost want to laugh at how wooloo he looks amongst a sea of fur, lying all crooked like that.

Instead I drop my bow and go to him, help him escape his furry prison, pull him down in a patch of empty durt.

I check his leg first, and it's not too bad, no worse'n my leg. A few bite marks, yeah, but we're Heaters, not some weakling group of pale-faced Glassies. His arm is worse, and I can see from the way he's holding it that it hurts something fierce.

"Am I gonna live?" Circ asks.

"Maybe, maybe not," I say, hiding my smile.

"I hope it's maybe," he says. "I'd miss you too much."

I touch his durty, blood-spattered cheek. "You'll live forever," I say.

Thirty-Six
Tristan

Even as the Sun Realm appears to be exploding from within, I rain down death upon the enemy. They fall before me, and even as their return fire whizzes over my head and skips off the ground next to me, I keep firing. Who am I to hide and live when those who would stand with me are falling and dying around me?

The black wall is advancing, moving up the hill toward us. I'm aware that it's not all of them, because the rest are heading the other direction, trying to hold off the moon and star dwellers pouring out of the tunnel. We have them surrounded but they still seem to have the advantage in numbers.

Something bites me in the left shoulder and I cry out, rolling behind the truck and clutching at my torn uniform, now slick with blood. Gritting my teeth, I look through the hole, seeing a chunk of flesh missing from my arm. A flesh wound, I think. The bullet went clean through.

My back against the truck, I watch men and women shooting past me at the enemy, their faces full of determination. One falls, then another. Not flesh wounds. Death wounds.

Taking a deep breath, I roll out, shooting with my good arm. But it's pointless; there are too many and they keep on coming, climbing over the dead like the bodies are sacks of dirt on an obstacle course. They're so close now that some of them are drawing swords, preparing for the hand-to-hand combat that's becoming more and more inevitable.

Their mouths are contorted into snarls, their eyes full of anger and violence, and they're running, running, shooting, and then suddenly...

They stop.

All of them as one, as if responding to a command. Just stop.

A few shots ring out, from both sides, but then even the shooting stops.

What the...?

The enemy soldiers are staring off to the right, down a side street, where—now that it's quiet, I hear it—the sound of a drum tap tap taps out a rhythm. But it's not just a drum; there are voices, too. Many voices, singing a song so familiar it's like coming home or seeing Roc or swinging a sword...

The Tri-Realms anthem.

A hundred, no, a thousand voices just belting it out, raising their voices as one, stopping the entire freaking battle in its tracks, like a pregnant woman crossing the street will stop traffic. I stand, step forward, toward an enemy who could shoot me dead in an instant, in awe of what I'm hearing.

There's still a mix of firing and explosions beyond, closer to the tunnel entrance, but even that slows and then stops as the song gets closer and louder. I take another step forward, drawn by the music.

In front of me there's shouting and grumbling and the wall of black slowly parts, opens up, making way for...

General Aboud.

He's waving a gun in each hand, pointing them at his own soldiers, threatening them to "Move aside or die!"

And when he steps out he looks right at me, narrowing his eyes, but then, even his anger is drawn away by the sound of the singing voices. "What is the meaning of this?" he says, turning to look down the street, but then he takes a step back, shocked by whatever he sees that we cannot.

He raises his arms, both weapons aimed down the street toward the singing. "Go home!" he shouts. "This is not your place!"

I raise my weapon, center my aim on Aboud's side, hesitate. If I start shooting, everyone might start shooting, and whatever happens, I don't want whoever is singing the Tri-Realms anthem to get caught in the crossfire.

I wait. Aboud yells, "Go home!" again, but the singing continues, so loud now it's practically on top of us.

Aboud takes another step back. And then...

A line of drummers emerges into the intersection, hammering out a beat, their heads held high, their backs straight, their eyes on Aboud. And behind them...

A line of people, then another, and another. Marching as one. Singing, singing, singing their hearts out.

"I'm warning you!" Aboud says, but everyone can hear it now. The doubt in his voice. The false promise.

The drummers surround him, and between the flash of their drumsticks I see Aboud drop his guns, cover his ears. The people are sun dwellers. Not soldiers, just everyday citizens, come out from hiding in their lavish homes to show us all where they stand. And where they stand is clearer than the red sky on the earth's surface:

They stand for Unity.

Hundreds upon hundreds of people, men and women and children, young and old, crippled and whole, pour onto the street that's become a warzone, splitting in both directions, surrounding the soldiers on both sides. A graying man with soft eyes grabs my arm, which I realize is still up, still aiming my gun into the crowd, and gently pushes it down, until my trembling fingers release their grasp and let my weapon fall to the ground with a clatter.

"President Nailin," he says, and I can see that while the look on his face is one of confidence, his eyes are wet. "No more. Be at peace."

And then he moves on, leaving me stunned, gone to disarm the next soldier.

Many of the people are carrying medical supplies, bottles of antiseptics and bandages and gurneys. They go to the wounded, to the dead, begin tending to them. I'm in awe.

Even over the singing and drumming, I can hear Aboud yelling and screaming and there's a commotion around the drummers. "Come with me," I shout to a soldier who's standing, weaponless, watching in amazement as the singing people walk by him. "You and you, too," I add to two others who look just as shocked by the whole thing.

They follow me as I push through the crowd, forcing my way toward the drummers. When we're close, one of them falls back, his drum thudding hollowly on the ground. Aboud stumbles through the gap. "You!" he shouts at me when he sees me, his finger pointed at my head. "You did this!"

But I didn't. All I did was ask the people...

It hits me. My words, they were a cry, a final plea for—

For Unity.

But I never expected...I didn't think...it's more and more and more than I could've ever hoped for. It shows that the sun dwellers are not my father, that they have minds that can think and make their own decisions and unite as one.

I stride toward General Aboud, stopping a few feet from him. "Aboud, you are under arrest for igniting a civil war in the Tri-Realms."

The three soldiers step past me, grab Aboud by the arms, pull them firmly behind his back. He's smart enough not to fight it. He knows when he's been beaten, not by bullets or soldiers, but by hearts.

A young woman steps up to me as Aboud is being led away. Her eyes are pale blue and she has hair as red as a sky she's never seen. "President Nailin," she says.

"Yes?" I say.

"Do it," she says, handing me a bullhorn.

I take it automatically, surprised, wondering what she means. But of course. I'm the leader. Someone needs to tell them what to do next. I look around, trying to find somewhere they'll be able to see me.

"Here," the young woman says, motioning to a wooden slab—a door, I realize, ornately carved and which probably cost a fortune for the sun dweller whose house it adorned, broken off its hinges and being carried through the crowd. A dozen people step forward to hold it up. Two of the drummers set down their instruments and offer me their hands to step into.

They lift me up onto the red door.

A hush falls over the crowd, except for a shout from somewhere near the tunnel, where I can see the uniforms of moon and star dweller soldiers making their way into the city. "He's going to speak!" the voice shouts.

So many people. All looking up, all looking to me, all listening to what I'll say.

What will I say exactly?

Of all people, it's Roc who pops into my mind, his advice to speak from the heart hitting me in the gut.

I raise the bullhorn to my lips. "The citizens of the Tri-Realms have spoken!" I shout. A cheer rises up from the crowd, although even as I scan the people, I can see those wearing the black clothes aren't smiling, aren't cheering—many of them are shrinking back, toward the edges, as if they might run.

"Let me first address those who fought against us, who followed the orders of General Aboud and the other rogue generals. You will not be punished!" The cheering stops in shocked silence.

One of my own red-clad soldiers looks up at me. He's carrying the body of a boy who looks far too young to be wearing a uniform. "They killed my brother," he says.

I put the bullhorn down to speak directly to him. "I'm sorry," I say, chasing away the swell of emotion that threatens to overcome me. "I can't bring him back, but together we can honor him by forgiving the soldiers who were only following orders given to them by those who would destroy us all."

Tears are running down his cheeks, but he's nodding. "I will honor him," he says.

Turning back to address the crowd, I say, "We need every last one of us to unite if we're to defeat the madness that's sweeping across the surface of the earth. President Lecter seeks to control you, to keep you underground, as my father did, and as his father did before him, but we can't let that happen. You all deserve the truth, and the choice to live where you want, whether it be deep underground or above, where the birds sing and the sun shines and the rain falls like water from heaven. Will you stand with me? Will you fight?"

There are cries of "Yes!" right away, but it's only when I see some of the black-clothed soldiers raise their fists in the air that I know my words have hit home. Although the Tri-Realms might still be a splintered mess, the Capitol at least, is united.

I step down, the world around me darkening as the artificial sun turns off and the moon and stars blink on. Night has fallen over day two in the Tri-Realms.

~~~

The reports are coming in fast from all over the Sun Realm. Bands of citizens, pouring from their homes, singing, surrounding the army splinter groups. In most cases the renegade soldiers didn't know what to do, who to shoot at. They allowed themselves to be disarmed. In some cases, however, the mutinous combatants opened fire on the innocents, killing many. Eventually, sickened by their own actions, they turned on each other, ending the battles quickly. Many died on this day that will be remembered in all history as the day the Tri-Realms was united, but many more survived because of the brave actions of ordinary men and women who found it in their hearts to be extraordinary.

A miracle like this doesn't just happen without planning, and this was no exception. It was planned over the communication network, starting as just an idea that spread like wildfire. While we were planning our assault on the renegades, the citizens were planning to stop it.

The moon and star dweller soldiers are now spread out throughout the many chapters of the Sun Realm. Like the sun dweller army, they're awaiting my orders.

It's late; I'm tired. My shoulder's bandaged, but it's nothing compared to the many injured who will lose limbs or maybe worse. I drop the reports on the desk, sit back and sigh. Was today one major stroke of luck? Or did it just prove everything that Ben Rose believed in, that the Tri-Realms were always meant to be united?

Even as I'm chewing on the question, Roc comes in. I've had him running around all over the place, carrying messages for me. There's simply not enough time to meet with everyone I need to meet with.

"Lowly messenger boy reporting for duty," he says, raising a hand in salute. I roll my eyes, but laugh inwardly. Without fail, he's been doing that every time he's come back from carrying a message.

"That's it for now," I say. "What did the lead scientist say about the transporters?"

"He's coming here," Roc says. "Now."

"Now?" It's got to be three in the morning.

"He said he has something to tell you. Something important."

I raise my eyebrows. "And he wouldn't give you any details?" I ask.

"He said he couldn't tell secrets to a lowly messenger boy," Roc says, keeping a straight face.

"You know, not that long ago I left you in charge of the entire Tri-Realms."

"How far I have fallen," Roc says.

"You did abandon your post within just a few days."

"To find your sorry as—"

There's a knock on the side of the doorframe. A bald man steps in. "Sorry to interrupt," he says. There are dark circles under his eyes.

"Dr. Kane," I say. "Meet my best friend, Roc."

The two shake hands. Roc says, "Lowly messenger boy will leave you to it. Goodnight."

"Say hi to Tawni for me," I say.

Roc leaves and Dr. Kane immediately moves to close the door behind him.

"Have a seat," I say with a wave.

Or not. Dr. Kane remains standing.

"I think your father lied to you about something else," he says.

"Shocking," I say, wondering when I'll really know everything that my father knew. Probably never. I think back to the message I had Roc take to Dr. Kane. I wanted to know how long it would take to transport ten thousand troops to the surface using the two small transporters we've got. What could he possibly have lied about? That they can only be used seven times before they self-destruct?

"Your message seemed to imply that you know of only two earth Cylinders." Cylinders! That's what they're called. I knew there was a fancy name for them.

"Yes," I say. "You're saying there's a third…Cylinder that my father didn't tell me about?"

Dr. Kane laughs, his face lifting into a jovial expression that seems out of place on his usually serious face. "A third? No, not a third."

Then what? "I'm not following," I say.

"Did you really think your father would allow Lecter to win?" Kane asks.

I let his words sink in for a moment. My father was a lot of things—cruel, evil, maniacal—but he was anything but a fool. He knew when he was beat. He had two Cylinders and Lecter controlled the exit for one of them, as well as the New City and its citizens. Plus, my father had a good thing going as leader of the Tri-Realms. But he *did* hate to lose.

"You're saying he was plotting to overthrow him?"

Dr. Kane claps his hands together like I'm a baby who's just said his first word. "President Nailin, your father, hated Lecter with a passion."

"At least we had one thing in common," I say.

He continues as if I hadn't spoken. "And he knew the one major advantage he had was in numbers. The New City was a fledgling compared to the mighty eagle your father commanded. A mass attack by a significant portion of the sun dweller army would undoubtedly be successful."

I rub my forehead, fighting the urge to close my eyes. "Yeah, but without a third transporter, a bigger one, there's no way he'd be able to get enough troops to the surface. Look, Dr. Kane, it's great getting an inside look at my father's twisted mind, but I really don't have time—"

"There's not just a *third* Cylinder," Kane says, cutting me off, "there's a fourth and a fifth and as many as there are subchapters in the Sun Realm." He smiles broadly, looking as fresh as if it was the middle of the day and not the middle of the night.

"What?" I blurt out. "You mean…" He can't mean…

"To answer the question from your message, we can get ten thousand soldiers to the surface in about five hours."

I stare straight ahead, wondering whether I fell asleep at my desk, dreaming about miracles, like the sun dweller citizens coming to save us. I want to pinch myself, but I resist the urge. "There are thirty-seven Cylinders," I say. "One in each of the subchapters and two in the Capitol." It's not a question, so Kane doesn't answer. But he doesn't deny it either. I continue thinking out loud. "And the thirty five that are outside the Capitol, they're much larger?" I do some quick math in my head. "They can carry fifty, sixty soldiers?"

Kane nods. "Fifty," he says.

"Holy crap," I breathe.

"That's what I thought you might say. Shall I get them prepped and manned?"

"Hell yeah," I say.

With a curt, businesslike nod, Dr. Kane exits, leaving me stunned, gripping the desk with two hands. I was expecting an answer more like *never*—not five hours. With only the two small Cylinders we could've only transported twenty to thirty soldiers an hour. We wouldn't even have a force worth attacking with until long after the Tri-Tribes had attacked and been massacred. And Adele? She'd be left on the inside with Lecter, to die a spy's death the moment she was discovered.

But now…

Now we can attack with numbers, destroy the Glassy army, and take down the madman at the helm!

I realize I'm standing, my chest buzzing with excitement, my hands clenched at my sides. I'm thankful there's not a mirror in front of me, because if there was, who would I see? Would I see Tristan, son of Jocelyn Nailin, fighting for the good of the people? Or would I see Tristan, son of President Nailin, seeker of power and control?

I shake my head. No. No. This isn't about power; it never was. I don't even want to be the president. I just want this to be over, to go back to getting to know Adele, to building a relationship with her that doesn't include secret missions and assassinations and the end of the world.

Taking a deep breath, I unfurl my fingers, bring them up and run them through my hair, which is longer than it's ever been. When this is all over, I'll get a haircut.

Exiting my father's old office, I make my way out of the governmental side of the palace and into the place I used to call home, where my memories are a collage of happy and sad moments, built on the foundation of a loveless marriage that ended in my mother's death. In the foyer is the photograph that was always my favorite, the one where my father looks like he'd rather be anywhere else, a rare moment where he was captured as he truly was. My brother, my mother, and I are all smiling, laughing, happy.

I grab it and smash it on the ground, scattering chips of glass around my feet. I extract the photo, stare at it for a second, and then tear it about a quarter of the way from the left. Setting down the larger piece on a table, I stare at the small strip in my hands. My father's angry, bored eyes look back at me.

"Bastard," I say, and then rip it once, twice, and again and again until the stack of paper's too thick for me to shred with my bare hands. A strange energy running through me, I toss the pieces in the air, letting them fall like rain around my shoulders, all the way to the floor, where they mingle with the broken glass.

I leave my father in pieces on the floor, taking the rest of my dead family with me to my bedroom, where I set the picture reverently on the table beside the bed.

As the wall clock flips over to four in the morning, I pull back the covers and crawl in, fully clothed, hoping to catch a few hours' sleep before day three really begins.

Thirty-Seven
Adele

I take her hand, which is cold and clammy. Even as she pulls me through the window, I can't stop staring at her, the dead woman before me. I can't reconcile what I'm seeing with President Nailin's words ringing in my ears, mocking Tristan even as he destroyed every last bit of childish hope he had left: *I killed her with my bare hands! And I loved watching the life drain out of her face; loved kissing her lips as I held her down and she took her last breath; loved feeling her body go cold as we lay in bed together one last time.*

It never happened. He lied about Tristan's mom. Not dead. Not murdered. Here, in the New City, in…Lecter's house? But why?

Even as she closes the window behind us, I whirl on her, anger bright in my eyes. "What are you doing here?" I accuse.

"Adele, it's not what you—"

I'm not listening to excuses, to more lies. "He thinks you're dead, you know? It crushed him, destroyed him, broke him. Even after your...husband"—I spit out the word—"was dead, he grieved for you."

There's genuine shock on her face. "Edward's dead?" she says.

"Sorry to break it to you," I say, still feeling flushed.

"Thank God," she says. I look around the room, trying to distract my anger. There's no time for this, no time for voices from the dead, no time for a woman who abandoned her children to the whims of an evil man.

Like everywhere else, the room is small and bland. But it does have a real bed, decent size, too, taking up most of the space. There's a pillow on the floor beside it, along with a blanket. Were those thrown there in haste when she heard the gunshots, or was she sleeping on the floor?

"Adele," Jocelyn says, cutting off my internal question. She's biting her lip and her eyes are wet, though no tears have fallen.

I take a deep breath. "I'm sorry I snapped at you," I say. "Tristan will be beyond excited that you're alive. I'm glad you're alive. But..." I let the thought float away.

"But you think it's pretty screwed up that I've gone from one dictator's bed to another's?" she asks, a tear finally falling.

I lift a hand to my mouth. She can't mean...she's not...she can't possibly be saying that...

"It's not what you think," she says quickly. "Well, not exactly what you think. I'm a prisoner here. When I ran from my husband, I didn't know where to go that he wouldn't look for me. I realized the earth's surface was the one and only place, so I came above, asked to become a part of the new society, not realizing what Lecter was creating here. I had hoped to return later for Tristan and Killen, but…"

"They let you in and wouldn't let you out." I'm still shocked that she's standing in front of me. "But you're here."

"Borg was so welcoming," she says, and I cringe at the way she says his name, like it's so familiar, that of an old friend…or more. "He helped me get on my feet, showed me around, ate meals with me…" She sits on the bed, but I remain standing.

There are more shouts outside and I glance at the window. "They won't look for you here," she says. "At least not right away. Here I might as well be dead, and sometimes I wish it."

"Don't say that," I say, for Tristan's sake, although I'm still mildly disturbed by the gentle way she had recounted her memories of Lecter.

She shrugs, as if talk of suicide is a part of her daily life. "I started asking questions when what I was seeing around the city didn't look right. The people, despite being the first in hundreds of years to live on the earth's surface, were unhappy. They depended on Borg for everything. He was in complete control." Her tone changes. Gone is the lightness. "I demanded to know the truth, and you know what? He told me. Every last detail. How he wanted to control everything, to create more cities like this one, to destroy the savages from off the face of the earth. I tried to run, to get away, to go back down to find my children, but his guards grabbed me and brought me here. I've been living here ever since."

"You're a prisoner," I say.

"Just like everyone else in this twisted city," she says, pursing her lips, which are now wet with tears. "Borg's a monster, and I fell for his charms just like I did for Edward's. I'm a fool."

Although I'm still confused and in a semi-state of shock, I can't watch Tristan's mother—who is very much alive—crying like that. The woman who brought me and her son together. The woman who loved her son enough to give him a chance at a different life. The one who gave Tristan his only truly happy childhood memories.

I sit down on the bed, wrap a tentative arm around her, and hold her as she silently weeps.

Suddenly her body stiffens and her head jerks to look at me. "You can stay here for a while, but not forever," she says. "They're looking for you; eventually they'll find you."

I stare at her. "Of course they're looking for me. I just killed three presidential guards. But they don't know who I am."

"They do," she says. She reaches over and snatches a controller off a table. It looks like the one in the room I'm staying in. She presses a button and one of the walls brightens. A vid screen.

"What are you doing?" I ask. Strange time to be watching the news.

I gasp when the image appears. Because it's…it's…

It's me.

~~~

Crap, crap, crap. This is not good. Beneath the photo that was taken at the *Get Chipped!* offices, is my false name, Tawni Sanders, and the words "Armed and Dangerous." At least they got that part right.

But how?

The image changes to a news report. A woman wearing a black dress and bright red lipstick speaks:

"The two soldiers who had been missing for days have been found. They were tied up in an electrical room in the army medical building. Suffering from severe dehydration and malnourishment, they're being treated as we speak. However, they have confirmed that the girl you saw on screen a moment earlier is their attacker. The army has not yet speculated on the reasons for her actions, except to say, 'She's a seriously disturbed girl.' President Lecter himself has urged all citizens to assist in the identification and capture of the girl calling herself Tawni Sanders, and a reward will be considered for information leading to her arrest. According to sources close to the investigation, Miss Sanders' chip was found moments ago in the room that was registered in her name. Somehow she'd managed to extract it and leave the building, suggesting assistance from another citizen."

The woman glances to the left, cups a hand to her ear. "What's that?" she says to someone off-camera. "Okay, okay." She turns back to face the screen. "This just in. We've just received reports of a dead night watchman. There are also rumors of three dead guards at the presidential quarters. Although no official statement has been issued, there are suspicions that the murders are linked to Tawni Sanders. More as this story evolves."

The image flashes back to my photo. Crap.

"The story has been looping for a while now," Jocelyn says, pressing a button that turns the volume off but leaves the video on. "Each time there's more information."

"Crap," I say aloud.

"What are you doing here?" Jocelyn asks.

Does she mean on the surface of the earth, in the New City, or in her room? I've got to tell her everything that's happened, but she's not off the hook yet.

"Look, I'll tell you what you need to know, but first I need some answers."

Jocelyn looks shocked. Since I crawled through her window I've snapped at her, held her while she cried, and now I've come full circle.

"You're so much like your mother," she says. Not what I expected her to say. "What happened to her?"

"She's fine," I say. "She's a general in the Lower Realms army. When my father died, she led the Resistance." I feel a swell of pride for the woman who raised me.

"That doesn't surprise me," Jocelyn says, and I feel a smile tug at the corners of my lips. "She was always a strong woman."

"So are you," I find myself saying. "You defied your husband, took a chance, did something crazy and unpredictable—we thought you were dead. Nailin told us you were dead."

She shakes her head. "I learned very early on in my relationship with Edward that you could never trust any words that passed from his throat through his lips. Even his body language was a lie most of the time."

"Tristan has to know; we've got to get you out..."

"Impossible. There's no leaving once you're here," Jocelyn says.

I feel something under my foot, on the floor. The pillow. The blanket. "Why are you sleeping on the floor?" I ask. The bed feels very comfortable, much better than the tiny beds in Lin and Avery's building.

She looks away. "I'm a prisoner," she says, which doesn't answer my question at all, and makes even less sense.

"You're a prisoner who can open your window? What's to stop you from climbing down and escaping?" I'm missing something. Something big. What is she not telling me?

"I—I've been slowly getting my privileges back," she says. I can barely see the tear that slips down her cheek. "Borg, he—when I found out the truth, and I slapped him, and I ran…he stuck me in a cell barely big enough to squeeze into, didn't feed me for a week. Gave me a squeeze of water from a sponge each day, dribbled it personally into my burning mouth. He—he thought he broke me."

My God. "But he didn't?" I ask, hoping I'm right. Tristan's mother seems weak, damaged, but not broken. Not yet anyway.

When she looks back at me, there's a fire in her eyes I haven't seen yet. Even with hot tears running down her cheeks she looks angry, strong. "No. I'm pretending. Day by day, hour by hour, minute by minute, I'm showing him that I've changed. And he rewards me. This room. An open window. He knows I can't escape because of the glass walls and the armed guards at the front. But one day he'll make a mistake, and then I'll be gone."

Not broken at all. Chipped a little, maybe, but not broken. She still hasn't answered my question. I motion to the floor.

She raises a fisted hand to her mouth, bites lightly on her knuckle, closes her eyes. "He makes me do things on this bed," she says. "The nightmares never end when I try to sleep on it."

I'm on my feet in an instant, my entire body tight and full of anger. I want to punch something—no, some*one*. Lecter. Borg, as this abused woman calls him. I stalk back and forth, staying out of view of the window. Why does she let him do this? If it was me, and he tried to so much as touch me, I'd freaking—

"I kicked him once," she says, snapping me out of my internal tirade. I turn to look at her.

She's wiping away the tears and nodding. "The first time he tried anything. I was playing along, trying to be congenial, acting like I didn't find him completely disgusting. He thought that meant I was…interested in him. He touched me, kissed me—and I let him. But then he took it a step further and I resisted. He grabbed me, his arms like iron. Shoved me down. Tried to climb on top of me. I kicked him, as hard as I could, right in his…"

"Stones?" I say.

She smiles. "Yes. It was the best feeling in the world, hurting him like that, seeing his face contorted with such pain."

It didn't end there. Surely she paid a price for her resistance. Her makeshift bed on the floor tells me that much. I don't ask, and she stands and turns away from me, so I think she's done talking. But then she grabs the sides of her white shirt and pulls it over her head.

I gasp, tears welling up and blinding the truth written all over her back in long, jagged scars. He beat the life out of her for that one kick.

When I've furiously blinked away the blurriness, she's got her shirt back on and has once more turned to face me. "I don't fear him anymore," she says. "He's taken everything he can from me. The only thing I fear is never being free of him, being his plaything for the rest of my life."

"That's not going to happen," I say. "Tristan is outside the Glass City. He's gathering an army of the natives. If I can find a way to get them inside the city, we will crush Lecter."

"My son," she says, and there's pure joy in her eyes. Knowing he's alive, that he's nearby. The best gift I could possibly give her without delivering her to him. "And Killen?" she says.

I shake my head. It shouldn't be me to tell her—it shouldn't be anyone.

"Tell me everything," she says. "Starting with how my husband died."

Thirty-Eight
Siena

The wounded've been bandaged, the dead've been buried. Surprisingly few died in the Cotee attack—maybe twenty—but no one avoided getting bitten or scratched. Except Skye, who, according to Feve, killed fifty Cotees herself. He said it was like the sun goddess had entered her body, giving her power and strength beyond her own. I'd say he was exaggerating if he wasn't talking 'bout Skye.

Grunt didn't die. He was one of the runners, turning tail the moment the Cotees came over the hill. I ain't blaming him—he ain't no warrior. I'm glad for him having the sense to let the fighters do the fighting. I couldn't bear to tell Veeva he didn't make it, 'specially 'fore we even got to the real battle. Hopefully most of our people stick around when it comes time to attack the Glassies.

We all know we've lingered 'ere too long. Nothing's changed. Tristan told us to attack on the third day. We hafta move.

Wilde leads us away from the piles of dead Cotees. If any of us survive the day, we'll come back to collect the meat. Though they tried to kill us, we won't disrespect 'em by letting their bodies go to waste.

I'm limping and Circ's trying to hide his limp. Hopefully a bit of walking will help the pain.

We head further east, making searin' sure that we come in from the northeast, where the Glassies'll least expect it. I'm hoping they'll think we're the ghosts of the Icers and drop their weapons and flee before us. If we had some mud paint and scary masks, maybe we could give it a go.

I'm 'bout to tell Circ my brilliant idea, when Wilde stops, her hand in the air. I crane my neck to see what's snatched her attention.

The forest. The huge, huge forest that extends all the way to storm country. And beyond that, to water country. We've reached the very eastern edge of fire country. Only one way to go now.

I grab Circ's hand and pull him to the front of the column, coming up next to Wilde and Skye. "So we head south now?" I ask.

"I thought I saw something," Wilde says absently.

"What kinda something?" I say.

She shakes her head. "Nothing. It was probably nothing."

"'Cause if it's a bunch of pale-faced Glassies, you should probably tell us," I say.

"It's okay. Let's keep moving. We'll angle our way to the edge of the forest from here." Wilde continues on, and we follow, but not until I catch Skye's eye.

"Did you see anything?" I ask her.

"No," she says. "If there was a Glassy to be seen, I'da seen him."

I don't doubt that.

The stretch of sand and durt 'tween us and the forest disappears a little with each step, until we're in the shadows of the trees, stretching out like dark clouds underfoot. I walk with Skye on one side and Circ on t'other. Wilde walks alone, and I swear she keeps flicking her eyes to the trees, like at any moment a Glassy fire chariot might burst through the leaves.

A bird chirps from a branch somewhere above us. Wilde stops, looks up.

"It was just a bird," I say. Why is Wilde being so paranoid?

"I just thought…" Wilde says. As if in response to the first bird, another one chirps further down. Wilde's eyes widen in horror.

The leaves rustle and there's a sharp whistle and a rush of air, and the pointer's coming so fast that we're all frozen…

Thunk!

Feather's protruding, the pointer sticks in the ground at our feet. "Get down!" Wilde yells and there's scrambling and scraping and the shriek of weapons being drawn, and I've got my bow out, pointer nocked, but there's nothing to shoot at but trees, and we're sitting 'zards out in the open desert like this.

Nobody moves. Nobody breathes. The forest is silent.

Then there's a laugh and I think we all 'bout jump outta our skins, 'cept maybe Skye, who don't seem to know the meaning of the word scared.

"Don't shoot," a voice says. It's as familiar as the durt stuck to my moccasins.

Nobody moves. Nobody breathes.

"Wilde, tell your shooters to relax."

Wilde looks at me, her mouth open slightly, dips her chin. And then, of all things, she stands. "Shooters! Stand down," she says.

I drop my bow 'cause there's something 'bout the voice in the woods…

A black-skinned girl steps from the tree cover, her dark robe floating 'round her heels. Holy tugballs! I know that girl, 'cause that girl is Sadie.

~~~

After the initial excitement dies down, we gather 'round to talk. The Stormer Riders are watering their horses and pretending like there's not a huge army of brown-skinned people setting in the durt, gawking at 'em.

I'm 'bout to burst with excitement and questions, but Circ's squeezing my hand so tight I know he's telling me to be patient. I ignore him. "Sadie, what in the name of the holy god of all things surprising are you doing here?" I ask.

Sadie looks at Wilde, who merely shrugs at her. "We've come to fight," she says.

"Fight who?" I ask, remembering the pointer stuck in the durt at Wilde's feet.

314

"Whoever needs to be fought," Sadie says. She looks at the giant Stormer setting beside her, Gard I think his name is.

"You can tell them," Gard says. "You were the one who garnered the support of the Riders."

"Well, it wasn't just me. Remy helped, too." She nods at the dark, lean guy setting on her other side, the one whose smile seems to come easier'n a hot day in fire country. If I remember correctly, they had some kinda a thing going, like what Circ and I have. "We talked a lot about what you"—Sadie gestures to Wilde—"said when you arrived in storm country. About how these people...the Glassies?...were threatening all the tribes. How they'd start in fire and ice country and then move to water and storm country. Remy and I decided we better do something about it before it came to all that."

"And then, unbeknownst to me, you convinced the vast majority of the Riders that this was the wisest course of action," Gard says. The twinkle in his eye doesn't match his words. Is he angry or does he find it funny?

"In the end you agreed, Father," says Remy.

"You could have talked to me first. I would have listened," Gard says.

"What difference does it make?" Sadie says. "We're here now, aren't we?"

I want to laugh at the almost identical look of embarrassment that flashes across Remy's and Gard's faces. But I don't 'cause I'm trying to be all serious the way Wilde and Skye are.

"We're glad you're here," Wilde says. She tells 'em about the Icers.

"Mother Earth," Sadie says. "This is real, isn't it?"

"Why are they doing this?" Gard says.

Wilde shrugs. "They fear what they don't understand."

"And their leader's a searin' baggard," I add helpfully.

"There's that, too," Wilde says, smiling grimly. "And what of the Soakers? Did they have an opinion?"

I lean in, curious for Jade's sake. After all, the last thing she did in storm country was kiss that Soaker boy, Huck Jones. If he's hiding in them trees, it'll be another person I'll have to protect. And the person I'll be protecting him from is Skye, who's leaning in too, her eyes gleaming.

"Admiral Jones agreed with us," Gard says. "He tried to convince the other captains but couldn't get a majority. After the way his father led, he refuses to force them to do anything they don't want to."

"I don't blame him," Wilde says. Skye and I lean back at the same time. I guess we'll be saving that fight for another time.

I glance at the sky above. Time's a-wastin'; the sun's already over its peak. Who knows where Tristan is, whether he'll come through for us, but we've gotta hold up our end of the bargain. "Uh, Wilde," I say.

"I know," she says. "We can't delay any further. It's time to move on the Glass City." We stand as one. "We'd be honored to fight with you by our sides," Wilde says to Gard, extending a slender hand.

Gard grabs it, his hand looking like that of a giant next to Wilde's. "We shall be victorious," he says.

"And go with honor and strength," Sadie says.

The way they say these words, I can tell they're more'n just words to 'em. They're important. Maybe they'll help us in some way we can't fully understand yet.

I think there's a lot I don't fully understand, that I haven't come to terms with. It's like I can't get my pebble-sized brain 'round the magnitude of what we're 'bout to do, like this is just another day and tomorrow I'll wake up and hug Circ and curse Perry and crack jokes with my sisters…

But it ain't just another day. This is THE DAY. More'n likely the last one. There's so much I need to do.

While the Stormer leaders go to organize the Riders, and Wilde and Feve begin preparing our people for the final leg of the journey, I grab Skye's arm. She looks at my hand and then at me. "Siena, don't," she says.

"I hafta," I say.

"You don't hafta do nothin'."

"Don't make me hurt you," I say, pulling her into a hug.

At first she struggles against me, all hard and sharp angles, but then she softens, squeezes back. "You ain't dyin'," she says.

"Then neither are you," I say.

Still locked in an embrace we pull back, looking at each other. "Siena, I—I might hafta put myself in more danger to do what I gotta do."

I glare at her. "I'll chase on after you wherever you go."

"Promise me you won't," she says.

"I can't," I say. "I ain't gonna live without you. Not again."

"Oh sun goddess," she says, trying to look angry but failing at it. "You can be so burnin' stubborn sometimes."

"I get it from you," I say. We hug once more and then she just walks away, toward the front, where Wilde and Feve are waiting.

Circ's standing nearby, the sun browning his skin and showing off the muscles of his bare chest. "Looking smoky," I say, whistling. "Just hanging out there looking pretty?" He should laugh. He'd usually laugh. He walks over. Serious Circ. "Don't," I say, realizing I sound just like Skye even as I say it.

317

"Don't what?" he says, putting an arm 'round me.

"Don't make a big thing outta this."

"Like you just did with Skye?" he says. "Siena, I'll make a big thing out of this, because it *is* a big thing. You are a big thing. You're everything."

"I'm just me," I say.

"You're all I want," Circ says. "All I ever wanted. And now…"

"Now you've got me and there ain't no fire-stick-wielding Glassy gonna change that. So let's give 'em scorch, you and me, just like the old days."

Finally, Circ laughs, 'cause he can't help it 'round me. "Okay," he says, pulling me into a big ol' hug.

A rumble of thunder and a cloud of dust fill the air as hundreds of Riders gallop past us, toward the front of the column. And still we go on holding each other, just a moment longer, then another. If this is the last time I'll ever hold him, I'd better make it good.

Finally, when my people have already started marching, and the Riders are leading the way, and the whole world is dangling from the edge of a cliff, we pull away.

The world can end now. I'm ready.

Thirty-Nine
Tristan

The transporters will make five trips to the surface, carrying fifty soldiers with each go. They'll be a mixture of sun, moon, and star dweller men and women, hand selected by the leaders in each subchapter. Although I've warned the leaders about the toxicity of the air, we've all agreed that masks won't be necessary for such a short amount of exposure. Soon we'll all either be dead or inside the filtered atmosphere of the Dome. In five hours we'll have nearly ten thousand troops positioned throughout the desert, all around the New City, surrounding it.

All the soldiers and their leaders have been briefed about what to expect up there, how hot it is, how big everything looks, but they won't fully appreciate it until they see it for themselves.

I don't know if it will be enough, but we can't risk delaying the attack any longer. If the people of the Tri-Tribes get there first…

I don't even want to think about the bodies in the sand. Seeing the Icers like that was enough tragedy for a lifetime.

I'm about to leave the palace when she walks in through the front door, like she owns the place. Her posture is upright, her face stern, her uniform unwrinkled. She's a leader and a soldier, through and through.

"I was wondering when I'd see you," I say.

"I was busy keeping my soldiers' emotions in check," General Rose says, "and I figured you were even busier." Then she smiles, and she's not a general, just a person, the mother of the girl I love. "Tristan, thank God you're alive."

To my surprise, she steps closer and hugs me, her embrace far warmer than I expected it to be. "Uh, thanks. You too."

"We'll find Adele, even if we have to smash every last pane of glass in the New City," she says. How does she know that behind my façade of leadership, my every waking, aching thought is of her daughter?

"I know," I say, even though I don't.

Pulling away, she says, "The first Capitol transporter just left for the surface. The other subchapters have sent theirs too." I'm amazed at how quickly she switches roles, from general to mother to friend, and back again, like they're cloaks she can swap in the blink of an eye.

"Good," I say. "We'll be on the last one."

She nods. "I want my daughter to be there," she says.

I don't understand. Where does she want Adele to be?

320

"Elsey," she clarifies. "She refuses to be left behind and I won't have it any other way. She marched to the Capitol with my soldiers, stayed at the very back with the medics and cooks."

"It's not safe," I say. "And there's only limited space. We need every—"

"—soldier we can fit," she says, finishing for me. "She's getting big, but I'm sure I can carry her on my shoulders for a half hour if I need to. This isn't a request."

I think of what it will mean to Adele to have her whole family together soon after we find her. "And she'll stay in the cave when we march on the city?"

"Of course," the general says.

"Done," I say. "Roc and Tawni can look after her."

"Did my nose just itch?" a voice says from the corridor. Roc walks in, holding Tawni's hand loosely.

Tawni immediately goes to Anna and hugs her. "I wasn't sure I'd ever see you in person again," Tawni says.

At that, General Rose laughs. "I might be getting old, but I'm still tough. And I suspect you're made of tougher stuff than anyone thinks."

"Trust me," Roc says, interjecting, "we all know the kind of stuff Tawni's made of. I can't say anything fresh without getting a palm print tattooed on my cheek."

"He gets slapped a lot," Tawni says.

"Why does that not surprise me?" Anna says.

"Because it's Roc," I say, without blinking.

"Soooo," Roc says, "why did I hear my name? And Tawni's too?"

"You're babysitting Elsey while the big kids go fight," I say. "You've been volunteered."

Roc frowns. "By whom?"

"Me," I say, punching him in the shoulder.

He sighs. "I'm sure my presence and wooden sword will be missed on the battlefield," he says, "but I *am* injured."

"Good," I say, glad to hear him agree without a fight. Even if everyone else I care about will be in danger today, at least Roc and Tawni and Elsey will be safe.

~ ~ ~

Time passes with the speed of an inter-Realm night train. Transporter after transporter leaves from what used to be the secret cave on the outskirts of the Capitol, and which now is as well known a place as the palace.

We cram as many soldiers as we can fit into each load, just like all the other subchapters are doing. The half-hour ride to the surface will be cramped and miserable, but surely no one's thinking about that right now.

I shake the hands of each man and woman that board the transporter, thanking them. It's strange to see sun dwellers and moon dwellers and star dwellers mixed together, like they're no different from one another, like they weren't trying to kill each other not so long ago. When I look into their eyes, I can't tell the difference. They're just people. Just soldiers. Why were they fighting in the first place? I'm not sure anyone really knows the answer.

I could have gone ahead with the first load because I've been to the surface before, but I'd rather make sure everything runs smoothly, that everyone leaves on schedule.

When the next to last transporter shoots up the glass tube, into the rock-lined tunnel, and out of sight, I sit with my back against the wall and close my eyes.

I see nothing but her. Her sparkling green eyes grim with determination. Her knuckles white as she grips the gun. A swirl of shimmering, obsidian hair as she turns, aims…

BOOM!

The eruption is sharp and real in my memory, but even it's a lie. When Adele shot the monster who was my father, I didn't even know it was happening because Roc was gasping for air, bleeding from a self-inflicted stab wound in his gut. Dying.

But not dead.

When I hear the camouflaged gate to the not-so-secret cave whir open, so do my eyes. The image of Adele's face fades as I blink away the false memory.

Tawni and General Rose enter, talking like old friends. Behind them, Elsey grips Roc's hand, swinging it. When she sees me, her eyes light up.

"Tristan!" she says.

She releases Roc and runs to me, her one arm swinging awkwardly and slightly off-balance, hugging me around the waist. As I squeeze her tightly to me, the gesture feels so…normal. Like I've hugged Adele's sister a million times over a million years. Like I've known her my whole life and like we never left to assassinate my father.

"I missed you, Else," I say, feeling my chest tighten at the sight of the stump that used to be an arm jerking and almost reaching out. Like it wants to hug me too, not understanding why it's not able to anymore, why it's not long enough to do so. Because of my father's command. The one that killed Ben and maimed Elsey.

"I missed you, too," she says, looking up. "I prayed for you every night."

I raise my eyebrows in surprise, still gritting my teeth at the memory of Elsey bleeding on the floor, screaming and screaming until the shock and the pain sent her into a fitful sleep. "You did?"

Elsey nods fervently. "You and Adele and Tawni and—"

"Not Roc?" I say, feigning astonishment. "Tell me you didn't pray for him, too."

She giggles and swats at me. "Of course I did. I prayed the most for Roc after he got hurt."

"He stabbed himself, you know."

"To save your sorry a—" Roc starts to say.

"Language," I say, cutting him off.

Elsey giggles again. "I've heard worse than that, you know," she says, matter-of-factly.

I'm sure she has. When her parents and Adele were dragged from their home and sentenced to life in prison, Elsey was taken to an orphanage in a rough part of the Moon Realm. Not an ideal place for a ten-year-old to grow up. I plaster a smile on, even though every muscle in my face is trying to pull my lips into a frown.

"Even still," I say, "Roc should be kept away from children whenever possible."

"I'm not a child," she says, hands on her hips. "And Roc is a perfect gentleman."

"See that, Tristy?" Roc says, grabbing me around the shoulders. "I'm a perfect gentleman." He does a perfect imitation of Elsey's overly formal way of speaking, all the way down to the high pitch and raised chin, which sends her squealing with laughter.

She tries to grab his hand again, but he darts away, and she chases him around the cave, leaving her mother shaking her head and the engineers cringing as Roc nearly crashes into something—a control panel for the transporter, I think—that looks expensive and complicated.

"You better watch out, Tawni," I say, "it seems you've got competition."

Tawni brushes a loose strand of blond hair away from her face. "Don't I know it. Since we met up, those two have been inseparable."

For a moment—just a moment—I forget where we are and why we're here. As I watch Roc dance out of another attempt by Elsey to grab him, I wonder whether we could ever experience true happiness in a better time, in a better place.

I hope so. Otherwise what are we fighting for?

Roc and Elsey don't stop their game of tag until the now-empty transporter descends slowly from the roof. No one speaks as the doors open, revealing the dimly lit interior.

"Ride's here," Roc says unnecessarily.

"This will take us above?" Elsey asks.

"Just wait," Roc says, "the surface is the coolest thing you'll ever see. Try not to get bit by the flying monkeys."

Elsey's eyes widen. "There are fly—"

"Usually the twelve-legged mountain lions will protect you from the flying monkeys," I say. "Don't worry."

"Although if they're really hungry, sometimes they prefer little girls to flying monkeys," Roc adds, tickling Elsey.

Giggling, she pushes him away. "They do not!"

"Guess you'll find out," I say, stepping into the glass enclosure.

General Rose presses a button to open the cave door, ushering in a dozen soldiers. "It's time," she says.

Roc, Tawni and Elsey step in next to me, followed closely by the final group of soldiers. Anna squeezes in last of all, barely able to fit.

The door closes and we shoot straight through the ceiling.

Forty
Adele

"And then I snuck into the New City," I say, ending my story. Twice I've had to stop because the sounds of the guards searching the area got too close for comfort. But like Jocelyn guessed, no one's looked in her room yet. But they will eventually.

The tears that filled her eyes when I told her about her husband pitting her sons against each other in a fight to the death finally break free, spilling down her cheeks, glistening like liquid diamonds.

She stands and looks away from me and I wonder if I've said too much, if I've broken her spirit. Should I have lied about Killen and let Tristan tell her the truth later? I know that even if I wanted to, I couldn't have lied to a woman who's been through so much.

She speaks to the window. "I've known for a long time that Killen had too much of Edward in him. I tried to undo the damage that my husband's brainwashing did to him, but I—I failed."

"No," I say, shaking my head. She still won't look at me. "He never had Tristan's goodness inside him. He never wanted it. It's not your fault. Nor Killen's. Nailin—I mean, your husband—is the only one to blame here. You did everything you could."

"Did I?" she says, turning suddenly and sharply to look at me. Her eyes are the clearest I've seen yet, as crystal blue as Tristan's. I know she's not really asking me—she's asking herself.

I let the question hang in the air, my gaze wandering past her to the screen on the wall, where a new image has appeared. I gasp, rising to my feet. "No, no, no, no," I say, my heart slamming around in my chest. But no matter how many times I refute the image with my lips, it remains, as clear as the sparklingly clean glass windows of the New City buildings.

Lin's face fills the screen, her expression frozen in a sneer, her eyes dark and stormy.

"You know her?" Jocelyn says, turning the volume on once more.

I don't answer, just listen. "This just in," a voice says. "As the ongoing search for the dangerous soldier calling herself Tawni Sanders tightens, at least one mystery has been solved. Sixteen-year-old Malindra Elliot, niece of Avery Elliot, has been taken into custody under suspicions of aiding and abetting Tawni Sanders. According to sources close to the investigation,

Lin has been uncooperative and somewhat belligerent during early questioning. Police are confident that, given time, they'll be able to draw the information they need from Ms. Elliot."

The room begins to spin. This wasn't supposed to happen, I think as I try to focus on the screen, which seems to be darting away from my gaze. I stumble and would fall if not for the hand that grabs my arm. Jocelyn guides me back onto the bed as the report continues.

"Dr. Wayne Zhou, government psychologist, has reviewed the facts of the case and his preliminary hypothesis is that Tawni Sanders is suffering from post-traumatic stress disorder as a result of her time spent in combat. Although no one knows exactly who she really is, or what unit she was stationed with, it's clear from the way she emerged from the desert into the New City that she's seen and experienced the terrible atrocities carried out by the natives on our people."

"BS," I say.

"It's normal," Jocelyn says.

"What is?" I say, massaging my temples, the room finally slowing its rotation.

"The propaganda. It's what Lecter does to control things. He controls the information so he controls the people."

"No one actually believes this crap, do they?" I ask, meeting her eyes.

"I don't know," she says. "I don't exactly get to interact with anyone other than Borg. But so far it's seemed to have worked for him."

"Why do you call him that?" I snap, unable to hide the fire in my words.

"What?" she says, like she doesn't understand.

"You keep calling Lecter, Borg, like he's someone you're fond of. Why?"

"He is...was...someone I was fond of."

I cringe, my hands balling in my lap. Look away. She's not the strong woman I'd built up in my imagination. Falling for psycho after psycho.

"It's complicated," she says.

"Then explain it," I say coldly.

She sighs. "I—I'd gotten so used to being treated like a rat, like a thing, by Edw—by my husband—that when Bor—Lecter"—she says his last name slowly, like she's not used to it—"treated me with kindness, I reached for it, like a drug, grabbed hold of it. I needed some kindness."

"Yeah, but—"

She rushes on. "And at first the way he talked about his plans...about equality for all people, expanding the population, feeding the hungry and clothing the naked and sheltering the homeless...it was exciting. It was what I wanted to hear. No, what I *needed* to hear. The exact opposite of my husband. I fell for it, grew fond of hearing his vision, of having normal meals with him, of talking to someone who seemed interested in what I had to say..."

"And then it all changed." I'm trying to hear her side, but I still can't understand how she could be so blind.

"Yes. The first time I questioned something that didn't make sense...let's just say I'll never forget his eyes. They were so dark, so full of anger, and then poof! The smile was back, the sparkling eyes, the happy-go-lucky expression. He very calmly and logically explained why I was wrong. But I knew something didn't make sense."

"And the more you questioned, the more you got the *other* Lecter," I say.

She nods. "But I still can't seem to make sense of him. How he could seem so kind and caring one minute, and so brooding and threatening the next."

"He's a liar," I say. "It's that simple."

Her face twitches, like she's been bitten or slapped. I can see the torment in her expression. This woman has gone from the devil to a demon and it's done things to her I may never fully understand. In her current state, she can't be reasoned with, so I just add, "But I can see how hard all of this has been." It's an understatement so deep I might as well be saying it from the Star Realm.

She just nods, her face going back to normal. "What are you going to do?" she asks.

That's the question, isn't it? I'm out of options. The streets are too dangerous, the chances of getting back to Avery slim to none. He's probably being watched anyway, if he hasn't been imprisoned along with Lin. There's no chance of me getting to either of the entrances to the city—the one from underground or the one from the desert—so I can't help Tristan and those on the outside.

I have only one choice, but I can't tell Jocelyn, can I? *I'm going to kill Lecter*, I think.

"I'm going to get you out of here," I say.

~ ~ ~

I awake to darkness. Where am I?

Mother? Elsey? I almost say their names, but my lips are too dry and chapped to speak.

I was dreaming, something that's left me feeling warm and alive. What was my dream about? Something about my family? I frown, trying to remember. Try to sit up.

Crack!

"Ahh!" I cry out as sharp pain rips through my skull. I slump back, raising one hand to rub my head and the other to feel for what hit me. Wood. Hard. Very hard.

The truth flashes back. Killing the presidential guards. Climbing the wall. Somehow, almost miraculously finding Tristan's mother, crawling through her window. Rolling under her bed to get some much needed sleep. No Elsey. No Mother. No Tristan.

There's a rustle beside me and I stiffen. "What happened?" Jocelyn's voice says. I must've woken her when I cried out.

"Hit my head," I say. "I'm okay."

"It's not morning yet," she says.

Though I should try, there's no way I'll be able to go back to sleep, not when Borg Lecter might already be back, sleeping under the same roof as me.

I hear Jocelyn roll over, and soon the soft sounds of sleep roll past me.

My head throbs, but I don't mind it. The pain helps sharpen my mind, pulls me away from sleep, from the dream...

Why can't I remember it?

I feel around with my left hand until I find what I'm looking for. Cold and solid and familiar. Metal. A gun. Three men dead because of how well I wielded it.

Before I slept I reloaded it with the last magazine. Today I'll use every last bullet on Lecter if I get the chance.

Will killing Lecter be enough to stop the genocide? Or has the ball started rolling so fast down the hill that no one can stop it without getting flattened too? If he dies, will someone else just step in to take his place?

I close my eyes and try to sleep, but the last forty eight hours continue to spiral through my mind. Watching it in a continuous stream like this makes me wonder if it's real. Only the pounding in my chest and head assures me it is.

At some point, the room begins to lighten, the surreal glow of real sunlight pushing its way through the window and sending a bright white line around the bedframe, just below the skirt, which hangs almost to the floor.

There's a knock on the door and Jocelyn stirs. Then, suddenly, she scrambles up and onto the bed, dragging her blanket and pillow with her, the mattress sagging slightly toward me between the wooden slats as it takes her weight. I hear the door open.

Light footsteps. A gentle voice. "Good morning, beautiful," Lecter says.

A groan that I know is faked. Jocelyn trying to keep her secret. That she never sleeps on the bed. "Tired," she says.

"You were kept up by the excitement?" Lecter keeps his voice low and soothing, but there's a piercing sharpness behind it.

"I thought we were under attack," Jocelyn says. "The guns were so loud. I was scared. I watched the news. Why is that girl doing this?" Her question is full of innocence. It even sounds true to me, and I know it's a lie.

"I think she's trying to get to me," Lecter says. I freeze. How does he...? "I think she's from down below." What?

"But the news said she was an unstable soldier. Post-traumatic—"

"You should know by now that sometimes the people don't need to know everything," Lecter interrupts.

"Then why are you telling me?"

The mattress sinks further as Lecter sits. He's right there. So close. Is this my one and only chance? Can I shoot him through the mattress? Or could I roll out fast enough to surprise him from behind?

The mattress shifts, undulating like a rippling lake, and I know he's moving closer to Jocelyn. Too close for me to risk trying to kill him. If I hit her by mistake...

"Because you're special..." Lecter says. The acid in my gut roils as I picture the scene above me. Is he touching her face, caressing her, his words whispered in her ear? Has her body stiffened, or is she melting into him, her movements so well-practiced they almost look real? Are they real? Can I trust her?

My heart races as I remember the soft and familiar way she said his name—*Borg*—like an old friend or lover. Is she pointing at the bed, secretly making Lecter aware of my presence? Is he slipping off, about to shove a gun underneath the bed skirt?

Quietly, quietly, my fingers tighten on my gun.

"And because I know you have no one to tell," Lecter adds with an arrogant laugh.

Jocelyn laughs like it's the funniest thing she's heard in a week. Sadly, it probably is. She hasn't given me up—at least not yet.

"We'll find her," Lecter says. "She'll be held accountable for her crimes." His words are as cold as stone and twice as hard. And then he's gone, his weight leaving the bed, his footsteps across the room, the door flung open, so fast that even if I'd been ready, there's no way I could've risked rolling out and shooting.

The door closes, opens. Lecter's voice again. "Breakfast will be up soon. I apologize that you'll have to eat alone today. I'll be conducting the search from here if you need anything."

"Thank you," Jocelyn says, but her words are only for me because the door is already shut again.

I let out a long breath and relax my fingers from the gun handle. So close...and yet impossibly far.

There's silence above me. I can't even hear her breathing, almost like she's dead. I follow her lead, lying still, breathing through my nose.

Minutes pass. Is it safe? Just as I'm considering saying something, there's another knock and the door opens. Under the cloth I see two feet and four wheels move into the room. "Breakfast is served," a woman's voice says.

"Thank you."

The feet leave but the wheels stay.

The door closes. Silence once more.

"Okay," Jocelyn says after another five minutes pass. "That should be the last danger for a while."

"Are you sure?" I say. If I get caught now, it will all have been for nothing.

"No," she says. "But they don't usually come back to collect the cart for a few hours."

I don't like the way that word—*usually*—echoes in my head. Words like that will get you killed.

I roll out from under the bed, ready to dive under at the first sign that someone else is coming in. From her perch, Jocelyn watches me with interest. Her hands are clasped, but I detect a

335

slight tremor. What did she think Lecter was going to do to her? What does he *usually* do to her? There's that word again.

"You okay?" I ask softly.

She nods, but it's not convincing. "We'll share the meal," she says, motioning to the cart. Three plates covered by silver domed lids form a triangle on a silver tray. A fork, a knife and a spoon rest beside them.

Keeping one eye on the door handle, I step to the cart. "Let me guess: one green, one brown, one yellow."

"What?" Jocelyn says.

I remove a lid. "What?" I echo.

It's food. Real food. Not the weird rectangular blocks of faux-food that everyone else gets. An oval of ham, pink and steaming with heat. The next lid reveals fluffy yellow-white scrambled eggs, flecked with pepper. The urge to use my hands as shovels shudders through me. Hands shaking as much as Jocelyn's, I open the third lid. Thick bread, at least five slices, browned on one side, damp with melted butter.

I don't wait for an invitation. Three pieces of toast are gone in less than a minute, my mouth bulging with buttery flavor and warmth. Three quarters of the eggs are next, the spoon moving ceaselessly from the plate to my mouth until I try the ham. In three bites the meat is gone and I'm chugging half the glass of water to wash it all down.

Finished, I stare in shock at the cart.

Oops.

"Uh, sorry," I say.

"You eat like Tristan," Jocelyn says, finally smiling for real. Her hands have stopped trembling. "It's fine though, I've had enough of the food here to last a lifetime."

"I thought you might turn me in," I blurt out, wondering why I'm saying it even as the words spill from my mouth.

Jocelyn stares at me. "Why would I...?" Something flickers in her expression. Understanding. "Because of how I talk about Borg?"

I nod. She sighs, looks down. Is that...embarrassment? "I'm sorry, I didn't mean to..." I say.

"It's okay," she says. "I'm screwed up. I have been for a long time."

"No," I say, but I know it's true. No one could go through what she has and not be a little scarred by it. Okay, *a lot* scarred. "We're all a little screwed up," I say.

"Thanks for saying that," Jocelyn says. She scoots to the end of the bed and eats what's left of the breakfast, taking each bite slowly.

"See?" I say. "I ate breakfast like a crazy person. You're eating normally."

She grins, but it doesn't reach her eyes. As she swallows the last bite, however, her expression turns serious. "I know what you're really doing here," she says.

Uh oh. Here it comes. The I-can't-let-you-do-that speech. She might hate Lecter, but she also doesn't want to see him die.

"I'll help you kill him," she says.

My mouth settles into a gaping "O." "What? Why would you do that?"

She re-covers each of the three dishes, placing the used utensils neatly inside each one. Finishes the water. Dabs the corners of her mouth with a napkin. I stare at her.

Finally, she turns to me. "Because until he's dead, I'll never be whole."

"Okay," I say, wondering if I'm making the biggest mistake yet.

Forty-One
Siena

The Glass City's ahead of us, but we ain't slowing down. Not one bit. We're charging ahead like there's something worth charging for, like home or a hot meal or even an old friend like Perry. Not death.

For a while the black Riders kept their horses in check, so as to not outdistance those of us on foot, but the moment the dome rose up 'fore us they took off like a brush fire, riding hard on wings of dust.

What will we do when we get there? Can we break through the glass? Will 'em Glassies come out to meet us? Or will we just set there ogling our enemy through the dome, us watching 'em and 'em watching us?

As we get closer'n closer, the dome gets bigger'n bigger. And inside the glass: the city rises up impossibly tall, structures so enormous they're like mountains. Mountains built by men and women. How can we defeat an enemy who can build mountains?

The Riders are almost to the dome when we hear the sound. A loud cry that ain't made by man or beast. Loud and shrill and a warning from the Glassy leaders to the people.

They know we're coming.

Tristan

Half the soldiers are laughing and the other half are pretending not to. Roc may not be able to fight, but he's helping the cause with his jokes and banter. Keeping things light. Cracking on everyone. Me and Elsey and Tawni, and even one ill-advised shot at General Rose that drew more laughs than any of them.

"Did you hear the one about Prince Tristan and the cannibal woman?" Roc asks the group. Laughter and shaking heads.

"And don't forget the prince's trusty sidekick, Roc," I say.

"Tristan cried like a baby when the old hag tried to gnaw on his leg," Roc says.

"And Roc peed himself when she started buttering his arm," I add.

More laughter. We're a hit. We should've been comedians. What the soldiers don't know is that we're only half joking about the story, which was freaking scary when it was actually happening.

The transporter slows and everyone suddenly goes silent. The constant wisecracking might've helped ease the tension during the ride, but now it springs back like a released bowstring. Twang!

Elsey, who's been holding Roc's hand the entire ride from the Sun Realm, grabs my hand and squeezes. She looks up at me with earnest eyes, as green as her sister's. A mini-Adele in looks only. "You'll protect my mother, won't you?" she asks.

I almost laugh, but her expression is so serious I don't want to offend her. "It's more likely she'll protect me," I say. "But I'll do what I can."

"Please bring my sister back," she says.

"That's the first thing on my list," I say.

The doors open and the soldiers at the front shuffle out, moving faster as they spread along the dark cave beyond, flashlights flicking on like glow worms.

We follow, Elsey between Roc and I, Tawni on one side, Adele's mother on the other. Not long ago I made the same walk, but with Adele, full of excitement and joy. How did we get to this place? Where the same journey could be stretched dangerously thin by fear and the anticipation of violence? The answer is simple: Lecter.

The bright white light at the end of the tunnel expands as we approach, until everyone is shielding their eyes with their hands. "Sunglasses," I say.

The flashlights are turned off and put away, and dark eye coverings with long, elastic bands are clasped around the back of each soldier's head. Even still, the sunlight is painfully bright after the artificial light of the Realms.

"So beautiful," Elsey murmurs when we're close enough to see outside.

"Wait until you see the night," Roc says. "A million stars in a million places."

"That was almost…deep," Tawni says, raising her eyebrows.

"See, there's more to me than tasteless jokes and ill-timed comments," Roc says.

"Yeah, like bullcrap and whining," I say.

"My feet hurt," Roc says. "And if it wasn't for my self-inflicted stab wound, I would lead this army to victory."

I laugh and clasp his hand, pulling him into an embrace. "See you soon," I say.

"Take care of yourself," my best friend says.

I turn and hug Tawni. "Make sure he gets three square meals a day and doesn't overexert himself," I say with a grin. "He's fragile."

"Are you his friend or mother?" Tawni asks.

"Sometimes I wonder." She smiles but it's tight and forced. She's fighting back heavy emotions.

"Bring her back," she says.

"I will," I promise to myself and her.

I lean down and Elsey practically leaps on me, clutching me fiercely. For once her passion seems to fit the gravity of the situation. "Don't laugh too much at Roc's jokes," I advise. "He might start to think they're funny."

"They *are* funny," Elsey insists.

I release her and look at Roc. "Congratulations. You've brainwashed her."

"All part of my evil plan to take over the world. As soon as Lecter's out of the way, I shall rise!" He pumps a fist in the air and shakes it.

"God help us all," General Rose says, taking her turn to hug Elsey. "Be safe, sweetheart. Listen to Roc and Tawni."

"Yes," Roc says.

"Or maybe just Tawni," Anna amends.

Roc groans and I say, "Good call."

"I'll pray for you every minute until you return," Elsey says. I know she's not lying.

Side by side, General Rose and I step out into the fullness of the light.

Outside, there are a few hundred soldiers, some lounging in the sand, or gazing at the big red sky, or touching the rough skin of the pricklers growing all around us. Exploring the new world that might be the last thing they see.

When we emerge, they cluster together in front of us. Ours is the smallest squad of all those gathering on the earth's surface, and in the vastness of the desert they look pitifully small, and yet determined.

Should I address them or should Anna? She touches me lightly on the shoulder. I take a deep breath.

"Without fighting today, the Tri-Realms could continue to exist, and our friends and families could continue to live underground, in the dark. But we'd have no choice. Today we fight for a choice. The choice to come aboveground, to see what you've seen today, to live wherever we choose." I pause, scanning the brave men and women who were selected by their leaders to represent the Capitol. Stalwart expressions, nodding heads, steely eyes. Soldiers from all three Realms, brought together for the first time to fight a common enemy.

"But that's not all we fight for," I continue. "We fight for the rights of strangers, people we don't know, people whose peaceful way of life is threatened by a tyrant who seeks to exterminate them like vermin. Already he's massacred an entire tribe. He must be stopped. It is our duty to stop him. Will you fight?"

343

A few heads nod, then someone claps and someone else shouts, "Yeah!" More clapping, more shouting. Soldiers doing what they do: whipping themselves into a frenzy.

I point out the direction for General Rose and she begins the march.

The time for speaking is gone. Actions will speak far louder.

Adele

According to Jocelyn, we may only have one chance to make this work. Clambering through the window the same way I came in the previous night is an option, but not a good one. After what I did, there will be many more guards on the prowl. They'll shoot us on sight.

The better choice is to walk out the door like normal people. Well, not exactly like normal people.

While I stand in the corner, she pounds on the door, gripping the breakfast cart with white-knuckled fingers.

My gun's in my hand, but my finger's not on the trigger as I don't plan on shooting anyone. Not yet anyway.

The lock clicks. The door arcs open, right toward me.

"What do you want?" a voice growls from outside.

"I finished breakfast," Tristan's mother says.

"Congratulations. If it wasn't for the president's strange obsession with you, I'd shoot you for making me come all the way down the hall just for you to tell me that." The door starts to close.

"Aren't you going to take the cart?" Jocelyn asks. She's doing a fair job of acting. If that door closes, we may not get another chance for hours, when someone comes to take the cart.

The shiny black barrel of a rifle pokes through the doorway. Aimed right at Jocelyn's head. She backs away, her hands over her head. I don't think she's acting now. "Do I look like kitchen staff?" the man says.

My muscles tense. Just a little bit further...

Jocelyn retreats another two steps, until her legs hit the edge of the bed and she sits down. "I'm just lonely," she says. "Borg's always busy."

"He's kind of in the middle of a war, stupid woman," the man says, his gun creeping half a foot inside. I can see his hand now.

Take one more step, you bastard...

He does, his foot moving forward, his head coming into view.

My hand lashes out like a whip, clubbing the hard steel of my pistol on the crown of his skull with a vicious *CRACK!* that makes me cringe even as I'm following through and watching him slump to the floor.

Jocelyn's eyes are wide as she stands. Things got very real all of a sudden. "Help me," I say, adrenaline shooting through my veins.

Together, we drag the guard away from the door and shove him under the bed. He's bleeding heavily, but we manage to wipe up the spatter with a pillow case, which we kick out of sight. With any luck, it'll be hours before he awakes and someone finds him. Either Lecter or we—or maybe all of us— will be dead long before that.

I hold a hand out to keep Jocelyn behind me as I peek out into the hallway. Clean tiled floor, bare, white-painted walls. Lecter's the poster child for minimalist living.

Moving out into the hall, I can feel Jocelyn behind me. I glance left and then right. Jocelyn motions left and I tiptoe forward, holding my gun in front, chest high. I'll shoot if I have to, but it's better if our approach is silent.

We're halfway to the archway in front of us when an alarm shrieks. Not possible. No one's even seen us yet. Well, no one who's still conscious and able to press an alarm button. I whirl around, surprised to find Jocelyn smiling. "It's our lucky day," she says. "That's a citywide alarm. The New City is under attack."

Siena

The wooloo non-human screaming continues even as we stare at the dome, frozen. Is a new Glassy weapon 'bout to be unleashed on us?

Red lights flash through the glass, almost like torches but without the orange and yellow parts.

One of the Riders thunders back toward us. The huge man—their leader. "What is that?" Gard asks.

"A warning," Wilde says.

"A warning to who?" I ask.

"Us. Or the Glassy people." Wilde shrugs.

"We can't stop now, can we?" I ask.

Wilde looks at Skye. Skye looks at me. "We ain't stoppin' for nothin'," Skye says.

Gard smiles wickedly and wheels his horse 'round, charges back toward his warriors.

Wilde faces the thousands behind us. "Today we fight!" she yells and a roar starts up, rolling 'cross my people like a storm country thunderstorm building in the clouds.

Just as we charge toward the Glass City, we see 'em:

Dozens and dozens of fire chariots tearing 'round the curved arc of the dome, packed with mask-wearing Glassies, their fire sticks poking out every which way like prickler barbs.

Heading right at us.

With a thousand screams, we race toward 'em.

Tristan

After an hour of walking, we see them. Soldiers. Many, many soldiers.

"Subchapter two," Anna says. "There are more than I expected."

"No..." I say, thinking. "That's more than one subchapter."

She glances at me sharply. "They've already started combining?"

I nod. "That's got to be at least four groups." A thousand soldiers. Suddenly our small band doesn't seem so inadequate.

A cheer rises up from the soldiers in front of us. We yell right back, me included, energy pouring through my bones.

I jog ahead with Anna, meeting the leaders of the other groups in the middle. Two men, two women. "Subchapters two through five," one of the women says. Her blond hair is cut short and dyed with strips of blue. A sun dweller, no doubt.

"Good," I say. "Any sign of the Glas—I mean, the earth dwellers?"

"Not yet," she says. "Based on the maps, we should only be an hour out."

"Then let's move," Anna says. If possible, her expression is even fierier than usual, perhaps a trick of the red sun cooking us from above.

As we march onward through the desert, we run into more groups from more subchapters, until our numbers climb above five thousand. The rest will meet us from the south.

Sweat-soaked and dry-lipped, we finally see it. The Dome. The New City. A fortress of shiny glass, so out of place amongst the yellow-white sand and brown rocks of the desert that it should be a mirage.

With renewed vigor, we march on.

Adele

There are shouts ahead of us, but they're moving away, declining in volume with each step we take.

"Will Lecter leave?" I ask.

Jocelyn shakes her head. "Not a chance. He'll let his army do the dirty work while he hides here. In the end, all he cares about is preserving his own life."

"Where will he be?"

"He doesn't let me out that often, but when he does he always takes me to his command room, where he can control the entire city." She motions down the hallway. "Straight ahead, down the stairs, and around the curving atrium wall. It's the room with the huge wooden doors. There will be guards."

I nod. "Stay close behind me," I say, turning away.

On a whim, I start to run, the blaring alarms masking my footsteps. I can't even hear Jocelyn behind me, but I know she's there. Where else would she go?

At the end of the hall, there's a staircase, just as she said. I pause for a quick second to listen. I can't hear anything except the continued shriek of the headache-inducing alarm.

Taking the steps two at a time, I reach the bottom in five seconds flat. A path curves away from me, glass on one side and a white wall on the other. Outside the glass there are a half-dozen guards running away from the building. Are they going to fight whoever is threatening the city? It has to be Tristan. Tristan and the Tri-Tribes. Can't think about that now. Tristan's giving me a chance and I have to take it. No, more than that. I have to grab it and squeeze it until it pops. Until it dies. It being Lecter.

Head facing forward, watching for any signs of movement, I sprint along the wall, gun trained on the space coming into view in front of me.

Crap! I slam on the brakes a split-second too late. The big wooden door rises up, flanked by two guards, one of whom has already seen me and is raising his gun, shouting, shooting...

I fall back, hoping gravity will be quick enough to save me.

A bullet whines over my head, shattering the window-wall behind me, sprinkling my face with shards of glass that prick and sting.

Rolling, rolling, rolling, I scramble out of sight, hugging the wall. I prop my gun hand on my elbow.

A guard runs around the bend, perhaps thinking I've run off, perhaps trying to be a hero, perhaps just scared and making a stupid decision. Right into my crosshairs.

BOOM-BOOM-BOOM! I pull the trigger three quick times in succession. The first shot hits him in the midsection, and each successive blast climbs higher up his body as the gun bucks in my hand. The final shot smashes into his chest and throws him back, his automatic weapon spraying bullets into the ceiling, raining plaster onto my head.

I hold my breath, waiting patiently, hoping Jocelyn's found somewhere to hide out of sight. Two guards. That's what Jocelyn said and that's what I saw. But what if there are more? I'll be screwed.

A gun pokes around the bend. Cautious. Careful. This guard saw what happened to his buddy and he doesn't want to meet the same fate. I aim at his hand, but there's no chance I'll hit him and I can't waste the bullets as I've used too many on the first guard already. Patience is the key.

His head snaps out and then back. He saw me. Knows exactly where I am and that I'm a sitting duck on the floor. No time to lose.

I scramble backward just as he flings himself into the open, fire spewing from the muzzle of his gun. Bullets chew up chunks of the floor I was occupying a second earlier.

BOOM! I shoot, miss, devastating the pane of glass to his right.

He shoots again, takes out more of the floor. Another blast and I feel a sharp pinch in my shoulder. I cry out, drop my gun, clutch at my injured arm, burning with pain.

No. It's over. No.

Wait.

"Jocelyn!" I cry out, rolling back, my eyes wildly trying to find her. She has to take my gun, has to shoot the guard, has to help me like she said she would.

350

But no.

She's gone.

Jocelyn is gone.

Siena

My pointer joins a flock of other pointers, swarming through the air, some clanking off the sides of the fire chariots and others hitting the Glassies riding 'em, sending the baggards flying off into the durt.

My injured ankle's burning like it's stuck in a fire, but I ignore it. The pain is nothing because…

My people are dying.

In front of me, my people are falling, dying, hit by magic or weapons or whatever the fire sticks do. They're bleeding and crying and all being ignored by the rest of us fighting for our lives.

I stop shooting when the black Riders reach the fire chariots, which stop to let the Glassies pile out. CRACKS and BOOMS and deafening blasts fill the air as their weapons seem to explode in their hands. Some of the horses topple over, right onto their Riders, while others lose their Riders but kick and gallop at the Glassies, fighting still.

And my people are all charging, taking advantage of the distraction caused by the Riders, a stampede of dust and sharp blades held above our heads so we don't accidentally poke one another.

Circ's beside me with Skye and Wilde in front, and Feve sorta diagonal. I spot Grunt not that far off, running faster'n I ever seen him do anything. He's red-faced and sweaty, but

351

looks determined too. Will he run away at the last moment like he did against the pack of Cotees? I almost hope he will, for Veeva's sake.

I hurdle a fallen horse, its black hide streaked with red stripes.

And then the Glassies are amongst us.

They're still trying to use their fire sticks, but more like clubs now, swinging at us or poking at us with these long spikes that are stuck to the front of some of 'em. Skye rips through 'em, slashing one and then another. Circ and Feve get in front of me and Circ shouts something I can't hear on account of all the screaming and the blaring of that searin' noise from the city, but I know exactly what they're doing. Protecting me so I can keep shooting.

I nock a pointer and release it into the neck of a Glassy who was pushing Wilde back. A dangerous shot, but these are dangerous times.

Another pointer finds its way into the gut of a Glassy who tries to double up on Circ, who's already grappling with an enemy soldier. He looks so strong I'd never guess he's got an injured arm and leg.

Circ's muscles strain and he gets the advantage, whipping the guy's neck hard to the side.

I reach for another pointer—the last one. Whirl 'round to find a good target. I see Grunt get hit in the side by a fire stick. He falls over, still gripping his useless sword. The Glassy points the stick at him.

Twang!

Thock!

The Glassy slumps over, feathers sticking from his chest.

Grunt's eyes are bigger'n the water country ocean. "Run away!" I yell, thinking only of my promise to Veeva. This is no place for Grunt. No place for any of us. 'Cept maybe Circ and Skye and Feve.

Grunt nods and scrambles to his feet, running on unsteady legs toward where we came from.

"Siena!" Circ shouts from the side and I spin 'round to see what he's hollering 'bout.

His cry was too late and I'm too slow, although I duck as the fire stick arcs toward my head.

Crack! It catches me in the face, but sorta on an angle so it doesn't get me with full force. Even still, it's enough to send me star-seeing to the ground, tasting durt and blood on my lips.

I look up to see three Glassies, identical, all pointing fire sticks at me. Circ's yelling something but it sounds so far away, too far away to save me.

The three Glassies shift and fade in and out and then combine into one man, wearing a snarl. "Die you little bitch," he says.

A big blur flashes from the side, yelling something, thumping into the Glassy with the force of a tug. The Glassy disappears from sight and I'm left staring at a puffy yellow cloud full of shards of light that I think are just a trick of my eyes.

Circ stands over me, speaking, reaching toward me. I can't hear him, just see his lips moving. He's saying something like, "Far two to fight." That can't be right.

I blink again, try to reach for his hand, but nothing's working right.

I see Feve behind him, thrusting his sword into the gut of a Glassy, shoving him down.

With a roar, my hearing comes back in booms and clanks and the sound of Circ's voice. "Are you all right?" he asks, and that makes much more sense.

"Who?" I ask, 'cause all I can seem to think 'bout is that tug of a human who came out of nowhere and saved me.

Grunt appears next to Circ. "I couldn't run," he says. "I saw you and I couldn't..."

"Shanker," I say, but I take his hand and he and Circ pull me to my feet, holding me up as I get my balance. I feel like I should thank Grunt, hug him or something, but there's no time to think or do anything, not when there's death all 'round.

I notice that it's not just Feve protecting us, but Skye and Wilde too. There are Glassies everywhere, and it seems like less'n less of my people and the Stormers are standing with every second that passes. We're being slaughtered, just like the Icers.

I give my head a shake and the cobwebs fall out and the stars fade and, although the pounding in my brain is still there, I'm steady on my feet. Drawing my short blade, I say, "We die t'gether."

As one, we charge into the fray.

Tristan

When we're less than half a mile from the New City, we hear the gunshots, hammering across the desert like cannon fodder.

Oh no, I think. The Tri-Tribes have arrived first.

"Move!" I shout, feeling somewhat sick all of a sudden. Memories of bodies in the sand flash through my mind. We have to hurry or I'll be seeing the same thing again, only it'll be brown bodies this time.

Like legions of ants, we pour over the final dune separating us from the city, gaining speed as our feet find purchase on more solid ground, cracked and hard, specked with small stones rounded by wind and sand. A loud sound is emanating from inside the Dome, like a siren or an alarm. A call to war perhaps?

Abruptly, it stops.

I have the urge to pause, to wait to see what happens, but we're like a flowing river now, moving forward until something stops us.

The gates—the ones Adele got in through—to the New City open.

Soldiers swarm through.

Adele

Even as my mind is stuttering over the fact that Jocelyn isn't behind me anymore, the alarm stops.

The silence that follows is eerie, almost as if more than just the gut-wrenching sound has been sucked away. Soulless. Dead.

My shoulder's on fire, like it's being roasted from the inside out. Not a clean wound. The bullet's in me somewhere. Blood squirms between my fingers as I try to stop the bleeding.

Glass crunches underfoot around the bend. Does the guard know I'm shot? He must, the way I cried out, but he can't know the extent.

My pistol is a few inches beyond my feet.

Slowly, slowly, I ease a toe forward, gritting my teeth because my nerves are screaming. I hook the gun and slide it back toward me. The sound of metal scraping against the tile is loud enough to wake the dead.

Crunch, crunch. The guard's gun comes into view. He's still being cautious, regardless of whether he thinks I'm hit or not.

My left hand leaves my shoulder to bleed.

Grips the gun, forefinger resting lightly on the trigger.

Breathe in, breathe out, through my teeth.

Heart racing—ignore it.

Drops of sweat quivering on my brow—doesn't matter.

Focus.

The guard steps out and fires, a heavy blast meant to end this game, but I've already shrunk back another foot and his bullets sing and chirp and glance harmlessly off the wall.

The moment he stops shooting, I push to my feet and rush forward, one arm damaged and dangling, and the other held steady in front of me.

He's reloading, scrambling to snap a new clip into his weapon.

I aim—

—point blank at his chest—

—and I fire.

He's thrown back by the speed of the bullet ripping through his skin and veins and bones and heart.

His gun clatters to the floor, along with the clip.

I approach slowly, my gun never leaving its target. The guard's not breathing, not moving. His eyes are open, unblinking. Dead.

I've made too much noise. Surely Lecter will be gone, having escaped through some back door. Or he's waiting inside with ten more guards. But either way, I have no choice. This is my mission, my destiny.

The heavy wooden door stands before me. What lies beyond?

My right arm is useless, so I have to stuff the gun in the back of my pants and use my left hand to turn the handle. It's unlocked and opens inward. Pushing it forward an inch, I grab my gun and kick it the rest of the way.

Crash! The heavy door reverberates off the inside wall, shuddering slightly.

It can't be. It can't. He's there, waiting, just staring at me from across the large room, seemingly weaponless.

The man from the propaganda videos.

Lecter.

With a wave of his arm, he beckons me inside, like an old friend.

I aim my gun at the thickest part of his body and step inside, trying to guarantee I'll hit him with the first shot. Just a step closer and there's no way I'll miss.

Before I can react, I feel the cold press of metal against the side of my head.

"Drop the gun," Tristan's mother says.

Siena

Feve goes down, hit by a fire stick. Wilde's got blood all on her front, bubbling from a deep slash 'cross her belly. Circ's being held from behind while another Glassy smashes his face. They don't have fire sticks, so they musta lost 'em during the battle. Even Skye looks 'bout ready to topple over, though she's still giving the Glassy baggards scorch.

357

Me, I'm surrounded by three Glassies. At any moment, they could send fire and magic shooting from their sticks, finish me off. But instead they're having fun with it, laughing and poking at me with the knives on the ends of their weapons. They think they've won.

I dance away from a jab and they roar with laughter.

I duck a slash and they taunt. "This one's still got fight in her! Might have to take her alive!"

But I won't surrender. They ain't taking me alive—that's one thing I know.

With a wild yell, I leap at the one who said that, slash at him with my blade. He tries to jump back, but I'm too quick and I slice open his throat. His last words bubble out through his neck.

Then I stumble over my own two feet, fall, almost on top of the man I just killed. Even as I land face down in the durt, I know it'll be my last clumsy, awkward moment, the last time my two left feet trip me up. But I roll anyway, 'cause if there's anything I learned from my big sister, it's that you hafta keep fighting, never give up.

Crack!

The sound of a fire stick exploding rings out so close I know I'm dead. I don't feel nothing, so I keep rolling.

And then:

A shout. And another. Some close, some far. What's happening? Why ain't I dead?

I look up and there're hundreds of boots running through the dust, thundering onto the battlefield. Familiar boots. It takes me a moment to place where I've seen 'em 'fore.

Water country.

The kind they wear on the decks of the ships.

The Soakers have arrived.

Still not dead, I push to my feet and see one of my tormentors taking aim at the newcomers. Rage filling me from gut to heart to head, I charge him, stab him from behind, not caring whether that's fair.

He drops his searin' stick. The third Glassy shoots fire from his stick and a Soaker falls in front of him, but there are ten more to take his place and they swallow him whole, trampling his bleeding carcass as they surge forward, moving on to other enemies.

I whirl 'round, the desert spinning like a dust devil: dead bodies and injured folks crying out and the Soakers finishing off the Glassies. And Skye, still fighting with 'em, killing another enemy, her brown skin glistening with sweat and exertion.

Somehow I always knew she'd be the last of us fighting.

I spot Grunt, who's pulling himself to his feet, staring in amazement as the remaining Glassies flee for the safety of the city. He's hobbling, one leg bleeding heavily from a hole near the top. He spots me and in his face I see horror and relief and pain, and the man who saved my life. I'll never look at him the same way.

I throw myself at him, and almost knock him over, but his sheer girth holds up my skinny frame. He's sweaty and durty and even less attractive'n usual, but I hug him with everything I got left. "Help me find Circ," I say to him, my chest heaving. We pick through the bodies. Each one I turn over chips away at my heart. My people. Dead. So many dead. The tears are flowing down my face, hot and dripping, but I keep looking, 'cause I hafta see him one way or t'other.

Grunt calls out and I stumble toward him, fearing the worst.

My legs give out when I see the body, which is too small to be Circ.

I slump over her, bawling, unable to hold back the tears flooding from my eyes. And then Skye's 'side me too, dripping all over her—all over Wilde.

She's barely breathing, her chest rising and falling in a way that ain't natural. The slash 'cross her stomach is so wide and deep it almost looks fake.

She's trying to speak, her eyes dry, her tongue moistening her lips. "You'll…"

"Don't," Skye says, choking.

"…always be my sisters."

"No," Skye says, but it's too late, 'cause Wilde's eyes are closed and she's gone. The sun goddess took her.

We huddle t'gether, crying, crying, pouring everything we got left out of the deepest pits of our souls.

Skye, always the stronger one, stops 'fore I do. She kisses my forehead, tucks my head to her chest. "We hafta find Feve and Circ," she says.

"No," I say, 'cause I can't do this again. I'd rather die.

"T'gether we can," she says, but I don't believe her.

She pulls me up and it's all I can do to cling to her arm, which is so strong. There're a few Stormers riding their horses toward the Soakers, who're coming back from chasing the Glassies to meet 'em.

More'n more brown-skinned folks are on their feet, not dead, helping to find and tend to the wounded, even though they're hurt too. None of 'em are Feve. None of 'em are Circ.

"C'mon," Skye says, pulling me forward. My feet barely scrape the ground.

We find Feve next. He's facedown and under the bodies of two Glassies, his blade still sticking into one of 'em. Even taking his last breath he was fighting.

I've got nothing left to cry so my whole body just shakes against Skye's as we mourn another friend, one who I'd only begun to believe in.

"Stay with him," Skye tells Grunt, who's sticking close to us, I think 'cause he don't know what else to do.

He nods and sits down.

"No," I say, 'cause I don't want to go any further. I'm done.

Skye scoops me up, carries me, trudging over bodies and 'round piles of the dead.

My heart's in my throat, which is burning and dry. My breath's coming in ragged heaves and shudders. How is Skye holding me t'gether when I'm in so many pieces?

I know every inch of him, so I spot him first.

It's just his hand, sticking out from a pile of the dead. Not moving, like he's sleeping. Just sleeping. *Sleeping, sleeping, sleeping,* I keep telling myself, again and again and again and again, and I'm not gonna stop saying it in my head, even when fresh tears burst out like blooming prickler flowers, even when a dreadful groan escapes my lips, even when my heart stops beating and I stop breathing.

His hand moves.

I squirm like a fussy baby in its mother's arms and Skye releases me. On all fours I crawl to him, to Circ, who's blinking at me, his eyes rolling 'round in their sockets. His face is puffy and bleeding.

"Where'reyouhurt?" I spew out in a single breath. Even if he's cut open like Wilde, I'm gonna fix it, hold him t'gether with my bare hands if I hafta.

"Siena?" he says, like he's all surprised to see me. "Thank the sun goddess you're alive."

"Areyouhurt?" I say. His eyes are having trouble staying open; is he dying, fading out like Wilde?

"My head," he says, reaching up to touch his hair, but stopping halfway there, touching my cheek instead. I run my fingers through his hair, feeling 'round 'til he winces. There's a big ol' lump on his head. "What happened?"

"The Soakers came," I say. "They saved us all."

He nods, as if not surprised. "I got whacked," he says.

"Wilde's dead," I blurt out. "Feve, too." And then I'm hugging him and crying into him and it's not all 'cause our friends are gone, but 'cause I'm ashamed that I'm feeling so much relief and joy right now. 'Cause Circ's alive.

We stay like that even as we hear explosions to the west.

Tristan

We're dying; they're dying; the world's full of smoke and blood and mortal shouts.

Even with our five thousand soldiers, the earth dwellers have the advantage in numbers, wearing sinister dark masks. Slowly, slowly, they're pushing us back, cutting us down, winning.

A truck roars toward where General Rose and I are ducking behind piles of the dead, using our fallen brothers and sisters to save our own lives. Anna pops up and shoots three times in rapid succession. One of the front tires bursts and the truck swerves and then rolls, flattening a soldier wearing star dweller blue. Earth dweller soldiers fly from the back, landing hard in the dirt.

"We can't hold them back much longer!" I shout above the gunfire. I pull the trigger and blast at an earth dweller who gets too close. She falls back with a cry.

"No," General Rose says. "But we have to try. There's nowhere to retreat to." She pulls a grenade from her belt, rips the pin out with her teeth, waits three heartbeats, and then hurls it toward an enemy pack, which scatter like a discarded handful of pebbles. The explosion is so loud it's as if it's inside my head.

I look around, trying to think. Our forces are spread out, disorganized, splintered by the strength of the earth dweller attack. We're pinned down, immobile. "We need vehicles," I say.

Through the smoke-filled haze, Anna stares at me. Nods. "Spread the word."

I peek over the dead soldier at the top of the pile, ducking as a bullet whines overhead. Then I run, keeping my head as low as possible. A crouch-run, awkward and slow, but the only thing that saves me from the enemy fire that buzzes around me. "We've got to get the trucks," I tell each living soldier I see.

I move on before any of them can so much as nod in understanding.

When I reach the truck with the blown-out tire, I pause to catch my breath. An earth dweller groans, trapped beneath the mangled vehicle. It's a wonder he's still alive.

Across the battlefield, I spot Anna, who's picking her way over to an abandoned vehicle, her eyes darting every which way, occasionally shooting the random enemy who gets too close. She reaches her goal and pulls the door open, slipping inside.

The truck springs forward and I rush out to follow its path, throwing caution to the gusting wind.

I can barely see her in the cab, as she's ducking low, practically steering blindly into the midst of the earth dwellers, hitting one, then another, throwing them up and over the windshield and roof.

Another truck is tearing for her, spitting up dust and rocks in its pursuit. No, not pursuing…joining! Another stolen vehicle. The word is out.

Could this work?

Just as a shred of hope fills my chest, I see them:

A dozen trucks erupt from the New City, heading right for General Rose.

Bright spots of gunfire rip from them, sending sparks dancing along the sides of Adele's mother's vehicle, spiderwebbing the windshield. Two tires burst at the same time and the truck flips, the back soaring over the front, crashing onto the hard ground, sliding twenty feet on its roof before coming to rest.

My heart sinks. There are too many, but if there's any chance Adele's mother is still alive, I have to get to her before the enemy does.

I steel my resolve and prepare to charge into the open.

That's when I hear the chorus of shouts, not from the New City, but from the south. I crane my neck, my breath hitching when I see them. The rest of the Tri-Realm soldiers, come from the remaining subchapters. Five thousand strong and already shooting at the enemy, which suddenly doesn't look like too many.

With renewed vigor, the soldiers around me are popping up and pushing forward, the weaker side of a pincer attack. I dart out, shooting at anything that moves, killing one earth dweller, then another, as they try to decide which direction to look.

One of the new trucks explodes, presumably from a hit to the gas tank.

The earth dwellers are dying in waves and some of them are losing their resolve and fleeing back toward the city, only to be cut down by the force from the south. We're winning. No, we've won.

I let the soldiers clean up the remaining enemies, veering off toward the upside down truck. Toss my gun aside. Dive to the dirt. Anna's slumped inside, covered in glass, the windshield having shattered inward. Her arm is contorted awkwardly against the steering wheel. But she's looking at me with blinking eyes.

"I'm gonna get you out of there," I say.

"That'd be good," she says.

"Are you okay?"

"I think my arm's broken," she says, whistling out a sharp breath through her teeth. "Other than that, I'm fine."

"This is gonna hurt," I say, getting a firm grip on the arm that looks okay.

"Just do it quick."

With everything I have, I pull her from the vehicle. Her mouth opens like she wants to cry out, but she doesn't, just screws up her face. She slumps over when she's free of the carnage. "Tristan," she says.

"Yeah."

"Find my daughter."

Adele

I could shoot—I could. But I'm not the best shot in the world, and if I miss or don't kill Lecter with the first bullet, then I'll be dead and so might the fire country natives. Tristan, too.

So I do it. I drop the gun, hating the dull thud it makes at my feet, and hoping I'll get another opportunity to kill Lecter.

I want to ask Jocelyn why she's doing this, but I don't, because I'm pretty sure I wouldn't understand the answer anyway. Her head is all screwed up, brainwashed by the very person she hates and loves.

My mission has failed because of the very person who started everything when she paid an unexpected visit to my mother.

"Bravo," Lecter says, clapping slowly. He walks across the room, which is full of screens with colored dots, and blinking lights on shining metal panels. The room where he controls the world he's created, where tracks the implanted chips of his people. "I'm glad I don't have to use this," he adds, holding out a gun I didn't even notice.

"Of course not, darling," Jocelyn says, her eyes narrowed. "I told you I'd do it."

"And you did," Lecter says. "You've come so far from the skeptical, questioning person you were a few years ago. I'm most impressed."

"You're sick," I say. "Both of you."

Jocelyn gives me a surprised look. "Don't you see, Adele? Borg has created everything that my former husband refused to. An equal world, where everyone gets the same amount of food, the same living conditions. There are no Realms. There is no poverty, no crime. It's a perfect world…one that deserves to grow."

"You're delusional," I say.

She shakes her head. "One day you'll understand," she says.

"No," I say. "I'll never understand either of you. Tristan would say the same thing."

Hearing her son's name, she jerks slightly, just in her face, her gun remaining firm against my temple. "You may be right," she says. "But I'm willing to try to explain to him too. To teach him, like I always did."

This woman can't be reasoned with, can't be talked out of the disease that's consumed her. I can't be a prisoner in this world. Even though it'll only take the slightest squeeze of her finger to end me, I have to try to do what I came here to do.

I don't tense my muscles in preparation. I can't give any indication of what I'm about to do.

"You're the crazed soldier," Lecter says. "Why are you doing this? Who sent you? Was it Nailin?"

"Nailin is dead," I say, trying to keep the conversation going, waiting for the perfect opportunity to make my move.

Lecter tries to cover his surprise, but I see it in his eyes. I've shocked him. "How?" he says.

"I killed him."

More surprise. "But why?"

"Because he was evil, like you."

"You're an assassin."

I've never been called that before, never thought of myself that way, but I guess it's not that far from the truth. I shrug.

"Kill her," Lecter says to Jocelyn.

I'm running of time. I've got to do something or Jocelyn might actually…

Jocelyn grabs my wrist with her other hand just before I start to bring it up to attack. "Don't," she says. There's something in her eyes, something different…

She pulls the gun from my head and aims it at Lecter, who doesn't even have his own weapon raised. "Die," she says and pulls the trigger.

A puff of red plumes above his scalp a split-second before he falls back, blood oozing from the hole in his forehead.

My eyes are bulging and my mouth is open in shock, but every instinct in my body is telling me to act, to seize the opportunity to gain control of the situation. I lash out, chop at Jocelyn's arm to dislodge her weapon, but the gun is already slipping from her grasp, falling to the floor. She collapses on top of it.

I just stand there, gasping, my heart bouncing around wildly. What just happened?

Lecter's not moving. There's no way he could survive a direct headshot.

Below me, Jocelyn's weeping, caved in, her knees to her chest and her arms wrapped around them. A broken woman. The savior of the world inside a damaged, abused shell of a person.

Kneeling down next to her, I rub her back with the palm of my hand. "It's okay," I murmur. "You did it. You're okay now."

It was all an act. Her words, her icy cold voice, the gun to my head. It was the only way she could make Lecter trust her, lower his guard, get him close enough to do what she had to do.

She fooled me and she obviously fooled him.

Beneath my hand, her body continues to shake with emotion.

"Tristan will be so proud."

Only at the mention of her son does her trembling cease. She opens her moisture-filled eyes.

"Where?" she says.

"Outside the city," I guess. "Attacking with the natives."

She grabs my arm and I pull her up.

Forty-Two
Siena

Sadie's alive, her horse too. She walks beside Gard and his son, Remy. Scant few Stormers survived the battle. Not that different'n the Tri-Tribes. Devastated by the Glassies.

There're many more Soakers, on account of how late they arrived, but all that matters is that they came. None of us'd be standing here if not for 'em.

I'm still setting next to Circ when I see him. Huck. The Soaker boy who captured the attention of my younger sister, when she was a slave on one of his father's ships.

I leap up, not 'cause I'm all excited to see him, though in some ways I am, but 'cause of Skye's words earlier when she found out what he'd done to Jade, how he'd beaten her with a whip.

I'll destroy him.

But I'm too slow, too late, 'cause Skye's already spotted him and she's running right at him. Still, I try to get in front of her, but a couple burly Soakers beat me to it. "Git outta my way," Skye says.

"Skye," I say, grabbing her arm. "Don't."

She pulls away from me, her eyes boring into mine for a moment 'fore darting back to the Soakers.

"It's okay," Huck says to his guards. "Let her through."

Although they don't look like they want to, the guards step aside, creating a gap. Huck pushes a wave of blond hair off his forehead. "Skye, Siena," he says.

But Skye's already pushing through the gap, bumping the guards as she passes by. She don't hesitate, just pulls her fist back and cracks Huck in the jaw, rocking him back. The guards are on her, but she elbows one in the face and kicks t'other in the midsection.

"That's for hurting my sister," she says to Huck.

On the ground, Huck's massaging his jaw. Skye extends a hand and he looks at it for a second before taking it. She pulls him to his feet. He stares at her, his arms sort of extended in front of him, as if they could ever protect him from the force that is my big sister. But she doesn't hit him again. Instead, to my surprise, she grabs him 'round the back and hugs him tightly.

"And that's for saving her, for saving us," Skye says.

Tristan

With no one left upright to stop them, the Tri-Realm army has managed to drive two trucks through the gates, parking one between each set of double doors, leaving an open path into the city. The toxic air is surely spilling through, but I'm hoping a few hours won't do any lasting damage.

"President," a soldier says at the gate. "What are your orders?" he asks. I realize then that he's a general from the Moon Realm.

"Get the word out to all the other generals. Sweep the city, but do not fire unless fired upon. Disarm and bind any soldiers who surrender. No more killing unless necessary."

"Yessir." He turns to go.

"Can I have a few of your soldiers?" I ask, stopping him.

"Shoe, Mags, Tilda," he barks. Two women and a man step forward from the crowd of soldiers manning the gates.

"Come with me," I say.

We climb over the trucks and into the city, the Dome arcing high above us. It's just as bright inside as out, one of the benefits of using glass, I suppose. We're on some kind of an army base. There's what appears to be a medical building in front of us, barracks to the left. Several unused trucks parked to the right. But not a single soldier. The place is deserted; every last soldier was sent into battle.

But where's their ultimate leader? Where's Lecter?

I stride across the stone courtyard, my protection unit flanking me. A high metal fence surrounds the complex, a closed gate at the center. Together we push it open.

Buildings grow like trees around us, glass running up their sides. Like the military base, the streets are empty. I remember the alarm. Warning everyone to get and stay inside. Thank God for that, I think. At least the innocents are safe.

Nothing here is new to me, because of when my father brought my family on a tour of the New City, but the three soldiers' heads are roving like searchlights, taking it all in.

The city is spotless, just like I remember it.

Is she here? Is Adele here?

Then I see her. I gasp, because it's not her, not really. Just her face, stone cold and unsmiling on a screen on the outside of one of the buildings. "Wanted," it says in big block letters above her head. "Reward for information."

Lecter's discovered her. He's got the whole city on the lookout. The only comfort I have is that if she's still on the screen then perhaps they haven't found her yet.

We march down a street, scan the vacant cross streets at the intersection, continue on.

I can't stop, have to keep looking.

I won't stop until I find her.

Adele

We exit Lecter's home through the shattered windows along the curving hallway. I've got three guns tucked in my waistband. Mine, Jocelyn's, and Lecter's.

Jocelyn's holding my hand, like she's afraid I'll disappear if she lets go.

Neither of us speaks. There's nothing left to say.

We walk past the vacated guard station. The city is quiet for this time of day. The alarms did their job well. The citizens of this city know how to follow orders.

I can only see the parts of the Dome that rise above the buildings; the edges are lost behind the hundreds of structures lining the streets. Somewhere out there is a battle. Did Lecter's final order result in another massacre, the end of another tribe? The end of him, the son of the woman whose hand is gripping mine so tightly it's starting to hurt?

Without discussing it, we both head in the same direction, down a lettered street, making our way to whatever numbered one will take us to the main gates. Where, soldiers or no soldiers, we both know we have to go. We'll shoot our way out if we have to. I don't think either of us can take one more minute in this damned spotless city...

We both stop at the same time when we see people. Crossing an intersection two blocks up. Stopping in the middle. Turning away from us, then back toward us. And when they do...

Jocelyn sighs, making a high-pitched sound from the back of her throat. And I realize I'm making a similar sound, because...

It's him.

It's Tristan.

Tristan

I turn and my chest fills with air when I see Adele. But no, it's not just her—there's a woman too. No.

No.

Impossible.

My skin tingles and warmth roars through me and my feet are so fast, far faster than those around me.

I run toward my mother, blinking furiously at the tears in my eyes.

Adele

I just watch them run at each other, though I desperately want to run too. But I can't be selfish. My time is later and nothing in the world can trump a reunion of a lost mother and son.

They smash into each other and Tristan whirls her around and I'd bet anything he wasn't big enough to do that the last time they saw each other. Jocelyn is crying and planting kisses on his face and Tristan's face is peeking around her, his eyes full of shock and joy.

And he's crying the happiest, most wonderful tears.

When they finally pull apart, Tristan leads her over to me, hand in hand.

His smile is as beautiful and bright as the first time I saw him. At the parade. From behind the prison's electrified fence. But this time it's real. So real.

He puts an arm around my head, tugging my face toward his. And his lips part and meet mine, warm and full and comforting.

"She saved me," I gasp when our lips unlock. "She saved us all."

Tristan looks at his mother with admiration, and I won't tell him anything else. Jocelyn can tell him as much as she wants to when the time is right.

Epilogue
Somewhere beyond…
Dazz

The Earth is unfolded before me like a map, crisp and sharp and vibrant. It's strange, I can see everything so clearly, almost like I'm still there, and yet it feels distant, worlds away, impossible to touch.

I'm ripped in half.

One part of me is curling the biggest icin' smile across my lips, so wide and filled with giddiness that I almost feel ready to explode with happiness.

But the other part of me is squeezing my heart, filling me with the ache of desperate longing, sending rivers of sadness down my cheeks.

When I died, I lost more than my life.

I can't be sad, though. Not really. It would be too selfish. Because they did it. They freezin' did it, and though I wasn't there to be a part of it, I know I was with them in different ways, living in the place it mattered the most: their hearts. And Jolie and Mother and Buff were there too. Even good ol' Abe and Hightower were rooting for them to defeat the Glassies, standing next to me, watching from…well, from wherever we are. Somewhere beyond.

Somewhere beyond the pain and the hopelessness and the despair of a world torn into little bits so small and bent that I was starting to wonder whether there was any possibility of putting them back together again.

But when Lecter (the Yag!) fell and his army collapsed, a cheer went up, so loud that the misty haze surrounding us turned blue for just a moment, before returning to its normal color, a white so pure it's like snow. Familiar. That's the word for it. Although it's not cold anymore, this place feels like home, in a strange way. A good way.

Even as I stare down at Skye, who's safe and alive and as beautiful as ever, I know it's better this way. I get to be with my family, and she with hers. And I know that one day—hopefully not anytime soon though—I'll get to be with her again.

I finally turn away from the Earth and a hand reaches out to wipe away my tears. "Thank you, Brother," I say. "But don't let Buff see you coddling me like that, he'll never let us live it down."

Wes laughs and it's the most brilliant sound I've ever heard, because I'll never have to miss my brother's laugh again. "Then quit crying," he says. "There's nothing left to cry about."

And though I know he's right, the tears keep falling, spilling from eyes overflowing, even as Jolie emerges from the mist holding Wilde's hand on one side and Mother's on the other. Her smile is as bright and welcoming as the sun over fire country. She's happy, so happy.

I never imagined I'd find so much life in death.

Buff and Feve appear next, laughing and telling stories. I have a feeling they're going to become good friends.

"Come. Look," I say, gesturing at the world that's no longer ours.

And they do, crowding around, more and more Icers and Heaters and Stormers and Soakers and Dwellers surrounding the portal, gazing at our old friends. Our people united.

They're okay and so are we and nothing will ever change that again.

New Wildetown
Sadie

This is a strange, strange land.

For one, it's boiling hot all the time, even when the sun goes down. Secondly, I haven't felt a drop of rain since setting foot in fire country. Storm country feels like it's millions of miles away.

Although my heart yearns for the cool ocean breeze, familiar storms, and lush, flat plains of storm country, I'm content to stay here for a few more days. After all, I don't know when we'll get the chance to see our unexpected friends again, and I've grown closer to Siena and Skye than I ever thought possible. Remy seems to be getting on well with Circ and Hawk and a few of the other guys, too.

But I know that whenever we do leave, it won't be forever. Already Gard's been discussing a potential trade agreement with the Tri-Tribe leaders, one that will ensure our friendship and joint preservation for years into the future. Remy and I have already agreed to visit at least once a year, preferably when it's slightly less hot.

Remy puts his arm around me and I'm tempted to lean into it, but I'm not that girl. Not yet anyway. Maybe someday I will be, when I'm old and decrepit and walking with a stick to support me.

Instead, I squirm away and wrap my arm around him, tucking him against me. It makes me even warmer, but it's worth it to see the amused look on his face. "One day, when you least expect it, you'll let me protect you," he says.

"I know," I say. "But for that to happen I'll have to be lying unconscious with both legs broken."

He laughs and just lets me hold him, and I'm glad he's not too proud to let me do that.

While the embers glow and my head touches Remy's and I look at the moon-brightened night sky, I see my mother and father and brother, Paw, smiling from somewhere else, somewhere that's not as far away as I always thought.

And I smile right back.

New Wildetown

Huck

Being here seems impossible.

Not two days ago I was arguing with the other captains, who were about as fun to talk to as a pile of rocks. I never thought I'd convince any of them to come, much less a full quarter of the sailors. And yet now I'm here, in fire country, three of the fleet's ships anchored to the south, just off the red cliffs. The battle was brutal and devastating—so many dead—but necessary work to defeat a tyrant, just like my father.

And the most amazing thing: I'm holding the hand of the girl who owns half of my heart. The other half belongs to the Deep Blue.

To this point in my fourteen yars of life, I've never been able to see my future a day ahead; but now, with the warmth of Jade's hand tucked into my palm, I can see yars and yars, a whole lifetime worth living. With her.

My only concerns are the muscles and fists and swords and bows and arrows of Skye and Siena, both of whom seem intent on staring at me with dark eyes for the entire night. But when Jade looks up at me with her intense brown eyes, the ones that, not long ago, were so mysterious to me, everything else fades away and I'm alone with her.

And she moves closer and her lips are so small and perfect and wearing just the tiniest grin, which makes me smile and almost laugh even as the fishlets are swimming and squirming through my stomach.

We kiss and everything's right.

I know people are watching but I couldn't care less.

I might kiss her for the rest of time.

New Wildetown
Siena

Jade and Huck are still kissing each other, and now even I have half a mind to knock him back to yesterday. She's still just a child, after all. But I know that's not entirely true anymore, 'cause she's grown up just like the rest of us have, and her guy's fought in two battles now and that should count for something in terms of his manhood. Plus, he managed to convince a quarter of his fleet to sail 'round the southern cliffs of fire country in order to help us. Seems only a man could do something like that.

So I just look away and lean into a kiss of my own from Circ.

"What was that for?" Circ asks. It doesn't sound like a complaint, just a curiosity.

"'Cause I can," I say.

He shrugs and gives me another peck.

Next to Circ, Lara and Hawk are arguing 'bout something, but they're holding hands, too, which I just can't get over. Who woulda thought? And yet, they seem like a perfect pair. Wooloo how the world spins and flips and changes faster'n Perry shouts insults at clutzy skinny girls in the desert.

The moon goddess is shining tonight, and she's so bright I know that Wilde's in there with her, watching over us, even now. We held a ceremony for her and Feve and all the rest who didn't make it. I gave Feve's wife and his kids a big hug each, and we cried t'gether. I'll never fully get over my friends' deaths, but Skye and me cut our fingers open and made a blood oath to be happy in honor of 'em. Then we smiled through the hurt and the pain and the tears staining our cheeks.

I talked to Veeva afterward, when I could tear her away from Grunt, who's hobbling 'round, milking his injury for all it's worth. But I won't dare call him a shanker—never again. Veeva thanked me for saving his life, but I told her he saved mine. You couldn't imagine the pride in her eyes. "That's my stallion," she said. They've been in their tent ever since, and I'm doing my best not to guess what they're doing in there.

Tristan, who followed through on his promise to return with an army, helped us get the people with small injuries back to New Wildetown. We rode in the Glassies' own fire chariots to do it, how 'bout that? The seriously injured are being fixed up inside the Glass City, something 'bout their Healers being better'n ours. We pray for 'em every night to the goddesses in the sky.

The Stormers and Soakers are staying with us for a while, in our camp. They sent Riders back to water and storm country to tell 'em what happened and ease their fears. Across the fire from me, Sadie's got her arm 'round Remy, looking up at the star-speckled sky. Even now that the war's over, she's always got to be in control. It only makes me like her that much more.

I don't know what's gonna happen with Adele and Tristan and all t'others who live underground, but I'm not worried 'bout it anymore, 'cause they seem to have things pretty much under control. Finally—finally!—I just wanna live my life, be with Circ and my family and friends. Honor those who died for us…by being happy.

And if anyone like my father or King Goff or Admiral Jones or President Lecter ever try to put on their big boy britches and knock us 'round again, well, I s'pose I'll fight for our freedom one more time. Or as many times as it takes. 'Cause I ain't afraid of nothing anymore.

Circ sighs as I run a hand through his thick hair. I knock a knee against his and he pushes back. Just like old times, so long ago and yet only a moment out of reach.

"I love you, Siena," he says.

And for the first time ever, I know why he does. 'Cause I say the wrong things sometimes and trip over my feet and shoot pointers like an expert and kiss mighty searin' good and am braver'n most. 'Cause I'm me, an imperfect part of a perfect pair.

Circ and me.

Me and Circ.

Surrounded by our families, by the ones we love.

Unity (the city previously known as the New City or Glass City)
Tristan

I've got the weight of a crumbling world on my shoulders, and yet I feel lighter than the birds soaring over the glass dome, which is once more sealed tight at the gate and providing filtered air to all who reside within its bounds.

I've got a million things on my mind, and more than a million people, but I'm spending today with my family and friends. A day off. Adele will join me later; she said she had something important to do.

My mother is sitting beside me, gazing at the birds high above, just like me.

"Do you think we'll ever be able to live out there?" she asks the birds.

I shake my head. "I don't know," I say. "Maybe this great earth will heal itself eventually, but at least for now we can live above."

"I don't think I want to," she says quickly.

I look at her but she holds her gaze far past the Dome, on the sky and the birds wheeling overhead, playing on the wind.

Something happened to her. Something bad. She's not the same person that she was. Slow to laughter, heaviness in her eyes. Every time I ask Adele about what happened, she tells me everything except about my mother. If I want to know those parts I have to ask her, she says. I haven't, and Mother hasn't exactly volunteered the information. Maybe someday…

"Where will you go?" I ask.

Finally, her expression lightens. "The Realm," she says.

I smile at the name, one of the many good decisions the Unity Council has made since its creation. No more "Tri." No more "Sun, Moon, and Stars." Everyone equal, living where they choose to live. In all honesty, the cramped caverns of the old Star Realm will likely be abandoned, possibly the old Moon Realm caverns too.

It all depends on how many citizens decide to come above, which was another awesome decision made by Unity, a unanimous vote. All humankind gets to choose where they live, whether underground or above, in the air-filtered glass dome, or outside.

Sun dweller scientists are already analyzing the air, trying to figure out what's wrong with it, something that should have been done by Lecter. So far they've found at least six toxins that are deadly to humans over time. We'll monitor them over the course of years to determine whether the levels are on the decline or consistent. Whether we'll ever be able to live long lives outside of our domed city. Maybe someday our children, or our children's children, can live like people used to, free to roam and inhabit the earth.

We've also abolished all the major systems put in place by Lecter in the New City, which has been renamed Unity. The first major human city on the face of the earth since Year Zero. Those living in Unity will be able to choose their jobs, what to eat, and where to live.

Because there's not enough space in the city for the millions from the Realm that are expected to choose to come above, plans are being made to create additional cities, but only if we get the approval of the tribes that live on the lands we want to build them on. It's not our world to take; it's our world to share. And we're the party crashers, so we have to play by their rules.

However, I fully expect Gard and Huck to approve our plans for a city on the eastern coastline of storm country, and the Tri-Tribes' leaders to allow us to build at least one more city in fire country. As for ice country, we'll be building a large memorial for the lost Icer tribe. It will stand for centuries to come as a reminder of the stupidity and tragedy of greed and intolerance. We can't change the past, but we can remember it so we don't screw up the future.

There are also early discussions about the potential to help the tribes build mini-domes over their villages, but only if they want them. Living in filtered air even part of the time could extend their lifespans by decades. But that's a choice they'll have to make. Of course, they'll also have the opportunity to move into our cities if they want. Either way, we'll respect their decisions and ensure they're involved in ours wherever they affect them.

It's all part of the New Constitution, which dissolved any forms of dictatorship and sustained the new council. The people will finally get their voice back.

"I'll miss you," I say, "but I'll visit all the time." I'm staying above, with Adele, a decision that was all too easy to make. We've both gotten too used to the real sun, and I have a feeling we'll become good friends with our new acquaintances to the west.

She smiles, and though it's not the full, eye-reaching smile I remember from the woman who used to read to Roc and I against the big tree in the palace gardens, it's a start. "You'd better," she says, putting an arm around me.

For just a minute, I lean in, a child in a man's body, allowing myself to be held by the woman whose bold and creative decision so long ago played a major role in shaping the world for the better. She had a vision, and I was but a tool in her loving hands.

My mother, my hero. From the look in Adele's eyes when she refuses to talk about what my mother did, I can tell she feels the same way.

"Hard at work, as usual," a voice says from behind. "Or is it hardly working?"

"It's my first break in days," I say without turning around.

Roc comes around the front of the bench we're sitting on. He's holding Tawni's hand and looking rather smug. "A few more days like this and my rise to the top of the Unity Council will be like taking candy from a spoiled prince," he says.

My mother stands and hugs Roc, who kisses her on the cheek, sending warmth through my veins. She might've lost a son, but she got two back, even if one isn't connected to her by blood.

"You can have this spoiled prince's job anytime you want it," I say. Joking aside, I was equal parts surprised and happy when Roc ran for a spot on the hundred-member Council. I was even happier when he got it. I might be the moderator for the meetings, but his vote counts every bit as much as mine. Although I've always considered him my equal—even when he was supposed to be my servant—it's gratifying for the rest of the world to feel the same way.

As my mother hugs Tawni—who she's taken a particular liking to—Roc says, "I don't want your charity, Tristy." He sits next to me on the bench and rests a hand on my shoulder. "Nor do I really want your job. I'd follow you to the ends of the earth if you asked me to."

Damn Roc, always jumping from joking to saying stuff like that. I turn my head and try to discretely rub the mist out of my eyes, but he's already laughing. "Cry baby," he says.

I may be the moderator of the Unity Council and a former president of an entire underground nation, but I can still shed a happy tear or two for those I love.

This world is far from perfect, and it always will be, but with people like Roc and Tawni and Adele and my mother in it, life will always be well worth the struggle.

Unity

Adele

It's strange to ride the elevator back up to a place I thought I might never see again. When I step out into the hallway, I can't hold back my smile. Because where there used to be gleaming, sterile, white walls, there are now beautiful, colorful paintings of the world outside the Dome. A lizard—or *'zard* as our fire country friends like to call them—bakes in the sun on a sandy dune; a forest-covered mountain rises almost to the ceiling; a ship crashes against a white-capped wave, sea spray spouting up and looking so real it's like I'm in the midst of it all. Vibrant colors and life and change.

The wall paintings are all part of a movement to add color to a place that desperately needs it. The movement, appropriately called "Color Me Up," is burning through the city like wildfire.

I stroll down the hall, admiring each painting, until I reach my destination. A blue door that used to be white. A smile spreads across my face as I lift my fist to knock.

The door opens just as I try to crack my knuckles against it, and I almost punch Lin in the face.

"Is that how you treat all your old friends?" she asks, grinning.

"Only my favorites," I say.

I give her a hug, favoring my injured arm, and she accepts it, but pulls away quickly. Hugging's not really her thing. "C'mon in," she says. "It's about time you visited."

"Sorry," I say, stepping inside the narrow apartment, now splashed with yellow walls and a red countertop. "Life of a councilmember's girlfriend. Hey, I like the new décor."

"Hey, kid," Avery says, looking up from where he's hunched over the small table. It's painted red, too. "You like the colors? They are my creations. I've become something of a paint mixer since you took down Lecter. Well, at least after I got out of prison."

I cringe. "Sorry you had to go through that," I say. "You too, Lin." One of the first things I did after Tristan told me the war had been won, was to go to the jail and release all the prisoners, including my two friends and the old man who's apartment I borrowed while he was imprisoned. Lin's still got a jagged scar just below her eye from being tortured, and Avery's nose is a little crooked, having been broken.

Lin grins, like the memory is one of her favorites. "No biggie," she says. "There aren't many people who've got 'Was tortured for information but didn't tell them a damn thing' on their list of life accomplishments."

I laugh because only she'd be able to put such a positive spin on a horrific experience, wearing it like a badge of honor.

"You feel the same way, Avery?" I ask.

"She's one of a kind," is all he says, but there's pride in his voice. "You're just in time for some food."

I groan. "Is it green, brown, and yellow rectangles?"

"Blech," Lin says, "I hope I never see rectangle-shaped food again."

Avery hands me a plate. "No, I call this earth dweller/fire country fusion cuisine. Or to the layman, eggs and prickler."

I stare at the fluffy white-and-yellow, green-flecked clouds on my plate. It doesn't look half bad. I take a tentative bite. "Mmm," I murmur. "This is awesome."

"Glad you like it," Avery says. "I've managed to transform this minimalist place into a half-decent kitchen. Apparently cooking and painting are more my skillset than street cleaning."

"He painted the hallway, too," Lin says, talking with her mouth full.

"You're kidding me?" I say. "It's breathtaking. You've got real talent."

Avery shrugs. "Who knew? I've been asked to do some other walls around the city."

I take another bite of deliciousness and sigh. I'm not sure what I'm good at other than punching, kicking, and assassinating maniacal dictators, but I can't wait to find out.

~ ~ ~

The sun is past its peak when I leave Avery and Lin's place with a promise to see them more often. "And bring Tristan with you next time," Lin says on my way out the door.

I stroll through the city, which is still shockingly clean and litter-free. Lecter didn't do much right, but keeping the city free of trash was one thing I agreed with.

Left turn, right turn, another left: the new park comes into view. Children are running and playing and I spot Elsey, not because of the unbalanced way she runs now—which, amazingly, doesn't seem to slow her down one iota—nor because she's the only kid with one arm, but because she's wearing the biggest smile of anyone. She tags a dark-skinned boy and then runs away laughing as he darts after her.

My mother's sitting nearby, alone, away from the other parents, her broken arm in a sling. I'm not sure whether everything she's experienced in her lifetime will ever allow her to fit in with everyone else, but that's something I love about her.

She gives me a raised-eyebrow smirk when I plop down beside her. "Did you get to see Lin?" she asks.

I nod. "She asked about you like twenty-four thousand times," I say. "I'm pretty sure she wants to be you."

"She's a strong girl," she says without so much as blushing at the compliment. That's another thing I love about my mother: she knows she's strong and she's not afraid of that fact. "You are too," she adds, and I *do* blush, warmth creeping into my cheeks. I guess being like my mother is still too new for me to fully understand it.

"Elsey looks happy," I say, watching her legs—which seem to grow longer each day—easily carry her away from the boy who's "it," until he gives up in search of slower prey.

"She's never let the world scar her the way other people do," she says. She's right, which is what makes my sister so special, because even though she wears a terribly real physical scar from the atrocities of life, inside she's pure and unmarked. Am I scarred? Is my mother? Will any of us ever be as pure as Elsey again? I hope so.

Elsey runs over, out of breath, giggling. She practically falls into my lap, even though she's getting far too big to do that. "I was only 'it' once, and that was because I let someone tag me," she says.

I laugh and push her off. "You're sweaty, you little bragger."

"Mother says sweat is a good thing. That it's what makes the world a better place."

I glance at my mother, who tries to hide her smile. "Yeah, but that doesn't mean I want your sweat on me," I say.

As I watch Elsey brush a moist strand of hair away from her face and charge off to rejoin the game, I feel an unexpected swell of emotion in my chest. Is this......*real?* Can life go on like none of the awfulness ever happened?

The answer comes to me as I watch Elsey let herself get tagged again. In a move that reminds me so much of myself, she immediately hones in on the tallest, fastest boy, chasing him across the lawn.

No, the world will not go on in denial about its past. And it shouldn't. But that doesn't mean we have to be afraid of the past, so long as we remember it and learn from it, united in our belief that humans are inherently good and that the evil is the exception, not the rule. Always hope and strive for a better future.

Elsey gains a step on the boy, then another. She's so close, her fingers swiping and missing his back by the tiniest margin. She springs forward, diving to try to make the tag, but a brown blur rushes in from the side, catching her before her fingers can find their mark.

Roc does an exuberant and overzealous celebration lap around the park, slinging Elsey—who's giggling and protesting—over his shoulder like a sack of potatoes.

Tawni shakes her head at Roc's antics and makes her way over to us. Her white-blond hair practically sings under the reflected rays of the sun. I stand and hug her, holding her longer than normal. "I missed you too," she says, understanding me the way she always has.

Behind her is Tristan, his arm around his mother, talking and laughing, his mouth closing only when he sees me and the way I'm looking at him:

With fire and ice and water and storms in my eyes. With the red sky and the yellow-white sand and the green grass. With gray rocks and dim lighting and painted walls. With life and love and memories.

Does he stop laughing because he sees all that in my gaze?

When he smiles I know that he does.

Because I see it in his eyes too.

A million memories and the future.

He hugs me and I'm home.

He kisses me and I'm never alone.

Whether our mothers had any idea what they were really doing when they stuck those chips in our necks, we may never know, but it doesn't matter now. Because we were always meant to be together and I can't imagine a life apart.

I'm his rock and he's mine.

And thus ends (and begins) the greatest adventure of my lifetime.

~*~

Keep reading for:

1) Three awesome Dwellers short stories

2) A long-awaited interview with Perry the Prickler

3) A sneak peak of *Brew*, the first book in David Estes' new YA paranormal dystopian series, *The Witching Hour*, coming January 16, 2014!

A personal note from David...

If you enjoyed this book, please, please, please (don't make me get down on my knees and beg!) consider leaving a positive review on **Amazon.com**. Without reviews on Amazon.com, I wouldn't be able to write for a living, which is what I love to do! Thanks for all your incredible support and I look forward to reading your reviews.

Acknowledgments

No way! *blinking quickly while pinching my arms and slapping my cheeks* It can't be over, can it? 7 books, more than 700,000 words, and 18 months later, and the combined Dwellers/Country Sagas are finished. I'm in shock. Complete shock. Speechless. Well, not completely, as us writers almost always have something to say. And what I have to say is mostly a whole lot of THANK YOUS.

First and foremost, to my wife, the real Adele, you have been more than just a support to me on this journey—you've been my partner in crime. You've suffered my endless babbling about plotlines and characters and promotions and rejection letters and on and on. You've been there for my greatest defeats and my greatest triumphs. You've sat with me and pored over copious amounts of beta feedback, helping me decide how to improve my early manuscripts. You've added your own critical feedback to my stories, never holding back, always being honest, determined to not let me be complacent in my earlier successes, to make each and every book the best that they could be. You are my best friend and the most important person in my life.

To my readers, you are the best, most wooloo people I've ever met and I'm so searin' glad to know so many of you on a first name basis through the David Estes Fans and YA Book Lovers Unite group on Goodreads. You people make me laugh, cry, and throw my laptop across the room on a daily basis, and I'll always love you for it. If you keep on reading, I'll keep on writing. Thanks for sticking with me.

A huge HUGE HUGE thanks to my cover artist for this book and for the other three Dwellers books, Tony Wilson at Winki Pop Design. Your art and designs have been PERFECT for this series and I'm never surprised when readers tell me how much they love the covers.

To my beta readers, many of whom have been around for all seven books, you all are so AWESOME I can hardly even put it into words. This is the seventh book in the series, and yet you took your job so seriously, challenging me on the smallest of minutiae, forcing me to think about the decisions I was making and why I was making them. The improvements I made to the story based on your feedback will undoubtedly be well appreciated by my readers. So thank you Laurie Love, Alexandria Theodosopoulos, Kerri Hughes, Terri Thomas, Lolita Verroen, Rachel Schade, Brooke DelVecchio and Anthony Briggs Jr.

And last but not least, to my remarkable Street Team, I love love LOVE reading your reviews of my ARCs, they keep me going sometimes when building a writing career feels like the hardest thing in the world. Thanks for all your reviews, support, and genuine kindness. You are the definition of good people. And a special thanks to Kelly in particular, who has been the ultimate street team member and has taught me so much about how to get the word out about my books. I appreciate everything that you do.

Discover other books by David Estes available through the author's official website: http://davidestesbooks.blogspot.com or through select online retailers including Amazon.

Young-Adult Books by David Estes

The Dwellers Saga:
Book One—The Moon Dwellers
Book Two—The Star Dwellers
Book Three—The Sun Dwellers
Book Four—The Earth Dwellers

The Country Saga (A Dwellers sister series):
Book One—Fire Country
Book Two—Ice Country
Book Three—Water & Storm Country
Book Four—The Earth Dwellers

Salem's Revenge:
Book One—Brew (Coming October 1, 2014!)
Book Two—Boil (Coming October 1, 2014!)
Book Three—Burn (Coming in 2015!)

The Slip Trilogy:
Book One—Slip (Coming December 1, 2014!)
Book Two—Grip (Coming December 1, 2014!)
Book Three—Flip (Coming in 2015!)

The Evolution Trilogy:
Book One—Angel Evolution

Book Two—Demon Evolution
Book Three—Archangel Evolution

Children's Books by David Estes

The Nikki Powergloves Adventures:
Nikki Powergloves—A Hero Is Born
Nikki Powergloves and the Power Council
Nikki Powergloves and the Power Trappers
Nikki Powergloves and the Great Adventure

Connect with David Estes Online

Goodreads Fan Group:
http://www.goodreads.com/group/show/70863-david-estes-fans-and-ya-book-lovers-unite

Facebook:
http://www.facebook.com/pages/David-Estes/130852990343920

Author's blog:
http://davidestesbooks.blogspot.com

Goodreads author page:
http://www.goodreads.com/davidestesbooks

Twitter:
https://twitter.com/#!/davidestesbooks

About the Author

David Estes was born in El Paso, Texas but moved to Pittsburgh, Pennsylvania when he was very young. He grew up in Pittsburgh and then went to Penn State for college. Eventually he moved to Sydney, Australia where he met his wife and soul mate, Adele, who he's now been happily married to for more than two years.

A reader all his life, David began writing novels for the children's and YA markets in 2010, and has completed 16 novels, 14 of which have been published. In June of 2012, David became a fulltime writer and is now travelling the world with Adele while he writes books, and she writes and takes photographs.

David gleans inspiration from all sorts of crazy places, like watching random people do entertaining things, dreams (which he jots copious notes about immediately after waking up), and even from thin air sometimes!

David's a writer with OCD, a love of dancing and singing (but only when no one is looking or listening), a mad-skilled ping-pong player, an obsessive Goodreads group member, and prefers writing at the swimming pool to writing at a table. He loves responding to e-mails, Facebook messages, Tweets, blog comments, and Goodreads comments from his readers, all of whom he considers to be his friends.

Dwellers/Country EXTRAS!

1) Three awesome Dwellers short stories

2) A long-awaited interview with Perry the Prickler

3) A sneak peak of *Brew*, the first book in David Estes' new YA fantasy dystopian series, *Salem's Revenge*, coming October 1, 2014!

1) Three Dwellers Short Stories by David Estes

The Shattered Stones of Fate
Adele

Originally posted on <u>Confessions of a Bibliophile</u> on July 21, 2013.

Hours before The Moon Dwellers...

Sometimes time ticks by at a pace so dismal you can almost see the stones of fate gathering moss before your very eyes. And other times...well, life seems to roar past with the speed of an inter-Realm through-train, whipping your hair around your face and forcing your eyes shut against the airborne debris.

Today starts with the former, but you can never guess which way it'll end.

Class is heavy and tight on my skull, full of "important" dates and wars and a history that only half sounds real. Did humans really live on the earth's surface once? It's hard to believe, and yet everyone says it's true. And if they did, why did they seem to be constantly in the midst of disagreement and strife?

My grandmother—may she rest in peace—used to say that being outside was like laughter and a warm blanket and the hug of a friend; but of course, those were the same things her mother had told her. No one really knows anymore—all we have are stories from the generations before us. Do I believe them?

Does it matter if I don't?

I massage a knot in my forehead, the beginning of a sharp headache. Something pokes me from behind. I ignore it.

Poke poke.

"Gannon, you do that again and I'll break your arm," I hiss.

"Ms. Rose...something to share?" Mrs. Hill asks, stopping in mid-lecture, her hands on her hips.

"No," I mumble, writing Gannon on my blank notebook page. When the teacher resumes her monologue about some kind of civil war, I slash through Gannon's name with a single stroke of my pencil.

Poke poke.

You've got to be kidding me. I whirl around, my pencil snapping under the strain of my fingers, which are already curling into fists. My chair falls over with a slam. "Do that again..." I say, pushing the unfinished threat out into the air.

Gannon's face is even whiter than usual, his big blue eyes as wide as false moons. "I—I—"

"Yeah, everyone's sorry," I say, feeling bad seeing Gannon look so scared. After all, he's one of the few people who are ever nice to me anymore. But my breathing is heavy, my blood running hot and angry through my veins. An overreaction. Something my father has always warned me against.

I try to swallow it down but all I get is a lump in my throat.

"Ms. Rose..."

Suddenly I'm aware of the many eyes on me, staring, some with open mouths of shock and others with smirks of amusement. I cringe and turn to face Mrs. Hill, who's placed her lesson plan on the table in front of her. Never a good sign.

I know I should apologize but the lump gets in the way. So I just stare at her, feeling my face redden.

"I'll not have students threatened in my classroom," the teacher says. I'm already grabbing my pack and pushing for the door when she says, "Detention. Now."

The grey-stone halls are empty and hollow, like the feeling I've had in my chest ever since the other kids started talking about my father a week ago. I asked Father about it, but he swears everything's okay, that it's no big deal, that the rumors and gossip are exaggerations. But his words don't match his eyes like they usually do. He's protecting me from the truth: a dangerous world has become infinitely more dangerous.

As I stride down the hall toward the detention room—my fourth such journey in the last week—the playground shouts hit me like bursts of gunfire:

"Your father's a dead man!"

"Better start looking for a new dad!"

"Complainer!"

I touch a hand to my gut, half-expecting to feel moist holes in it, but all I get is the brittle texture of my school-tunic. *Dead man! New dad! Complainer!*

Are things really that bad? If they weren't, would I have broken those three kids' noses? Would I have two black eyes and fire roaring through my skin?

When I reach the detention room, I glance through the window and see the regulars: Drummer, the heavily pierced kid who can't seem to stop tapping his fingers on his desk; Gina, the girl with the spiked purple hair and unexplained scars up and down her arms; Chuck, the dude who smells funny and is addicted to pulling bad pranks. Freaks. Am I one of them?

I stride past the room and push through the school doors. Mother will be furious when she finds out I ditched school again, but she'll just have to deal.

There are a couple of punks on the corner, smoking something that doesn't smell like normal cigarettes. "Try it," one of them says as I pass, holding out a joint.

An insane urge to kick him rolls through me, balanced only by a desire to take him up on his offer. I ignore him and run past, wishing my feet had wings—that I could fly: out of subchapter 14 of the Moon Realm. Out of the underground world of caves and rock and disappointment. Excitement shivers down my spine at the thought, making me feel nauseous because of the conflicting emotions, like I'm spinning and spinning.

Turning a corner, I take the next block in stride. It's only when I reach my neighborhood that I slow to a jog, hoping Mother will be out.

She isn't.

Worse, she's standing in front of our house, looking right at me, like she has delinquent-radar or something. I stop, consider turning and running in the other direction, think better of it, and cautiously approach her.

"I know what you're going to—" I start to say.

"Come inside, I'll make you something to eat," Mother says, cutting me off.

She turns and makes her way back to our small stone cube of a house, holding the door for me. I follow her inside, wondering whether this is one of those mom-pretends-to-be-your-friend-as-punishment teaching moments. I hope not—I'd prefer a harsh punishment dealt by a swift hand any day.

"I shouldn't have left school," I say, dumping my pack and my words in a heap on the floor. My only hope is to control the conversation.

"No, you shouldn't have," Mother says. She doesn't sound angry. Why?

She starts chopping something with a dull knife. Potatoes. I gawk at her, unable to feel my feet, like I'm floating. Who is this woman?

Before I can consider the possibilities, Father pushes through the back door. "Hi, Adele," he says, as casually as if school *and* work are meant to be over.

"Why aren't you at the mines?" I ask, more sharply than I intended.

"Why aren't you at school?" he counters, but a smile plays on his lips. His eyes disagree with his mouth, remaining downcast and tired, like he's just woken up.

"The school called," Mother says, stirring a pot. "Adele was supposed to go to detention but she left."

God. Word travels fast. Mrs. Hill must have expected it. "I hate school," I say. I hate people, I don't say.

"I know," Father says, to my surprise. If Mother is a clone, Father is a robot. Where are my real parents?

I stare at him. He stares at me, his smile gone. Mother nonchalantly stirs a pot.

The unanswered question springs back into my head. "Father…why aren't you in *the mines*?" I ask again.

He sighs, scratches his head, looks more vulnerable than I've ever seen him. "Oh God," I breathe.

"They let me go," he blurts out, turning to head back outside.

"They what?" I say, following him onto the back patio, a familiar place where we've trained every morning for the past ten years. Now a place so foreign and frightening I barely recognize it. "You lost your job?"

He nods. "I guess I stood up for one too many people," he says.

"Fix it," I say, a knot forming in my stomach. People don't just lose their jobs in the Moon Realm. There are always repercussions, especially when it's related to a complaint.

"I can't."

"You can," I protest.

"It's unfixable," he says, and before I can contradict him, he throws a punch at my head.

I duck, grabbing his arm and swinging a low kick at his legs, which he easily hops over. He lets me try again, this time with a hooking fist, but at the last minute he ducks and my momentum of my wayward punch spins me around. He grabs me from behind, trying to lock my arms, but I manage to twist out of it before his hands can get a good grip.

I whirl around, my chest heaving, my blood flowing, my adrenaline higher than the dim and rocky cavern ceiling that arcs above us. I charge my father, aiming dual jabs at his chest.

He grabs my arms, pulls me into him. I'm squirming and clawing and bucking...and then I hear it.

A strange sound, low and guttural. A groan. I stop moving, listen to the slightly disturbing noise.

"Adele," Father says, hugging me, crushing my face into his chest. "It's going to be okay." That's when I realize: the strange sound is me. Grunting and groaning and protesting the truth.

"Nothing's okay," I manage to wheeze out, breathless. A hot tear spills down my cheek and I wipe it away angrily. "Nothing."

Father's eyes are sad, and this time they match his lips, which couldn't form a smile if we were suddenly rich and living in the Sun Realm. "Be strong, Adele," he says. "For your mother, for your sister, for me, for yourself."

"No," I say, even though I know I will. It's the only way I can be. It's the way he's built me.

"No matter what," he reminds gently.

I push away and go to bed early, eating my pathetically unfulfilling supper alone in the room I share with my sister and parents, wishing I was oblivious the world that's about to end.

And times races on and on and on, shattering stone and bones and lives, twisting fate into a blind whirlwind of grief and splintered moments.

I awake to the sound of our front door slamming open.

~THE END~

The Runaway
Tawni's Story
Originally posted in Furthermore: an Anthology.

Even when you know it's the right thing to do, running away from home is never easy.

Although my small bag is packed and dangling from my shoulder, my nondescript black boots are laced, and the door is open, I linger on the threshold for a moment, and gaze back at the house I've called home for as long as I can remember. Everything I see—from the flat-screen telebox, to the sturdy stone table, to the photos of my parents and me hanging on the wall—should be familiar, but it's not. It's as if I've never seen any of it before. Ever since I overheard my parents talking last week, my entire world feels foreign.

I cannot wait any longer or I know I might change my mind. Swiping a long lock of straight, blond hair away from my face, I take a deep breath, close my eyes, and try to muster what little courage I can.

It's such a normal thing, stepping through the door, something I've done a million times. But this time it feels so *un*normal, like it's not me, not my legs—someone else. Not me. When I close it behind me I feel an errant rush of wind through the cave; it washes over my face, my arms, through my hair, as if the unlikely breeze is cleansing me, washing away the sins that are mine by association. Having left the house in which my parents are still sleeping, I feel cleaner already.

They're not good people. I can't stay here anymore.

With practiced steps I zigzag through the rock garden in our front yard. Most moon dwellers can't afford to waste perfectly good stones for decoration—but my parents are not most moon dwellers. Now that I know why my family is so wealthy amongst such poverty, seeing the polished and shiny stones makes me sick to my stomach.

It's still too early for the broad overhead cavern lights to be on, but I don't risk illuminating my flashlight for fear of drawing the attention of one of the Enforcers that roam our subchapter at all times. This deep below the earth's surface, we don't get much electricity anyway, so I'm used to seeing in the dark. But still, I take extra caution with each step, being careful not to stub my toe or kick a loose stone.

As I exit our walled-in property, I feel the pace of my heartbeat pick up. Although I'm walking slowly, my heart is racing. I might be walking, but in my heart I'm running away.

I'm running away.

I'm.

Running.

Away.

The words feel prickly in my mind and I wince as the dull throb of a headache starts in my left temple. I feel a trickle of sweat slide intimately down my back beneath my gray tunic. Ignoring the sweat, my racing heart, and the icy stab of the truest words I've ever thought in my head, I take another deep breath, reposition my shoulder satchel, and walk faster, stepping on the tips of my feet to remain as quiet as possible.

The night is quiet.

The neighborhood I grew up in, played in, made friends in, disappears beneath the soles of my boots, like the cool night air vanishes in the wake of the wings of a bat. With each step I gain strength in both my legs and my heart. Another suburban block slides away behind me.

My goal is to make it to the train station before the morning rush. Then, when the mass exodus of workers seeking work begins from our faltering subchapter, I might be able to blend into the crowds and escape the roving eyes of intra-Realm security. I bought my ticket in advance, which doesn't require an intra-Realm travel authorization; however, when I go through security I'll be required to provide my pass. Unfortunately, there's no way a sixteen-year-old girl would be granted such authorization, so I was forced to hurriedly purchase a cheap fake from a shady guy at school.

I hope it'll pass the scrutiny of the security guards.

Travelling intra-Realm without authorization is a serious offense that automatically requires time in the Pen, our local branch of the Moon Realm juvenile detention system. A lot of kids that go in there don't come out alive. My best friend, Cole, got sent there three months ago when an Enforcer tried to rape his sister. Cole killed the guy, but then his buddies killed Cole's sister and parents. They sent him to the Pen for life.

I still cry for him sometimes at night, especially after I get one of his letters and I miss him all over again. If I do end up in the Pen, at least I'll get to see him.

I'm not sure what I'll do if I get out of subchapter 14. I guess I'll just keep running, moving from underground city to underground city, until things cool off and my parents and the authorities forget all about me. Then I'll try to make things right with the girl named Adele Rose.

My thoughts are running amok and I know it, but I can't seem to turn them off as I turn a corner, cutting a path through the back roads that will eventually get me to the heart of the city, where the train station lies. The strange route will add twenty minutes to my trip, but might protect me from the Enforcers.

In the darkness of a rarely travelled street, I feel somewhat safe, which is the first lesson I'll learn out on my own: you're never safe.

Feeling safe, I pass right by a stone stoop that sits just off the road at the front of a small house. There's a flash of red in my peripheral vision and I jerk my head to see what caused it. That's when I smell the bitter smoke from a freshly lit cigarette. My eyes zero in on the scene before me, taking in every awful detail before my brain can put it all together. Two men, both smoking, gazing off to the side, away from me, smoke curling around their heads. One of them is an Enforcer, dressed in bright sun dweller red, a gun and a sword hanging awkwardly from his belt as he sits on the steps, one knee raised higher than the other. An open door revealing the soft glow of candlelight.

Engrossed in their own thoughts, they haven't seen me yet, staring absently out onto the small front patio.

You're never safe.

But I do have half a chance because they're oblivious to my presence. My heart pounding in my chest, I back away slowly, retracing my steps in reverse, holding my breath as I move further and further from their field of vision.

Three steps from safety.

The non-Enforcer—a moon dweller who likely owns the house and trades cigarettes to the Enforcer in exchange for freedom from persecution—can no longer see me, as I move behind a wall.

Two steps.

The angle of the wall is such that I can still see the Enforcer, the crimson of his uniform like a warning beacon on the edge of my vision.

One step.

As if some inner instinct alerts him to my presence, his head snaps to the side and his black eyes lock on mine. He smiles.

I run.

Although I can't see him, my ears pick up the scuff and scrape of his shoes on stone as he moves off the stoop. He's not wasting any time coming after me, probably already feeling the excitement of the chase that will add some fun to his boring night. Maybe a juvenile girl breaking curfew is about the most excitement he ever gets, who knows? My only chance: get out of sight as quickly as possible. I might not be a fighter, but I am a runner.

I hear a shout as I cut a hard right down an alleyway. It's the obvious move, but the only one available. Lengthening my already-long strides, I abandon my quiet footsteps and thunder down the narrow path between the houses. The alley is longer than I'd like, and I know the Enforcer will enter it before I get to the end.

Get out of sight.

I listen to my own advice and swerve to the left, using a hand on the top of a chain-link fence to propel myself over it. Landing in a crouch on the other side, I make for a gap between the houses, cringing as I hear the rattling of the metal fence in my wake. I feel a sting of pain and warmth on my hand from the sharp barbs at the top of the fence, but I bite it back and dash to the front of the house.

I don't have time to open the front gate so I hurdle that, too, stumbling when I land awkwardly on the street. *Keep moving*, I urge myself, using my uninjured hand to catch my balance. From the property I just exited, I hear another shout, this one closer. Despite my efforts, the Enforcer is catching up.

Doing my best to ignore a twinge of pain in my ankle and the burning in my hand, I sprint down the road, running faster than I ever have before, my breathing ragged and gasping, my heart like a jackhammer in my chest. Up ahead there's an alley on the right and one on the left. Although it shouldn't be, it feels like a crucial decision. Right or left. Freedom or capture. Neither feels right as I approach the intersection, but I lean toward the left and prepare to dive in that direction, hopefully before the Enforcer gets out onto the road.

Just as I bend my knees and start to push off with my feet, I feel a rough hand grab a handful of my tunic and yank me hard to the right. Unless the Enforcer has been blessed with inhuman speed, it cannot be him; more likely it's another Enforcer that I didn't see or that was radioed in by his buddy. Either way, I'm toast.

And then I'm in the alley to the right, a firm hand over my mouth, kicking and clawing and bucking like a wild animal, desperately trying to get loose. A harsh voice hisses in my ear. "Quit yer fightin' or that Enfo will catch the both of us!"

I have no reason to obey the voice, but instinctively I do. I guess I've just always been a rule follower, not one to disobey an order. The second I calm down, the hand moves away from my lips and clamps around my arm, urgently pulling me further into the alley and behind a dumpster. I try to get a look at my captor (hero?) but all I get is a flash of thick, long dark hair attached to a sturdy frame. He's dressed in all black, nearly invisible even to my used-to-the-dark eyes.

He turns to face me and I catch a glimpse of a very young-looking face, before he whispers, "Under here," and throws a thick blanket over the both of us, casting us into darkness. "Get down," he commands.

I'm not sure how a blanket will protect us, but I have no choice but to trust this young stranger, who seems just as intent on avoiding detection by the Enforcer. I sprawl out on the rock alleyway, unconcerned with getting scraped and dirty. The guy with the young face is closer to me than I've ever been to a boy, and instantly I feel warm—hot even. The heat might have been slightly pleasant, if not for the putrid odor of rotting garbage that assaults my nostrils.

But now is not the time to complain, so I do my best to breathe through my nose and remain perfectly still. We're in place not a moment too soon, as we hear the pound of boots on rock, a pause, and then urgent footfalls heading right for us.

They get closer and closer until I swear he's about to step on us, and then stop with a suddenness that throws my heart into a frenzy. There's heavy breathing and a grumbling voice. "If I find you, you freaking little blond-haired bitch, we'll have a little fun before I turn you in, you mark my words. Damn strays, always making things harder than they have to be." There's a clang that almost makes me jump out of my skin as the Enforcer opens the dumpster lid. He's literally right next to us, searching through the garbage in case we're hiding inside. But why doesn't he see the blanket with the two human lumps under it?

After a few minutes of rummaging in the garbage, the lid slams shut with a frustrated *bang!* and the guy mumbles, "…might just have to kill you for putting me through all this trouble…" before scuffing away, his footsteps becoming more and more distant until they disappear into the night altogether.

Neither of us move or speak for what feels like hours, our bodies close and warm and covered in a haze of nose-plugging odor.

Finally, he speaks, his voice a low rumble under the blanket. "You okay?"

It feels like such a strange question after the rough way he manhandled me to safety. And yet, I sense he's not just being polite, but genuinely wants to know that I'm uninjured. "I think so," I say, flexing my sore ankle to check for a sprain. It's twisted, but not sprained. Definitely walkable. "I need to get going," I add.

"That guy will be back with more Enfos," he says. "We need a better place to hide."

"Better than a blanket?" I say, not meaning to make a joke, but unable to stop my mouth.

He laughs softly, which sounds even stranger under the circumstances. "It's a special blanket," he explains, which doesn't explain anything.

He stands up, simultaneously lifting the blanket off of me. The relatively fresh air hits my sweaty skin, immediately cooling it and raising goose bumps. "Here," he says, offering a hand.

I'm not one to deny a gentleman his small pleasures, so I take it, allowing him to pull me to my feet. It's probably just my imagination, but his fingers seem to linger on mine for a split-second longer than is necessary. Ever so slightly, the world lightens, as dawn begins when the panel lights on the cavern roofs switch on. With the added light, I see his face for the first time. He *is* young, perhaps my age, perhaps a year or two older. He's also indisputably handsome, with a strong jawline made rugged by the dark stubble of a three-day-old beard, dark brown eyes, and full, pink lips that appear to smile even when I know they're not. When he tosses the blanket in a pile next to the dumpster, I realize why the Enforcer missed us. The blanket is covered in garbage, to the point where you can't even see the fabric. With us under it, it would have just looked like a slightly bigger pile of trash, nothing worth investigating.

"Very clever," I say.

"They only ever check the dumpsters," the guy says. "They've got a lot of firepower, but they're not too bright."

"I take it you've done this before?"

He smiles, flashing a set of nice teeth. "You could say that. Let's go inside."

"The door will be locked," I say, pulling on the handle of a rusty metal door. As expected, it doesn't budge. "See."

"Don't tell me something as small as a locked door will stop a girl as motivated as you," he says, laughing at me with his deep, brown eyes.

I shrug, not knowing what to say. I'm too embarrassed to tell him I've never done *any* of this before.

"Don't worry, I could tell you were a *caker* from a mile away," he says.

I frown. "*Caker?*" I say, confused.

"Rich kid. Family with money. Cake eater."

Uh oh. This is the moment that always occurs when I try to make friends. It's happened to me my whole life. I meet new kids, try to be nice to people, but eventually they find out I

417

belong to one of the few wealthy moon dweller families, and then—

—they hate me.

Except for Cole. He was never one to act like the other kids. But now, my short acquaintance with this guy is over, because he guessed where I come from. We didn't even get to the stage where we exchange names. He might even turn me in to the Enfo.

"I'm Roan," he says.

Huh? I just stare at him, waiting for the punch line, waiting for him to spit in my face, maybe even throw stones at me, like kids used to do before Cole put an end to all that.

He stares back, a goofy smirk resting easily on his face. "This is usually the point where you tell me your name, but if you don't want to…"

"My name?"

"Yeah, you know, like what your mother hollered out when the doc smacked you on the butt after you were born. Or did you want me to guess it?" Before I have a chance to say anything, he continues on, as if we're not hiding from the Enforcers in a deserted alleyway. "Hmm, I'd say you're a Violet. No wait, that's not it. You're Trudy, right?"

Is this guy serious? "Umm, Tawni."

"That was my next guess," he says. "So, *Tawni*, you coming in, or what?"

I gaze down the alley, expecting to see flashes of red as Enforcer reinforcements charge around the bend. But all I see is gray. Hiding out for a few minutes might not be a bad idea. "I've only got fifteen minutes," I say.

"Just enough time for breakfast," he says, sticking a hand in his pocket and pulling out a thin metal stick. "Step aside and make sure you're wearing your safety glasses—this might get messy."

Not having a clue what he's talking about, I move away from the door. With a couple of deft and experienced twists and turns of his wrist, he jams the stick—which I now realize is a pick—into the door's lock. I hear a clatter and a click and then the door opens, creaking slightly.

I just gawk at the door. "That was…" I murmur.

"Awesome, amazing, fan-freaking-tastic? Any of those will do, take your pick. Get it—*pick*," he says, holding up the metal wand.

I nod excitedly. "All of those things. It was really impressive. But is it legal?"

"Is whatever you're doing legal?" he retorts.

Even though I already know I'll have to break a number of rules along the way, his question still stings. Breaking the law doesn't come easily to me. "Fair enough," I say.

"After you," he says with a sweep of his hand. His second gentlemanly act.

I enter first, instinctively flicking on my flashlight amidst the inky darkness. The beam doesn't cut very far through the murk, but provides enough light to illuminate a concrete stairway immediately inside.

"Not much to look at, is it?" Roan says, stepping inside and easing the door shut. He reengages the lock by twisting a latch. "But it's still home."

"Your family lives here?" I ask incredulously.

"My *family* sold out to the Enfos a long time ago. I didn't stay with them after that. They never really liked me anyway."

I turn and take in Roan's shadow-darkened face, searching for a lie. There's none to be found. "I'm sorry," I say. "I'm leaving my family, too."

"Follow me," Roan says, barely brushing against me as he slips by and begins climbing the steps.

When we get to the top, he reaches back and grasps my hand, tugging me gently into a mostly-bare room off to one side. A thin bed pad and lantern sit on the dusty stone floor against one of the cracked walls. The stones, while mostly gray, have a greenish tint that looks anything but natural. The air smells musty and old and faintly of stale cigarettes. Releasing my hand, he says, "This is it. Home, sweet home."

I'm shocked. I've seen plenty of poverty in the Moon Realm, but this is beyond poverty. Roan has nothing. He should hate me for all that I have, but he doesn't seem to. Unless he's been biding his time, acting nice to get me inside, where no one would ever hear me cry out—

"I'm not going to hurt you," he says, an eyebrow raised.

Did he just read my mind? "How did you—"

"You look like someone just punched you in the gut. I know what you're thinking, and you're right not to trust people…like me. But I'm not like that. I just wanted to help you escape, to talk to you. I don't get the chance to make a lot of friends."

Oh. I feel rotten for having the thoughts I did. I can understand why Roan would be lonely in this place. It almost feels like a prison, only without bars on the windows and doors.

I want to change the subject. "Hey, can you teach me that lock-picking trick?"

His eyes light up. I've hit a happy topic. "Sure! It'll come in handy on the streets."

The streets. The phrase sounds so ugly, because...well, because it's true. The streets are my home now. I shrug it off. "Great," I say, trying to sound excited.

Grabbing my hand again, he pulls me outside the room and closes the door behind him. Looking so seriously into my eyes that it makes me blink faster, he says, "See, most locks have metal pins inside, the trick is to get them to all line up, as if there's a key in there..."

For the next twenty minutes—or is it an hour?—he teaches me, showing me sometimes, holding my hand to help me other times, and finally, letting me practice on my own. Just when I think I'll never get it, the lock clicks open!

"I did it!" I exclaim.

"Well done," he says. "You're a good student."

"You're a great teacher," I reply.

There's an awkward silence when he ducks his head sheepishly, as if not accustomed to being complimented.

"Well, I..." I start to say.

"Do you want some breakfast?" he asks suddenly.

"I should really be going..." I say.

"Another time then," he says, "do you know where you're going to live?"

"I have to leave subchapter 14," I say, realizing too late how stupid it is to share my plans with anyone else.

"Leaving? But why?"

"It's a long story," I say, not wanting to reveal any more than I have to. "I need to catch a train."

His dark eyes slowly brighten as he cocks his head to the side into the beam of his flashlight. After a few seconds chewing on his lip, he nods, as if he's made up his mind about something. "I'll take you to the station," he says. "You know, for safety," he adds.

"You really don't have to…"

"I *want* to," Roan says, shrugging.

Well, if he wants to… "Sounds great."

Although I've lingered far too long at Roan's place, we make up a lot of time on the way to the train station. Roan takes me on a crazy and convoluted route that I could never repeat on my own. Although we get within eyeshot of Enforcers several times, we never get close enough to feel threatened. By Roan's side, I feel safer than I thought I could possibly feel away from home. Even though I don't really know him, I feel like I trust him. If he wanted to hurt me, he already could have. It feels good being with someone, and I'm dreading reaching our destination. It's weird: I'm actually sort of enjoying running away while I'm with him.

But all good things have to come to an end.

Standing on crumbles of broken glass, we can see the entrance to the train station from our vantage point at the end of a shadowy alley. I've missed the beginning portion of the morning rush from our subchapter, but there are still plenty of late arrivers to keep things busy and hectic, which is exactly what I need.

Here goes nothing.

"Thank you, Roan," I say, meaning it. His kindness was an unexpected—and life-saving—part of my journey to this point.

He shrugs as if it's the kind of thing he does every day. "Sure. So there's nothing I can do to change your mind about going?" The smile that accompanies his words generates a burst of heat on my cheeks. I certainly wouldn't mind looking at his face a little while longer, but I've already delayed this too long and I'm afraid if I don't take the first step now, I never will.

"This is something I have to do," I say, trying to make my voice as deep and bold-sounding as I can.

He nods, like he already guessed my response. "Be careful, Tawni. If I'm lucky we'll meet again."

"I hope we do," I say, wishing I could drag the moment out a little longer. I've never liked goodbyes, even ones from people I don't know very well—or in this case, at all. But I manage to square my shoulders, face the train station, and find a tiny splinter of courage somewhere in my bones. I'm doing this to atone for the sins of my parents. If I can find Adele Rose, I'll tell her the truth about what they did to her family, and I'll do everything in my power to make things right.

My legs are suddenly like lead, but even that can't stop me. I lift one foot and force it forward, following it with the other foot. With each step I feel lighter, as if bits and pieces of a heavy burden are crumbling down from my shoulders. I feel alive.

I slink into a stream of adults making their way to the train station. Keeping my eyes straight ahead, I avoid looking at them for fear that "Alert! Delinquent!" might be written all over my face. But no one seems interested in me. They all have their own problems, which they face by trudging to the train every day, zombie-like expressions on their blank faces, hoping that they'll earn enough today to feed their families. Yeah, they've got bigger concerns than a sixteen-year-old girl who should be getting ready for school.

And then I'm inside the train station, so quickly that it almost feels like I blinked out of existence and back into it, not even passing through the arched entrance. I nearly forget to prepare my ticket and travel pass until I notice a woman who's scrambling for hers. Swinging my pack around, I locate the ticket and forged intra-Realm travel authorization card under a sachet of rice.

The automated turnstiles loom ahead, spinning as each rider scans their ticket and, depending on where they're going, their travel authorization. I've never ridden a train before, never left my subchapter, so I watch each traveler, memorizing the order of things. Ticket first, then pass, green light, push through the gate. Not so hard.

There are only five people in front of me, no more than ten seconds. The moment of truth. Will there be flashing lights and blaring alarms? Or will the green light blink, beckoning me through to a new life?

Four people. No wait, three people—two passed through while I was worrying.

Green light. Two people.

I realize I'm sweating profusely from my forehead. Make that my armpits. And kneepits, if there is such a thing. Everywhere, really. I'm a sweaty mess.

Green light. One person—the woman who was as unprepared as I, who now has her ticket ready, just like me.

My heart's pounding, both in my chest and my head. My knees feel rubbery, as if my bones have melted under me, congealing into a moldable substance that wobbles and totters like a two-year-old who still can't walk properly.

Green light. The woman passes through the turnstiles and for a moment the metal rungs look like scythes, cutting her to ribbons, severing her limbs like scissors against the arms of paper cutout dolls. I blink away the thought.

My turn.

I just stare at the ticket scanner, wondering what fate it holds for me. My mind goes blank. What goes first again? Pass or ticket? I know the answer should be obvious, but I just can't seem to remember. My mind is more muddled than bean stew.

"Move it," a gruff voice says from behind me.

If I don't hurry I'm going to draw a lot more attention to myself than I want. Ticket first, I remember. I scan my ticket, which I already know is valid. A dull beep sounds and a robotic voice says, "Please scan your travel authorization now."

I'm dead. I know it. I should just turn and leave now, before it's too late. Forget the strange and annoyed stares I'll get from the other passengers. Forget the shame I'll feel inside for having chickened out. Go back to Roan's place and let him teach me the ways of the street.

"Hurry up, kid!" A different voice this time, angrier than the first, and identifying me as a "kid," which is exactly the sort of tag I don't want. The instinct to run grows stronger and I start to turn, but then something pops into my head that stops me.

A face from the news. I watched it with my parents on the telebox, knowing full well it was them that had created this news story. The face of a young girl—my age. Adele Rose. Black, obsidian hair. Pale skin, like mine. Fierce, emerald-green eyes. Full lips. Pretty. A look on her face that could only be described as ugly. It was a face that told a tale of betrayal, of having her parents sold to the world as traitors, of being ripped from her family and sent to the Pen until she turns eighteen, and then to an adult prison, the Max, until the day she dies. All because of the actions of my parents. Not me—my parents. And yet I feel responsible.

The memory of her face stops me. Only I can turn her expression pretty again.

I turn and scan my fake travel pass, ready to be arrested if that is my fate.

The light turns green.

I can't help the smile that lights up my face as I stride forward, placing my hands on the push bar, which is cold and hard, but with rounded edges, not like the razor-sharp blade of a scythe at all. I did it—I'm leaving the subchapter at long last! I'm so full of elation that I literally feel bubbles of air rising in my chest, lifting my posture higher, buoying my spirits. I start to push the bar forward.

"Wait just a minute, kid!" I hear from behind.

When I turn I see red: a uniform, clean and bright; an Enforcer, his Taser raised, aimed directly at my chest; his face, a duplicate of the man I saw smoking a cigarette on a moon dweller stoop earlier this very morning.

"I told you I'd catch you," he snarls, pressing a button on his Taser.

Just before the snake of electricity pulls me into unconsciousness, I think, *I'm coming, Cole.*

~THE END~

The Life Lottery
A Story from Year Zero
Originally posted in Furthermore: an Anthology.

Today is The Lottery. It's been the only thing anyone's talked about for the last week.

My mom said it would never happen, that the government would come to their senses, come up with a new plan. My dad said the whole world's gone crazy. Now that the day is here, it looks like my dad was right.

The guy on the news says that the countries aren't speaking to each other anymore, that it's every country for itself. That just seems sad to me. I once had a pen pal named Sophia from France. I worry about her. I wonder if France has a Lottery too.

The Lottery in the U.S. is "a bag of baloney," my dad says. By that I think he just means it's not a good system. I pretty much agree with him, because I don't want to be split up with my family. The way it works is that every person of every age has the same chance of getting picked. The government says that's the only way it can be equal, because if they did it by family, the smaller families would have an equal chance of being selected as a larger family, and it might mess up the number of people who are allowed to go underground. Only three million can fit in the caves, they say. No exceptions! I can still see the President's finger pointing at the camera, as if he's yelling at me personally.

I might be only twelve years old, but even I don't think it feels like the right rules. I mean, what if my dad gets picked and not my mom? Or my sister, Tina, and not me? Or what if everyone *except* me gets picked? What would I do then? Who will I live with until the meteor comes?

But there's no arguing with the government people. Once they decide something, that's it. End of story. Only for the rest of us, it's not the end of the story—it's only the beginning.

My mom gave me this diary this morning so I could "share my experiences and pass them down to my children." I think she's being rather optimistic, but I didn't tell her that. I'm scared I'm not doing a very good job with it so far; I mean, I haven't even told you my name. Anna Lucinda Smith. There—I guess that covers that.

At school I have lots of friends, but it's not like I'm stuck up about it or anything. I just get along with most people, I guess. Not that we have school anymore. Ever since the announcement, pretty much everything's been cancelled. My parents won't even let me go outside, because everyone's going crazy and breaking into stores and stealing stuff and all that nonsense. I've seen all that on the news, but not in person. My neighborhood has mostly been quiet, with people just staying inside, spending time with their families. It would actually be kind of cool getting out of school for a few days if it weren't for the whole world-ending thing.

It's been a little boring, too, so I started playing this game I made up. I cut up a hundred strips of paper. On four of them I wrote "Anna", "Tina", "Mom" and "Dad". Then I put them in a bowl and mixed them all around. With my eyes closed, I take turns picking out a name. After reading it and marking it on a score sheet, I stick the name back in the bowl and try again. Most of the time I just get a blank piece of paper, which means some random stranger was selected to go underground. But every once in a while I get a hit. So far I've picked random strangers eighty six times, my mom twice (she's always been the lucky one in the family), my dad once—and even I got picked once. Only Tina hasn't come up yet, but I think that's because she'll be the one to get chosen in the real Lottery. Anyway, the game passes the time.

My parents are out for some registration thing they had to do in advance of The Lottery tonight, and my sister is in her room listening to her iPod and obsessing over some guy that she hopes will get chosen with her. She thinks it would be so romantic to go underground with this guy, like something out of a movie. Although I've seen the guy, and he *is* cute, this isn't a movie. In any case, I'm alone again so I play my game for another two hours. I pick out one hundred and thirty three strips of paper.

None of them have a name on it.

Not a good sign for tonight.

I'm thankful when my parents get home because I'm feeling depressed about the game. I don't tell my mom though because she's been telling me all week not to play it.

Mom makes lunch—salami and provolone cheese, my favorite!—while Dad scoops ice cream into tall glasses and pours Root beer on top. All the while they keep up a constant chatter about how nice and sunny it is outside—cold, but nice—how we should all go in the backyard and spend time together later, and how beautiful the leaves are now that they're changing. I've never heard them so cheery, which scares me.

After lunch, the day whizzes by, like it's sprouted wings and flown south for the winter. Tina refuses to come out of her room. I don't feel like going outside either, but I finally give in to my parents and follow them to the backyard. We sit cross-legged in the grass for a while, which feels weird and awkward, probably because it's something we've never done before—I mean, why would we?

Dad has a ball, which we pass around. Each time someone catches it, they have to say something that they love about the person who threw it to them. Although I know what Tina would call the game—"Totally cheese ball!"—I kind of like it. Not only do my parents say some really nice things about me— my dad says I'm "as pretty as a flower," and my mom says my sense of humor "is as good as your father's," which is saying something, because Dad's pretty funny—but I also get to hear them say some nice things to each other. I'm not embarrassed to admit that I'm disappointed when the game ends and we go inside to eat dinner.

Tina finally makes an appearance, although she doesn't talk much, just types out "later texts" on her phone, which I guess are texts she'll send to Brady—her guy—after The Lottery is over. She says they're all positive messages which will help their karma, so they both get picked. I don't ask her what messages she's sending for me so I'll get picked. I also don't tell her that she never gets chosen in my game.

Dinner is delicious: my mom's famous meatloaf and creamy mashed potatoes, drowned in brown gravy. Hot fudge sundaes for dessert this time, compliments of Dad.

When we finish, we get dressed in nice clothes, as if we're going to church. Dad says there will be lots of photographers at each of the local Lotteries, taking pictures for future history books. I wear a medium-length purple dress with amethyst beading that Tina once admitted makes me look "all grown up." When we meet downstairs she gives me a nod as if to say, "Nice choice," which makes me smile. She, on the other hand, tries to slip past Dad in a tiny black skirt and a tight, low-cut red blouse. He makes her change twice before she finally gets it right. I guess even on Lottery Day, he's still a dad.

Dad wears his best suit and a pink tie that almost makes him look like another person. Mom is in her favorite blue gown—the one with all the sparkles.

Like everyone else, we walk to the school, where The Lottery will be held. It's slow going, because Tina and Mom are wearing heels, clopping along with short strides. I'm glad I wore my ballet flats.

Dozens of other families are doing the same, and we greet many of them with cheerful cries of "Hello!" and "How are you?" They answer with the same forced cheerfulness.

We arrive at the school and enter the auditorium through the propped-open double doors. Dad hands some papers to man at a desk who then signals us forward. Already the hall is half full. Ushers direct us up one of the aisles and into the next available row. Normally I'd want to sit by one of my friends, Maddy or Bridget or Haley, who I spot sitting a few rows forward, but I know tonight is meant to be spent with family. Even Tina sits with us, which she never does these days.

Despite all the greetings and warm wishes that were exchanged outside of the auditorium doors, once inside, no one speaks to each other, or even smiles. It's like we all know that the others are our enemies, people who will strip us of our winning ticket in The Lottery, take away our family and friends.

Not long after we arrive, the auditorium fills up. I stare at the empty stage, where I once stood dressed like a tree in the school play, *The Wizard of Oz*. Now it looks barren and desolate, like a hot, dusty stretch of desert. Mom checks her watch and shows it to me: one minute until eight o'clock. Time for The Lottery.

She squeezes my hand and holds on.

All is silent in the hall, not even a whispered comment breaking the quiet. Footsteps echo onto the stage as a man who I recognize from TV moves across to a podium in the center. A local politician. The mayor or governor or something like that. The man in charge tonight.

When he reaches the stand, the microphone cuts his face in half, so he lowers it until it's even with his lips. He speaks, his voice magnified and deep, like the real Wizard of Oz from the movie.

"Residents of the Sawcutter School District of the great state of Pennsylvania. Today is a momentous occasion in the history of our great country." Although he looks up every couple of words, his voice sounds stiff, scripted, like he's reading off of something, perhaps a hidden paper on the podium. "I know you all must be scared, because you have little control over the random selection that is about to be made, but remember that this is an opportunity to defeat the cosmic powers that strive to wipe us off the face of the earth. For the first time in history, a species has had the wherewithal and foresight to prepare for just such an event. We will not be forced into extinction! We will fight to survive, whether above or underground! We cannot be defeated!"

He spouts the last three sentences with such conviction that it's like he's leading a pep rally, trying to get us all pumped up for The Lottery, but his words fall flat on our ears and we just stare at him. Mom glances at Dad and he rolls his eyes.

"Well, uh, I guess we should get started then," the guy says when no one applauds. "First, the formalities. The names of all five thousand, two hundred and forty six residents of this district have been entered into a database, sorted alphabetically by last name. When I press a button, the computer will randomly select a name from the database, simultaneously removing it from the list. I will read out the name. I ask that you try to keep your celebrating to a minimum so that I can move on to the next name. As announced by the President of the United States a week ago today, each citizen of this country will receive a one in one hundred chance of being chosen, and therefore, I will read out fifty two names for this district. Good luck."

He pauses and I remember my game, remember how excited I got when I opened my eyes to see that I'd picked one of my family members. If I magnify that feeling by a million, that's how excited I know I'll be if all of us get picked today.

He reads the first name: "Helen Chambers."

Somewhere behind us a woman squeals in delight, but I don't look back. That name is foreign to me. I close my eyes, wait for the next name.

Another stranger—a blank strip of paper. No one worth getting excited over.

Ten more names—ten more strangers. I flinch with each one. And then—

Maddy gets picked! My eyes flash open and I look where I know she's sitting. She's smiling as her mother puts an arm around her shoulders, hugging her, but she also looks kind of scared and I know why: no one else in her family has been chosen.

More names, more exclamations of excitement, more blank names on white pieces of paper. Although I've tried to keep track, I've lost count of how many names have been called. One of my neighbors gets picked, a guy who's always been nice to me, bought Girl Scout Cookies from me and said hello when I walked by, but I realize I'm not happy for him…because he's not my family. Like the rest of the people around me, he's the competition.

Three, four, five, six names: not us. Enemies.

There's a pause and my breath catches in my throat. Is that it? Has The Lottery ended so quickly without warning? Will my family go home without a ticket, left to face the meteor with the rest of those not chosen?

"Ten spots left," the man says, and I let out my breath. A warning. A bone. A shred of hope. Almost like a redo, like in my game when I pick out a blank paper, I can just put it back and try again. Ten more tries.

"Morgan Rivers." A stranger in the front row.

"Willow Meadows." Sounds like a made up name.

"Robert Dorsett." Who?

Seven left.

Three no-names and then a man my father works with. Three left.

"Meghan Taurasi." Never heard of her.

"Brian Henderson." An older man two rows in front of us tips his brown bowler hat at the stage.

One left. He pauses, scans the audience, as if he's taking in each of the faces, knowing full well he has bad news for most of us. Ten seconds go by and I wonder if I miscounted, if Mr. Henderson was the last name the computer has for us.

But then he clears his throat and speaks: "Anna L. Smith."

~THE END~

2) An Interview with Perry the Prickler

Originally posted on <u>Lola's Reviews</u>. Awesome questions by Lolita Verroen, who conducted the strangest interview of her life.

Lolita: Hi Perry! I am so excited to have the chance to interview you today! You are definitely one of my favorite side-characters of Fire Country!

Perry: Well, thank you for that. I wish you'd tell the natives, they can be extremely sour and unpleasant sometimes, bitching and moaning about their little "problems." Meanwhile, they're the ones trying to chop me and my brothers up to make salad or stew or some other such local dish.

Lolita: So Perry can you tell us a little something about yourself (like who and what you are)?

Perry: Well, as you mentioned, my name's Perry. Well, it's not really. I never really had a name, until this strange black-haired girl came along and starting talking to me, which nobody had ever done to me before, and well, she called me Perry and it kinda stuck.

What am I? Hmmm, I understand that most of your readers are from the 21st century, so they'd probably understand the term "cactus" although the people of fire country refer to me as a "prickler." Basically, I'm a thick-skinned plant that grows even under the harshest conditions, like in fire country, where's there's not enough burnin' water to barely quench my thirst. I've got spiky little buggers all over me, so watch out if you get too close—Siena learned that the hard way when she ran smack into me. I'm able to store loads of water in me, so the natives like to use me for a quick drink and something to munch on, if they can get past my pricklers that is! Sometimes I bear beautiful flowers, but only if we get enough rain, which is rare, so usually I'm just plain old gray-green Perry the Prickler.

Lolita: How old are you?

Perry: If treated well, I'm immortal, able to last for centuries even out in the desert, but because of the Meteor god, who became angry with the humans, all desert plant life was pretty much wiped out. Somehow, somewhere, some prickler buds survived though, and sure enough, I started growing once the great dust clouds rose and disappeared, and the searin' humans started crawling from their hiding places. Long story for a short answer, I know. I'm approximately exactly Four hundred and eighty nine years old, by the humans' reckoning. In prickler years that makes me twenty one, so I'd like to say hi to all the ladies out there looking for an extremely eligible bachelor. Hiiiii!

Lolita: What is your favorite color?

I love a deep magenta with a yellow border. I sprouted these flowers once that were exactly like that. Absolutely breathtaking. A nasty baggard by the name of Keep picked them clean offa me and gave them to a female inmate up here in Confinement, trying to win her affections and such. Well, she spat in his face. But then she wore my flowers behind her ears until they withered away to nothing but brown mush.

Lolita: What is your favorite time of the day?

Perry: Nighttime, when the searin' humans are sleeping. Not that a little darkness ever stopped Siena. In fact, she seemed to talk to me more at night than any other time, always going on and on about conspiracies and her father and blah, blah, blah. I was like, hey girlfriend, can a guy get a little shut eye? Not that I have any eyes, but I still need my beauty sleep.

Lolita: How is it like to be bound to one place?

Perry: Bound? Oh, I wouldn't call it bound. I mean, I ain't got any feet, but that don't stop me from walking far and wide. Maybe not in person, but through the eyes of other pricklers. You see, all pricklers are connected. We see what each other see, we hear what each other hear, we know what each other know, you get me?

Ha! I could see it in your eyes that you bought that whole load of tugblaze! I was just screwin' you around a little, all in good fun of course. Honestly, it really sucks sometimes, not being able to move from one place. I've got to rely on all the action coming to me up in Confinement, but I still feel like I miss so much of the goings on in fire country. But I guess it could be worse. I could be one of those pricklers stuck in the middle of the desert with only 'zards, Cotees, and vultures to keep them company. Or worse yet, one of those pricklers that end up in someone's prickler salad, all cut up into little chunks.

Lolita: How does your normal day look like?

Perry: Well, when the sun comes up and turns the sky all red and the clouds all yellow, I usually start with some stretching, reaching for the sky, working the kinks out. Then I do mental jumping jacks, just pretending, trying to get some exercise. It's almost the same thing as actually doing them, and I swear I would do them if I had legs and well, arms.

What next? Ahh, yes, I drink a smidgen of the water I've got stored inside me, just enough to quench my thirst and keep me from drying out and getting too brittle. Nobody likes a brittle prickler! Then, if there are any brambleweeds being blown past by the wind I do my best to catch them on my spikes. You know, like sort of a game. It's fun. I mean, I can only lean a centimeter or two to either side, but sometimes that makes all the difference.

When I get bored in the afternoon, I usually take to taunting anyone who's nearby. I'm an avid taunter, did you know that? Of course, I'm sure you do. I pretty much taunted Siena every second of every day she was stuck in that cage of hers, and even when she wasn't. I tend to taunt those I like the most, so she got a very healthy dose.

As night falls I always watch the sunset, because hey, I got the best seat in the house and who doesn't like a good sunset?

Nighttime is for listening, and although I've got a big mouth, I can listen pretty searin' good if I put my mind to it. The desert has so much to say at night with creepy-crawly things, well, creeping and crawling and slithering and scurrying. And Cotees howling too, a mournful, eerie sound that makes you shiver in the best way possible.

Lolita: What do you like doing in your free time?

Just having fun mostly. I mean, what else is life about but having fun. So I usually try to keep things exciting by making up new taunts I can use on any passing humans. Or I might scare a passing 'zard with a loud "Argh!" in their face. That always gets me laughing. But really, I don't have too much free time, what with all the humans passing through to observe. Then it's my solemn duty to pass any information I get through the mental telepathies of all the other pricklers....Ha! Got you again! I wouldn't know a prickler on the other side of fire country from a prickler sitting right next to me.

Lolita: Can you tell us something about your first meeting with Siena?

Perry: Well, first of all, you should read her book, Fire Country, because it'll tell you everything that happened. But if you want to know one thing, it's that I didn't mean to prick her with my spikes. I tried to move, I swear it, but my two-centimeter lean wasn't nearly enough to get out of her way. And when she crashed into me and my spikes got her, I felt awful, terrible really, for maybe five, ten seconds. And then I just thought it was really funny and I couldn't stop laughing, because who runs into a prickler!

Lolita: Can you tell us something interesting you have seen happen in the confinement of Fire Country?

Nothing really. These humans are so wooloo, I never know what they're thinking. They shove people in these cages, which is pure foolishness, because what a waste it is to have perfectly good arms and legs and not be able to use them. That's why I was really happy for Siena when she used her perfectly good arms and legs to bust out of Confinement, not once, but twice! Impressive, really, although I couldn't help giving her a hard time about it. A human's gotta be free and a prickler's gotta laugh, right?

Lolita: Thanks so much Perry for letting me interview you! I think it was one of the most fun interviews I have ever done ☺!

Perry: Wow, is that it? Is that my fifteen minutes of fame? But I'm not done yet, I have so much more to tell, I just want to say—

It was at this point that a tugskin was thrown over Perry's spiky head to convince him it was nighttime and that he should be sleeping. Thankfully, he fell for it and shut the scorch up

3) A Sneak Peek
BREW
BOOK 1 OF SALEM'S REVENGE
Available anywhere e-books are sold October 1, 2014!

PART ONE

SALEM'S REVENGE

In the black of night,

'Midst shattered dreams,

Come darkest terrors, once unseen.

Hidden amongst us,

Wielding ancient power,

'Til the wraiths step forward, for the witching hour.

Salem's Revenge, Rhett Carter

One

The witches don't deserve to die.

As I chuck my football cleats in my duffel and zip it shut, my foster mom's words ring in my head. For months she's been focused on the whole Salem's Return debacle. The new laws, the hunt for real, live witches, the executions. And, after the news today, she's up in arms all over again.

Number of Witches May Stretch into the Thousands, the headline read.

It almost made me laugh, but I held it in because of the grave expression on my mom's face. Witches? Come on. There's no such thing, not in real life anyway. Between the pages of the books I love to read, however, that's a different story. And that's where they should stay. All the rest is nothing more than fear, just like it was during the original Salem Witch Trials.

"Bye, Mom!" I shout as I push through the front door, shouldering my backpack and football gear.

"Have a good day, Rhett!" Trudy Smith calls back, but her head never turns, her eyes glued to the continued Salem's Return news coverage.

The world is a scary place. One big hot mess. While we should be focused on our real problems, like the thousands of homeless living—and starving—on the streets, the ever-rising cost of healthcare, and the ticking time bomb that is the social security system, the lawmakers are focused on…drumroll please…witches. Really?

I weave my way along the familiar path through the Atlanta suburbs, making my way to meet my friends, Beth and Xavier. Well, Xave's a friend, and Beth—she's more than a friend. The thought brings a smile to my face, instantly erasing the negative energy from this morning's news.

On the opposite side of the street, I see a couple of my teammates getting into their car. They glance in my direction, pausing to smirk at me. I'd wave, but I don't really like them very much—like, at all. Unfortunately, the "mates" part of "teammates" is used loosely in my case. Maybe if I partied more and read fewer books I'd be more popular on the team. But alas, the star quarterback, Todd Logue, has decided to make me the target of ninety-nine percent of his jokes. And these two punks are two of his besties.

So I look away from them and just keep walking, breathing a sigh of relief when they don't do more than honk obnoxiously at me as they roar past, filling the air with a foul-smelling cloud of fumes.

"This week I decided the school newspaper should discuss Salem's Return," Beth says when I meet her and Xavier in front of their neighboring houses.

"Good morning to you, too," I say, leaning down to sneak in a quick kiss. To my delight, Beth returns it, her lips lingering on mine for three awesome beats of my heart.

"They should outlaw kissing in front of friends," Xave says, turning away from us and shielding his eyes. My best friend, as usual, looks like he's heading to some private prep school. Wearing a red and blue sweater vest that perfectly matches his brightly colored belt, he could be the son of a politician or a CEO. Beneath the vest is a spotless white button-down shirt.

"You might not be saying that if you had a boyfriend," I say, pulling away from Beth.

"Yes, I would," Xave says, starting down the sidewalk. A carpool full of students zooms past, radio blasting.

"I guess you saw this morning's news then," I say, returning to Beth's initial topic of choice. "So you're going to write about the revival of the Salem Witch Trials?"

Her big, brown eyes light up the way they always do when she talks about her latest project as editor of the school paper. "Yes," she says. "I've been doing some initial research, and something about it all just doesn't add up. I don't think the government is telling us everything."

"Do they ever?" I say.

"You mean, like a conspiracy?" Xave says, leaning in. He's always liked a good conspiracy to start the day. I smile, because why not? The sun is shining, I'm with my two best friends, and no one has tried to pick a fight with me today. All in all, it's a good start to a Wednesday.

"Exactly," Beth says. "It's still early on, but I'll let you know what I find out."

"Correction. You'll let the whole school know what you find out," I say.

"No. The whole world!" Xave says, laughing. I try to disguise my own laugh as a cough, but Beth hits me anyway. Although Beth's articles are only published in print in the school newspaper, she also shares them with the respectable following she's managed to amass on her collection of favorite social networking sites.

"Laugh all you want, boys, but when I'm running a real paper you'll learn the true power of the press." I don't doubt her words, not for one second.

I rub my shoulder even though her whack was the equivalent of getting hit by a raindrop. "So what do you think they're holding back?" I ask. "Everyone already knows the witches aren't really witches."

"How do you know?" Beth says, firing me a frown. "You read books about witches all the time, and yet you don't even think they could be real?"

"That's fiction," I say.

"Seems like half of what's in old science fiction books has been coming true for years."

"Yeah, but that's grounded in reality. In science. Now we're talking fantasy. Magic. Not. Real." We make another turn, which seems to prove my point. More nondescript cookie-cutter houses line another cookie-cutter street in suburbia. One of a million such neighborhoods across the country that have many things in common—including no real witches.

"Anyway," Beth says, "it doesn't matter whether they're real witches or not, they're being murdered for nothing other than existing. It's not right."

"Now that I agree with," I say. "I can't wait to read everything you find out."

My comment draws a smile from my girlfriend, which I much prefer to the glares she's been giving me for the last few minutes. She wraps an arm around my waist and pulls me into her side.

"Well, I know one thing," Xave says, "if I ever come across a male witch, I won't turn him in—I'll ask for his number. Witches are hot."

"There's no such thing as male witches," I say.

"Always gotta be a know-it-all," Xave says. "I meant warlocks, or wizards, or whatever Harry Potter is."

"You've got a crush on Harry Potter?" Beth says, raising her eyebrows.

"Not Harry specifically, although when he fires a curse it definitely gets my heart pumping. More like Draco Malfoy. Now he's a stud."

"You always preferred the bad boys," I note.

Beth chuckles, and Xave says, "True. At least I'd know what to do if I came face to face with a witch. You two would be hopeless. Beth would probably ask for an interview, and Rhett here would either freeze up or run away screaming."

Ever since I met Xavier in the foster system when we were five, he's been like a brother to me. And, like a brother, he knows me all too well. He's fought for me at least a dozen times, while it's always been my preference to use words—rather than fists—as my weapon of choice. I owe him more than I can ever repay.

So I don't even mind the insult, not when I can feel the warmth of Beth's body seeping through our clothes. The school comes into view and I let out a silent groan. I squeeze Beth one more time and then head toward the opposite end of campus, to the athletic locker rooms. I have to stow my football gear before I make my way to class.

"See you guys later," I say, still thinking about what Beth said about witches being real.

~~~

Football practice. Although I don't mind sports, I'd rather be hanging with Xave and Beth than smashing into sweaty guys. However, according to my foster father, my height, build, and athletic abilities make football my best shot at a college scholarship. I'm taller than most guys on the team, and when I wear contacts Beth says I almost look like a football player. But I know she prefers me with glasses—we're two nerds in a pod. Xave says we're a cute couple because we're opposites in so many ways. Her brown eyes are light; mine are dark. She's petite; I'm, well, not. Her nose is small, like a button; according to Xave, mine is too big, although Beth says it's cute.

So here I am, on the sidelines, waiting for Coach to arrive, thankful that my dark skin isn't particularly sensitive to the hot Georgia sun.

"Jacob's search for true love is something every teenage boy can relate to," a voice says from behind. I sigh, hating the way my own written words sound so pathetic and stupid when spoken by the human gorilla.

I finish tying my cleats and turn around to find Todd Logue and three of his football buddies laughing at me. "Do you need something?" I say, unwilling to rise to the bait.

"Me?" Todd says, feigning surprise. "All I need are more of your blog posts. They touch me in ways I never knew were possible." He makes a vigorous and exceptionally lewd gesture with his hand. His goons laugh louder.

Knowing that people like him are able to read my posts almost make me want to give up book blogging. Almost.

"I'm so glad," I say, offering the fakest, broadest smile I can muster. I grab my helmet and head left toward the field.

The foursome move in tandem, blocking my path. Determined to avoid them, I turn toward the right. Again, they block my escape.

"We'll let you by if you recite something from your last blog post," Todd says. "You know, the one I printed two hundred copies of and posted around the school."

He didn't. I want to believe myself, but I know it's exactly the kind of thing he would do. A crowd starts to gather as some of the students who were there to watch the football practice realize something's about to go down.

"Screw you," I say, moving back to the left to try to get past. I refuse to let him goad me into a fight. One of his goons pushes me back.

Someone in the crowd yells, "Fight!"

"Leave him the hell alone," a familiar voice says. Crap. I glance over where Xavier has just emerged to stand beside me. His pudgy face is pulled into a frown.

"Xave, I'm fine," I hiss. "Get out of here." When he looks up at me with those fiercely loyal brown eyes of his, I know he's not going anywhere. When did he get so much smaller than me? While I've grown up, he's grown out, his plump belly making him as big a target of bullies as me.

"Oooh, has your fat boyfriend come to save you?" Todd taunts.

Although a few chuckles dance through the crowd, I see plenty of kids shaking their heads, not amused by Todd in the least. And yet none of them step forward to help. I don't blame them. Why make yourself a target when staying under the radar is so much easier?

Xave doesn't understand the meaning of "flying under the radar."

"At least Rhett's ancestors didn't swing from trees," Xave says, not backing down. He rummages through his bag and finds a banana, which he tosses over Todd's head. "Fetch!"

There are a lot of laughs from the crowd, which only seems to infuriate Todd, his eyebrows pinching together. "You'll pay for that, homo," he says, stepping forward.

He swings at Xave's head, but I step in front of him, taking the punch in the chest. It hurts like hell, but I stand my ground, ushering Xave, who's trying to get around me, further back. The next punch catches me in the face and twists my head around, blood exploding from my nose.

The four huge guys surround us, all smiles and wisecracks.

"Bring it, losers," Xave says as they close in. Sometimes I wish my best friend was a little more scared of pain.

I tense up, ready to take the worst beating I've had since my second foster father, Big Hank, used to regularly use Xave and me as punching bags, when a flat, hard voice says, "I'd stop while you're ahead, Todd."

Todd stops mid-punch, whirling to glare at the girl who would dare threaten him. Soft brown skin. Intriguing brown eyes, flashing with anger. Glasses that give her a trendy, intelligent look. Her hands are on her hips, a look of utter contempt screwing up her otherwise pretty features.

Not again, I think. Beth. She wasn't supposed to make it to watch practice today, her duties as editor of the school newspaper consuming her afternoon.

"I won't hit a girl," Todd says.

"How chivalrous," Beth says.

"But you're awfully tempting," Todd says.

"Like a guppy to a shark."

"So why don't you get out of here so we can finish with these two?" Todd says.

"I've got a better idea," Beth says, a somewhat vicious smile forming on her pink lips. "Why don't you go back to what you do best—throwing a ball—and we'll pretend this never happened."

Silence. I can tell Todd's confused, his face switching between laughing and frowning. Evidently he doesn't know what to make of the spitfire standing before him. I'm equally dumbfounded, wondering how the hell Beth is planning to get Todd to back down. But there's one thing I know about Beth: She always has a plan.

"And why should I do that?" Todd asks.

Beth motions for him to come closer. He stands stock-still, then shrugs and saunters over to her. The kids in the crowd are whispering to each other, their hands over their mouths. Our little scene is better entertainment than reality TV.

When Todd gets close to her, she motions him even closer, toward her mouth. The tall quarterback has to bend to get to her level. She whispers something in his ear and he stiffens, pulling back. His eyes are wide and white for a moment, and then he sneers, "C'mon, boys. These losers aren't even worth our time."

Although the other players don't look like they want to leave, one by one they follow their leader as he jogs back onto the field.

"Break it up! There's nothing to see here!" Beth shouts, motioning for the audience to go back to whatever they were doing before.

"Wow!" Xave says, watching the crowd dissipate. "That was incredible. I didn't even have to get all bloody and bruised, like I usually do when I defend Rhett."

I cringe, hating how I always feel when my friends have to come to my rescue.

Like a big wimp.

"Those idiots deserve more than a free pass," Beth mutters, but flashes a real smile. "A swift kick in the groin would've been more satisfying."

"Ooh," Xave groans. "Remind me never to get on your bad side."

"Sorry," I say, feeling about half my six-foot, four-inch height.

"About what?" Beth says, wrapping an arm around my waist.

"Involving you guys in my problems yet again."

"We involved ourselves," Xave says, beaming. "It's part of our job description. Personally it's not my favorite part of the job, but I'm pretty used to it by now. Like, remember when Big Hank came home drunk and decided you needed 'toughening up'?"

"Not this story again," I say, wishing Xave had a shorter memory.

"Oh, have I told this one before?" Xave says, raising his eyebrows theatrically. "Let's just say that I took the licks for you. It's the only time I've had two black eyes and a bloody nose all at the same time."

I chew my lip, remembering that night. After all, it was only eight short years earlier that Xave and I met when we were both sent to live with Big Hank and his wife, Cindi. For almost a year it was a nightly ritual for him to come home drunk, driving a beat-up pickup proudly flying a Confederate flag, unleashing a barrage of obscenities at Cindi, who would spew all sorts of vile threats right back.

Big Hank would stomp up the steps and, with his alcohol-breath hitting us in a nauseating blast, he'd pick one of us and then proceed to "beat the black out of us," as he liked to say.

On more than one occasion, Xave, who was bigger than me back then, would volunteer to take the beating for me. I cried most of those nights, listening to Xave's screams.

Two days after the final beating Xave took from Big Hank, Cindi shot and killed her husband when he tried to touch her.

Xave, who was still recovering in the hospital from his "bad bike accident," and I were split up and moved to different foster homes.

Neither of them was as bad as staying with Big Hank and Cindi. But neither of them was much better either.

"Ooh, wait, I've got one," Beth says, raising a finger in the air.

"Not you, too," I say. "You know, you two would make really good bullies. You've mastered the art of ganging up."

Ignoring me, Beth says, "Remember how we met?" Ugh. Why can't we be a normal couple with a cute story of how we got together? Like someone knocks her books out of her arms and I pick them up. Or she sees me catch a game-winning touchdown pass and interviews me for a school article. No such luck.

"No," I lie.

"Then let me remind you. Much like today, you and Xave were surrounded by thugs."

"I was throwing punches like a tornado," Xave says, chiming in.

"None of them connecting," I mutter.

"And Rhett was just standing there letting his face get tenderized," Xave continues.

"I shouted, 'Cops!' and the bullies and crowd took off running," Beth concludes.

"See," I say, "if not for my knack for attracting attention, we might not even know each other."

"I still don't get why you don't stand up for yourself," Beth says.

"Rhett wouldn't hurt a fly," Xave says. "It's just not in him."

"What should we do after practice?" I say, changing the subject.

"You're a freaking giant, Rhett," Beth says, continuing on as if I hadn't spoken.

"A real Big Foot…" Xave adds.

"I barely come up to your waist," Beth says.

"…with fists the size of meat cleavers," Xave says.

I throw my hands up. "Okay, okay, I get it. I should be doing the hitting, not getting hit. I should be book blogger turned Superman, right? Defender of the weak, protector of the bullied. Look, I just don't like violence. The thought of hitting someone's"—I make a face—"nose or chin or cheek grosses me out." Even talking about violence is making me queasy. I can't help it—I've always been this way. When the other boys were wrestling and playing "Cops and Robbers" I was more interested in books, happy to get lost in someone else's adventure.

"Then aim for their stomachs," Beth says.

"Or their kidneys," Xave says, waggling his eyebrows encouragingly. "Or if you want to act like a little girl, a good shot to the nuts will drop 'em like the sacks of feces that they are."

I swallow the lump in my throat. None of those options are any more appealing to me. "Pass," I say.

"You're hopeless," Beth says, but from her smile and the way she squeezes my waist, I can tell she won't hold it against me. "Well, I'd love to stay and talk strategies for inflicting pain on jerks like Todd Logue, but I've got to run. Our issue spotlighting the inequality of Salem's Return won't get written and edited by itself."

She gives me a quick peck on the lips and skates away, adjusting her glasses when they slip down her nose.

"Hey, Beth!" I say, stopping her.

"Yeah?"

"What did you say to Todd?"

Smiling, she strolls back over and stands on her tiptoes to whisper in my ear. "I told him I had a source that told me he used to wet the bed, and that I'd run the story in next week's newspaper if he didn't leave you alone."

I snort out a laugh. "Whoever told you that about Todd has a death wish," I say.

"I made it up," she says.

"But...how'd you know it would work?"

She offers a sly grin. "Because bullies like Todd are always overcompensating for their own insecurities," she says.

Shaking my head, I grab my helmet off the ground, reacting to Coach Bronson's whistle. After kissing Beth on the cheek, I run onto the field.

"What? No smooch for me?" Xave calls after me. He has a knack for embarrassing me in front of my teammates, as if they need any more reason to make fun of me.

Beth hoots and hollers and claps. "Superstar!" she shouts.

My face warming, I turn and look at the bleachers so I won't have to see the rest of the players—whose stares I can feel on the back of my neck—but Beth and Xavier are already huddled over his tablet, immersed in homework or a funny video or my latest blog, which they never fail to give me a hard time about.

A burst of energy plumes in my chest as I watch them. My embarrassment vanishes like a ship in the Bermuda Triangle. Beth and Xave and me. Inseparable.

Two

"How's the Salem's Return issue coming?" I say to Beth when she and Xave meet me to walk home.

Beth frowns. "The more research we do, the more the whole thing stinks," she says.

"Like Rhett's football cleats?" Xave says.

"Worse," she says. "Do you know how it all started?"

Of course. Everyone does. A woman who could breathe fire. A circus performer. But not just her—there were three of them. Sisters, calling themselves The Pyros. Only it wasn't just that they could breathe fire, but that they could seemingly create it from thin air. Snap their fingers and a flame would appear. Of course, it was all just an illusion. Magic isn't real. However, the Pyros were so good that people started to think they were real witches. A couple of religious groups accused them of being devil-worshippers. Of course, it didn't help that a national media organization had a slow news week and grabbed onto the story, broadcasting snippets from the sermons condemning the witches. Like every other snowball that gets a big push down a hill, the story got bigger and bigger, until the story became an issue, and the issue became a problem.

Enter the politicians, who only made things worse. Because of the potential for panic, a law was signed preventing "real" magic from being performed—whatever that meant. The media coined it Salem's Return. I can still remember the first trial. My mom was obsessed with it. She said it would redefine the type of country we'd be for the next century, that it was the most important event since the Civil War. When the Pyros were sentenced to burn, she wouldn't leave the house for three days. Said we'd become monsters.

According to the judge, death by burning was justified because of the unique circumstances surrounding the guilty. They were witches. Burning them was "the only way to destroy their evil." Of course it didn't help that when they tried to burn the sisters, they supposedly wouldn't burn.

"Yeah," I say. "But the whole thing was a trick. Someone wanted to incite fear so they made it look like the so-called witches wouldn't burn."

"They showed it live on TV," Xave says.

"Yeah, so they could prove to the world that the sisters were REAL witches," Beth says. "I think it was all staged. Another illusion, just like the tricks the Pyros did with fire. Whatever the case, it worked. When they couldn't burn them, they—"

"Drowned them," I say. I remember my mother's face after it happened. After months of protesting she looked defeated. She didn't say a word that day. Since then they've used burning as the primary method of execution, with drowning used only if burning doesn't work.

"Sometimes the government makes me want to move to Switzerland," Xave says.

"Why Switzerland?" I ask, raising an eyebrow.

"Mostly the chocolate and the cheese," Xave says, not missing a beat.

"That was a decade ago," Beth says, bringing the conversation back to her favorite topic. "The fires haven't stopped burning since." Although there have been many groups protesting the anti-witch laws, in which my mom is a proud member, their efforts have been unsuccessful. More than a hundred witches have been executed so far, although it's hard to keep count with the death toll rising by the month. The executions barely even get any news coverage anymore; they're as normal as car accidents in L.A. and murders in Detroit.

"No one even cares about the death count anymore," I point out.

"That's where the conspiracy gets a little interesting and a lot disturbing," Beth says. "There are all kinds of theories out there, most of which contradict each other, but one thing everyone seems to agree on is that the reported witch death count is but a fraction of reality."

"You mean, like, it's closer to two hundred witches?" Xave asks, huddling closer to Beth's side as we walk.

"No," Beth says. "Try a thousand."

My mouth drops open. "A thousand?"

"And that's on the low end of the estimates. Some sites say they have sources that peg the number of executions at more than five thousand witches."

"But that's..." The word I want to say leaves a bad taste in my mouth as it rolls around on my tongue.

"Genocide," Beth says, reading my mind.

"It makes the Salem Witch Trials look like a child's birthday party and lethal injection appear as boring and humane as giving a child a timeout," Xave says.

"It's just not right, and that's what I'm going to say in the newspaper," Beth says.

With at least half the students' parents likely in support of the anti-witch laws, her article will mean even more bullying for the three of us. But that's Beth—she'll never back down from something she believes in. And that's just the way I like her.

"We're behind you all the way," I say.

~~~

When I get home, I leave my dirty cleats on the front porch and push through the door. My mom is folding laundry on our beat-up brown couch in front of the TV.

"Hi, Mom," I say, the word not even sticking in the back of my throat the way it used to.

"Hey, Rhett," she says, her gaze fixed on a news program. "How was practice?"

"Not terrible," I say.

"How's Xave?"

"He's Xave," I say.

"How's Beth?" She pulls her stare from the TV for just long enough to waggle her eyebrows. Yep, she's the closest thing to a real mom I've had in a long time.

"She's great," I say.

"There's fruit on the table if you're hungry," she calls after me as I head to the kitchen. I dump my sports duffel and backpack on a couple of chairs and grab a banana, peeling it as I move back into the TV room.

There's a rattle of footsteps scurrying down the stairs as Hurricane Jasmine approaches from upstairs. "Rhett!" my seven-year-old foster sister cries. "I thought you'd been kidnapped." She throws her arms around me and I almost drop the banana.

"Um, why?" I ask.

"The witches," Jasmine says, looking up, her chocolaty skin vibrant in the late-afternoon light.

"Jaz, I already told you," my mother says, turning to face us with a swirl of blond hair. "The witches aren't dangerous. They're not even real witches. They're just people, like you or

460

me. They're not the ones to blame for all of this. We're to blame. Our fear and hate." Finally I realize what my mom's watching on TV—what had her so engrossed.

"A curfew?" I say, reading the headline at the bottom of the screen. A newswoman is jabbering on about how the witch threat level has just been raised. How there are more of them than we first thought when Salem's Return began years earlier.

"The witches are starting to fight back," Jaz says, her voice no more than a whisper. "They say no one should be out after dark."

"Seriously?" I say in disbelief.

"Seriously," my mom says. "It's utterly ridiculous. The whole country's gone half-crazy."

"More like full crazy," I say, slipping my cell phone out of my pocket when it rings.

When I press a button to answer it, Beth says, "Have you seen the news?" before I can say anything.

"My mom's ready to march on Washington D.C.," I say, which earns me an eye-roll.

"Is that Beth?" Jaz asks, tugging at the side of my shirt.

I pull away from her, shaking her off. "Now do you think I'm wasting my time with my article?" Beth asks.

"I want to talk to her," Jaz whines, trying to grab the phone.

I hold it higher, out of reach. "I never said you were wasting your time," I say. "I just said witches aren't real. But that doesn't mean the fake witches should be killed."

"Here here," my mother says, raising a pair of my underwear like a banner.

"What about the curfew? Do you think that'll stick?" I ask, holding Jaz off with one arm.

"Who knows?" Beth says. "Before all this started, I'd say no. But now…"

"Hey, my sis wants to talk to you," I say, hoping to avoid getting clawed by Jaz's purple-painted nails.

"Sure. I love your sister."

When I offer the phone, Jaz grabs it with two hands and starts all over again with, "I was worried you and my brother had been kidnapped!"

As Beth tries to reassure my sister, I turn my attention back to the TV, where the newswoman is elaborating on the current situation. "Multiple anonymous threats from pro-witch organizations have evidently come through various law enforcement agencies over the last forty-eight hours. Although our sources were unable to provide specifics, they did say that the threats were violent in nature and suggested a large-scale response to Salem's Return. Citizens are being urged to remain in their homes with their doors locked whenever possible."

"Unbelievable," I say.

"As if," my mother says. "More likely I'll be accused of being a witch and get tied to a stake than a 'witch' attacking our house."

"Don't say stuff like that," I say. The last thing we need is cops on our doorstep because my mom joked about being a witch.

Jaz hands me the phone. "Beth says she'll talk to you later. She has conspiracies to unravel."

"Thanks, I think," I say.

Just before I head upstairs to get a shower, I notice Jaz locking the front door. "What are you doing?" I ask.

"The witches," she says, as if that explains everything.

I shake my head and take the steps two at a time to the second floor.

A half hour later I'm showered and back downstairs watching TV with my sister while my mom makes dinner. The front door rattles as someone tries to open it.

"The witches!" Jaz cries, clutching my side.

There's a click and the door eases open. "Anyone home?" my father hollers.

Jaz runs to him, wrapping her arms around his leg. "You're not a witch," she says.

"I guess you've all heard the news," Dad says, walking inside with Jaz still stuck to his leg. He hangs his tool belt on a hook in the closet. After retiring from the military, he became a handyman, quickly gaining a reputation for being able to fix almost anything.

"Jaz thinks the witches are going to kidnap us, Mom thinks the government is made up of fools, Beth thinks there's a major conspiracy, and Xave wants to move to Switzerland."

"And what do you think?" Dad asks me, picking Jaz up and throwing her on the couch beside me while she laughs gleefully.

"I think there are no witches and the sooner we all realize that the better," I say. "I mean, didn't we learn our lesson after the Salem Witch Trials? We were idiots then and we're idiots now. Some things never change."

"I'm with you, Son," my dad says.

As he moves to the kitchen to kiss my mother hello like he always does, I wonder how it's possible that my life is this good. Maybe I'm not connected to any of the people in my life biologically, but I love them just the same. My parents, Jaz, Xave, Beth—they are the best of the best. That thought sticks in my mind all through dinner until I lay down to sleep. When I think back on my darker days, they almost feel like just a bad dream. A distant nightmare. I smile as my eyes flutter closed and sleep takes me.

Three

Shrieks and screams tear me from an already forgotten dream. They're not human, the howls. Well, maybe some are, but certainly not all—not the ones closest.

As I sit up sharply, heart leaping forward to sprinting speed, another ear-rending

screeeeeeech!

shatters the night. Metallic. That's the only way to describe the sound. Like we're in Oz and the tin man is being ripped in half by impossibly strong hands, reduced to shredded hunks of scrap metal.

Screeeeeeech!

I flinch away from the window, as if it might burst inwards, but no...whatever's tearing through the metal is outside. At least for now.

Voices from the other room, muffled at first and then raised, shout, "Jasmine! Stay in your room!"

"What's happening?" my sister cries through her door.

"Just stay inside!" Dad's voice thunders through wood and plasterboard. "Rhett! You, too! My gun, Trudy!"

"Take it," my mother says. There's a double click—chook-chook!—and my father's heavy footsteps pound past my room and rumble down the staircase.

Kicking my legs over the side of the bed, I almost trip on the sheets, which are tangled around my ankles like vines. I high step and manage to slip free. Two long strides and I'm at the window, peering into the unlit yard, searching for the source of the ruckus.

Under the glow of the half-moon, the wrought-iron fence around our front yard is shining, mangled, and ripped in several places. The white, wooden gate at the end of the brick path is missing…no, there it is! Two jagged halves lie on opposite sides of the yard, splinters scattered like straw. Whatever did that is strong beyond imagination…

There are shadows on the lawn.

The dark echo of the big rosebush, tenderly cared for by my father; a wheel barrow, still half full of mulch, casts a black spot amongst the lush, green grass; the shadows are moving. Not the roses or the barrow, but others, darker and lurking, creeping toward the front door.

There's a bright flash of light and the rosebush bursts into flame, its thorny stems painted with chaotic red and orange strokes. Glowing orbs appear in the midst of one of the moving shadows and they're—they're—

—staring at me.

Unnaturally large eyes in the dark. The shadow raises a finger, points at me through the glass…

The wheelbarrow rockets through the air, spinning and sending clumps of brown mulch flying in all directions, heading right toward me…

I dive and duck just as the window explodes inwards, glass shrapnel raining all around, tinkling like crystal wind chimes. There's a whoosh! and a whoomp! and a heavy crash as the barrow bashes into my door.

A scream. Jasmine.

A shout. My father.

A gunshot. Then another.

Covered in shimmering glass shards, I push to my feet, ignoring the spots of blood welling up from my skin and the pinpricks of pain. The wheelbarrow is on its side in the hall, having destroyed my bedroom door. I barely spot my sister's bare foot as she climbs past and toward the staircase.

"Jasmine, no!" my mother shouts, clambering over the barrow after her. "Rhett, stay here," she says through a mop of unkempt blond hair.

My entire family is running toward the danger and I'm frozen, glued to the floor, unable to speak, unable to act.

There's a roar of agony from somewhere downstairs, another gunshot, and then my sister's scream, a wail of fear and terror. Something snaps inside me and I can move again, charging through the opening, leaping over the barrow, rebounding off the wall, half-stumbling down the hall. I take a sharp left and bound down the steps two at a time.

A cool breeze hits me in the face, unimpeded by the front door, which is wide open and hanging awkwardly by a single hinge. To my left the couch is overturned, splinters of ceramic from a broken vase littering the wooden floorboards around it.

Where's my family?

I glance into the yard, where the rosebush is nothing more than a glowing pile of ash. The moving, bright-eyed shadows are gone. Are they inside?

"Mom?" I say, surprised when my voice comes out more than a whisper. "Dad? Jaz?"

No answer. Silence. Silence. And then…

A scream. Not inside—but somewhere else, down the street perhaps. Another house. Can't worry about that now. Have to find my family.

I tiptoe into the living room, stubbing my bare toe on something hard. My father's gun skitters away, clattering across the wood as more screams fill the night. Screams of terror and pain. Neighbors, friends…what's happening?

I bend down and reach for the gun, my brown skin appearing even darker in the shadows…

"Death finds you," a voice says from behind.

My heart skips a beat as I whirl around, instinctively taking a step away toward the tipped-over couch. Fluorescent bulbs stare back at me, too bright to gaze at directly. I shield my eyes with a hand, trying to discern who or what is connected to the blinding light. "Where's my family?" I say. A black cloak, thin at the top and flared out toward the bottom, sits below the eyes.

"You won't need them anymore," the eyes say.

I reverse another step, feeling the gun clatter against my heel.

I crouch down, watched by the animal eyes the entire time. Blindly grab for the gun. It's warm and soft. For a moment, I risk tearing my gaze from the black-cloaked menace standing before me.

I'm holding a small, dark-skinned hand.

Screaming, I drop it and fall to the side, my breath coming in ragged heaves, my heart in my throat, my brain finally catching up to my senses.

"No," I breathe. And again: "No."

Jasmine watches me with wide, white unseeing eyes. Her neck is wet and glistening with spilled life.

Tears blooming like dewdrops, I wail at the presence, at my sister's body, at the empty room, my cries joining the screams and shouts that seem to be everywhere now, a cacophony of despair. "What have you done?" I cry. I'm dreaming—oh please let this be a nightmare. Pinch myself. And again, harder.

A groan gurgles from the back of my throat, a cry of rage and hurt.

I jump to my feet and charge the shadow, forgetting my father's gun because I don't need it, don't need anything but my own two fists and unbridled anger.

I blink and it's gone.

Ohcrapohcrap.

"You can't fight me," the voice says, behind me again.

I whirl around to face it, my heart stuttering in my chest, my every instinct urging me to get the hell out of the house. The shadow is hovering over my sister's dead body.

It's a woman's voice. I only now realize it. What is she?

"Get away from her," I growl through my teeth.

A laugh. How could she be laughing when Jasmine is broken beneath her? Who is this psychopath? "I'm afraid I can't do that. Your family"—she points at the couch and it flips over as if it weighs no more than a feather, revealing the still bodies of my parents—"is waiting for you in hell."

They're not moving, not breathing: dead like Jasmine. Just like before. Not again.

I clamp my eyes shut as a flash of pain sears through my skull.

When I open my eyes, they're still there. My newest family, the first one I've felt comfortable with in a long time—since after I lost my first foster family—gone to a place I can't follow. The glowing eyes are still there, too, still staring. I run at the she-demon, and this time she doesn't vanish, and I hit her so hard, like I'm hitting the tackling machines at football practice, but it's like crashing headfirst into a stone wall. Her icy hands clamp around my throat and she picks me up like I'm not big for my age and over six feet and a hundred and ninety pounds. Like I'm the size of one of the dolls Jasmine will never play with again.

"Guess we're doing this the hard way," she says, and I can see her teeth, straight and white and in perfect little rows above and below her lips, not rotted and sharpened into fangs like I expected. She squeezes my throat and I can't breathe and I'm surprised when I realize:

I don't care.

Breathing doesn't matter. The sharp rap of the heartbeat in my chest doesn't matter. Nothing matters now that they're gone.

And then something hits me, and at first I think it's the demon, but we're both flying backwards, and her grip loosens and she releases my neck. I crack the back of my head against the fireplace before slumping to the floor, my skull aching, acutely aware of the writhing presence beside me. A flash of metal cuts through the darkness and she disappears, like before.

Three dark-skinned faces appear, each identical and framed by well-trimmed gray hair and webs of wrinkles. I shake my head and the three faces become one.

"Mr. Jackson?" I say, glancing at the long sword my neighbor's carrying in his left hand. Hastily, he shoves it into a loop on his belt.

"She's gone, son," he says, bending over and picking up my body as easily as the demon did, surprisingly strong.

"So are they," I say through the tears and the wave of dizziness that assaults me, and he nods with sad eyes.

"Salem's Revenge has begun a day early," he says gruffly, just before my vision fades and I lose consciousness.

Brew by David Estes, coming October 1, 2014!

Made in the USA
Middletown, DE
12 December 2014